'Part mystery, part war story, part romance, *The Winter Soldier* is a dream of a novel – impeccably researched and totally immersive'
Anthony Doerr, author of *All the Light We Cannot See*

'One of the finest prose stylists in American fiction'
New York Times

'Utterly convincing and written with a lyricism that belies the horror so unflinchingly describes'
Daily Mail

'A powerful tale'
Sunday Times

'Held by the throat from the first lyrical page to the last'
Emma Donoghue, author of *Room*

'A tour-de-force. I was immersed in the grandeur of Imperial Vienna the frozen battlefields of the Eastern front'
Abraham Verghese, author of *Cutting for Stone*

'So rich and detailed, that the room in which I was reading vanished'
Andrew Sean Greer, author of *Less*
and *The Story of a Marriage*

of the best books I've ever read'
Elizabeth Macneal, author of *The Doll Factory*

'Captivating . . . A novel to get lost in'
Herald

'A powerful tale of a medical student in the First World War'
Sunday Times Culture

'A touching, intensely human story of longing and love'
ucky Ones

THE WINTER SOLDIER

DANIEL MASON is a physician and author of the novels *The Piano Tuner* and *A Far Country*. His work has been translated into twenty-eight languages, and adapted for opera and theatre. A recipient of a fellowship from the National Endowment for the Arts, he is currently a Clinical Assistant Professor of Psychiatry at Stanford University, where he teaches courses in the humanities and medicine. He lives in the Bay Area with his family.

ALSO BY DANIEL MASON

The Piano Tuner
A Far Country

DANIEL MASON

THE WINTER SOLDIER

PICADOR

First published 2018 by Mantle

This paperback edition first published 2019 by Picador
an imprint of Pan Macmillan
The Smithson, 6 Briset Street, London EC1M 5NR
Associated companies throughout the world
www.panmacmillan.com

ISBN 978-0-3304-5833-7

1 3 5 7 9 8 6 4 2

A CIP catalogue record for this book is available from the British Library.

*Entry of the Wedding Procession of Constance of Austria and
Sigismund III into Cracow*, artist unknown.

Map artwork by Jeffrey L. Ward.

Typeset in Janson Text by Jouve (UK), Milton Keynes
Printed and bound by CPI Group (UK) Ltd, Croydon, CRO 4YY

Visit **www.panmacmillan.com** to read more about all our books
and to buy them. You will also find features, author interviews and
news of any author events, and you can sign up for e-newsletters
so that you're always first to hear about our new releases.

For Sara

Certain affections have an unfortunate destiny.

— André Léri, 1918 *Commotions et émotions de guerre*

THE WINTER SOLDIER

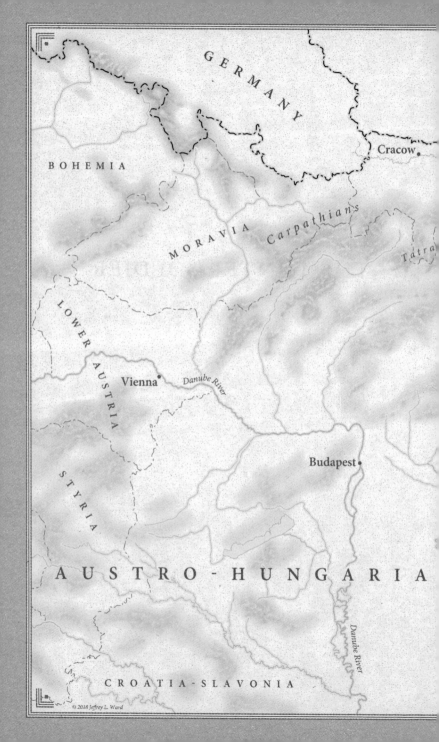

1

THEY WERE FIVE hours east of Debrecen when the train came to a halt before the station on the empty plain.

There was no announcement, not even a whistle. Were it not for the snow-draped placard, he wouldn't have known they had arrived. Hastening, afraid he would miss the stop, he gathered his bag, his coat, his sabre, pushing his way out through the men who filled the corridor of the train. He was the only passenger to descend. Further down the line, porters unloaded a pair of crates onto the snow before jumping back on board, slapping warmth into their hands. Then the carriages began to move, chains clanking, stirring his greatcoat and swirling snow around his knees.

He found the hussar in the station house, with the horses brought in from the cold. Their ears flicked against the low ceiling, their long faces overhanging a bench where three peasant women sat, hands clasped over their swaddled bellies like fat men content after a meal. Feet dangling just above the floor. Woman, horse, woman, horse, woman. The hussar stood without speaking. Back in Vienna, Lucius had seen regiments on parade with their plumes and coloured sashes, but this man was dressed in a thick grey coat, with a cap of worn, patched fur. He motioned Lucius forward and handed him the reins of one of the horses before he led the other outside, its tail whisking across the women as it passed beneath the Habsburg double-headed eagle on the door.

Lucius tugged on the reins, but his horse resisted. He stroked her neck with the back of one hand – the broken one – while he pulled with the other. 'Come,' he whispered, first in German, then in Polish, as her back hooves broke from the ice and frozen dung. To the hussar at the door, he said, 'You've been waiting long.'

It was the last thing he said. Outside, the hussar lowered a leather mask, cut with slits for eyes and nostrils, and heaved himself onto his horse. Lucius followed, rucksack on his shoulders, struggling to wrap his scarf over his face. From inside the station house, the three old women watched them until the hussar wheeled his horse around and kicked the door shut. Your sons aren't coming, Lucius wanted to tell them. Not in any state you'd wish to see. There was scarcely a young man with two legs who wasn't trying to lift the Russian siege of Przemyśl now.

Without a word the hussar began to ride north at a trot, his long rifle across his saddle, his sabre on his waist. Lucius looked back to the railway, but the train had vanished. Snowflakes had begun to cover the track.

He followed. His horse's hooves clattered on the frozen earth. The sky was grey, and in the distance, he could see the mountains rising up into the storm. Somewhere, there, was Lemnowice, and the regimental hospital of the Third Army where he was to serve.

HE WAS twenty-two years old, restless, resentful of hierarchy, impatient for his training to come to an end. For three years he had studied alone in the libraries, devoted to medicine with a monastic severity. Onion paper feathered the margins of his textbooks, licked and pasted in by hand. In the great halls, on gleaming lantern slides, he'd seen the ravages of typhus, scar-latina, lupus, pest. He had memorized the signs of cocainism and hysteria, knew that the breath of cyanide poisoning smelled of almonds, and the murmur of a narrowed aortic valve could be heard in the neck. In tie and jacket, freshly ironed for the day, he'd spent hours staring down from the dizzying heights of the surgery theatre, straining his neck for a line of sight through the restless coveys of his classmates, over the neatly combed heads of senior students, over the junior professors, the surgeon's assistants, across the surgical drape, and down into the cut. By the time war was declared, he was dreaming nightly of the the-atre: long, demanding dreams in which he extracted impossible organs, half-man, half-pig. (It was on butcher's scraps he prac-tised.) One night, dreaming of an extraction of the gall bladder, he had such a distinct impression of the wet, leaden warmth of the liver, that he woke certain he could carry out the surgery alone.

If his devotion was total, its origin remained a mystery. As a child, he had gazed with wonder at the wax cadavers at the Ana-tomical Museum, but so had his three brothers, and not one of them had turned to Hippocrates' art. There were no doctors in his line, not among the Krzelewskis of southern Poland, and certainly not among his mother's people. At times, cornered by some peahen at one of her unbearable receptions, he endured a condescending speech on how medicine was a noble calling, that one day he would be rewarded for his kindness. But kindness was not interesting to him. His best answer to what drove his endless hours of study was the joy of study itself. He was not a person drawn to religious devotion, but it was in religion that he found the words: revelation, epiphany, the miracle of God's creations, and by extension, the miracle of how God's creations failed.

Study itself: this was, at least, the answer that he gave in his moments of greatest exultation. But there was another reason he had turned to medicine, one he only considered later in the hours of his doubt. Of the two other students he could call his friends, Feuermann was the son of a tailor, while Kaminski, who wore empty spectacles just to look older, was on a scholarship from the Sisters of Mercy. Although they never spoke of it, Lucius knew they all had come to medicine for its promise of social mobility. For Feuermann and Kaminski this meant *up*: from the slums of Leopoldstadt and the charity school. For Lucius, whose father came from an ancient Polish family that claimed descent from Japheth, son of Noah (yes, *that* Noah), and in whose mother's veins coursed the same cerulean blood as that Great Liberator of Vienna and Saviour of Western Civilization, Jan Sobieski, King of Poland, Grand Duke of Lithuania, Ruthenia, Prussia, Masovia, Samogitia, Livonia, Smolensk, Kiev, Volhynia, etc., etc. – for Lucius, such mobility meant not up, but out.

No, from the beginning he hadn't belonged among them, an accidental sixth child born years after the doctor told his mother she couldn't conceive again. Were he not the spitting image of his father – tall and big-pawed, with skin pale as alabaster, a shock of blond hair fit for an Icelander, and old man's ducktail eyebrows even as a little boy – he might have wondered if he was another's child. But the flushes of ruddiness that gave his father the hale glow of a knight who has just removed his jouster's helmet, in Lucius looked more like blotches of an embarrassed blush. Watching his brothers and sisters glide through his mother's receptions, he could never understand their ease, their grace, their force. No matter what he tried – holding a stone in his pocket as a reminder to smile, writing lists of 'Chatting Topics' – spontaneity eluded him. Before the parties, he would slink through the salon, attaching to each piece of artwork an idea for conversation: when he saw the portrait of Sobieski he was to speak of holidays; the bust of Chopin should spur him to ask about his guest. Yet, no matter how he prepared, it happened: there would be a moment, a pause – just a second – just a catch – before he – spoke. He could move easily through the shifting choreography of soft gowns and pressed field marshal trousers. But the moment that he approached a cluster of other children, their easy laughter stopped.

He wondered whether, if he had grown up in another time or place – among a different, silent people – his discomfort would ever have been noticed. But in Vienna, among the eloquent, where frivolity had been cultivated into a faith, he knew that others saw him falter. *Lucius*: the name, chosen by his father after the legendary kings of Rome, itself was mockery; he was anything but light. By his thirteenth birthday, so terrified was he by his mother's disapproval, so increasingly uncertain of anything to say at all, that his unease began to appear in a quiver of his lip, a nervous twisting of his fingers, and at last, a stutter.

In the beginning, he had been accused of feigning. Stutters appear in childhood, his mother told him, not in a boy his age. He didn't stutter when he was alone, nor when he spoke of his science magazines or the bird's nest outside his window. Nor did it afflict him at the aquarium in the Imperial Zoological Collections, where he went to stare for hours at the *Grottenolm*, blind, translucent salamanders from the Southern Empire, in whom one could watch the almost magical pulsing of blood.

But at last, conceding that something might be wrong, she hired a speech expert from Munich, famous for his *Textbook of the Disorders of Speech and Language* and a metal device called the *Zungenapparat*, which isolated the labial, palatal and glottal movements from one another and so promised the repair of sound and speech.

The doctor arrived on a warm summer's morning, gnawing a hangnail. Humming, he appraised the child, palpating his neck and peering into his ears. There were measurements, sour fingers probed his gums; his mother grew bored and left. At last, the apparatus was applied, and the boy was told to sing 'The Happy Hiker'.

He tried. The clamp pinched his lips. The tongue prongs cut, and he spat blood. 'Louder!' cried the doctor. 'It is working!' His mother returned to find her son baying like a dog, mouth foaming red. Lucius looked between them – Mother – Doctor – Mother – Doctor – as his mother seemed to grow bigger and pinker and the doctor smaller and paler. *Oh, you have no idea what you have got yourself into*, thought the boy, watching the man. And he began to giggle – not an easy task with a *Zungenapparat* – as the doctor gathered up his tools and fled.

A second doctor tried to hypnotize him, failed, and prescribed herring for oral lubrication. A third, cupping his testicles, declared them sufficient, but finding no movement when the boy was shown the fleshy gymnastics in an illustrated edition of *The True Secrets of the Convent*, he removed his notebook and scrawled 'Insufficiency of the Gland'. Then he whispered to Lucius's mother.

A week later, she had his father take him to a house specializing in virgins, certificated free of syphilis, where he was locked in the plush Ludwig II suite with a country girl from Croatia attired like a singer of the opera buffa. As she was from the south, Lucius asked her if she had heard of the *Grottenolm*. Yes, she said, her frightened face brightening. Her father had once collected the little salamanders to sell to aquaria across the Empire. Then the two of them marvelled at this coincidence of their lives, for, just that week, one of Lucius's favourites in the Zoological Collection had spawned.

Afterwards, when his father asked, 'And did you do it?' Lucius answered, 'Yes, Father.' And his father, 'I don't believe you. What did you do?' And Lucius, 'I did what was to be done.' And his father, 'Which is what?' And Lucius, 'What I have learned.' And his father, 'What have you learned, boy?' And Lucius, remembering a novel of his sister's, answered, 'I have done it in a fiery way.'

'That's my son,' his father said.

In silence, he endured his parents' receptions until they allowed him to escape. He would have skipped them altogether, but his mother said the guests would think she was like Walentyna Rozorovska, who hid her crippled daughter in a crate. So Lucius followed as she made her rounds. She was distinctly proud of her narrow waist, and he thought she sometimes kept him near because nothing pleased her more than to have another woman say, 'Agnieszka, after six children – so *sportive*! How can it be?'

Whalebone! Lucius wished to shout. The conversation horrified him. He thought such comments about his birth were vulgar, as if they were complimenting her on her genitalia. He was relieved when she spoke instead of music and architecture, and showed particular interest in the industrialists' wives and where their husbands had been travelling, and it was only when he was older that he realized how strategic, and ultimately ruthless, such questioning had been.

The King is always hunting, and the Queen is always pregnant, ran the joke about his family, paraphrasing Goethe. But he thought, *In many ways, this Queen is both*. His sweet-toothed father, a major in the lancers, had been shot in the hip by the Italians at the Battle of Custoza, and had intended to spend the rest of his life happily lounging about his garrison in Kraków, drinking slivovitz and perfecting hand shadows to scare his children.

For the first decade of his marriage, fearing disruption to his idyll, the war hero tried to hide the sleepy family mines from Lucius's mother. Iron? *There?* Nothing but bat droppings. Copper? Oh, my dear, that's just a silly rumour. What, they told you there was *zinc*?

He had known his wife too well. No sooner did she have her hands on the balance sheets than a great rumbling was heard over southern Poland. Within three years, the Krzelewski mines had gone from providing buttons for the army's tunics and brass for its trumpets to steel and iron for the new railway to Zakopane. Soon she had moved them to Vienna so as to better grip the heart of Empire. It was only fitting, she liked to say. Vienna owed her family, ever since Sobieski liberated Austria from the Turks.

This of course was mentioned only in private. In public, she had no hesitation in acquiring the necessary imperial trappings. Commemorative ceramics from Franz Josef's jubilees soon graced their mantelpieces. She had Klimt paint her portrait, first with Lucius at her side, and then, because she was enthralled by the patterns of gold on the portrait of Adele Bloch-Bauer, she had Lucius painted over. Their dynasty of Irish wolfhounds – Puszek I (1873–81), Puszek II (1880–87), Puszek III (1886–96), Puszek IV (1895–1902), etc. – were all descended from none other than Empress Sisi's beloved Shadow.

Each of her children, save the eldest, had been born in Vienna. Władysław, Kazimierz and Bolesław, Sylwia and Regelinda: names like a procession of Polish saints. By his second decade, they had all moved on. Later Lucius would learn that there were divisions among them, deep divisions, but for most of his childhood, their unity seemed impenetrable. The men drank and the women played piano very well. The men, disappearing with his father on pre-dawn hunts from their estates in Poland and Hungary, drank a lot.

HE WAS NOT surprised, therefore, that when he had first announced his intention to study medicine, his mother told him it was a field for arrivistes.

He responded that many sons of nobility became doctors. But he knew the answer before it was uttered from her thin, drawn lips.

'Yes. But our kind of doctor is not the kind of doctor you will be.'

She relented in the end. Better than anyone, she knew his limitations. Alone in the beginning, unwelcomed in the German medical student associations, he had found Feuermann and Kaminski similarly excluded, trying to hide their discomfort as the other students laughed among themselves.

From the first day, Lucius had thrown himself into his studies. As opposed to his two companions, who had studied at the trade-oriented *Realschule*, and so had already completed much of the basic sciences, Lucius's education at the hands of his governesses had consisted mostly of Greek and Latin. To his gang he said that his zoological and botanical studies had stopped at Pliny. When they laughed with him, he was amazed, as he hadn't meant it as a joke. After that, he pretended he had never heard of Darwin, and liked to say, 'This whole gravity business is quite a craze.' But he didn't mind the remedial courses; there was magic in the choral recitations of Linnaean classification, in the luminous Crookes tubes brought out for physics demonstrations, the lesser alchemy that bubbled in the lines of Erlenmeyer flasks.

If he loved Medicine – yes, this was the word, this giddiness, this jealous guarding against fellow suitors, this pursuit of increasingly delicate secrets to be indulged – if he loved Medicine, what he had not expected was for *Her* to return his affections. In the beginning, he noticed only this: when he spoke of *Her*, his stutter vanished. There were no exams until the end of his second year, and so it was only one cold day in December, during his third semester, that there came the first hint that he possessed, in the words of that year's assessment, 'an unusual aptitude for the perception of things that lie beneath the skin'.

The lecturer that day, Grieperkandl, the great anatomist, was of that species of emeriti who believed that most modern medical innovations (such as hand-washing) were emasculating. It was in a state of general terror that the students attended his classes, for each week Grieperkandl would call a *Praktikant* before him, take down his name in a little notebook (always a *his*; there were but seven women in the class, and Grieperkandl treated them all as nurses), and proceed to submit him to an inquisition of such clinically irreverent arcana that most of their professors would have failed.

It was during a lecture on the anatomy of the hand that Lucius was called to the front of the class. Grieperkandl asked if he had studied for that day – he had – and whether he knew the name of the bones – he did – and whether he would like to recite them. The old professor was standing so close that Lucius could smell the naphthalene on his coat. Grieperkandl rattled his pocket. Inside he had some bones. Would Lucius like to select one and name it? Lucius hesitated; there was nervous laughter in the tiers. Then cautiously, he slid his hand in, his fingers settling on the longest and thinnest of the bones. As he went to remove it, the professor grabbed his wrist. 'Any fool can *look*,' he said. And Lucius, closing his eyes, said *scaphoid*, and withdrew it, and Grieperkandl said, 'Another,' and Lucius said *capitate* and withdrew it, and Grieperkandl said, 'Those are the two largest – that is easy,' and Lucius said *lunate*, and Grieperkandl, 'Another,' and Lucius said *hamate, triquetrum, metacarpal*, removing each in turn until at last a tiny bone remained, peculiar, too stubby to be a distal phalange, even that of the thumb.

'Toe,' said Lucius, realizing he had sweated through his shirt. 'It's the little toe.'

A hush had come over the class.

And Grieperkandl, unable to prevent a yellow smile from spreading across his face (for, he would say later, he had been waiting twenty-seven years to make the joke) said, 'Very good, my son. But whose?'

An unusual aptitude for the perception of things beneath the skin. He copied out these words into his journal, in Polish, in German and in Latin, as if he'd found his epitaph. It was a bracing thought for a boy who had grown up mystified by the simplest manners of other people. What if his mother's pronouncements were false? What if all along he had been simply seeing *deeper*? When the first *Rigorosum* came after two years, he scored the highest in the class on all his subjects but physics, where Feuermann edged him out. It seemed impossible. With his governess, he had nearly given up on Greek, cared nothing for the causes of the War of Austrian Succession, confused Kaiser Friedrich Wilhelm with Kaiser Wilhelm and Kaiser Friedrich and thought philosophy stirred up problems where there were no problems before.

He entered his fifth semester with great anticipation. He had enrolled in Pathology, Bacteriology and Clinical Diagnosis, and the summer would bring the first lectures in Surgery. But his hopes to leave his books and treat a real, living patient were premature. Instead, in the same vast halls where he had once attended lectures on organic chemistry, he watched his professors from the same great distance. If a patient was brought before them – and even this was rare in the introductory classes – Lucius could scarcely see them, let alone learn how to percuss the liver or palpate swollen nodes.

Sometimes he was called forth as *Praktikant*. In Neurology, he stood next to the day's patient, a seventy-two-year-old locksmith from the Italian Tyrol, with such severe aphasia that he could only mutter, 'Da.' His daughter translated the doctor's questions into Italian. As the man tried to answer, his mouth opened and closed like a baby bird. 'Da. Da!' he said, face red with frustration, as murmurs of fascination and approval filled the hall. Driven on by the lecturer's aggressive questioning, Lucius diagnosed a tumour of the temporal lobe, trying to keep his thoughts on the science and away from how miserable he was making the old man's daughter. She had begun to cry, and she kept reaching for her father's hand.

'You will stop that!' his professor shouted at her, slapping her fingers. 'You will disturb the learning!' Lucius's face was burning. He hated the doctor for asking such questions before the daughter, and he hated himself for answering. But he also did not like feeling he was on the side of the patient, who was inarticulate and weak. So he answered forcefully, with no compassion. His diagnosis of early brainstem herniation and the relentless destruction of the breathing centres and death, was met by rising, even thunderous, applause.

Following his performance, some of the other students approached him and asked him to join their groups. But he had no time for their inadequacies. He couldn't understand the laziness of those who hired artists to help them remember the anatomy of their cadavers. He was ready to move on, to touch his patients, to cut them open and take out their disease. Even the clinics frustrated him – crowds of eighty would follow their renowned instructor, and merely ten or twenty of them would be allowed to probe a hernia or examine a tumour in a breast.

Once, and only once, he was left alone with a patient, a wispy-haired Dalmatian from whose ear canals he extracted enough wax to make a small but working votive candle. The man, who had been diagnosed as deaf for fifteen years, stared at Lucius as if Christ himself had just returned. But the praise, the blessings, the lachrymose kissing of Lucius's hand embarrassed him. This was what he had trained for? Mining? That his esteemed professor had attributed the deafness to dementia only left him more depressed.

He returned to his books.

By then, only Feuermann could keep up with him. Soon they left the others and studied alone, pushing each other to ever finer diagnostic feats. They memorized poisoning syndromes, the manifestations of obscure tropical parasites, and mischievously applied defunct physical classification systems (phrenology, humoralism) to the other members of their class. When Feuermann said that he could diagnose a dozen conditions by watching a patient's gait, Lucius countered that he could do so by *listening* to the gait, and so the two sought out an empty corridor, and Lucius turned to face the wall. Feuermann walked back and forth behind him. *Slap* went his feet, and *slap slap* and *slide-thump* and *slide-slide* and *plop plop*. The answers were: sensory ataxia, spastic hemiplegia, Parkinson's and fallen arches.

'And this?' asked Feuermann, and his feet went *pitter-pitter plop*.

But that was easy.

'Dancing, wretched type, chronic, most likely terminal.'

'I have been defeated!' roared Feuermann, as Lucius, utterly pleased with himself, began to tap as well.

He felt at times that Feuermann was the only person who could understand him, and around Feuermann alone, he felt at ease. It was his friend, handsome, already with a bit of a reputation for flirtation among the lay nurses, who persuaded him to go to the brothel on Alserstrasse by arguing that it had once been frequented by the legendary doctors Billroth and Rokitansky; Feuermann, who taught him, with reference to *Structure and Function of the Genitalia of the Female* (Leipzig, 1824), the principle of *titillatio clitoridis*. And yet never in the past two years had they spoken of anything that wasn't at least partially related to medicine. Not once had Feuermann accepted an invitation to Lucius's palatial home. And Lucius never asked what had happened to Feuermann's parents that led them to flee their village near the Russian border when his friend was still a baby, or why he had no mother. He knew only that his father was a tailor, outfitting his son with suits assembled impeccably from scrap.

Billroth, said Feuermann, would dine on gherkins after coitus; Rokitansky never took his lab coat off. *Titillatio* had once been prescribed by the great van Swieten to treat the frigidity of Empress Maria Theresa; it was what saved the Empire. Once, from nowhere, Feuermann said, 'Perhaps one day we might marry sisters.' Lucius said he thought this was a fine idea and asked if he had read Klamm's paper on bromides for palpitations, of unknown cause.

BUT OF ALL the cases he studied, it was the neurological ones that fascinated him the most. How extraordinary was the mind! To sense a limb years after amputation! To see ghosts at one's bedside! To create all the symptoms of pregnancy (swollen abdomen, amenorrhea) by wish alone! The thrill he felt when he solved the most difficult cases was almost sexual. There was a beautiful clarity in the patterns, the possibility of locating a tumour simply by whether it destroyed language or vision, the opportunity to reduce the complexity of other people to the architecture of their cells.

At the university was a professor called Zimmer, famous for his dissections of the thalamus done back in the '70s, who had later published a book called *Radiological Diagnosis of Diseases of the Head*. It was Feuermann who found it, Lucius who couldn't put it away. Soon he was spending so many hours with the library's copy that he purchased one himself.

Page after page showed radiographs of the head and face. Little arrows illustrated the growths of cancers and subtle hairline fractures. He learned to make out the thin, twisting courses of the sutures, the 'Turkish saddle' that held the pituitary, and the darker swirlings of the skull base. But his eyes kept travelling to the smooth dome of the calvarium. There, the light was hazy, like puffs of smoke blown into the skull. Nothing to see . . . just cloudy shades of grey and lighter grey, tricks of shadow that played upon the eye and yielded nothing. And yet! *Thought* was there, he told himself, astounded. In that grey haze lay Fear and Love and Memory, the countenances of loved ones, the smell of the wet cellulose, even the vision of the technician the moment the film was shot. Dr Macewen of Glasgow, one of his gods, had called the brain *the dark continent*. Before the radiograph, one could only see the living brain in the tiny pearl of optic nerve inside the eye.

He approached Zimmer unannounced in the Department of Neurology.

What was lacking in his book, said Lucius, seated before the old professor, in a room piled high with specimens and slide boxes, *What was lacking, with all due respect, Herr Professor Doktor,* were images of the *vessels*. If one could invent an elixir that that could be picked up by the radiograph, if one could inject it into arteries and veins and show the twisting tributaries ... if one could just resolve this haze ...

Zimmer, with the stringy hair and overgrown muttonchops of a professor long sent to pasture, licked something off his monocle before polishing it and placing it before his eye. He squinted as if in disbelief at the student's impudence. On the wall behind him were portraits of Zimmer's professor, and his professor's professor, and his professor's professor's professor, as much a royal line as any in medicine, thought Lucius, who prepared himself to be dismissed. But something in the boy's gangly tactlessness must have intrigued the old man.

'We inject mercury to show the vessels in cadavers,' he said at last. 'But with live patients, it can't be done.'

'What of calcium?' asked Lucius a bit vertiginously, but pressing on. 'Iodine, bromine ... I've been reading ... if you could see the vessels, you could watch blood flow, you could see the outlines of tumours, strokes, the narrowing of arteries—'

'I know what you could see,' said Zimmer sharply.

'*Thoughts*,' said Lucius as the old man marked the end of the visit with an arch of his eyebrow, releasing the monocle and catching it in his hand.

But two weeks later Zimmer called him back.

'We will begin in dogs. We can prepare the solution here and inject it at the X-ray machine in the School of Radiology.'

'Dogs?'

Zimmer must have read the unease on the student's face. 'Well, we can't just use Professor Grieperkandl, can we?'

'Professor Grieperkandl? Well, no, Herr Professor.'

'Our findings would not be generalizable, would they?'

Lucius hesitated. The possibility that a professor of Zimmer's stature was making a joke about a professor of Grieperkandl's stature was so far beyond contemplation that Lucius took the question literally at first. But what to answer? *Yes*, and he would be agreeing to vivisect his old instructor. *No*, and he would imply that the great anatomist was so abnormal . . .

'We are not going to experiment on Professor Grieper-kandl,' said Zimmer.

'Of course not, Herr Professor!'

His hands twisted. Then Zimmer, clearly amused, opened a tin on his desk and popped a sweet inside his mouth. He held another out across the desk.

'Caramel?'

His fingers were dark with tobacco and smelled of chloroform; now Lucius noticed an open jar containing what appeared to be a brainstem on his desk.

For a moment Lucius hesitated, eyes darting to the jar and back.

'Of course, Professor. Thank you, Herr Professor Doktor, sir.'

THE MAIN HOSPITAL was nearly a kilometre from Zimmer's lab. For two weeks Lucius brought the dogs there. As none of the fiacres would stop to transport the animals, he had to push them in a cart. In the streets, the dogs – those that had survived the procedure – were prone to seizures. On the crowded pavements, people turned to watch the pale young man in his loose-fitting suit, wheeling the twitching animals along. He steered far away from children.

The X-ray machine was often broken, and the lines to use it were long. One day he had to wait five hours while the Royal Family had themselves radiographed with their decorations.

He returned to his professor. 'How much is an X-ray machine?' he asked.

'To purchase? Ha! Far beyond the budget of this laboratory.'

'I understand, Herr Professor Doktor,' said Lucius, his eyes cast down. 'What if it were purchased with a donation, from a family of means?'

For the following weeks, he returned home only to sleep, taking the grand staircase three steps at a time. Past the bust of Chopin and portrait of Sobieski, down the grand hall, with the medieval tapestries and the gilded, Lucius-less Klimt.

He rose before dawn. He injected mercury salts and solutions of calcium, but the images were poor. Oil suspensions provided brilliant images of the veins, but they formed emboli. Iodine and bromine showed more promise, but too much killed the animal, while lesser quantities didn't show up on the films. His increasing frustration was equalled only by the enthusiasm of his advisor. *Zimmer's elixir*, the old man took to calling the substance that was yet to be, and he began to speculate whether minute increases of blood flow could be detected in areas of greatest activity. Ask them to move an arm, said Zimmer, and we might see a corresponding flood of light within the motor cortex, while speech would illuminate the temporal lobe. One day, with men.

And Lucius thought, *I said that the very first day we met.*

The dream of being able to see another person's thinking was all that retained him.

Soon it was clear that they were far from any discovery. The few images they had were too blurry to be of much use, and Zimmer refused to publish them out of fear that another professor would steal his research. Now Lucius regretted having ever proposed the idea. He was sick of killing the poor dogs – eight by spring. At home, Puszek (VII) fled him, as if he knew. He had wasted time. Now Feuermann teased Lucius that it reminded him of the days when, slipping brain sections into their microscopes, the two of them pretended to see the snake-like curl of envy, or desire's glimmering curve.

'A lovely idea, Krzelewski. But you must know when to stop.'

Still, Lucius would not relent.

Most classmates made up for limited clinical training by spending their holidays volunteering in provincial hospitals. *Lancing milkmaids' boils*, his mother called it, so Feuermann went alone, set broken legs, repaired a pitchfork wound, pronounced a man dead from rabies, and delivered nine babies to fertile country girls so robust they sometimes walked in from the fields in labour. Three weeks later, back at their table at Café Landt-mann, Lucius listened as his friend described each case in detail, his tan, child-birthing forearms waving his confident, child-birthing fingers in the air. He didn't know what made him more jealous: the meals the peasants prepared in gratitude or the sunburnt girls who kissed Feuermann's palm. Or the chance to deliver a baby using procedures he had only practised on the satin vagina of a manikin. He had spent the month chasing a mix of iodine and bromine, only to find that Zimmer had switched the labels on the flasks.

'I can't describe it, truly, words can't do it justice,' said Feuermann, flipping a coin onto the waiter's silver platter. 'Next summer, we'll go together. You haven't lived until you've held one in your arms.'

'A milkmaid?' Lucius joked weakly.

'A baby, a real live baby. Pink and lusty. Screaming with life.'

THE LAST STRAW came in May 1914.

That afternoon, Zimmer called him conspiratorially to his office. He needed Lucius's help, he said. He had a very peculiar case.

For a moment, Lucius felt that old excitement. 'What sort of case, Herr Professor?'

'A perplexing condition.'

'Indeed.'

'*Very* mysterious.'

'Herr Professor is being youthfully playful.'

'A case of severe *coccygeal ichthyoidization*.'

'Sorry, Herr Professor?'

Now Zimmer could not control his giggling. 'Mermaids, Krzelewski. In the Medical Museum.'

Since beginning medical school, Lucius had heard the rumour. The museum, with objects from the famous Cabinet of Wonders of Rudolf II, was said to contain, among its centuries of priceless artefacts, a pair of dwarfs, three formalin-preserved angels, and several mermaids gifted to the Emperor after washing up on foreign shores. But no student had ever been inside.

'Herr Professor has a key?'

His answer was a smile, mischievous, revealing gums and pebbly teeth.

They went down that night, after the curator had left.

The hall was dark. They passed tables of torture implements, jars of foetal malformations, a collection of dodo beaks and pickled terrapins and a shrunken Amazonian head. At last they arrived at a distant shelf. There they were. Not some lovely young girls floating in a tank, as Lucius had always imagined, but two shrivelled corpses the size of babies, the dried skin of their faces pulled back over the teeth, the torsos narrowing before they merged into a scaly tail.

Zimmer had brought a rucksack. He opened it and motioned for Lucius to set one of the bodies inside. They would take it up to the X-ray machine, to see if the lumbar spine articulated with the vertebrae of the tail.

'With all due respect, Herr Professor,' said Lucius, feeling a faint despondency sneak into his voice, 'I really doubt it does.'

'Look at the surface – one sees no glue, no thread.'

'It is a very good *hoax*, Herr Professor.'

But Zimmer had his monocle on and was peering into the first one's mouth.

'Herr Professor. Do you really think it is wise to take them? They look . . . crispy. What if one breaks?'

Zimmer rapped it gavel-like against the shelf. 'Very strong,' he said.

Lucius took it, gently. It was light, the skin like dry leather. It seemed to be pinching its eyes shut. It looked outraged.

'Come,' Zimmer said, slipping it inside the bag.

The Medical Museum sat in the basement. They climbed the stairs and walked down the main hall, lined with statues of Vienna's great physicians. Only a distant light was on. Lucius was thankful that it was evening and his classmates had gone home. The sound of the mermaid rubbing against the canvas of the bag seemed even louder than his footsteps.

They were about to exit, when they heard a voice. 'Herr Professor Zimmer!' They stopped, and Lucius turned to see the rector, with a small, dark-haired woman at his side.

The rector approached Zimmer with a broad smile, lifting his arms in greeting.

Zimmer scarcely noticed him. Instead he took the woman's hand.

'Ah, Madame Professor. What brings you to Vienna?'

'A lecture, Herr Professor,' she answered in accented German. 'It's all lectures these days.'

The rector now had noticed Lucius. To the woman, he said, 'This is one of Vienna's finer students. Kerzelowski . . . *ahem* . . . Kurslawski . . .'

'*K-she-lev-ski*,' said Lucius, despite his better instincts. 'In Polish, the *Krze* is pronounced . . .'

'Of course!' The rector turned. 'You've heard of Madame Professor Curie?'

Lucius froze. Madame Marie *Skłodowska* Curie. He dropped his head. 'A great honour,' he murmured reverentially. *Two* Nobel Prizes: in the Polish community of Vienna she was a saint.

Madame Curie smiled. In Polish, she said, 'Krzelewski – a Pole?'

'Yes, Madame Professor.'

She leaned in conspiratorially. 'What a relief! My God, how sick I am of speaking German.'

Lucius looked uncomfortably at the men, who seemed pleased to see that Madame Curie had found a conversation mate. Not knowing what to say, he replied, 'Polish is a beautiful language.'

But the great chemist seemed not to have registered how awkward this sounded. In German, she said to the rector, 'Might we bring them to supper? I am happy to meet a fellow countryman.' Then in Polish, to Lucius, 'These old men are so boring! I am ready to die.'

Lucius looked to Zimmer, hoping his professor might intervene and suggest they drop the rucksack off at his office, but he seemed to have forgotten that Lucius was still carrying it beneath his arm.

THEY DINED that night at Meissl und Schadn. Madame Curie asked to stretch her legs, and so they walked. Along the Ringstrasse, they were followed at a short distance by a pair of mangy dogs, who whined hungrily at the rucksack. At the door, the maître d' offered to take the bag, but Lucius said politely that it wasn't necessary, and as deftly as possible, he slipped it beneath his chair. At the beginning of the meal, Zimmer spoke at some length about his radiological work, and Madame Curie asked sharp questions about contrast agents, most of which Zimmer asked Lucius to field. They had just begun dessert, when the great chemist asked the two professors for permission to speak in Polish.

'Of course!'

To Lucius she said, 'What's in the bag?'

'The bag, Madame Professor?'

'Don't play stupid, young man. Who brings a rucksack into Meissl und Schadn and tries to hide it under the table? It must be something *really* precious.' She winked. 'I have spent the last half-hour palpating it with my foot.'

'It is a mermaid, Madame Professor,' said Lucius, who did not know what else to say.

Her eyebrows rose. 'Indeed! A dried one?'

'Yes . . . a dried one, Madame Professor. How did you know?'

'Well, she's not preserved or we would smell the chloroform. And she's not alive, as I'd imagine she'd be struggling. *I'd* be struggling. It is a she, isn't it? Our exotic things are always female.'

Lucius looked anxiously about. 'I have not been able to confirm, Madame Professor. I am unfamiliar with the anatomy.' Then in horror, he realized the unfortunate way this could be misunderstood. Thankful for the dark light of the restaurant, he added, quickly, 'I have never seen a mermaid before.'

She lowered her voice. 'May I see?'

'*Now*, Madame Professor?' asked Lucius.

'*After*,' she said.

When the meal ended, she said, 'Can the student walk me home?'

The rector, who seemed to want this honour for himself, reluctantly agreed. Zimmer, by then completely drunk, waved Lucius off.

She was staying at the Metropole. Inside the lobby, as they waited for the lift, Lucius could sense the eyes of the bellboy appraising the rendezvous. *Oh, but it is not what you are thinking,* thought Lucius, though a little flattered by the suggestion. *Just looking at a mermaid, that is all . . .*

Upstairs, she led him into the bathroom, which had a tall four-legged tub. Lucius opened the rucksack, and she lifted the creature out.

'Oh, dear,' she said. She held it close to the light. In the mirror, Lucius could see all three of them. 'How very ugly!' She turned it. 'The face looks very much like the old American president Theodore Roosevelt, don't you think? If she had a little moustache and glasses . . .'

'Yes, Madame Professor. If the American president were desiccated and had a tail, I think they would look very much the same.'

Lucius, who had the student's habit of answering in complete sentences that recapitulated the question and expanded it slightly, had actually not meant this to be a joke, but Madame Curie began to laugh. Then she shook her head. 'Why in the world are you carrying this?'

'Professor Zimmer . . . wanted to radiograph it . . . It is from the collection of Rudolf the Second. A gift from the Sultan. He thought he might see if the vertebrae of the tail and thorax articulated . . .'

'Articulated? He actually believes it's real?'

'It is a possibility he – we – have considered.' In the mirror, Lucius could see his face turning bright red. 'The radiograph has allowed the investigation of phenomena . . .'

She interrupted sharply, 'And what does the student think?'

'I think it is a hoax, Madame Professor. I believe it is a monkey and a sarcopterygian fish.'

'Why is that?'

'Because I can see the thread, Madame Professor. See, if you look closely, under this scale.'

He showed her.

'Oh, dear,' she said. 'You're trapped, aren't you?' She handed the mermaid back. Then, 'The rector speaks of you with admiration. If you don't mind some personal advice, between countrymen. Save yourself. Genius favours the young. You are running out of time.'

BUT LEAVING his professor was not that easy.

Against his better judgement, he could not help but feel a filial affection. By then, he had begun to dream the two of them addressed each other with the informal *du*. So when Zimmer declared the radiographs 'inconclusive', Lucius told the old man that he needed to spend more time back in the library, in order to find a compound that could better serve their needs.

He began to attend class again.

Pathological Anatomy, with lab and lectures.

Pathological Histology, with lab and lectures.

Pathological Anatomy, with autopsy work. (Feuermann: 'At last, a patient!')

General Pharmacology, with its long lists of drugs to memorize, but no one to prescribe them to.

Back in the amphitheatres, peering down onto the stage.

And on. Until the summer of his third year, when, with two years of studies remaining and his impatience again almost unbearable, fortune intervened, this time bursting from the pistol of Gavrilo Princip in Sarajevo and into the bodies of the archduke and his wife.

2

AT FIRST LUCIUS did not appreciate the opportunity of war, declared that July. He saw the efforts of mobilization as disruptive to his studies and feared the rumours that classes would be suspended. He did not understand the patriotism of his classmates, so drunk with a sense of destiny, vacating the libraries so that they might attend the marches, lining up together to enlist. He did not join them when they gathered around maps showing the advance of the Austro-Hungarian Imperial and Royal Army into Serbia, or the German march through Belgium, or the engagement with Russian forces at the Masurian Lakes. He had no interest in the editorials exalting 'the escape from world stagnation' and 'the rejuvenation of the German soul'. When his cousin Witold, two years his junior, and recently arrived from Kraków, told him with tearful eyes that he had enlisted as a foot soldier because, for the first time in his life, the war had made him feel as if he were Austrian, Lucius answered in Polish that the war had also apparently made him an idiot, and he would do nothing but get himself killed.

But the celebrations were hard to ignore. It seemed as if the entire city reeked of rotting flowers. In the city parks, errant streamers tangled themselves in the rose bushes, and everywhere Lucius saw garlanded soldiers walking with beaming girlfriends on their arms. Cinemas offered war-time specials with short clips like *Our Factories at Work*, and *He Stops to Bandage a Friend*. In the hospital, the nurses debated the problems of gauge coordination for Austrian trains advancing over Russian rails.

Portraits of the enemy appeared in the papers to illustrate their brute-like physiognomies. At home his nephews sang,

> *Pretty Crista,*
> *At the Dniester.*
> *How she cried!*
> *Cossack bride.*

He ignored them.

Zeppelins flew past, dipping their noses above the Hofburg palace in deference to the Emperor.

Then, a few weeks in, rumours of physician shortages began to come.

THEY WERE ONLY rumours at first – the army would not publicly admit to such poor planning. But quietly changes were announced at the medical school. Early graduation was offered to those who would enlist. Students with but four semesters of medical studies were made medical lieutenants, and those with six, like Lucius, offered positions on staffs of four or five doctors, in garrison hospitals serving entire regiments of three thousand men. By late August, Kaminski was at a regimental hospital in southern Hungary, and Feuermann assigned to the Serbian front.

Two days before his friend's departure, Lucius met Feuermann at Café Landtmann. It was covered with bunting and overflowed with families on one last outing with their sons. Since his enlistment, Feuermann seemed to be whistling constantly. His hair was trimmed; he wore a little moustache of which he seemed unduly proud. On his uniform he had pinned an Austrian flag next to his Star of David badge from the Hakoah sports club where he swam. Lucius should reconsider, he said, sipping from a beer decorated with a black and yellow ribbon. If not out of loyalty to the Emperor, then loyalty to medicine. Didn't he understand how many years he would have to wait before he saw such cases? Galen learned on gladiators! Within days Feuermann would be operating, while Lucius, if he stayed in Vienna, would be lucky to be the twentieth to listen to a patient's heart.

In the street, a band led a festooned ambulance from a Rescue Society, followed by a rank of wasp-waisted women in white summer dresses and fluttering hats. Little boys wove through them, waving streamers of coloured crêpe.

Lucius shook his head. More than any of his classmates, he deserved such a posting. But in two years they would graduate. And then on to academic posts, *real* medicine, to something worthy of their capabilities. Anyone could learn first aid . . .

Feuermann removed his glasses and held them to the light. 'A girl kissed me, Krzelewski. Such a pretty girl, and on the lips. Just last night, in the Hofgarten, during the celebration parade.' He put his glasses back on. 'Kaminski said one actually threw him her knickers at the train station. Frilled and all. A girl he'd never even met.'

'You don't think that she was throwing them to someone else and Kaminski intercepted?' asked Lucius.

'Ah ha!' laughed Feuermann. 'But to the victor go the spoils, right?' And he kissed his fingers like a satisfied gourmand.

Then he brought out a surgical manual, and they read through the standard hospital kit.

Morphine sulphate, mouse-toothed forceps, chisel, horsehair sutures . . .

On and on, like two children poring over a catalogue of toys. 'Well?' asked Feuermann at last.

But Lucius hadn't really needed to read past *chisel*.

At the recruitment office, he waited in a long queue before a single clerk. He left as a medical lieutenant, with a drill handbook detailing bugle calls and the hierarchy of the salute. After, with Feuermann, at a wine tavern out in Hietzing hung with garlic braids, he got drunk with a group of Hungarian recruits. They were rough, heavy country boys, who spoke scarcely any German, and yet they all drank together until they could scarcely stand. They seemed completely unaware of the whispers that it was Austria's war, that the so-called Territorials – the Poles and Czechs and Romanians, etc. that made up the rest of the Empire – were being asked to sacrifice themselves in Austria's name. By the end of the evening, they were singing that they would die for Lucius, and Lucius was singing that he would die for them. None of it seemed real. Hours later, stumbling home through the hot night, he turned a corner to find himself facing a shirtless, gap-toothed child, ribbon tied around its head. For a moment they paused, staring each other down. Then the child grinned, raised his fist and cocked a finger, whispered, *Bang*.

BACK AT HOME, his mother was thrilled by his enlistment, but felt that medical duties, out of the line of fire, would seem like cowardice. So she bought him a horse and called upon a friend in the War Ministry to cancel his commission and speed his entry into the lancers, like his father, even though he'd last ridden when he was twelve.

Lucius received this news with quiet fury. The calculus was clear. Krzelewski Metals and Mining was about to be made even richer by the war. Every sabotaged railway would have to be rebuilt, only to be destroyed again; again rebuilt, destroyed, rebuilt again. But in the end there would be a reckoning. She needed at least one patriot to prove they weren't profiteers.

His father, overjoyed by the prospect, now filled with affection, spent hours versing Lucius on the history of the Polish cavalry, lavishing especial praise on the lancers. He had often dressed in some version of his old uniform, but now the outfit that emerged was something of an altogether different register of splendour: scarlet jodhpurs, bright blue tunic with a double rank of buttons, boots polished until one could see the far-off reflection of the plumed *czapka* on his head.

In his library, he brought down volume after volume of military history. His eyes grew teary, then he sang some very dirty cavalry songs. With the lights off, he showed Lucius hand shadows he had last performed a decade before: the War Horse, Death Comes for the Cossack, and the Decapitated Venetian. For a moment, Lucius wondered if he had been drinking, but his father's eyes were clear as he gazed into his great regimental past. No, God had made no greater warrior than the Polish lancer! No one! Unless, of course, one counted the Polish winged hussars, who rode with great, clattering frames of ostrich feathers on their backs.

'Of course, Father,' Lucius answered. The winged regiments had been disbanded in the eighteenth century; this remained a sore point with Retired Major Krzelewski. Since childhood, Lucius had heard this many, many times.

His father smiled contentedly and stroked the *czapka* strap, which bifurcated his smooth white beard. Then his pale blue eyes lit up. He had a thought!

Two full coats of winged armour flanked their entrance stairs. Together they hauled them creaking back up into the ballroom and strapped them on. The wings were so heavy that Lucius almost tumbled back.

'Can you imagine!' said his father, amazingly upright, looking like a wizened knight. Lucius wheezed; the breastplate had ridden up his thin chest and was choking off his breath. He wondered how long he could stand there without collapsing. But his father was lost in fantasy. '*Can* you imagine!' he said again, when, for a moment – finding his balance, the light glinting off the armour, a breeze from an open window fluttering the feathers, the image of the two winged men reflected in the ballroom mirror – for a moment, Lucius could.

'We should wear them out to supper with your mother,' his father said, and drummed his knuckles on the armour of his chest.

Later he realized Lucius didn't know how to shoot.

'Father, I'm enlisting as a *doctor*,' Lucius repeated, but his father didn't seem to hear. He opened all the doors along the grand hallway and the window that looked out onto a tall oak outside. From his study, he withdrew his old service revolver. He led Lucius to the far end of the hall and handed it to him.

'See the knot?' he said, and Lucius squinted, his gaze coursing the corridor with its portraits and statues.

'I see a tree,' said Lucius.

'The knot is on the tree,' his father said. 'Now shoot.'

His hand wavered. He squinted, pulled. In his mind, bits of marble burst from the busts of his parents, chunks of plaster fell from the ceiling, vases imploded. Again he fired, and again, the tapestries in threads, glass shattering from the chandeliers.

The revolver clicked, the chamber empty. His father laughed and handed him a bullet. 'Excellent. This time open your eyes.'

His mother turned the end of the hallway and entered his range, Puszek trotting imperiously at her side.

Lucius lowered his arm.

'Zbigniew, not again, please,' she said to his father when she reached him, lowering the muzzle with two fingers while her free hand stroked the dog.

She motioned behind her to a little man who had taken shelter behind the marble bust of Chopin. 'Come,' she said. 'They're harmless.' He scurried forward, easel beneath his arm. The portraitist: Lucius had almost forgotten. A servant followed with one of his father's old uniforms, which the painter had to pin so it didn't hang so loosely about Lucius's neck.

The portrait took three days. When the painter was finished, his mother took it into the light. 'More colour to the cheeks,' she said. 'And his neck is thin, but not *this* thin. And truly are these the shape of his ears? Amazing! How extraordinary the things a mother overlooks because of love! But do even them out – his head looks like it's flying away! And this *expression* . . .' She led the painter into the dining hall where the old portrait of Sobieski hung. 'Can you make him more . . . martial?' she asked. 'Like this?'

When the first portrait was finished, she sat with Lucius for another, for three more days. 'Mother and son,' she said. 'It will hang in your room.' And he almost heard her say, *When you are gone*.

BY THEN ZIMMER had also heard.

Lucius was in the library when his professor found him. 'Come with me,' he said.

Outside, Zimmer made no effort to hide his anger. He understood Lucius's patriotic impulse. Were he not so old, if he didn't have this rheumatism, he would also serve! But to go to the *front*? If it was a military appointment Lucius wanted, this could be arranged. He could be given an assistant position at the University Hospital here in Vienna. With the expected influx of cases he was sure to find many new responsibilities. He would be wasted on the front lines. That wasn't medicine anyway – it was butchery. War medicine was for nurses. A mind like his would not be content assisting amputations.

Lucius listened impatiently. It wasn't patriotism, he thought. *Morphine sulphate, mouse-toothed forceps, chisel* – that was why he was going. Feuermann, on the front already, had written about a giant magnet for extracting embedded shrapnel. In Vienna, the senior surgeons would take all the best patients for themselves – they, too, were eager for the complex wounds that war would bring. At best, he would be given abscesses or dilation of urethral strictures secondary to gonorrhoea. More likely he would be assigned to examining recruits. No: Lucius, first in his *Rigorosum*, would not spend the war telling eager volunteers to turn their heads and cough.

Zimmer called upon the rector, and the rector offered Lucius a position as Second-Level Assistant at the Empress Elisabeth Hospital for the Rehabilitation of the Very Injured.

Second-Level Assistant! Lucius didn't bother to respond.

He took the train a half-day south to Graz, where his family wasn't known. There he presented himself again at the recruiting office, giving the address of his boarding house. In the previous weeks, the Russian army had advanced into Galicia, the strip of Polish-speaking Austrian territory that descended the northern flank of the Carpathians. With Germany tied up in the west and north, Austria was forced to divert the Second Army from Serbia. To his great fortune, the Graz garrison was being transferred soon. For the entire Second Army of seventy-five thousand men, they had scarcely ninety doctors, forty of whom were medical students from the university in Graz.

He did the mathematics in his head.

His application was accepted instantly. The recruiter spent more time asking Lucius about how well he spoke Polish than questioning his medical training. Waving his hand vaguely towards the north, he said, 'No one can understand each other out there. They give our officers Territorials to command, and the men don't understand a word. How can you fight a war like this?'

Then he caught himself, and shouted, 'God bless the Emperor!' but this seemed to make his blasphemy only worse.

The knob of the seal was burnished down to the red wood, and the stamp was barely legible. *Thump*, it went, on seven papers, seven times. In his life, Lucius had touched four living patients in addition to the old man he had liberated from ear wax: three men and one blind old woman, the last who, truth be told, had clawed desperately at anyone nearby.

In Kraków, in his first communication home, he asked his mother to send his books.

LITTLE DID he know, but it would be nearly six months before he reached the front.

In Kraków, he was assigned to a field hospital near Rawa Ruska, but the day he was to leave, he was told that Rawa Ruska had fallen, and instead he was to go to Stanislau. Then Stanislau fell, and he was assigned to the Lemberg garrison. But Lemberg fell, too, as did Turka and Tarnów. The Austrian line was disintegrating, pushed back against the foothills; it appeared as if Kraków itself might soon be taken. From the train stations, on the wide roads that led out of the city, regiment after regiment departed for the east. Despite the losses, it was impossible not to feel awe at the immensity of the Empire: its spangled cavalry and multitudes on foot, its balloons and motor cars, its bicyclists, their chains clanking as they peddled out over the rutted roads, rims flashing in the sun.

To think how these men need us, he wrote to Feuermann, hopefully, *that they cannot live without our hands!*

Still he waited for his assignment, pacing the city, his officer's sabre slapping impatiently against his boots. The boulevard chestnuts turned gold, then red. Day after day he went to the hospital, trying to assist in surgeries. But medical responsibilities in a regiment other than one's own required a Document M-32, he learned quickly, and the train carrying the paymaster's batch of Document M-32s supposedly had vanished somewhere between Vienna and Kraków. Fortunately, explained an irritated clerk the fourth time Lucius visited, they had received an extra delivery of N-32s, *Regulations Regarding Marching Bands*. Would Lucius want one of those?

He would have laughed were he not so frustrated. In the hospital tents, shuffling priests hurried past the orderlies to administer extreme unction, and little women slipped inside to deliver icons to the dying. It seemed as if he were the only one without a purpose. Then, in late October, following yet another reorganization, he was assigned to Boroević's Third Army, which had just lifted the siege of Przemyśl, by then the sole Austrian holdout on the Galician plain. Again he prepared to leave. He had his tunic pressed, his boots polished, and he neatly folded his long underwear to keep his textbooks from getting bumped. But Boroević pulled back into the mountains, and Lucius's deployment was cancelled yet again.

By his fourth reassignment, he'd begun to give up hope. In his billet at the Kraków Natural History Museum, in the Room of Large Mammals, amid skeletons of whales and sea cows, he tried to study. But the surgical textbooks seemed to mock him with their discussions of cancers in the elderly, while the medical texts devoted pages to rest cures for pneumonia, hardly useful for an army on the move.

The army-issued medical manuals were not much help, either. They consisted of:

— five pages on applying whale oil to the inside of boots to prevent abrasions

— ten pages on latrine building

— a chapter on 'Moral instruction for the soldier who misses the comforts of the wife'

— a glossary for Austrian medical officers attending to the needs of Hungarian soldiers ignorant of German, with such phrases as:

Hazafias magyarok! Mindebben mindannyian együtt vagyunk!
Patriotic Magyars, we are all in this together!
Nem beteg, a baj az a bátorság hiánya!
He is not sick, his disease is no bravery.
Persze hogy viszket Somogyi őrmester, nem kellett volna olyan szoknyapecérnek lenni!
Of course it itches, Sergeant Somogyi, you were out of control.

— a page on abdominal surgery, which concluded, after consideration of the opinions of various world-famous experts and some statistical discussion – *abdominal wounds generally exceed 60 per cent mortality despite intervention* – that abdominal surgery should not be done.

He wrote to his mother again, this time asking her to send textbooks on wound care and basic first-aid techniques.

Briefly, he was appointed to a delousing detail, to prevent outbreaks of typhus among eastern refugees, mostly Jewish families fleeing attacks on their villages. The camp was set up in a cattle market, south of the city. It was miserable. A deep antagonism had developed between the medical personnel and the refugees, the most religious of whom resisted shaving their hair. The camp director was a former headmaster of a primary school, a viperous man, angry that the army was wasting

Austrians to defend Poles and Jews. To Lucius, he said he was happy to have the company of another man of science, and in the evenings he liked to lecture him on his theories of heredity and the natural uncleanliness of certain races. Not once did Lucius see the camp director try to explain to his wards why they were rounded up and shorn, their ritual clothes taken from them for steaming. When at last Lucius grew sick with watching sanitary personnel tear off the hats and kaftans, he went alone to one of the rabbis and tried to explain to him why the measures needed to be taken. But the old man wouldn't listen. He kept repeating how his people were being treated like animals. There had been no cases of typhus yet; why were they the only ones being harassed so? Lucius tried to explain the transmission cycle of typhus to him, that it took time for the disease to develop, that rats and fleas were present, and already they had outbreaks in other camps.

'What is it caused by?' the man asked, and Lucius had to answer, 'We ... I mean, science ... doesn't know. Something unseen, a bacillus, a virus.'

'So you are burning our clothes for something unseen,' said the rabbi, shaking his head. 'For a disease which has not been found.'

In January, he received news of his fifth redeployment, to a small village in the Galician Carpathians called Lemnowice. On the map it sat in a narrow valley, on the northern slope of the mountains, a finger's breadth from Uzhok Pass on the Hungarian border.

Uzhok, thought Lucius, a memory stirring. *Uzhok:* of course. For it was there a famous meteor had lit the sky two weeks before his father was shot in battle, an augury that had become part of family lore.

The Uzhok meteorite had been collected and brought back

to the Natural History Museum in Vienna; a painting on the wall illustrated the event. Yes, he remembered this . . . he used to go there with his father. It was perhaps his only memory of sharing anything that didn't have to do with the lancers, although, in a roundabout way (meteor–bullet–hip), it did.

But he couldn't get there from Kraków – the war was in the way. He would have to travel to Budapest, they told him, and from there on to Debrecen, where he would board yet another train.

Given his disappointments, he didn't believe it. He heard nothing for the next four days. But then, back in Vienna, in the Trains Division of the Headquarters of the Imperial and Royal Army, a Second-Level Clerk rose from his desk and, carrying a ledger, made his way to the corresponding Second-Level Clerk in the Medical Division, two flights down, returning with an order bearing a double-headed eagle stamp, which he presented to the First-Level Clerk in Trains for another stamp, then walked down four flights of stairs and out the building and through the snow to the Ad-hoc Office for the Eastern Theatre, where the order with both stamps was delivered to a corresponding Second-Level Clerk in the Transportation Division, who entered the name into a ledger, applied his own stamp, returned the order, wrote out a second order, and sent it down to the Head Clerk for Trains, in the Medical Division, Eastern Theatre, who, after a lunch of stale rye and egg sprinkled so heavily with paprika that it would stain the oily fingerprints he left in the margins of the page, rose, and with the ledger tucked inside his coat, went outside, stopping briefly to appreciate the beauty of the falling snow on a pensive putto above a doorway and on the glistening rooftops, before he crossed the boulevard to the military post office.

The route to Budapest passed back through Vienna. There,

just across the inner city from his home, Lucius only had time
to buy a pickle from a station vendor before he had to board
again. Three days later he was in the barracks in Debrecen,
when he received the orders that he would take a final train
to a place he had never heard of, called Nagybocskó, beyond
another place he'd never heard of, called Máramarossziget,
where he would be met by an escort from the hussars.

An escort from the hussars. An image, then, of standing with
his father in their ballroom, the great wings fluttering above
their heads. *Near Máramarossziget.* He said the word slowly, like
a child pronouncing the secret name of a fabled land.

To Feuermann, he wrote, *At last.*

THE NIGHT BEFORE his departure, distracted by anticipation,
Lucius was crossing the market square when a child dashed
from a carriage and with a squeal ran straight into his legs. The
street was slick with ice. He took a step forward to steady himself, caught his sabre between his legs, and tripped, hearing his
wrist snap when he reached out to break his fall.

For a moment he lay on the ice, clutching his arm. He
waited for help, but the street was empty. Like a ghost, the child
was gone, likely swept up by a mother afraid of the punishment
for knocking down an Austrian officer.

Back in his quarters, he removed his greatcoat and undid the
buttons of the cuff. The standard procedure would have been to
get an X-ray, but he was already certain what had happened: a
Colles' fracture of the carpal extremity of the radius, the bone
displaced dorsally, the sharp edge now palpable. Already it was
so swollen that he had trouble opening the cuff. He cursed, furi-
ous at the child and his own incaution. He still had feeling in
his fingers – at least there'd been no injury to the nerve. But the
fracture would need to be reduced.

It would be safest just to report to the hospital, he knew. But he also knew that if he did so, there was no way he would be sent on to the front.

It could have been a joke. What does the Imperial and Royal Army call a one-handed medical student with no clinical experience?

Doctor.

He pulled lightly on his wrist, thinking that if he could bear it, he might reduce the fracture himself. But the pain was too great, and the muscle was in spasm. His will failed him. He needed help from someone strong.

He left the barracks and wandered towards town. He hoped to find a local doctor; even a veterinarian might do. But most of the signs were in Hungarian, and he couldn't understand them. At last he saw the word *Kovács*, above a painted anvil – *Blacksmith*. Knocking on the door, he was met by a woman with a coat thrown over a nightdress. She stared at him suspiciously. In German she said, 'We are full. No more billets. Already sleeping on the floor.'

'I don't need a billet.' He lifted his arm to show his swollen wrist.

She disappeared inside and returned with a man of such shoulders and such a big, black beard that Lucius wondered if he had not stumbled upon Vulcan himself. Lucius showed him his arm, and the man whistled through his teeth. But he seemed completely unsurprised that an unknown soldier had appeared at his door in the middle of the night with a broken wrist. One of their boarders was a medic, he said, should he get him? Lucius shook his head – the medic would tell him to go to the hospital, he knew. He just needed a strong pair of hands.

The blacksmith led him to his worktable and lit the lamp. A pair of soldiers were sleeping on the floor. Speaking in a whisper, Lucius instructed him to grab the hand and forearm and draw them apart.

'That's all?'

'That's all,' said Lucius, though really he had no idea. His old textbook had an illustration that made it seem as if the bone simply popped back into place.

The man left, returning with a greasy cup of spirits. Lucius thanked him and downed it in a gulp. His eyes teared up; he presented his arm. The blacksmith was tentative at first, and because the muscles in the forearm were in spasm, Lucius had to instruct him to pull harder, then harder still. He could feel the edges of the bone scraping. He bore the pain until he couldn't any longer, pulling away with a cry.

His head spun; he was afraid he would pass out. Mumbling gratitude to the blacksmith, he stumbled outside and into the cold air. He needed some kind of narcotic, not only to relieve him now, but also to endure the coming journey by horse.

The hospital was across the street from the barracks. The hall was dark, the soldiers sleeping. He passed a pair of nurses at the nursing station, but he acted as if he knew where he was going. Somewhere there would be a supplies cupboard. He passed through another ward. At the far end he found it, slipped inside, and rummaged until he found ampoules of cocaine and morphine, a syringe. He slipped them into the pocket of his coat.

The train was scheduled to depart at dawn. Back in his room, he broke the cover from a histology textbook, lined it with a shirt, and fashioned a rough splint. With his good hand, he set about packing his bags. He didn't sleep – he was too worried that the swelling might cause compression of the nerve. Then he would have no choice but to report the injury, for they would have to open his wrist. He told himself that if he could still feel his fingers by morning, he'd press on. In any case, his destination was a hospital, where he'd get care if needed. There he could claim that the fracture had happened en route. And there, he decided, they wouldn't send him back. He'd learn while it healed. When it was ready, he would work.

In the morning, he removed the splint and let his hand hang free. Only once did he have to lift it, to salute the officer who took his papers at the station. When the train began to move, he splinted it again.

He reached Nagybocskó in the late afternoon, where the hussar escort was waiting.

FROM THE LITTLE station house, they followed the road through snowy fields before it entered a valley thick with pine. Milky layers of ice glinted on the branches, which clattered as the wind came through. Teardrops froze in the corners of Lucius's eyes and on his lashes, and the shawl that wrapped his face grew thick with rime. Binding his reins about his good hand, he tried to brace his broken wrist, but the narrow road was hard as metal, and the horses slipped from time to time. When at last the pain grew unbearable, he called out for the hussar to stop.

He fumbled with his rucksack until he found the ampoules of cocaine and morphine. They had frozen, so he slipped them into his mouth to warm them. He injected the cocaine directly into his fracture, then paused, ready to inject the morphine, but stopped. No. Best to be sparing; he didn't know how far they had to go.

The land rose, the valley steep but broad. Soon they reached a wooded pass. The road descended, crossed into another valley, and began to descend again. They passed the entrance to a village, marked by a painted sign with a primitive Death's Head and the words FLECKFIEBER!!! – *typhus* – and BEWARE SOLDIER! DO NOT ENTER HERE! DEATH AWAITS!!! in German, Polish and what he assumed to be the same in Romanian, Ruthenian and Hungarian.

The hussar crossed himself, and though they were far from the village entrance, he gave it a wide berth. As if something fanged and taloned might burst out and chase them down.

Lucius's arm began to throb again. Again he called to the hussar to stop, uncapped the old needle, broke the morphine ampoule, and injected it into his arm.

The forest thinned. They passed empty fields, now scarred by war. Bomb craters, abandoned bulwarks, trenches. From a tree, something was hanging: a body, now encased almost entirely in ice. At the far end of the field lay a dark pile of what seemed like boulders, but as they approached, Lucius saw that they were frozen horses. There were perhaps fifty, half-covered in snow. Garish, dark-red flowers bloomed from their heads. In the shadows of the forest, he thought he saw others. The hussar slowed.

A scrap of livery fluttered lightly from one of the exposed saddles, the letters *k.u.k.* still visible.

Kaiserlich und königlich. Imperial and Royal. *His* army. Suddenly Lucius was afraid.

'Cossacks?'

Shadows danced deep in the woods. He saw the horsemen, creatures of so many childhood dreams. Then nothing but the trees.

'Cossacks don't execute horses,' said the hussar, disdainfully, from behind his mask. 'This is Austria in retreat.'

At first Lucius didn't understand. But he was embarrassed to show his ignorance, and it was only as they rode on that he recalled the stories of surrender, the animals shot to keep them out of enemy hands.

It was close to dusk when they passed their first set of

travellers, a refugee family leading a goat cart down the snowy road. There were four children, two on the cart, two walking, their faces swaddled like mummies, jackets stuffed with straw until they were nearly bursting at their seams.

In Hungarian, the hussar commanded them to stop. He pointed to the cart and spoke. The woman protested. Lucius couldn't understand the words, but it was clear what she was saying: nothing here, some old rags – that's all. The hussar dismounted from his horse and walked, somewhat stiffly, over to the cart, where he began to search. The woman followed him. *'Nincs semmink!'* she cried, both hands in prayer. *'Nincs semmink! Nincs semmink!'* But by then the hussar had found what she was hiding. One by one, he drew them out: rabbits, twitching, eyes wide, breath steaming, kicking their long back legs against the air.

Cries rose from the swaddled faces of the children. The hussar offered Lucius a rabbit, holding out the steaming creature in his extended hand, like a priest before a sacrifice. Lucius shook his head, but the hussar threw it to him anyway, and he caught it with his good arm, against his chest. Then he hesitated. He wanted to return it to the family, but he could feel the hussar watching him through the thin slits in his leather mask.

The rabbit kicked as he slipped it inside his greatcoat. It wriggled out. He caught it by its leg and this time tucked it inside his shirt, against his skin, where, out of terror or from some physiological change provoked by the change in temperature, it released a stream that trickled down his belly and his legs. Lucius could feel its heart thrumming against his skin. He did not understand why the hussar hadn't killed the rabbits there, but this choice, before the children, seemed almost kind.

He kept his eyes from the family as they rode on.

They returned to the road. After another hour, the hussar stopped and dismounted slowly, even more stiffly than when he'd stopped before. He fumbled with his trousers as if to urinate, and Lucius looked away to give him privacy. But when the man hadn't moved for several minutes, Lucius looked back. Now something seemed wrong. Another minute, and Lucius heard him curse, then groan as if straining, before he gave up and climbed back on his horse.

Close to evening, they entered an empty village, stopping to billet in an abandoned house. The walls were bare; the kitchen was empty, the cabinets open, the floor covered with broken plates. An icon of St Stanislaus of Poland lay in an open drawer, as if it had been hidden there and then discovered.

Poland, thought Lucius. *Galicia*. Somewhere, in the woods, they must have crossed the border. On a table, inexplicably, was a beautiful ceramic music box, which played an unfamiliar tune. The bed had been lanced open and emptied of its straw.

They kept the horses inside, in the dining room. Gathering bed straw, tearing off the last remaining doors from the cabinet, the hussar lit a fire, killed and skinned the rabbits, and boiled them in a pot he carried on his horse. Without his mask, his face looked drawn and hollow now, and Lucius saw he ate only tiny bites. 'Are you ill?' he asked at last. The man grunted, but didn't reply. When they'd finished eating, they lay down, clothed, beneath a single blanket. Lucius remained awake. The anaesthetic had begun to wear off, and his wrist was throbbing. Now he regretted his ambition to push on. How far was Lemnowice? He had enough cocaine for one more day. Constantly, he wiggled his numb fingers, worried again about a compression of the nerve. But the room was freezing – he could scarcely feel the fingers of his other hand, either.

He was still awake when the hussar stirred, rose, and went to the wall to urinate. As before, he remained like that a long time, perhaps five minutes, more, before he began to groan and then to strike himself, his thighs or lower abdomen or penis – Lucius couldn't see, only that the man did so with increasing violence.

Lucius sat up. '*Corporal?*'

The man stopped. His fists were balled. He lifted them high above his head and began to moan.

'*Corporal?*' Lucius said again. Then, very tentatively, uttering the words for the first time in his life, 'I am a doctor.'

There was silence. Cautiously the man appraised him from dark, sunken eyes above unshaven cheeks.

Then tentatively, he said, 'It does not come out. It is stuck . . . It hurts, here . . .'

It took Lucius only a moment to put the signs together. In the textbooks there might be a dozen different causes for an obstruction, but on the Eastern Front, with its garrison towns lined with whorehouses, there was really only one explanation in an otherwise healthy man. Back in Kraków, the clinics cared for a steady flow of men receiving urethral dilatation for gonorrhoeal strictures. He had seen massive, stoic soldiers reduced to sobs.

Lucius said, 'Tomorrow, at the hospital, they'll take care of you.'

The man said, 'Nothing comes out.'

Lucius said, 'I understand. Tomorrow, we will reach the hospital . . .'

'*Nothing!*'

'I understand. I . . .' He took a deep breath. 'When did you last go?'

But the hussar didn't answer. Instead, he turned, holding his penis in his open palm, as if to say to Lucius, *look*. Lucius hesitated. Then, lighting a candle from his rucksack, he crouched before the hussar. *Think. Remember the lectures on the anatomy of the bladder.* Except he'd skipped them to work in Zimmer's lab.

He told the man to bear down, and a single drop of urine appeared at the tip of his penis. Gently, Lucius palpated the man's belly. It was tense, his bladder full. Once, chronic venereal disease was the kind of problem he might have joked about with Feuermann, hardly the glorious surgery he'd expected on the front. But now the possible consequences of an untreated obstruction ran through his mind. Did the bladder actually rupture? Or the urethra? Or did the kidneys shut down before anything tore?

'Tomorrow at the hospital . . .' Lucius began.

The man shook his head. 'I can't get back on the horse.' He bent over, pushing his fist so hard into his belly that Lucius was now certain something would burst.

Leaving me alone with a dying horseman in an abandoned village, he thought. He didn't know where he was going, nor how to return to Nagybocskó.

The soldier said, 'Every month, I go . . . they use a little rod . . .'

'I know,' said Lucius. 'It is called a *bougie*. But I don't have one.'

The two men looked around the room, eyes passing over the saint's icon, the music box. Then the hussar said, 'For my rifle, there is a rod assembly . . .'

Lucius felt his stomach turn. 'I can't. They use petroleum jelly . . . For the rod to advance, we need . . .'

But the man was rummaging through his saddlebags, returning with a three-piece collapsible brush, with one piece screwing into the other. It looked like a medieval torture implement. But the pieces without bristles were thin and smooth, and even

47

tapered at their threaded ends. From the bag, the man removed a tube of gun oil.

Lucius had two ampoules of morphine left, and he gave the hussar one, using the needle still dirty with his own blood. He told the man to lie down, and waited until the morphine took effect. Then he squeezed rifle oil onto the rod. Again he tried to recall what he'd read in the textbook. If he remembered correctly, the urethral canal took a sharp turn at the urethral sphincter. If he pushed too far, he could pierce through the wall of the canal. But if the stricture were closer, he might stand a chance. He took a deep breath. 'Grab here,' he said, and had the hussar pull his penis straight. He placed the rod at the urethral opening and advanced it slowly in. The man tensed. Lucius stopped, now remembering that one of the risks of the procedure was opening a false passage. His left hand was trembling, and he braced it with his right. He found himself recalling how in Kraków, in the mess hall, he'd heard a pair of sappers talking about a certain kind of shaking that beset them as they gently wound the wires of their bombs. He advanced the rod further, and then it reached resistance. He backed up, slipped it forward, again felt it stop. Then, with a push, past. Then the hussar roared, twisted away, leaving Lucius, rod in hand, stumbling back, piss-sprayed as the man shattered a wall plank with his fist.

He'll kill me, Lucius thought. But then the hussar began to laugh.

The next morning he was in tremendous spirits.

He sang as he urinated in many directions. '*Orvos!*' he said, embracing Lucius as he half-spoke, half-sang something in Hungarian, none of which Lucius understood. Save *orvos*. Doctor. It was enough.

They set out. Their trail joined with a rutted, empty road that climbed steeply into the hills. Now the hussar seemed positively garrulous. He sang and whistled and drummed on his thighs. It was good that Lucius was a doctor, he told him. Lots of patients. He made a sawing motion with his hand.

They stopped only for Lucius to inject more anaesthetic into his wrist. By then the signs of war were gone, the forest clear. The only person they saw was an old man in the middle of a dark wood, rummaging through the snow. When the hussar slowed, Lucius was afraid that he would rob him just as he had robbed the others, but he only asked the way, and the old man pointed with a turnip as he leaned unsteadily on his stick.

Dusk was falling when they came over a low hill and at last found themselves before a village. It was tucked in a softly slop-ing valley, with two streets of houses descending from a single wooden church of rough-hewn logs. Above the church, the road kept rising. Below, the valley widened into snow-covered fields that flanked a frozen river. 'Lemnowice,' said the hussar. They followed the road down to the fields and then up past the houses. They were low-ceilinged huts, made of wood, straw-thatched, with tiny windows, all covered with wooden shutters so that it was impossible to see inside. There were no chimneys. A pair of drays lay in the road, seemingly abandoned, half-buried in snow. There was a flutter over one of the rooftops, and a huge black crow took off into the sky.

There was not a soul in sight. He saw no garrison, no sign of the army at all, certainly nothing that could be a hospital. Perhaps it lay beyond the hill, he thought. Unless, this, too, had been a mistake. Unless, after such a journey, he would have to turn around.

The hussar stopped before the church, motioning Lucius to descend. He obeyed, approached the door, and knocked. He waited. There was a narrow window in the door that reminded him of a castle arrow slit. The hussar told him to knock harder, and only then did he hear movement, the sound of footsteps. In the window, an eye appeared.

'Krzelewski,' said Lucius. 'Medical lieutenant. Fourteenth Regiment, Third Army.'

Then a key in the lock, a clang of the mechanism. The door opened to reveal a nursing sister. She wore a stiff grey habit, and in one hand held a Mannlicher rifle, standard issue of the *k.u.k.*

'May I speak to the supervising physician?' he asked in German.

When she didn't answer, he tried Polish.

'The doctor?' she replied, still staying back, in the shadows. 'Didn't you just say you're him?'

3

THE NURSE'S NAME was Margarete. She gave no surname. It was not the custom of the Sisters of St Catherine to do so, she would explain. Even Margarete was a name she had assumed with her vows, abandoning her earthly appellation to the life she led before. Her face floated in the darkness of the narthex, and it was only when Lucius turned to see the hussar kick his horse and ride away (*flee*, thought Lucius later) that she opened the door more widely, motioning for him to step inside with a sweeping of the gun. Then she threw her shoulder against the door. He stood in total darkness while she secured it, first turning the iron lock, then heaving a crossbar into the cleats. Turning to follow her movement, he heard a key slip into a second door, then the sonorous clanging of the mechanism as it engaged. Then, weapon swinging in her hand, she led him into the dim light of the nave.

As Lucius's habit upon entering a house of God was to look up at the majesty of the ceiling, his first impression was that the church of Lemnowice was much like any other of the dozens of wooden churches he had visited in the Tatras, further west, though this, with its heavy dome and tiny windows, suggested more an Eastern rite. A row of six wooden columns supported the ceiling, from which a pair of chains dangled, now empty of their chandeliers. In the distance, the north transept was illuminated by a lantern. The rest of the church was dark.

It was the sounds and smell that made him look down. A low moan from somewhere in the darkness. A cough, a laboured

51

breath. An acrid odour, something animal, like spoiled meat. He stared. The pews were gone, and in their place were lumps of blankets, and it was only when he saw one stir that he understood they were men.

Three rows, perhaps fifteen or twenty lumps in each.

By then Sister Margarete had finished locking the second door and appeared at his side. Softly, she said, 'If I may speak?'

Lucius nodded, unable to take his eyes off the bodies.

'The doctor, Szőkefalvi, a Hungarian,' she said, 'Szőkefalvi, your predecessor, vanished two months ago under circumstances which perhaps Pan Doctor Lieutenant should understand.'

Now Lucius turned, struck by her form of address, a combination of Polish honorific and German military rank. For a moment, he studied her. She was more than a head shorter than him, and her face was framed by the impeccably crisp folds of her wimple, which pressed in upon her cheeks. Her eyes were of indistinct colour, glassy, her lips parted with the impatience of one who wished to speak. He guessed she was a year or two older than he was. The giant key hung like a cross from a chain around her neck, and she had yet to set down her gun.

Again, she seemed to await his blessing. 'Yes, please, go on,' he said. Then, quietly, drawing him aside so that she could speak without being heard by the soldiers on the floor, she began.

'In the beginning there were seven of us, Pan Doctor Lieutenant: myself and Sisters Maria and Libuše and Elizabeth and Klara, and two doctors – one whose name deserves no utterance and Szőkefalvi, poor Szőkefalvi, whom I've come to forgive. We were but a simple casualty clearing station then. Patch up and send along, as they say. It wasn't until September that the High Command appreciated our sheltered position in the valley and upgraded us to the status of a regimental hospital, receiving the wounded from the battlefield and caring for them until they were ready to be evacuated to the rear. We had an X-ray machine and a bacteriology laboratory, and with daily prayer and sharp knives and carbolic acid for antisepsis of the wound, we performed a great service for the brave young men serving this smaller, terrestrial king. For three months, we attended to them: castigations of mine and sword, of howitzer, ecrasite and poisonous earth. We resurrected men shot through with every bullet in the Devil's armoury, men struck by high explosive and Cossack swords, men who lost their feet and hands to the winter when they fell asleep. Such was our glory, Pan Doctor, it brings tears of joy to my eyes to contemplate it once again. Even when the X-ray machine was taken off to Tarnów, and our last drop of eosin had illuminated the mysteries of the last bacteriologic slide – even then we prevailed. For two more months we prevailed. But with so many prayers rising to heaven, Doctor, not only here in Galicia, but from the Pripet, and from the Bukovina and Bessarabia, and – now I have heard – far and beyond, from the cities of Flanders and Friuli, from Serbia and Macedonia, and from the great city of Warsaw – yes, with so many lips turned towards our Lord's ever attentive ears, and His angels labouring without rest, deflecting bullets with their angelic breath and giving heat to frozen bodies in the snow – with so many lips turned to heaven, one could not expect His eternal protection for ever. So we forgave Him and took no affront when the fortress of Przemyśl was seized, and He sent His angels on to that city and left us to the mercy of the Louse.'

She paused. For the last word, she had spoken in German – *Laus* – and with it her face contorted briefly in disgust.

'You are familiar with the Louse, Doctor. I had known Her too well as a child, and indeed from the very first days of the war She was with us. But never have I known Her in such abundance as in this house of prayer. As the war drew on, we found ourselves confronted with ever greater infestations. Never, never, dear Doctor, have I seen such extraordinary fertility in any beast; indeed, in my moments of least faith I have wondered if it was the Louse that is God's favoured child. For it seemed at times that one could subtract all matter from our worldly domain but the Louse, and still Earth's contours could be seen. Oh, Doctor, as a child I had imagined the animals of Noah to be tame, clean creatures, with soft, sweet-smelling hair and soft noses. No! Now I realize that they all must have been infested, not only the rat, but the lion and weasel, the vicious giraffe: veritable arks themselves, for worm and tick and louse.

'For you cannot imagine the infestations of our men. Everywhere! On every layer of clothing, in every stitch and seam. In churning clumps, they teemed, they stirred, like embers. They came out upon our combs, grainy, like wet meal. Oh, sir, the Devil has had time to practise since poor Job! For if the Beast truly wished to try that man's faith, he would have given him a field dressing in Galicia. No, there is nothing that arouses a louse like the moist, warm dressing of a wound, nothing that heightens their incest more. A dressing applied one week prior in Lemberg would be teeming with so many rutting creatures that one could hear the soft thumps of the clots as they fell onto the floor.'

She took a deep breath.

'Of course, the Louse might torture, but as I've learned, She doesn't kill alone. The first case of typhus appeared in December, Doctor. I still remember the boy, the warmth of his skin, the rash as it spread across his chest and limbs, the peculiar thoughts that entered his mind and made him cry out. Try as we may, we couldn't save him, and it was not long before a second soldier, there –' and she pointed to the far corner of the room – 'and a third – there – and a fourth – there – came down with the disease. Night and day we worked to save them, but no amount of lime or cresol could clean them. No quarantine could stall their advance. And no matter how tight we made our clothing –' and her eyes traced the edges of her wimple – 'it did not matter. In the evenings, when I inspected the skin of Libuše, and Libuše Elizabeth, and Elizabeth Klara, and Klara myself – we would find the creatures on our very own flesh.

'Oh! Such was the state of affairs, Pan Doctor Lieutenant, when fear of Her first entered the heart of the good Hungarian doctor Szőkefalvi. Even now, I feel such love for Szőkefalvi – with his books and his patient lessons in nursing, with his innocent jokes of how he might like to join in our hours of delousing. He did not succumb at first, brave soul! I know so well the terror that seized him as he stood at the operating table and felt Her upon him. I saw him fight to direct his thoughts back to the case beneath his hands. Yet once you feel Her, you can't escape; once the itching begins, you cannot stop it, no, Pan Doctor Lieutenant: the slightest hair, the slightest tickle of wool is enough to conjure armies crawling across your skin. Even now if I am not strong, I can imagine Her crawling upon my knee, rising, her little prickling legs, her probing tongue. No! Oh, no, no, no! No, Pan Doctor Lieutenant Krzelewski: to survive, one must learn to fight such fantasies. But not so poor Szőkefalvi. In the middle of surgery, gloves wet with gore, I would see him twitch. Not a great motion at first, I tell you, just a pause with the knife, but I knew that he had felt Her. That deep within his woollens She had begun to crawl. Up his leg or foot or belly, and he would start to cut again, and She would crawl, and he would stop, and start, and stop, and all of a sudden put down his knife and tear off his gloves, the once steady hands trembling as he tore at his clothes for the offending itch. At first this man respected rules of modesty, moving swiftly into the vestry to disrobe. But as the weeks passed, he became so panicked, so harried, that he forgot my very presence, baring those parts that shouldn't be seen.'

Her eyes bore into him. 'Can you imagine the shock? I too feel Her crawling, Doctor, but I am of a nursing order, and if it is my fate to fall by Her bite, then it is so. I do not lose my dignity. St Catherine ate the scabs of the afflicted, and so I remain strong before my wards. This is my duty. Looking at a crushed skull, I feel no fear. I do not falter before gangrene. No! I see not death before me, Doctor, I see the glimmer of my heavenly crown. I do not hear screams, but the chorus that will greet me. And when I feel the Louse upon me, I do not thrust my hands into my habit like some Orang-utang of Portugal, but turn my thoughts to my Father on his throne. But Szőkefalvi, Doctor, gripped by such fear, was not so strong. Nowhere was he safe. Even in the fields, on his walks, I saw him tearing at his clothes, stripping madly in the cold. At night, I heard him weeping, begging our pest to leave him alone. So often did he wash himself with cresol that his skin began to peel away, which made matters worse still, for then it was impossible to know whether it was the Louse or his own mortified flesh that tickled in his brain. Yet no words could get him to change.'

She stopped. Now she seemed to be awaiting his response.

He said simply, 'And this other doctor, Szőkefalvi, he left?'

'In December.' She lowered her voice. 'If you will excuse your servant in venturing an opinion, I think he lost his mind. One morning I awoke and he was gone. But what do I know? You have studied in the great city of Vienna. Perhaps there you have heard of such a madness?'

But Lucius was looking over the vastness of the room. 'And the other nurses?'

'The other nurses, Pan Doctor Lieutenant?'

'They fled, too?'

'Oh, no. Sister Maria died of typhus and Libuše died of typhus and Elizabeth of typhus, too. All save Sister Klara are with the Lord. She *will* be judged. Oh! It has been weeks since I have had a companion. I must apologize for talking too much – it has been a vice since I was a child, worsened by the loneliness. There are the orderlies and the cooks, and I have the patients, of course – all these men are companions, but one must be careful, being the only woman, not to let affections develop, lest one follow the sad fate of Sister Klara, and be caught simulating married life in the vestry.' Now a blush passed over her face, visible even in the very low light. 'Must I say everything at once! You wish to rest. Can I show you to your quarters?'

She looked at him. It was a simple question, but at that moment Lucius could think of nothing other than going home. *How* exactly was beyond him – the hussar was gone, and two days of winter lay between him and the railway station. But certainly there were some means by which he might extricate himself. It was only a matter of explaining: he was not a true doctor yet, the Medical Service had made an error; perhaps with other doctors he could return and help. But alone? No ... he couldn't. Certainly, she would understand. Certainly, she was well aware of the incompetence of the High Command, of the growing debacle of a war; certainly she had heard of the entire Third Army sent against the wrong front; certainly she had seen the shoes made of cardboard, the summer coats given to alpine patrols. And if he didn't tell her now, his inexperience would soon become apparent, she would realize it the moment he touched a scalpel ...

'Sister ...' A pause. But what could he say? *My heartfelt apologies? There has been a mistake? I've never operated, I've cured two patients in my life, one of impacted ear wax and the other of a gonorrhoeal stricture?* Now, standing in the dim light, he could feel not only her eyes upon him, but also the eyes of the soldiers on the floor. *Primum non nocere.* But what did that mean here? Certainly he would do more harm to leave?

They, too, have not asked for this, he thought. *They did not ask to be sent into winter without coats. They, too, were not prepared.* Closest to them, he could see a young man with his head bandaged, staring at him with a single open eye filled with such pleading that Lucius had to look away.

Hope, gratitude, but there was also something else. It was hard to recognize it at first, but then he saw it: a demand – no, an expectation, perhaps even a threat. What would so many injured soldiers do when he told them he couldn't help?

'Pan Doctor?'

He turned back to her. Now his words seemed to come from someone else. 'It is important that the patients not be disrupted in their schedules. What was Szőkefalvi's custom at this hour?'

'Rounds, Pan Doctor. If there were no emergencies, he would make evening rounds.' Her voice soft, her relief palpable, a little constellation of candlelights flickering in what seemed to be her brimming tears.

'Then we should waste no time.'

'You will stay then? Even if you feel Her, you will stay?'

Lucius already felt Her. From the moment Margarete began to describe Her, he had felt his skin crawling and had done everything in his power to keep from tearing off his clothes.

'We each have our appointed hour,' he mumbled, aware it was something she might say. Something, before this moment, he would never have believed at all.

He shouldered his bag and she led him along one of the paths between the patients. She spoke as they walked. 'They are provisionally organized into wards. The nave is where we keep the lesser injuries – the fractures and amputations. We operate within the crossing – the light is best. The south transept is where the dying men are kept, out of sight of the others. The head wounds are in the chancel, where they can be watched.' Lanterns hung at even intervals. He was aware now of the walls, painted with scenes from the Bible. An ark, a serpent, crucifixions set amid what seemed to be Carpathian villages, entwined with Latin verse. Gilded saints above the colonnades. A Last Judgement on the sacristy partition, its tree of fire ornamented with monks and hog-tied sinners, marching on a devil's tongue.

At the end of the nave, beneath the Annunciation, they stopped. In the floor of the north transept was a crater, nearly a metre deep. A light dusting of snow covered its walls and the steps of a pulpit. Now he realized that the light he had seen earlier was coming from a jagged hole in the high ceiling, poorly patched with wood and tarpaulin. Sister Margarete said nothing.

'What happened?' he asked, pointing.

As she smiled, the wimple pressed into her cheeks. 'What happened, Pan Doctor! Well, there is a hole in the ceiling and a crater in the floor.' And she began to laugh as if this was the funniest question she had ever heard.

When he set his bag down by the pulpit, she began to speak again. There were approximately sixty patients in the church of Our Lady of Lemnowice. Most came from the Third Army, though with regiments garrisoned across the mountains, there were others there as well. The most recent truckload of men had arrived the week before – sixteen soldiers, three dead on arrival, five with wounds requiring immediate amputation. Since then it had been silent. The war had moved off, she said. This was its way. Sometimes the fighting was very close and they could hear gunshots, sometimes only distant shells. Once, the Russians had taken the town. Other times, she wondered if they had been forgotten. What a blessing that would be! The town still had a few people left – women only, Ruthenians whose allegiance likely had once been to Russia, until the Russians had taken all the men when they withdrew. The hospital had enough food to last the winter; in addition to the rations last delivered in mid-January, the church had stores of grain and turnips, sunflower seeds, potatoes, beetroots. As long as supplies continued to come, they could make it through spring, that most difficult of seasons, and come summer there would be apples and pears, and they could work their own fields, and grow wheat . . .

But Lucius had stopped listening. 'Dr Szőkefalvi left in December?'

'December, Doctor.'

'Two months ago.'

'Yes, two.'

'But you just said there have been amputations?'

'Since December, there have been forty amputations, on twenty-three men, Pan Doctor. Eight legs above the knee, fifteen below. Ten arms above the elbow and six below. One jaw that did not survive.'

Lucius looked at her, his heart beginning to beat faster. 'And who, Sister Margarete, has performed the amputations?'

'*He* has, Pan Doctor,' and she rolled her eyes beatifically towards the hole in the north transept.

Lucius did not drop his gaze. 'And whose hand was *He* directing, Sister?'

She held up her little hands, scarcely half the span of his.

'And are those patients here?'

'Yes.'

'All of them?'

'All that have survived, yes, who have not been evacuated.'

'How many have survived, Dear Sister?'

'Fourteen have survived, Pan Doctor.'

'Fourteen . . . of twenty-three.' He paused, thinking of the regimental hospitals in Kraków, the daily removal of corpses. 'That is a not a bad survival rate.'

'No, Doctor.'

'And God has worked by those hands alone?'

A pause, a little smile, as if she understood the impact of what she'd said.

'Sister?'

'God has given us morphine and ether, Doctor.'

'Yes,' said Lucius, staring. 'Yes, yes. He has.'

Then she said, 'One last thing, Doctor. I have given the men permission to use firearms on the rats, but they must shoot into the floor and not at one another. The typhus, thank God, has abated for now, and we have our procedures for keeping it away. But the rats! Pan Doctor, we are at the mercy of the rats. I have boarded up all the holes in the walls of our church. Sometimes they fall from the hole in the transept, though with winter, this has stopped. Traps have been laid in all corners, but still the creatures come, like mushrooms after a rain, everywhere. You will not be frightened by the occasional shot.'

He thought back to her heaving the crossbar in the narthex.

'Is this why you barred the doors, Sister?'

'Oh, no, Pan Doctor. I barred the doors because of the wolves.'

THEY MADE THEIR rounds that night by lantern light.

She announced him, briefly, from the pulpit, with the brevity and authority of a field marshal: this was the new medical officer, Krzelewski, from Vienna; there would be no change to procedures, they would continue to make rounds twice daily when not attending to new casualties; questions should, as before, be directed to one of the orderlies, or to herself.

They started in the nave, near the door, in Fractures and Amputations. Traction ropes hung from the roof beams, and little towers of wooden scaffolding with rope and counter-weights had been set up on the floor. They were joined by one of the orderlies, Zmudowski, another Pole, with a heavy, red-orange beard. Like Margarete, he wore a greatcoat in the cold of the church. He followed her closely, hovering behind her as she knelt by the first soldier, an Austrian cavalryman crushed beneath his horse the week before. She had amputated his leg above the knee and reset a wrist fracture, and kneeling, she inspected the wounds quickly, showing them to Lucius. She was clearly proud of her stitches, and Lucius, who had never seen a healing amputation site, and certainly not by lantern light, pre-tended to appraise it with a studious air. Then on, to the next patient, another Austrian, from the Graz fusiliers, shot through the shoulder. She had done little other than stabilize the fracture and suture the exit wound. What else was one to do with a shoulder fracture? But it was healing beautifully, she said affec-tionately, didn't Lucius agree?

'Beautifully, yes.'

She looked down again with pride. Then: 'Earlier, I heard you can speak German?'

He nodded.

'Please tell him that I saw him playing cards. This is fine. But he is not to use that arm unless he wants to tear the wound open again. We are short of suture material. Next time I will have to use thread from his coat.'

The man nodded sombrely as Lucius translated. Then to Margarete, in Polish, Lucius asked, 'We are short of sutures?'

'Sutures, no. At least not yet. But the men are like little children. They would eat their laying chicken, as the saying goes. There is no self-restraint. One must be strict.'

They moved on.

'This is Brauer, Pan Doctor Lieutenant, of Vienna, frostbite, both feet; this is Czerny, of the Hungarian Fourteenth fusiliers, gunshot wound to the left femur, amputated last week; this is Moscowitz, also of Vienna, a tailor, he has been quite helpful to us, bilateral foot amputation, also frostbite, now healing beautifully, as you can see. This is Gruscinski – a Pole. Gangrene of the feet, quite ugly, but God was on his side despite his habit of making pleasure with the whale oil. Kirschmeyer, shell-strike. This is Redlich, a professor in Vienna. He believes a monkey gave birth to a human woman—'

'Ahem,' began the man, who was lying on his belly, wincing as he turned. 'Not exactly. I told you there was a process, a slow process of variation and natural selection—'

'Yes, of course, Professor. A *monkey*, Doctor, can you imagine? Anyway, he was shot by Cossacks. In the rear. Next to his tail.'

They moved on. 'Corporal Sloboda, of a Czech bicycle infantry, another frostbite amputee. Tarnowski: left arm. Oh, dear, careful, Corporal, keep it elevated – that's why God gave us slings. This one is Sattler, an Austrian, prays constantly, too often really, it is its own disease. Oh, yes: chest wound; he also used to be among the dying, until the Holy Spirit intervened.'

At the end of the aisle, they stopped. 'And this one . . .' She knelt. 'Our Sergeant Czernowitzski, another Pole, though of this I'm not so proud. Amputations of the leg and arm. Show the doctor, Sergeant. See how they are healing nicely? But we have helped him not only with his *physical* wounds, Pan Doctor, but spiritual ones as well. See, Sergeant Czernowitzski had some trouble when he arrived in knowing the proper way that one is to address a nursing sister. But we learned! We learned that a nursing sister is not a tavern girl, with whom one can enjoy insinuations. Isn't that correct, Sergeant?'

'Indeed, Sister,' said the man, looking down.

'Tell the doctor. "Do you need anything, soldier?" is an innocent question, isn't it, Sergeant?'

'That is correct, Sister. It is a medical question.'

Standing next to her, Zmudowski was doing his best to look severe behind his beard.

'That's right, a *medical* question,' said Margarete. 'And what do we say when we are asked this medical question, soldier?'

'We are gracious, Sister. We recognize the gift God has given us to be alive, and we honour Him by our decorum and good deeds.'

She turned with a satisfied smile on her face. 'See, Doctor, he's so polite.'

When they were out of earshot, Lucius said, in a low voice, 'He seems chastened. If I may ask . . .'

Her eyes flickered. 'As I said earlier, Doctor, God has given his children morphine. But He has also given the discretion to withhold it, too.'

She smiled briskly, and for the first time he saw her little teeth. A memory came to him, of a soldier in Kraków, screaming during a shortage of narcotics.

Then she must have recognized his unease. 'I am alone, Pan Doctor. It is either morphine or the Mannlicher.' There was a long pause. Then she looked to Zmudowski and the two began to laugh. 'It is a joke, Pan Doctor Lieutenant. I haven't shot any of them, yet.' Another pause. 'Well, at least not in Lemnowice. Oh, Doctor, that was also just a joke. Don't look so frightened.

Ever since we've started, you've looked like a condemned man waiting to be hanged.'

THEY PRESSED ON. Up one row, down the second. They were lucky, she told him: often on rounds there were one or two amputations that had begun to sour, but that night it looked as if they had been spared. 'Yes,' he answered. They were lucky, he thought, still wondering if now was his moment to confess. They all were lucky, lest he be asked to intercede.

But he didn't confess. Down the second row and up the third, now into Medical, with its fevers, coughs and dysenteries, kept behind a small partition in a pathetic effort against contagion. Puschmann, Mlakar, both with pneumonia. Nadler: terrible abscesses of the tonsils. Kulik, Doctor, poor Kulik: chronic diarrhoea since his mama deliberately poisoned him at his going-away dinner, hoping to defer his deployment to the front.

And on . . . Yes, *poor Kulik*, thought Lucius. But *your* mother was trying to *keep* you from the war.

Now Heads, the chancel. The first two cases were both comatose, with drains leaking pale fluid into bedside pans. At the third, Margarete stopped and turned.

'No name. An Austrian by his uniform,' she said. 'But we couldn't find any papers. He came two days ago, discovered on the road. There were at least three fractures in his skull, though the membrane was intact. Szőkefalvi said there is great disagreement of when one should proceed with decompression. That some say it should be done quickly, at any sign of increased pressure inside the skull, while others believe any surgery only worsens matters. For now, I've waited. But since yesterday, he hasn't woken up. I'm not certain what to do.'

She had turned back to look at the soldier. *She wants me to answer*, Lucius thought. Again his heart began to beat faster. It was like being back in school, called up before the lecture hall. But he had stood before legendary members of the professoriate and didn't feel as afraid as he did before this nurse. He recalled the old Italian whom he'd examined long ago as *Praktikant*. A week later, the man had his skull drilled to remove the pressure on his brain caused by the tumour. Even then, it seemed barbaric. Now he couldn't bear to think of the kind of tools Margarete was using.

He knelt at the man's side. The soldier's face was gaunt, his cheeks covered by a thin beard. His breath soft and shallow. The gauze around his head was yellow, like the yolk of an egg.

For a long time, Lucius just looked at him, frozen, afraid not only that he didn't know what he was doing, but that he would cause the man more harm.

'You can examine him, Doctor.'

Still he waited.

'Pan Doctor Lieutenant?'

But he was now trying to remember the basic neurological exam. He could recall the pages in his textbook, but the order of the exam had fled. Assess orientation . . . then cranial nerves, then muscle tone, then . . .

At his side Margarete spoke again, softly. 'Szőkefalvi usually checked his eyes.'

Grateful that the darkness hid his blushing, Lucius leaned closer and asked the man to open his eyes. There was no answer. Again he paused.

'When I said examine, I meant you can touch him, Doctor.' Now something else had crept into her voice, a worry, inlaid with irritation or impatience. 'Perhaps back in Vienna, you are more cautious. But out here, if we are going to drill a hole in his skull, we can't be afraid of touching his eyelids. Unless Pan Doctor Lieutenant is used to doing things differently?'

'No ... no ...' said Lucius, flustered. He gently parted the man's eyelids with thumb and forefinger. Margarete handed him a candle before he could even ask. He wanted to snap at her, to tell her that he knew about pupillary reflexes. Swelling of the brain caused it to push the brainstem down, compressing the third cranial nerve, with its fibres controlling pupillary constriction. He had read this, dissected it in human and pig cadavers. He swung the light back and forth and said, as formally as he could, 'The *nervus oculomotorius* seems intact.'

She didn't answer.

'The *nervus oculomotorius* seems intact,' he repeated. 'That argues against advanced herniation.'

'Yes, Pan Doctor,' answered Margarete tentatively. 'The oc-u-lo-motorius. What a lovely word. Now, would you drill, or wait?'

A cold wind whistled across the patched-up shell-hole in the roof. Glinting snowflakes drifted down.

She leaned towards him and whispered, so the others couldn't hear: '*Szőkefalvi, Doctor, would wait.*'

Quietly, he nodded his assent. Below him, the man gasped briefly, before his soft, low breaths returned.

They stood. Margarete said, almost kindly, 'Perhaps it is better if I examine the other cases myself? We will finish here, in Heads, and then you'll rest. We usually do not bother the dying men in the transept this late at night.'

'Yes, Sister,' he said.

She asked him no other questions. There were seven more cases, all recently arrived. Once or twice, he added something he remembered from his texts, but his contributions only seemed to emphasize his ignorance. Soon he stopped speaking at all.

It was close to ten when they finished.

'Thank you,' she said at last to Zmudowski, who saluted

Lucius before he left. He too had been privy to the failure, though mercifully he let nothing show.

For a moment Lucius and Margarete were alone, in the crossing, before the operating table, which he now saw was made from a pair of pews. She looked at him directly now, her eyes appraising, weighing her own options, most of which by then must have seemed quite poor.

She was silent for no more than a few seconds, but when she spoke, he sensed that a decision had been made.

'We will make do,' she said.

He waited, realizing how much he was revealing by not asking what she meant.

And then she added, 'Perhaps now you can tell me what happened to your wrist.'

4

Lucius's quarters were in the former priest's house, a separate building that sat across a courtyard spanned by a massive beech tree, its upper branches high as the church steeple. The snow of the courtyard was packed down in paths between the two structures and a third, smaller house with two rooms, one for bathing and one for quarantine. Beyond this he could see a gate marking a graveyard, the crosses barely high enough to clear the snow.

There was a separate entrance to Lucius's room, but it was locked, and Margarete led him around to a second door, which opened on to a kitchen. There two men sat peeling potatoes next to a set of field stoves and pots. One of them was missing a hand.

'This is Krajniak, head cook.'

A poplar-thin man with a red nose sniffled and saluted with his stump. 'Humbly report, Herr Doktor! I hope you like pickled cucumbers, sir.'

'Ah. I haven't told you that,' said Margarete. 'In January they accidentally delivered two hundred kilos of cucumbers instead of cleaning lye. It is not to be mentioned to anyone. Agreed?'

At the far end of the room, the skinned corpses of pigs and chickens dangled from the ceiling. A third man sat in the corner, a shotgun across his lap. Margarete greeted him with a nod. 'That one is Croatian, speaks some German. I don't understand a word he says.'

'The gun is also for the rats?'

'Very good, Pan Doctor,' she said. 'I would have thought you'd say it's for the Russians, but my, you're learning fast.'

On a plate, she placed a hunk of bread and a pair of boiled turnips, then led him into a second room, a laundry with pots for disinfection, strung with rope from which hung a maze of drying uniforms and blankets. Together, they pushed aside the wet, frozen wool until they reached the door to his room.

It was a small space, four long paces across, with a straw mattress and a sheepskin blanket, a desk, a chair, a wood-burning stove. It had been Szőkefalvi's room, Margarete told him, and they had left it alone after his departure, waiting for the new doctor to take his place. She went and unlocked the bolt on the far door that opened on to the courtyard. 'So you don't have to crawl through potatoes each time you need to get to bed,' she said. There was a small window, already fogged by their breath, glowing with a gold nimbus from the light of the church. She set his food on the desk next to a casebook, and turned back the blanket on the bed, a gesture which at first appeared an act of hospitality, until he realized she was inspecting it for lice. The blankets lay directly on the mattress. No bedsheets: of course, he thought, embarrassed that he had even noticed.

Inspection complete, she turned back to Lucius. For a moment, he thought she would ask him something else, but she pressed her hands together and curtsied slightly.

'My quarters are in the sacristy. There is a bell outside the door if you need to call.' She turned, and then turned back.

'Oh, and, Doctor?'

'Yes?'

'Don't take your boots off.'

'No. My boots . . .'

'To run, Doctor, in case you need to run. And keep your

papers on you – the Austrians have a bad habit of thinking everyone without their papers is a spy.' And with that she hurried into the night.

Lucius set his bag down on the floor and walked over to the desk. The food was already cold, but he was starving, and as he chewed, he turned the pages of the casebook. The names and injuries ran well into the hundreds, all recorded in the same careful hand. He tried to conjure up the man who had preceded him. Margarete had said nothing more about Szőkefalvi, no mention of his age or rank or training. Lucius imagined an older man, because to him all doctors were older men, but now thinking back, he realized there was nothing to suggest the Hungarian wasn't also a student, perhaps an assistant to the other unmentioned doctor whose crime he suspected by then had something to do with Sister Klara's. Nothing to suggest Szőkefalvi hadn't been sent off to serve with just six semesters of study. Nothing, except that Szőkefalvi, whoever he was, apparently had known what to do with a skull fracture, while Lucius knew how to take an X-ray of a mermaid's spine.

He sat. Thoughts of the mermaid led to Zimmer, and then to Feuermann, now somewhere in Serbia. Had his friend also been so misled? But the hospital described in Feuermann's letters, though small, was functioning, with other surgeons and sanitary officers and Red Cross personnel, a steam laundry, an X-ray machine and bacteriological laboratory, not some freezing first-aid station with an armed, half-mad nurse and an operating table salvaged from the pews.

He ran his good hand through his hair and lay back on the blanket, still in his coat. Was he supposed to sleep in his clothes, then, too? He imagined himself fleeing a horde of screaming Cossacks in nothing but his boots. But it wasn't funny. He felt frightened by everything, the bomb-hole in the church ceiling, the rats like something from a nursemaid's tale. Was this what his parents had tried to protect him from? Was it too late to ask them to help him to transfer? Oh, but this brought its own worries. If his father had his way, Lucius might find himself a lancer, joining a cavalry charge against a line of howitzers and mortar fire, while he tried to steer an unfamiliar horse.

He turned on his side, his wrist throbbed, and his sabre poked into his hip. He had almost forgotten the pain; fear made a good anaesthetic, he thought. When Margarete had learned of the injury, she had asked to examine it, carefully touching the tips of his fingers to assess for nerve damage and palpating the fracture to see how it had set. She had given him some vials of morphine from the supply closet beneath the altar. But now he was grateful for the injury, which was all that stood between him and total humiliation. He unclipped the sabre and hung it from a bedpost. Yes, he thought: he was lucky for the scuttling child, the icy street. If Margarete was truly performing the amputations, then he could watch her, study, and perhaps, by the time he had healed, he could know enough to start. If a nurse had learned, he thought, then he could, too.

With this thought, he pulled himself further onto the bed. His feet felt massive in the boots. He closed his eyes. Now sleep seemed futile, but he wanted to be absent, if only briefly, from his fears.

And somehow, he must have slept, for he was awakened by a knock at the door.

It was Margarete again. She wore a second greatcoat over the first, her wimple hidden in the hood, dusted now with snow.

'Quick,' she commanded. 'Come.'

*

IT WAS STILL dark as they crossed the courtyard.

A fire was burning in the quarantine, its light flickering through the swirling snow. Beyond the gate, men carried shrouded litters out of an ambulance. It was a small vehicle, scarcely longer than a man and not quite as tall, but its supply of injured seemed almost inexhaustible. Lucius turned to Margarete, seeking some instructions, but she had vanished, leaving him alone. From around him came shouting, the crunch of footsteps, the clattering of doors, but all was muted by the falling snow. A pair of search dogs circled, as if someone had forgotten to tell them that their job was done. Polish *ogars*, hounds familiar from his father's hunts. They were almost otherworldly, like eels in their constant gliding, smooth coats glistening, noses cutting shallow tracks across the powdery snow.

At last, one of the ambulance men, with a vulgarity that suggested ignorance of Lucius's rank, shouted for him to help. He hurried into the lorry, nearly slipping from the snowy gangplank, lurched, and struck his head against a lantern hanging over the entrance. Thankfully, no one had seen him. He ducked inside, recoiling instantly at the smell. Two men remained, on litters that were stacked on racks. He hesitated. A face appeared at the entrance, shouting for Lucius to grab his end of the litter. He obeyed, realizing only as it left its bracket that he had forgotten about his wrist. Pain bolted up his arm, and he faltered, the body almost slipping off.

No one even acknowledged his incompetence. Another man climbed in, pushed him aside and took the body, and then the final litter was brought outside. He descended. Then the ambulance was empty, moving. Snow sloughed off in the vortices of lantern light. He saw his shadow swing against the wall of the church, and they were gone.

Inside the quarantine, Margarete hung her greatcoats by the

door. He saw Zmudowski already at work, and two others that he hadn't met. A pot of broth was steaming on a stove in the corner. The air was heavy, rank and damp. The wounded had been arranged on straw beds around the fire, and Margarete moved swiftly between them, asking questions while checking for a pulse.

Of the fourteen, eight were already dead and rigid. One had frozen in a seated position, his clothes in tatters, his mouth wide open in a scream. Lucius couldn't tear his eyes away. He had never seen such a scream, teeth glittering in the crimson mouth . . .

'Oh, my God.'

'Doctor.'

'That man . . .'

'Please, Doctor, don't stare, come.' Margarete pulled him on.

'That man, he lost his jaw, it's—'

'He's dead. He's God's. Not ours. Now, hurry, come.'

By then the living had been separated off. Three gunshot injuries to limbs; two head wounds and an abdominal wound. Almost all had frostbite. Margarete covered them with blankets and ordered soup for those who could drink. 'Shouldn't we bring them to the surgery?' Lucius asked. She shook her head. 'Not yet. Not until they are warm and deloused. Unless they are heavily bleeding, Doctor, we clean them first. No one goes into the church until they are deloused. The last patient to bring a louse into the church killed fourteen soldiers and three nurses. I won't let that ever happen again.'

Zmudowski had begun to strip the soldiers one by one, scrub them from a foamy bucket, and then send them shivering into a smaller, second room, where the others quickly swaddled them in clean clothing, powdery with lime.

Crouching by the moaning soldier with the abdominal wound, Margarete called Lucius over.

'See?' she said, lifting up the man's fingers, his nails clotted with skin. 'He's been scratching. This, Pan Doctor, is the Beast.'

His tunic bore the insignia of a sapper unit. Beneath it someone had packed the wound with a sock, dinner linens and photos, and as Margarete removed them, Lucius saw the lice, cupfuls of them, sloughing off in grainy clumps. There was a shout from the other side of the room, and Lucius turned to see that the patient with the head wound had risen and was heading towards the door. Margarete leapt for him, leaving Lucius alone. On the body before him, Lucius saw a last layer, a woman's shawl that had adhered to the soldier's abdomen by dried blood. He began to pull it off and found his hands full of intestines. Then Margarete was at his side. 'What did you do? Oh! Mother of God! Never! Never remove the final layer until you have a new dressing ready. On the abdomen, no!' He tried to keep the intestines off the floor, but they continued to slip out in hot wet rolls. The sapper began to gasp. Lucius felt he was witness to a metamorphosis, a man turning inside out.

'Move, Doctor!'

Lucius fell back, sleeves wet with peritoneal fluid. Margarete grabbed a clean dressing and swaddled the man's guts in one swoop and pushed them back inside, dirty with debris. She unrolled more dressings. With her free hand, she wrapped his belly.

She faced Lucius. 'Wash your hands. Come with me. *Now* we operate. We'll start with the head wounds, then amputate this foot, this leg, that elbow, this forearm – that arm we can let be.' She paused. 'With Pan Doctor's permission.'

'And this soldier?' Lucius asked, still looking at the sapper.

'Smelling like that?' She shook her head. 'He'll be dead by

morning. Don't worry. You didn't do it; he was on his way. We keep him warm. If he wakes up we tell him he's home; if he calls you his father, you call him son. Perhaps it is different in Vienna, but this is how we do it here.'

To the orderlies, who had whispered something Lucius couldn't hear, Margarete said, 'The Doctor broke his hand. Soon it will heal. Until then, we will continue as before. Come, Doctor.'

But Lucius couldn't turn his eyes. The soldier expelled something from his mouth and began to cough, his face twisted in pain. All around them the light seemed to have changed. The smells filled his nostrils, his head felt hot and damp . . .

'*Come*, Doctor.'

Then, to Zmudowski, she said, 'Get that soldier morphine, now. See, Doctor, he will feel better. He doesn't know what's happening. I know it's hard, but you'll get used to it. Come.'

They burst into a cold blue light. Dawn was breaking. A glittering of snowflakes drifted from the beech. In the church, she grabbed a jug of amber liquid from the foot of the operating table, took a quick swig and splashed it over her hands, then passed it to Lucius.. He sniffed, eyes smarting.

'*Horilka*, Doctor,' she said. 'Village speciality. Doctor Szőkefalvi called it Surgeon's Courage. Keeps the hands sterile, the belly warm. Perhaps the only thing that's not in shortage yet.'

A crate had been set out so she could reach the body on the table. Once more she washed her hands, this time in carbolic acid, its tarry odour lingering as she slipped on her gloves. She began with the soldiers with head wounds. The first was a young man, unconscious, a crush fracture extending from the top of the ear to the centre of the forehead. It had been packed in the field, and when she removed the new dressing, she exposed an abscess extending deep into the brain. She whistled, 'Our

Mother in heaven. This is days old.' Slowly, she picked away the looser skull fragments, cleaned out the pus, and irrigated the wound, stopping to inspect the grey-pink tissue with a candle. 'To think that's where the thinking is!' she marvelled, but she didn't explore further. Instead she placed a rubber drain and secured it with packing. The orderlies gave him anti-tetanus serum and brought him away. She washed her gloves in carbolic and *horilka* as the second patient was brought to the table. This one had a simple fracture that did not extend past the dural membrane, and she only cleaned and dressed the scalp. Then she called for the amputations.

Zmudowski appeared with an ether mask and bottle, positioning himself at the head of the table. By afternoon, she had removed two feet and a hand with Lucius at her side, watching as she tied the limb off with a tourniquet, incised the skin and retracted the muscle, and with a single, fluid motion, sawed off the bone. She threw loose loops into the muscles and drew them together before setting the flap. To a patient with a shrapnel wound to the thigh, she asked, 'How long ago did this happen, Private?' The answer was January. When he went under, she began to carve it away, murmuring as she went along, her voice like someone praying, cutting back the dead tissue until only pink, fresh bleeding flesh was left. By then, most of his thigh and hamstring were gone. The soldier stirred. They gave him more ether and cut off his leg.

By then, darkness had come, and Zmudowski returned with his lantern. Hopefully, Lucius wondered if they might break to eat, but then rounds had begun, as before, at the east end of the nave: the Austrian cavalryman, the Hungarian officer, the Czech sniper, and on. It was swifter now, the need for introductions gone. Halfway along the first row, flies circled above a soldier, an Austrian dragoon. She pointed. 'God made flies to tell us where the rot is, Doctor.' She knelt to inspect the stump of his arm. 'There,' she said. 'It's beginning. Can't you see?'

He nodded.

'Now smell it,' she said. He hesitated a moment. 'Closer, Doctor, with your nose.' And he leaned in, the sharp odour making his stomach turn. They brought the man back to the table, exposed an abscess reaching almost all the way to his axilla, and amputated the rest of his arm. An hour later they were back in the nave. Gruscinski, Redlich. Czernowitzski, docile as a lamb. Then into Fevers and Medical and Heads.

There she stopped suddenly, walked the length of the church, and returned with a shovel. 'Move,' she said to a patient, his head wrapped in gauze. As if in drill, he rolled to the side, and she brought the shovel down hard upon his pillow of straw. She stirred it, and a pair of pink little heads rose up, twisting in the air. She brought the shovel down hard again.

'*Szczur*,' she said, as if it needed naming. *Rat*.

Zmudowski hurried off to get a pan. There were three more cases to see in Heads, and then the six men in Dying, down from eight the day before.

That night, Lucius slept again in his greatcoat, too exhausted now to be afraid. When dawn broke, there was a knock at his door, and they began again.

THE NEXT DAYS were the same.

The ambulances arrived out of the black night, out of snow-storms, out of sun-glittering fields of ice. In his quarters, in the crossing, rounding in the church, he would hear the whistle, or the shout, 'Incoming!' and the orderlies would deploy to help the stretcher crews while Margarete, in her two coats, breath steaming, directed them to the quarantine. They came from the mountains or the snow trenches dug into the sloping hills, many already dead from their wounds or from the cold, the others crying or staring out with terrified eyes as they were stripped and disinfected, as clods of frozen dirt and blood were dissolved in water, and tourniquets applied.

In the beginning, Lucius only watched. But by the end of the month, his hand strong enough to grip a scalpel, he began to assist Margarete with the simplest cases. *Yes, a butcher's work*, he thought, this carving out of necrotic flesh, as Zimmer had promised. Yet it was extraordinary to think that he was allowed to do this, that he had been given permission, that there was no one there to ask him questions designed to humiliate him before the others, no famous professor to scold him for greeting the patient, no crowd of other students with whom to compete.

The first amputation he carried out was on the hand of an Austrian rifleman. A frostbitten purse of crushed bone, a single violet finger remaining, the hand had held together in the field by the simple virtue of having frozen, and once in the church it began to melt apart.

'A deep breath, Doctor.'

Margarete stood close to him as his scalpel pressed the fore-arm and finally broke the skin. He prepared the flap as she had shown him, dissecting back the muscle from the bone. But as he went to get the saw, she stopped him.

'Perhaps this is how it is done in Vienna, but in Galicia, you'll need to cut a larger flap. In Galicia, that flap will never reach across the stump.'

'Of course. Like this?'

'More.'

'This?'

'No, more. Don't be so shy.'

'Like this?'

'Like that.'

He looked up, glad his mask now hid a silly grin.

She handed him the saw. 'Now go. Don't stop. Zmudowski will hold him down if he awakes.'

But in Galicia, Pan Doctor . . .

Perhaps in Vienna they cut their suture knots too close; perhaps in Vienna they let their dirty sleeves dangle in a wound; perhaps in Vienna they forgot cotton in a wound after they closed it, or left tourniquets on when they were no longer necessary and the patient was writhing.

But in Galicia, it's done like this.

Perhaps in Vienna they took off the whole foot when only a toe was needed.

Perhaps in Vienna they were stingy with their drains, and made messes out of everything.

Perhaps in Vienna they didn't step away to sneeze.

But in Galicia . . .

He learned.

GOOD, PAN DOCTOR.

Yes, that's right. Stick your finger in, explore it. If you don't do it, no one else will. Get the bullet out.

Good. Now tie off, Pan Doctor. Go.

Good. Very good.

Lovely.

Yes. Good. There.

Who taught you, Doctor? They should really be honoured with a decoration.

There. Yes.

Go.

5

February turned to March.

New storms swept through the mountains. Outside, the fighting slowed. The snow blew steadily across the valley. Inside the church, it grew so dark they fashioned torches from pitch and rope hemp. Above, the murals glistened with frozen condensation from their breath.

Between rounds and cases, he took his meals with Margarete at a small table that had been set up at the edge of the bomb crater. She had initially brought him his meals in his quarters, as regulations dictated that officers should eat apart from the enlisted men. But Lucius hardly considered himself a real officer – to him, an officer was someone like his father – and, regardless of rank, he didn't want to be alone.

The room grew quiet as the men ate, their voices low as if in deference, their spoons clinking against tin. Like the soldiers, Margarete attacked the food. She ate hunched so as not to lose anything to the floor, always saved her bread to wipe up her soup, and like the others, unapologetically wiped up any missed drops with her fingers.

'One must hurry, Doctor – we might be bombed during a meal.'

At first they spoke mostly of their cases, of who was getting well enough to leave with the next convoy returning over the passes, and who – in lower voices now – would die. They reviewed their supplies obsessively: how much morphine was remaining, how much catgut, how much iodoform, how much lime. As the weeks went on, however, and he came to know the patients and their wounds, he found their conversation shifting. She had opinions about everything, not simply how to prepare antiseptic solutions or apply a dressing. She thought it a great mistake the army had pushed forward in winter. The generals didn't understand the snow, she said. One did not defeat the snow; one let it come and waited, like a bear in hibernation, one did not send soldiers where they didn't belong. And how did they make their decisions to dress men in cotton socks and such absorbent puttees? And, oh, the shoes they gave them! And then to think that they had the nerve to send conscription officers to canvass the wounded! The last had come shortly before Lucius's arrival, a horrid man who had taken any soldier he thought could march another step. Men with fevers! Missing fingers! Headaches that wouldn't go away. She cursed him. May his feet be eaten by maggots, may he lose his teeth on stale bread, may his family die of plague!

In the flickering torchlight, snow hissing against the windows, Lucius let her speak. He realized how she must have been waiting for someone to talk to, and there was something to her breathless stories that lightened his constant fear.

Other times, her cheeks reddening with the warmth of the soup, she asked him about medicine. For all her practical skills, he was struck by the great gaps in her understanding. She knew almost nothing about the fundamentals that had made up his studies, none of the names of bones or muscles, the rules for memorizing vessels. But her curiosity was endless. Was it true, she asked, that tuberculosis was caused by a tiny animal? And what caused a goitre? How could memory vanish, then reappear?

'Oh, I have too many questions!' she apologized. Szőkefalvi said it took years to study to be a doctor. She couldn't expect to learn everything at once.

He didn't mind, he told her. What he didn't add was that unlike most of the conversations he'd endured throughout his life, he looked forward to talking to her, didn't spend his time wishing for the moment to end. That he had *always* preferred to speak of medicine. It is like it was with Feuermann, he thought. Urgent and important and free from the byzantine structures of decorum so important to his mother. And silence, when it came, came naturally, because a question had been answered, not because he'd failed.

From medicine, her questions wandered. She asked him about the university, the lectures and examinations. And what of the city, could he describe the monuments to her? Szőkefalvi had told her about the tramcars – had he ever driven one? Then she spoke for a while about the castles filled with paintings and statues, and it took a moment to realize she was describing a museum.

It was only when her questions drew closer to his family that he hesitated, uncertain how to explain. He had thought of them often since his arrival. Austria, true to its epistolary trad-itions, had done its utmost to preserve its mail service, and in early March, a pair of letters had somehow made their way to him. Now that he was gone, his parents' stance towards him had softened. His mother, enclosing a sky-blue box of hard Polish toffee, wrote that her friend, the 'famous Polish doctor Karpiński,' had assured her that many of Europe's most eminent surgeons had gained their skills in wartime, and his father had enclosed a map showing the battles fought between the Polish–Lithuanian Commonwealth and the invading Cossack and Tatar hordes. The map was more than two hundred and fifty years old, and the area around Lemnowice was obscured by an image of a screaming Cossack impaled on a stake, but Lucius was oddly touched by his father's pride that his son was 'continuing the tradition'. He had also provided a list of Cossack memorabilia that he would cherish for his collection, with little illustrations of daggers and sable caps and decorated sabre sheaths. And they had the sad news of the death of Puszek to report to him, of ripe old Irish wolfhound age.

Lucius said nothing of this to Margarete, and at first he hid the toffees. He had grown up accustomed to seeing people's manner change the moment they learned of his bloodline. Instead, he invented a humble apartment on Schumanngasse, not far from the university; his father was a dentist who had moved from Kraków to find more work.

She thought this curious. Were there not enough toothaches in Poland?

Digging his hole a little deeper, he gave what sounded like a short lecture on the history of the Polish diaspora in Vienna, and swiftly tried to move along. He regretted lying, regretted the distance it placed between them, even if she didn't know. At the same time, he was well aware that she told him nothing of herself. In the beginning he had enquired cautiously about her training, her convent, what she had done before the war. She wouldn't answer. To speak of life before she joined her order would violate her vows, she said, fixing her grey eyes on his. What mattered was her holy service now.

Still, some clues she couldn't hide. She slushed her *s*'s – *sh* or *zh* – nasalized her *n*'s and *m*'s, and her vowels often seemed on the verge of song. The languages she spoke – an archaic Polish splintered with Slovak, her Hungarian and market Ruthenian, her mix of Austrian and Polish pronunciations of place-names – all put her origin in the mountains, somewhere to the west. Because she seemed so quick, he was surprised to find her handwriting was that of someone scarcely literate, her spelling abominable. But he had no polite way of asking how far she'd gone in school. And then there was the matter of her faith, the Demons of Spleen and Devils of Liver, her endless invocation of the Louse. The angelic interventions that seemed less a part of the world of the sombre Latin prayer Lucius had grown up praying, than some animistic rite.

So he contented himself with letting her lead, and following. What were dissections like? she wondered, now cracking on a piece of toffee. And could he tell her again about his experiments with radiography? Back before the army had taken away their X-ray machine, she had always wondered how they saw inside. And the amputees: did he understand how the feeling of a hand remained after the hand itself was gone?

SOMETIMES, THEY WERE joined by Zmudowski and the other orderlies, named Rzedzian and Nowak, and occasionally Krajniak the cook.

The men had all arrived at different times over the winter. Zmudowski was from a farm just outside Kraków. He had been a postman in his former life, and now sorted through the hospital mail and removed stamps for his collection. The war, he explained, one night in March, during a calm, was an extraordinary time for philately: families who had not written letters for years were digging through their drawers for any postage they could find. Already, he'd found some rarities, a 1908 10-kroner with no perforations and an 1899 10-heller blue. He kept them mounted in a little red book he carried always in his pocket, where he also kept his single photo of his daughter, a studio snapshot of a sombre baby sitting alone on a cushion, covered with a rug.

He showed it to Lucius.

Only it wasn't a cushion: it was Zmudowski.

'Look, Doctor: there, you can see my hand.'

And sure enough, emerging from the dark rug were two pale fingers holding the baby by the wrist.

The others apparently had also fallen for the trick.

He had loved to take the little girl on postal rounds. She was mad about it, he said. He hoped one day she would be the world's first Polish postwoman. In addition to the great orange beard, dense enough to store a thermometer when he needed both hands free, he had ruddy skin and coarse orange eyebrows that overhung a pair of close-set eyes. The eyes, the sunburnt skin, a pair of missing teeth, a nose broken twice during his youth: all gave the impression of a certain oafishness, as if Nature had cast him more for the role of a stable hand than an agent of His Majesty's Post. But he had a postman's meticulousness and a postman's spatial memory, and more than once, when Lucius was lost among the dozens of blanketed bodies, Zmudowski remembered which wound was where.

The second orderly, Rzedzian, was originally from Drohobycz, some two hundred kilometres to the north, where he had worked in the oilfields before the war. Rzedzian's great claim in life was that he had the same name as a character in the epic novel *With Fire and Sword*, save that the Rzędzian in the novel was spelt with an '*e* with a little tail,' while Rzedzian of Drohobycz was spelt with just an *e*. How the famous author had decided on this name for his character was a great mystery to Rzedzian. No, he, Rzedzian had never met him, though he heard he lived in Kielce, not that far away. And no one in Rzedzian's family had ever heard of any relative named Rzędzian. But since his discovery of this fact, at the age of nine, it had become one of the defining features of his life. The book was so famous, that often, when he met someone he didn't know and said his name, they would ask, 'Like Rzędzian who rescued Helena Kurcewiczówna?' and he would get to tell the story of the *e*. This happened almost every time they had a new Polish patient.

Then someone decided to call him 'Rzedzian without a Tail,' and he stopped telling the story, though by then it was far too late.

Rzedzian was very big, nearly two metres tall. His hair was black, and he wore a dangling moustache in the Cossack style, which he liked to chew in contemplation. In civilian life he had once won a *kielbasa*-eating competition, and his speciality in the oilfields had been lifting. Barrels. Timber. Reels of rope, which they dropped into the wells. He claimed it had nothing to do with strength and only mental domination over the object to be lifted. Anyone could do it, even weaker people, Doctor, no offence.

None was taken; what had served in Drohobycz also made him an excellent orderly: they needed patients lifted all the time. He also had amazing lungs, utterly untouched by the haze of lime they used in disinfection. His only weakness was his sentimentality, for he cried each time they lost a soldier, which meant sometimes he cried every day, tears running over his coarse cheeks until they streamed off the ends of his moustache. Like Zmudowski, he had a wife and daughter, but no photograph, though when he got home he was going to try the trick with the rug.

'But your daughter's sixteen. The whole point of the rug is for you to hold a child still.'

This was Krajniak, the cook. Twenty years old. Pale and thin, with an eternally drippy nose. A Ruthenian from a nearby village, he was one of the few people who could speak the language of the village women of Lemnowice. He had been in trade school when the war broke out, enlisted out of love of Empire, and lost his hand at Lemberg. But it had still been early enough in the war then that he hadn't lost his patriotism, and he re-enlisted as a cook. He was, he said, sniffling, with due respect, Doctor, the most powerful man in Lemnowice: he controlled the pickles, and who got sediment and who just broth.

Zmudowski, wiping *horilka* from his beard, concurred: they were indebted to the famous sneezer. And he and Rzedzian began to sing.

> *The French dine out on foie gras,*
> *The Brits beef in a pot,*
> *The Italians fettuccine,*
> *And we eat Krajniak's snot.*

He had no wife, no daughter. His mother, who was illiterate, paid a woman in the local market to write him long missives telling him to wear warm clothing, stay away from fish when summer came, and be extra careful of the local girls, who, meeting a man from trade school, might surprise him in a haystack and so wrangle him with child and cut short the great trajectory of his life.

And Nowak? An utterly unremarkable man who had once worked in his family's dog-fancier shop in Kraków, where he had met his fiancée in the months just before the war. In his pocket he carried a lock of her hair, quite a large lock really, which Rzedzian said looked more like her scalp.

He was proud of his hands, which his beloved had once told him were manly. In truth, they looked like normal hands, but because of this vanity he didn't wash them with the corrosive soap, contracted dysentery from a patient, and died in February, shortly after Lucius's arrival. He was replaced by another Pole named Nowak, whom they called Second Nowak, whose most noticeable feature was the straw-coloured moustache that he combed constantly throughout the day.

'But it *is* beautiful, don't you think, Doctor?' said Rzedzian. 'It's really so smooth. It makes me want to comb it myself. I am not sure who he thinks he is planning to make love to – the villagers would castrate him with their scythes. But if he is sad, all he has to do is remind himself that it is there, below his nose . . .'

'. . . *and* above his lip,' said Krajniak.

'Both places, Doctor, at once. That is why he's always smiling. For the rest of us, this place is hell. But this man is always filled with bliss.'

THEY TOLD STORIES. They had already, Lucius realized, a mythology of the little hospital. The founding legend, the early plague, the exodus of X and VII Corps, the great deluges of soldiers from the plains. With awe, they spoke of the whirl and welter of the winter storms, the wolf pack that had attacked the Russian line in December, the Austrian dragoon who had come back to life despite being frozen two days in the middle of a river.

The Tale of the Mysterious Tinned Sausage. The Stewed Boot. The Winter Bicyclist. The Czech's Rash. The Hungarian Platoon that Convinced their Austrian C.O. a Pornographic Novel was a Copy of the Catechism so they Could Read it All the Time. Iskandar of the Wrong Army. The so-called Brothel of Uzhok Pass. The Man Who Vanished. What Schottmüller's Wife Did to Him When She Saw What He Brought Back from Przemyśl. The Miracle of the Dud.

And when Margarete wasn't around: Margarete and the Cussing Hussar. Margarete and the Fate of the 'French' Postcard. Margarete and the Perfectly Capable Slovene who Wouldn't Clean His Tin.

Then, when they realized that Lucius was going to stay,

could be trusted with a secret, they told him the story of Zmudowski and the Russian stamps.

IT HAD HAPPENED over Russian Christmas.

For weeks, the line was very close, just down the valley outside Bystrytsya; at night they could see the light of shellfire. Fighting was heavy. The church was full, the mountain passes snowed in, all but blocking evacuation. Zmudowski was in Bystrystya, working in a dressing station. For the previous few days the front had been quiet, spies had seen what seemed like an escort departing down the valley, and a rumour had arisen that the Russian commanding officer had retreated for the holiday, when on the morning of Christmas Eve a lone man appeared from the enemy line, walking across a pasture, carrying a white sheet raised high above his head.

They let him approach. A thin man, with a scraggly beard, eyes lined with fatigue, woefully underdressed. He spoke some Polish, and one of Poles spoke some Russian. The man carried no weapon, only a flask of Russian vodka. A peace offering, he said, for Christmas, an invitation for the soldiers stationed in Bystrystya to come and drink. Their captain had gone back to occupied Nadworna to celebrate Christmas in the officers' garrison, leaving in charge the first lieutenant, who was tired of the fight.

There was much debating. A trap, some said. But others believed the soldier. At last, the Austrian squadron leader agreed to send a single envoy, and the two men trudged off together across the snowy field.

Two hours later, he returned. It was true, he said. The soldiers were alone. There were perhaps thirty. A handful were Ruthenians who could speak with the local women; it seemed like some had hit it off. There was dancing, not much food, but lots to drink.

They went. Nearly fifty soldiers crowded in a tiny barn. Candles flickered on the tables. Several of the men from both sides were good musicians, and now that they could play without being afraid of giving away their location, they made a band with fife and bagpipe and basolia, rummaged from the village. They joked how when the captain returned, they would be punished for fraternizing with the enemy. But to the devil with the captain, with his Christmas dinner and his officers' whores!

The barn had been used as dressing station and communication headquarters. It was when they were moving a crate to expand the dance floor that Zmudowski saw the stamp.

Until then, the story had been a communal endeavour. Now Zmudowski took over alone.

'So, the first thing to understand, Doctor, is that from a philatelic perspective, Russia really should not be considered one country, but many: it's simply too large. Thus, immediately after the introduction of the first national adhesives, the Rural Councils, or Zemstvos, started to organize their own local posts. I had become aware of such Zemstvo stamps early in my collecting years, and had managed to obtain a precious copy of Chudovsky's 1888 *Description of the Russian Zemstvo Stamps, Envelopes and Parcels*, which gives some order to the three thousand Zemstvo stamps issued before then. However, it was extraordinarily rare to encounter such a stamp arriving in Kraków, given its dedication to local use. Most of the stamps are decorated with provincial arms, so for example, one can recognize those from Perm by the bear, or from Tambov by the beehive, even without understanding Cyrillic. But more extraordinary are the quaint and irregular printing processes, leading to the so-called *tête-bêche* varieties, in which one stamp is printed upside down, or in the case of the extraordinarily rare first issues of Zolotonosha, even sideways. However, the greatest appeal for the Zemstvo collector . . .'

Rzedzian cleared his throat and suggested that Zmudowski 'move things along'.

'But the story won't make any sense unless the doctor has the background.'

'I think he has the background.'

'I *don't* think he has the background. It will seem I took unnecessary risks . . .'

Rzedzian turned to Lucius. 'So he saw a stamp from Astrakhan.'

There was a long pause. Zmudowski furrowed his brow, pinched his lips, and breathed heavily through his nose. 'You ruined it.'

'I didn't ruin it. Tell him about the stamp.'

Zmudowski lifted his hands helplessly.

Rzedzian twirled his long moustache. 'The *fabled city of Astrakhan*—'

'—on the Black Sea,' interrupted Zmudowski quickly. 'Yes. I'd never seen one in my life, not even in Chudovsky's book. From the Russian who spoke some Polish, I learned it belonged to one of their soldiers who had died two weeks before.'

'"Is it valuable?" the Russian asked me.'

'Here I knew I had to play my cards carefully. Valuable? It depended on what one meant. It was no 1868 Kharkov one-kopek blue—'

'Definitely not,' said Rzedzian.

'—no 1871 Saratov black. But for someone interested in a complete collection, it had great sentimental value, I told him. It . . . But there he stopped me and said I could have it for a cigarette. I hardly had time to assent when he asked if I wanted more.

'The soldier led me to the postbag of undelivered letters. It was testament to the horrific casualties that there must have been a hundred. He could not let me have the letters, of course, but if I wanted the stamps . . .'

So while the others danced and drank, Zmudowski spent the rest of the night before a boiling kettle, steaming stamps off. He was a little disappointed, he admitted; most were common Russian imperial stamps, but he found at least a dozen Zemstvos. By then, the soldier had come to understand which ones interested Zmudowski. If he wanted more, the soldier told him, this could be arranged. The mail depot for the Russian Seventh was now at Delatyn. He was due to go there tomorrow and would be back in one week. He had a cousin in Kiev who collected stamps, too, he said; Zmudowski would bring him Austrian stamps, and he would bring the Zemstvos. A trade. But there was a catch. By then, their little armistice would be over, and they would be trying to kill each other. If Zmudowski returned to the village, surely he'd be captured, if not shot.

The Russian had thought for a moment, and then led Zmudowski outside. There, at the end of the road, a second path led down to where a great willow tree dipped its bare branches into the frozen river. They would meet there one week hence; the Russian would arrange to be on sentry duty. They agreed upon a signal by matchlight. One, two, one.

Back in Bystrystya, the others told Zmudowski this was *definitely* a trap. How convenient that the Russian remembered he had a cousin only *after* Zmudowski had shown such interest! The time for fraternization was over. Already the shelling had resumed. He would be taken prisoner; for his capture, the Russian would certainly be rewarded with more than a bunch of useless stamps.

But Zmudowski insisted. The great Chudovsky wouldn't have backed down and nor would he. Unless one was a millionaire and could buy one's way to greatness, this was how collections were made. So the next week, he hiked back up to Lemnowice, avoiding Margarete, whom he knew would stop him, and gathered together what he thought was a good representation of Austro-Hungarian stamps for the Russian's Kiev cousin. And on the pre-ordained night, he put on his hat and gloves, wrapped a blanket beneath his coat for extra warmth, took a rifle, and headed into the night.

The sky was clear, and the moon was full; anyone watching would have been able to see a figure slowly making his way through the bare woods. But no one was out. An owl called; far up the slope, he heard what might be wolves. But he pushed on, the snow at times above his waist. By then his mind was filled with fantasies of what the soldier might have found for him: blocks of shiny green Viatkas, *tête-bêche* Saratovs, dark-blue sheets from Novgorod. Now he regretted he hadn't given the soldier a drawing showing how to recognize an offset, or told him to look particularly for those without heavy franking . . .

Oh, but he was getting greedy!

He reached the river, struck his match.

Nothing.

Again he repeated the signal.

Nothing. His heart fell.

Then, from across the river, from the darkness of a dugout, came the light. One, two, one.

Slowly, carefully, he began to make his way across the frozen expanse. This was the moment of greatest danger. Until then, he had been able to stay mostly in the trees. But now he was totally exposed, the snow deep. Were they to fire, he'd be trapped. He thought of his daughter now in Kraków. How stupid of him to take such a risk! Rumours were coming that new Hungarian divisions would be arriving to reinforce the line. Soon the Russians would be pushed back. By summer the war would end. And here he was, in broad moonlight, begging for a bullet, all for some stamps.

But what stamps!

He pushed on. Faster now.

He reached the bank. He was shaking, though he didn't know whether it was from cold or fear. At his side, a rustling. He turned, but before he knew it, his head was in a headlock, a gloved hand over his mouth. He was dragged off behind the willow. Hands gripped his face and he found himself nose to nose with the Russian soldier. The Russian raised a finger to his lips to caution silence, then slowly let Zmudowski go. By way of hand motions, he let it be known that someone had seen them. A patrol was coming.

Motioning for him to follow, the soldier led him downstream, through drifts of snow. Now, from above them on the bank came voices. Lanterns now, casting gigantic shadows of men across the snow. Crouching, the two men huddled together. The Russian was taking an immense risk, thought Zmudowski. At a certain point, he would decide it wasn't worth it and turn him in.

But neither moved.

At last the sentries, satisfied or just too cold, turned back. A name was shouted; the soldier at Zmudowski's side replied with what must have been a joke of sorts, for it was answered with a satisfied guffaw.

It was safe now, the soldier whispered. Go.

The stamps!

Of course!

A rustling. Envelopes exchanged hands. Neither looked. 'Good luck!'

Back at Lemnowice, hands held before the stove, Rzedzian laughed. He never tired of the story, he said.

'And the stamps?' asked Lucius. He was aware then that Margarete had appeared, still working, but hovering near their circle so that she could also hear.

'Total rubbish. Not a single Zemstvo. I probably could have bought them in the Kraków stamp market for a couple of heller.'

'But at least you have the Astrakhan Zemstvo,' said Lucius.

'So, it turns out *that* also was a mistake. I must have *wanted* it to be from Astrakhan. But I misread the Cyrillic. It's from Arzamas. That made more sense. Astrakhan was under Cossack administration – it never issued Zemstvo stamps.'

'By the expression on your face, I'm guessing Arzamas stamps aren't so rare,' said Lucius.

'Oh, some are. Just not those issued last year.'

'I see.'

Zmudowski shrugged, smiled and looked wistfully into his lap.

'The stamp is worth about as much as it costs to mail a letter, Doctor,' said Rzedzian helpfully. 'In case you were going to ask.'

Zmudowski opened his little book. Mounted on a page of its own was a tiny sky-blue rectangle, showing an even tinier deer. Lucius lifted it to the light, to stare at the little creature against its backdrop of snow and woods.

'There you have it,' said Second Nowak, stroking his moustache and rising. 'War.'

6

As the winter progressed, the offensive to liberate Galicia from Russia faltered. At Przemyśl, the Austrian commander shot his horses, fired off his artillery, and destroyed his guns with overloads before surrendering. By late March, snow still thick on the ground, fighting came within a few kilometres of Lemnowice, rising slowly up the valley like a flood.

All day long they could hear the rumbling of artillery. At times the shells struck so close they shook dust from the cross-beams. Then, for a few weeks, a field camp occupied the village, and Lucius found himself working alongside other doctors, while a trio of severe Hungarian nursing sisters joined Margarete in the sacristy.

The doctors were named Berman and Brosz, both Austrian, both ten years his senior. Brosz, small and thin, with hands so delicate as to give the impression of fragility; Berman, plump and always laughing, with a large port-wine stain across his cheek.

In the beginning, he expected them to be surprised by the limited supplies, the lack of an X-ray machine or bacteriological equipment, his single nurse. But the last hospital had been even worse, they told him, the morale abysmal, with the neighbouring garrison's commanding officer resorting to punishing suspected shirkers by *Anbinden*, stripping them and binding them to trees.

'In the winter?'

'In the winter.'

Lucius thought of the ice, the driving wind. 'But I heard *Anbinden* had been banned.'

To this they only laughed. When eventually they asked him about his training, they seemed surprised to hear he had enlisted as a medical student, before Berman said, 'At least you're not a veterinarian like the last one.' Before the war, Berman had specialized in nervous and mental disorders, while Brosz had operated a sanatorium for tuberculosis. So in some respects, they were as inexperienced as him.

But how had he learned to operate?

'There was another doctor who taught me, Szőkefalvi, a Hungarian who has since moved on.'

In a way, it was true. And he knew, even if Margarete hadn't told him with a flashing of her eyes, that he was to say nothing of her.

But they had little time to talk. The stretcher bearers, dragging the wounded by sledge or dray, or skiing in with them on chairs bound to their backs, came almost hourly up the valley. Soon the quarantine room was converted into a ward of its own, and then the bathhouse, and then the hospital began to spread into the neighbouring houses of the village. Lucius saw Margarete trying futilely to impose some order, pleading with the doctors and nurses to carefully check the men for lice. They didn't listen, not even when Lucius took her side. But what could they do? There were simply too many wounded. There weren't even enough blankets to go around.

Sometimes, on his rounds, he was joined by Rzedzian or Zmudowski, but usually just by Margarete. In the village, visiting the soldiers in the low, dark huts, she spoke in broken Ruthenian to the women. It was the first time Lucius had been in any of the houses, crowded with rough-hewn tables and pens for rabbits and chickens, these empty now. Wooden cradles hung above the beds, and the light came from saucers of tallow with burning wicks of cloth. On the wall hung woollen festival ribbons, wreaths of bells. In comparison to the church, with its constant clamour, the huts had the hushed, sacred air of death-bed scenes, the light barely illuminating the pallid faces of the soldiers, the village women moving slowly in their dark shawls, their children sitting in transfixed vigil by the beds. For these, Margarete always had a crust of bread, a piece of carrot. Some-times Lucius entertained them by showing them his father's hand shadows, other times by letting them listen to their hearts. Their wide eyes grew wider with the cold bell of the stetho-scope, not seeming to understand what they were hearing, but astonished nonetheless. Manifestly, he did this out of kindness, or a sort of effort at improving relations, though in truth there was something fortifying in the chance to touch skin without gangrene, without fever, the bodies without a wound.

He was aware, too, that Margarete was watching him in these moments, occasionally exchanging words with the women, but these he didn't understand.

THEN ONE MORNING he woke to an eerie silence.

It was late April. For two weeks, the artillery had pounded them, contrapuntal with the storm.

Sitting up in his bed, in his greatcoat, beneath his blanket, in his boots, he waited for the sound of shelling to resume. The small window, behind weeks of snow, glowed silver. He rose.

Outside, the sun was out, the courtyard glittered. He walked beyond the church's shadow and stood a moment, his eyelids warming in the light. From the distance, he heard a shout and a man on skis appeared. He wore a gunpowder-grey trench coat and aviator goggles. Snowflakes glittered on his pale blue cap. He was pink-faced, out of breath. Fighting had stopped down in Bystrystya, he told Lucius. The Russians had pulled back overnight.

By the next day, messengers had arrived from Nadworna, on the plains. The story was confirmed. The Austrian Third would be pushing north. The soldiers billeted in the village were given an hour to gather their belongings. Soon they stood shivering in formation before the church, rucksacks loaded, lips steaming. The field kitchen, communications station and artillery equipment that had accompanied them, were all loaded onto lorries, drawn by tiny Panje horses.

Then, with a whistle, they began to march.

Berman and Brosz had been given orders to report to a field hospital being established in Nadworna. Lucius was with Margarete when the news came, and he feared he would be summoned too. On and on, the courier intoned the orders. But there was no mention of his name.

When the man finished, Lucius realized that he had been holding his breath. He sensed Margarete standing very close to him, and wanted to turn, to see her face, now that she knew that he would stay.

APRIL TURNED TO May.

The sun grew warmer. The snow began to melt. Harp strings of light broke through the nave.

Everywhere the valley was filled with crinkling whispers, the whine of shifting snowdrifts, the rustling of rills. Beneath the ice, the river began to murmur. Deep holes formed under dripping icicles on the corners of the roof. Stones gleamed in the run-off, and boughs heaved as they released their burdens, the snow shattering in its descent. Life appeared, incautious roe deer, boar, astonished waxwings flurrying as if released from the melting snow.

In the courtyard, lime-green buds speckled the tips of the beech tree, still streaked with snowmelt. A world yet unknown to him – graveyard, hedges, discarded wagon wheel – began slowly to announce itself. Fallen fences around the village houses. Mouldering haystacks. Pig troughs, though no pigs. A gravelled walkway across the courtyard. A pair of tiny wooden statues of Christ and Mary, both so weathered as to be almost identical, were it not for the liberty the carver had taken with Her bosom, and His mountain-man's beard.

Stone urns. A pile of grey firewood. Then: colour. Blue sky. Green leaf. A yellow burst of goldenrod. The waggling crimson crest of an unanticipated rooster. A tiny field of rose and purple asters on the first bare slope.

There were few new patients. Now with the fighting distant and the passes melting, the routes of evacuation had also shifted down on to the plain. At first this was met by everyone with some relief. Lucius slept his first full night in months, in early May. He shaved and bathed, and wrote his letters home. Margarete, too, seemed to relish the hiatus. The rings disappeared from around her eyes. In her step, he noticed a new lightness, which he hadn't known she'd lost.

One afternoon, he ran into her as she was leaving the washroom, her cheeks rosy, her skin damp. Though she was fully dressed, her wimple neatly arranged, she seemed almost embarrassed to be caught like this, as if he had actually stumbled upon her bathing. But he understood. He, too, had lingered in the washroom, his skin alive to the same hot water and same rough stone.

Soon, the soldiers awaiting evacuation began to colonize the courtyard, to smoke and drink *horilka*, whittle dolls as gifts to send home to their children, and play *bocce* with the garden stones. Yes, it was good to have been forgotten, briefly. And then as the weeks drew on, and the supplies left by the departing army dwindled, they began to realize that with the shifting of the front, the food wagons seemed to have forgotten them as well.

The pickles were the first to vanish. Then the rice, the hocks of gristly meat, the potatoes. Then onions, lentils, carrots, the tins of cooking fat. The bags of flour: three, two, one.

They began to grow hungry.

The cooks diluted the soup, cut thinner slices of bread. They finished the turnips.

Przednówek, Margarete said.

The Scarcity. Lucius also knew the word, an old farmer's term for springtime, when last year's rations had begun to grow low, but it was too early yet to plant.

They sent Second Nowak north to Nadworna to request supplies, but he came back empty-handed two days later, saying the plains were all but impassable for the mud, the road littered with abandoned lorries and harried squadrons trying to advance.

They thought of sending someone south, but the road through the pass was even worse.

THEY TURNED TO the woods.

Those able to walk set off together. It was Margarete who taught them how to gather, showed the city men from Budapest and Kraków and Vienna how to identify goosefoot and club-rush, to select saddle fungus and pig's ear mushrooms from the tree trunks, horsetail cones from the river, sweet calamus shoots, and tender bracken stems to roast. On the green, open slopes, they picked pot-herb: sorrel and saltbush, dandelion, lungwort, goosefoot, swine thistle. They found fresh pine needles to stretch their bread, made gruel from the green seeds of manna grass; they fermented hogweed in ammunition tins and boiled the budding leaves of the lindens. She showed them how to strip bark from the lindens, the birches, the maples, the hazels, to dry and roast and bake into their breads. To make soups of birch buds. Butter out of birch sap. Bread from the roots of quack grass, sweet snacks from mallow seed and roots of cock's foot and polypody. She warned them against the roots of the calamus that would make them see ghosts.

When they split into pairs after a week, she said, 'The doctor will come with me.' Lucius was made self-conscious by his selection, sensed the men exchanging glances, and yet he told himself that it was only natural; she remained cautious of soldiers, as she should. She wore a single soldier's greatcoat, hemmed so as not to drag in the mud. Over her shoulder, she hung a burlap sack from the muzzle of her rifle, as if it were a milkmaid's yoke. It was clear now that his early speculations as to her origins in the mountains were correct. He struggled to keep up. She was swift, moving over stones and fallen logs without breaking stride. She plunged her hands gloveless into dirt or snow, tore bark from the trees, brushed off a tuber before testing it with a bite. He was struck by how she never hesitated. But this was a familiar movement from her approach to wounds.

They spoke little while they walked. Around them, the whole world seemed to be turning to water. The earth was sodden, the trails shimmering with run-off. Ferns the colour of mantises unfurled from the black rotting mosses. Steam rose from the wet bark, and from the upper slopes, the remaining snowfields calved in little avalanches, thundering through the trees.

At times they passed women from the village, similarly following the narrow paths in search of food. He felt uneasy then, as if it were *their* woods in which he was foraging. But the women seemed less suspicious there, in the forest, smiling with a kind of fellow spirit as they passed each other on the trail.

They were hesitant to wander beyond the valley, at first, distrustful of reports that the war had moved off. But as the snow melted away, they ventured further into the neighbouring valley, where another river tumbled, swollen with run-off. There Margarete broke apart calamus and handed him the inner shoots to eat, or brushed dirt from chanterelles. Her hands still had the tarry smell of the carbolic, but the mushrooms were like nothing he had ever tasted, and he had come to like the smell of carbolic by then. When she was thirsty, she asked for his canteen. He was acutely aware that her lips were touching the same place his had touched, but he dismissed this as simply another habit from where she had come from, just as she seemed to think nothing of his taking food from her fingers, that it meant little else.

It was on their fourth or fifth sally, some time in April, that she asked him if she could sing.

Of course, he said, surprised, but she didn't seem to think it was strange at all to ask. From then, when they weren't talking, she sang softly, usually to herself, but at times, it seemed, for him. Nursery rhymes and cradle songs, love ballads and battle hymns, songs of summer, of horsemen, of sweethearts and stolen kisses, dances, christenings, weddings, midsummer, songs of night spirits and glen witches, wolves and cats and kittens, swallows and pines. Songs of sounds, wordless, rhymed. There were times he recognized them, distant cousins of the folk songs sung mostly by his governesses, but the tunes were different, wilder, the singing at times nasal and strange. She tried at times to teach him, but he was shy and always a bit breathless, and preferred to listen anyway, as he watched her figure move ahead of him, greatcoat and habit swaying, allowing himself briefly, very briefly, to imagine the form beneath.

One day, she took him high in the valley to see the ancient ruins of a watchtower. Grass grew from between the lichen-covered stones, and the vague outline of a spiral staircase could be made out amid the rubble. Wind-stunted pines and chestnuts grew in what had once been rooms. As they arrived, a band of crows took off, leaving behind a scattering of shattered pine cones.

She had first found the ruins last September, she told him. The chestnuts were abundant then, and throughout the autumn she'd come to gather them. Later, on days when so much sickness became almost too much to bear, she came there, too, to seek guidance for questions she couldn't answer. Or to imagine that the war was over, that she would return to Lemnowice to find the hospital had become a church again.

Her cheeks were still red from the exertion of the climb. They were sitting close to each other, and he could sense her warm, human smell, distinct from the forest, the wet moss, the upturned mud, the sappy, savaged cones. She was quiet. He wanted to ask if, back in September, she had brought anybody else along.

Instead, she spoke first. 'What were they like, Pan Doctor, the nurses you worked with in Vienna?'

He looked at her, surprised by the question, the undisguised curiosity about his relations with other women. The answer was that he didn't really remember. Vaguely, he could summon up the starched white habits, the unrelenting efficiency, the court-like decorum with which they seemed to run the wards. But that was all.

'You are remembering someone,' she said, with a smile.

He shook his head. 'Oh, no. I was just thinking how mostly I was terrified of them. I was a student, remember. Mostly they just told us what we did wrong.'

'Like me, Pan Doctor.' She laughed. 'When you first came. Remember?'

He noticed then the lashes of her eyes, and the way the grey iris seemed to capture the green of the glen. Her fingers stained with berries, a tiny mark of violet on her lip. 'Yes, like you.'

A wisp of hair had broken from her wimple, now silhouetted in the sun. She must have sensed him notice, for she tucked it back.

A pair of squirrels chased each other on the low wall of the ruins. He picked at the grass about his feet.

'Do you know what you'll do after the war?' he asked.

She turned to him, then looked off. With the stock of her rifle, she pushed a thin path through the pine needles. For a moment he felt as if he were with someone very different from the nursing sister of such fantastic devotions who had met him when he first arrived. Different even from the hunter of mushrooms and pot-herbs, from the steady companionship he'd come to know.

She sniffed and rubbed her nose with the base of her palm. She looked up.

'I don't know.'

He waited, wanting her to say more. To speak of her convent, or home.

At last she said, 'And you, Pan Doctor?'

'After the war?'

'After the war.'

He rolled an awn of grass between his fingers. 'Go back to medical school, I guess. I haven't really any choice.'

'And then?'

'After that? I don't know. Perhaps I will try and work at the university.' He paused. It sounded as if he were asking for permission. 'It is what I was planning on before the war,' he added, but that world, with its amphitheatres, its gleaming lantern slides, its corridor statues, now seemed so far away. A question came to him, one he had often thought of, but never asked. Now, as offhandedly as possible, he said, 'One day, I might . . . depending on where I go, of course . . . I might need to find a nurse to work with me . . .'

She turned and studied him. He was aware of a little tilt to her eyes, a slight movement at her mouth, as if she had lightly bitten the inside of her lip. For a moment she seemed almost joyful, and then just as quickly, something darker crossed her face.

The wind blew. The pines and chestnuts shivered, and thin showers of catkins fell about them. A hubbub of birds suddenly descended, saw them, and just as suddenly departed, as if ashamed to interrupt.

Still the question remained unanswered. He waited, wondering if he should apologize, if he should take back what he'd said, afraid now that he had risked the happiness of the day.

She brushed a catkin from her knee.

'There will be a lot of chestnuts this year, Pan Doctor,' she said. 'With so much snow over the winter. We will just need to find them before the cursed squirrels. This autumn, when we come back.'

He nodded, a little miserable to think that she had changed the subject, before he realized that the future she had spoken of included him.

ON THE HIGHEST peaks, the last snows melted.

In the gardens of the village, the women began to sow their

fields. Now a kind of giddiness settled over the men. There were about thirty then, and they began to joke that they had been forgotten. Medical duties became few – the dying had died, and many of the others had recovered. Slowly, the hospital seemed to transform itself into a little village of its own. There was a carpenter among them who led the men in repairing the church. They finally secured the hole in the roof of the north transept and raised pallets in places where floor had turned to mud. There was even a cobbler, Austrian, in his late forties, forehead dented like a tin can, blind in one eye and missing an ear, who spent hours cursing the High Command for their carelessness in shoe construction as he mended the others' boots.

Cautiously, small patrols slunk into neighbouring villages. They brought back sheep's cheese and hen's eggs. Margarete interrogated them as to how they had obtained them, and when it became apparent that a lamb had been spirited away from its owner, she marched the soldiers back like guilty schoolchildren, threatening to report any man caught stealing, if she didn't shoot him herself.

Still they prowled. In an abandoned country house in a neighbouring valley, they found a hidden cupboard with old vintages of Romanian wine and stores of sugar, and a private library with the promising titles of *Ten Beauties of Munich* and *The Touch of Satin*, though the former was a travel guide and the latter about home furnishing. Back in Lemnowice, the wine was washed down with *horilka*. Krajniak, newly rheumy with the arrival of spring pollen, baked a cake. Nightly, there was singing; a soldier who had been a clarinettist in civilian life cobbled together an instrument of ingenious construction from trench wire and ammunition tins. There was an outbreak of gonorrhoea, contracted from God knows where.

Rats returned. Briefly, typhus flared, taking two soldiers, then Rzedzian.

Lucius was sleeping when Margarete came to share the news. The orderly had been ill for scarcely three days, insisting it was just a flu.

'One should not grow attached to other people, Doctor,' said Margarete, when he came to the door, and he didn't know if she was speaking for him or for herself. Her eyes were red, and he wanted to comfort her, but he couldn't think of what to say. He had thought he was inured to death by then, even prided himself by the calmness with which he absorbed the news of the most recent passing. He who had once stared in shock at the frozen soldier without a jaw. But the great Rzedzian's body seemed horribly small, the stiffening fingers too familiar, and the way his lip drew back over his teeth reminded him of the corpse of an animal.

They buried him beyond the blossoming pears in the grave-yard behind the church. As his duty as the orderly's commanding officer, Lucius wrote a short letter to his widow and daughter, struggling to capture all that Rzedzian had brought, his impious humour and excess of sentiment, his extraordinary way of lifting the soldiers, which seemed, at times, to transfer some of his strength to them.

He was my friend, he wished to write, but the words were too painful, and he told himself that such familiarity wasn't befitting for a commanding officer. *He was a friend to many*.

For a day, Zmudowski disappeared, returning reeking of *horilka*, his thick beard matted with dirt, his eyes red, knuckles on both hands bruised and swollen.

It rained. A rat's nest was discovered beneath the chancel. Margarete set about on a campaign to mate the village cats. She tied a female to a chair in the sacristy and then conscripted all the local tomcats, one by one. The queen mauled four in quick succession before she was overpowered by a golden tom, 'Tatar-style'. The patients planted a garden, planning for the winter to return.

AN EVACUATION DETAIL arrived at the end of June. There was space only for ten men in the wagon, so the others stayed. Later, Zeppelins were sighted on their way to the east, and the men who could stand helped carry the others outside to watch. Lucius stood beside Margarete, in the crowd of the others, aware of the brush of her habit against his arm, waiting for her to notice his touch and move away. She didn't. Instead, together they stared upwards, watching the pair of giant fish drift slowly across the sky.

At the end of July, a small company of Austrian dragoons passed through. In the courtyard, they set out a table and the officers joined them for the midday meal, while a half-dozen kittens batted the tassels on their boots.

The men shared news from the front. Since the May break-through in the Russian lines near Gorlice, Przemyśl and Lemberg had been retaken. Now they expected even Warsaw to fall. Everything was shifting north. They should prepare themselves to move.

For weeks Lucius waited for new orders. They finally came in August, carried by a lone horseman from the north. Germany, fed up with the ineptitude of the Austrian High Command, had taken control of operations on the Eastern Front. The church, further from the front lines, would be reclassified as a Second-Level Field Hospital, given more doctors, an X-ray machine, a laboratory, more drugs. It was, thought Lucius, what he had imagined when he first enlisted. It likely meant a larger kitchen, books, a regular post, sheets on the officers' beds.

'This is good, no?' said Margarete.

'Yes . . . good,' said Lucius. They were sitting in the garden, eating pears, sweeter than any he had tasted in his life. A kitten rubbed itself against his leg. He wondered if at a Second-Level Field Hospital the nurses might be kept apart. But then another month, then two, passed without any news.

In late October, the first snow fell, a light dusting that vanished instantly. Then it was winter again, and Russia invaded Bessarabia and the Bukovina, places which once had been just the mystical words of map edges, now just over the mountains to the east. Once again snow filled the valley, and once again the wounded began to come. It was as if time were repeating itself, he thought, and it might have, had not one February evening a man appeared out of the cold.

7

It was late afternoon when a whistle at the entrance announced a new patient had arrived.

Lucius found Margarete outside the church, with a peasant draped in a giant sheepskin cloak.

A coating of hoar frost glistened on the wool like finely shattered glass. Steam rose from a great grey beard, which he had tucked into his collar. Over all: a cape, also of sheepskin, and atop this mountain a black sheepskin hat.

'Look,' said Margarete.

The man leaned over and pulled back a blanket covering a wheelbarrow to reveal a body, curled up among a pile of roots. 'Alive,' said the man. 'From over the valley. But it doesn't move. It doesn't speak.' His Polish was halting, heavy, thick with Ruthenianisms, all throat and hum.

Snow was falling. They replaced the blanket and led the peasant through the gate and along the beaten path to the quarantine. By then Zmudowski and Nowak had arrived. As the orderlies prepared a fire, the visitor hooked his thumbs inside the hempen belt that bound his cloak. He spoke. It was his wife who had found the soldier. They had been up by the pass, searching the woods for *brukva* – Lucius didn't know what this was – when they came across a wagon. It must have been abandoned only recently, as it had yet to be stripped for firewood. Intact, too, no sign of shell-strike, just abandoned. A Christian truck, the man said, with a big red cross on its side. Inside were the men. All dead, nine of them, all but this one, buried at the bottom, beneath the other bodies. No life anywhere nearby but this one, and barely life at that. They had brought him here, for reward.

'Did he say anything when you found him?'

'No. No speak. No move. Breathe, just. If no breath, we don't know it was alive.'

By then the orderlies were ready. Again, Margarete removed the blanket. Before them the soldier in the barrow was completely still, the only movement the flickering deliquescence of the snowflakes dusting his coat. For a terrible moment Lucius thought that between the church and the quarantine house, the man had died.

Then a wisping of a piece of dried grass on his lip betrayed his breath.

Gently, Lucius touched his fingers to the man's shoulder. 'Soldier?'

Instantly, the man recoiled. In truth, he only twitched, but the suddenness of it, and the stillness of the moment that preceded it, made it seem as if a small explosion had just detonated in the barrow. His head turned, his arms drew across his chest. Lucius stepped back. The man's eyes were wide, whites visible around a pair of dark brown irises. His nose flared as he tried to take in breath. But no words, nothing save the flinch, the stare. Unbidden came the memory of the rabbits pilfered by the hussar on their journey to Lemnowice, ears back, too terrified to move.

'There,' Lucius said. 'There, there. You're safe. You're in a hospital. You'll be okay.'

Still the eyes.

'Hospital,' Lucius repeated, in German. Then again in Polish, Hungarian, Czech. He could have gone on. These words now part of him in so many tongues. *Doctor, hospital. Quiet. Still.*

'We should get him warm and dry,' he said, looking to Margarete.

She knelt then, stroking the soldier's hair. This time he didn't draw away. His eyelids were puffy, his cheeks reddened from exposure, the swelling giving them a slight cherubic quality. A fine beard covered his cheeks, and a wing-shaped blur of mud ran down the flank of his nose. Gently, Margarete cleaned pine needles from his eyebrows, his lashes, brushed his forehead clean of dirt. She looked at Lucius to signal that it was okay to touch him. He knelt and showed the man his empty hands before beginning to palpate around his head and neck. He tried to assess his back, but the barrow was too tight.

'Gently now.'

Zmudowski had joined them. Fearing an injury to his spine, they tried to lift him from below, but the barrow's walls sloped inwards, like a coffin's, and they couldn't get their hands around him. It didn't matter. The man's limbs were clenched so tightly that they could lift him almost by his arms alone.

They set him on the stretcher, where he remained in the same position. 'There,' said Margarete at his side. She hushed him, though he wasn't making any noise. Again she stroked his hair. In a soft voice, in Polish, she said, 'You're cold, your clothes are wet. We will check you for lice, get you new clothing. Nothing bad will happen. Now you're safe.'

The sound of words seemed to calm him, whether or not he understood.

Again she looked up to signal they should start.

Slowly they began to strip his clothes, first the greatcoat, heavy, stuffed with what seemed to be paper. Then a second, thinner mackintosh, two sweaters, a blanket. Two layers of long underwear. The man inside was moist and pale, like the pulp of a nut. Both hands, pink with chilblains, were swollen up like gloves.

Zmudowski carried off the clothing to be disinfected, as Krajniak approached with the cresol and began to spray. For a moment the man was naked, while Margarete searched his skin for any signs of lice, her fingers swift, making no concessions to modesty. They wiped him down, covered him in a blanket, his body still coiled tight.

'Soldier,' she asked, 'who are you? What's your name?'

But he only stared back, eyes dark above the red sheen of his cheeks.

'Doctor, look.' Across the room Zmudowski crouched over the pile of clothing, disinfectant bucket in one hand. He rose as Lucius approached. 'Look.' He had extracted a sheaf of papers from the lining of the coat. They were wet and matted, stained with ink, now dusted with clotted lime. Lucius took a stack and gently began to peel them apart. They were sketches, of men, soldiers, trains, mountains, all drawn in the same skilled hand. Then others: children, a woman, naked, then details of her hand, her breasts, her legs.

'You drew these?' asked Zmudowski, looking at the soldier. There was no answer. He waved one of the nudes. 'Can I keep it?' he asked, smile flashing within his beard. He lifted the coat and pulled out another clump of papers, then another. Lucius was still amazed by what the men stuffed into their coat linings for insulation. Military circulars, love letters, scavenged news-print. He could have made a museum by now, he thought. The 1915–16 Lemnowice Exhibition of Material Used for Warmth.

Now he remembered the peasant in his furs, still waiting just inside the door.

'Thank you,' he said, turning to the man, and then to

Krajniak: 'See what you can find in the kitchen. Some onions maybe, a bottle of schnapps.'

The Russians paid in meat tins for their wounded, said the sheep-man.

'Please,' said Margarete. 'You'd be lucky if they let you keep your coat.'

By the time Zmudowski had returned, they had dressed the winter soldier in the same clean clothes that had been worn by several dozen men.

The peasant counted the onions.

'You can stay the night,' said Lucius, but the man only grunted, and with the rank, wet smell of stable, he was off.

Lucius turned back. 'I thought I was generous.'

'Very generous,' said Margarete. 'There is more belly beneath that cloak than on all of us combined. We should be asking *him* for food.'

She turned back to the silent soldier. 'Now, this one. Shall we bring him to the church?'

'Please, Sister,' said Lucius.

'Diagnosis?'

'No wound? For now, we call it *Nervenshock*, I guess.'

'Yes, Doctor. This is also what I thought.'

Nervous shock. But what did this even mean? Back in Vienna he had never heard of the condition. No mention by Wagner-Jauregg, Professor of Psychiatry and Neurology, great Crown Counsellor to the King. No word of it in the textbooks, nor the military manuals distributed by the Medical Service. All he knew came from Brosz and Berman. A new disease, born of the war, they told him. No sense to its symptoms, which seemed to simulate damage to the nerves, without yielding anything on autopsy. No agreement as to cause. The penetration of the skull

by microscopic particles of ash or metal? A concussion of air?
Or the effect of terror? In the field stations, in the regimental
hospitals, they couldn't even agree on a name.

*Granatkontusion. Granatexplosionslähmung. Kriegszitterung.
Kriegsneurose.*

*Shell-contusion. Shell-explosion paralysis. War-trembling. War
nerves.*

It was even worse in the west, they told him: an epidemic,
like some kind of virus first stirred up in Flemish soil, now come
east.

And treatments? he had asked them then. There the two had
laughed. How do you treat something when you don't know
what it is? But he was earnest and they tried to answer. Many of
the men got better just with rest. And the others ... In the
beginning, the sicker cases were sent back to Budapest and
Vienna, for rehabilitation, which might take months. But now
there were new cures, electricity applied to the limbs to stimu-
late movement, to the throat to get mute soldiers to talk. It was
not clear if the electricity worked because it caused the frozen
muscles to contract or because it also hurt and scared them.
Sometimes they attached it to the eyes or testicles. Dr Muck of
Essen had devised a metal ball to drop down the throat of soldiers who had lost their speech, the sensation of suffocation
causing them to gag, gags turning to sounds, then sounds to
words.

'These men are cured?' asked Lucius, and Brosz had raised
his finger. 'Ah, but since when was our goal to *cure* them? It's to
return them to the front.'

In Lemnowice, his first case of *Nervenshock* had been in late
February, scarcely two weeks after he'd arrived. An Austrian
private, one Georg Lenz of Wiener Neustadt, one of three
men to survive when a shell struck his foxhole near Dolina. He

had arrived pockmarked with tiny bits of gravel but otherwise unscathed. Except that his legs had ceased to work. His knees buckled when they tried to walk him, and when they asked him to move his toes, he stared at them with a strange indifference, as if his feet belonged to someone else. But his reflexes were normal, as was the function of his bowel and bladder. From an anatomical perspective, the injury was impossible, and yet Lucius couldn't bring himself to diagnose Lenz as faking. There was something to the soldier's terror, the way he watched the others, his screams at night, that couldn't be feigned. They had found bits of the other soldiers in his hair and pockets. He had stayed just three days before he was evacuated to the rear.

The others followed similar patterns. A shell-strike against a foxhole, a trench, a transport vehicle. And then, sometimes after hours, the symptoms. The tremors, the paralysis, the twitching, lurching gaits, the bizarre contortions of their arms.

But there wasn't always a blast. In May, a young Czech sergeant had been found wandering across the battlefield after he shot a dog for food and found a child's hand inside its mouth. It had taken days before he said what happened. By Lemnowice, he was hollow-eyed, emaciated, gagging every time he tried to eat.

They kept the men in Heads, on the assumption that the injury was to the nerves, to the brain, but also because the other soldiers, with their missing hands and feet, didn't take well to men without a wound. As they were often the only soldiers medically stable enough to make the journey back across the pass to a second-level hospital, they usually didn't stay long. But when they did, and when duties were light, Lucius returned to their bedsides, intrigued, to repeat their exams, to try to wrench from them the story of what had happened. He wrote to Feuermann, then at a regimental hospital in Gorizia, and received similar stories in return. Feuermann subscribed to a psychological explanation for the injury, that the *horror of the fighting produced a disruption in the fibres of the brain.* But Lucius wasn't satisfied by this. The *horror?* he replied. Since when was this a scientific term? And a *disruption of the fibres?* Brosz and Berman said the autopsies on men who'd later died showed nothing; their brains looked like everybody else's. What was the *mechanism?* he asked Feuermann. War and fear had been with them for ever. But cases like these had never been described.

It is like the mystery we once searched for beneath the microscope, he wrote, aware that his words were getting lofty, but unable to hold back. *Or that I once was seeking with my X-rays and my dogs. Something beneath the skin, imperceptible, waiting to be found.*

IN THE DAYS that followed, the winter soldier didn't leave his bed.

'What's your name?' they asked him in the morning. 'Where are you from? What happened?'

The questions yielded nothing. Sometimes the man watched them with his wide eyes, his gaze shifting from one person to another, before settling on something hovering in the air beyond. Other times he squeezed his eyes shut and pursed his lips tight beneath his nose, almost cutting off his breath. He didn't speak, didn't rise; he soiled his blankets and his clothes, leaving Zmudowski cursing as he shovelled away the rank, wet straw.

After accepting the broth on the night of his arrival, he began to refuse his meals.

Margarete sat vigil at his side, gently pressing his lips with the edge of the spoon, wiping his chin and neck as the soup dripped down.

'You're safe here,' she said. 'Whatever happened to you in the woods, it's over now.'

But he never swallowed when she fed him, and the mess of food only attracted the rats, who sniffed about his neck without eliciting a stir. His eyes took on an empty gaze, his eyelids seemed almost translucent, his skin became like crêpe paper and tented when Lucius pinched it. His blood pressure began to drop.

Is this what it looks like to die from losing one's mind? Lucius wondered.

He returned to his books, but he found nothing.

The hospital had a spare nasogastric tube of India rubber, untouched since the last soldier using it had died. They boiled it and slipped it through the new man's nostril and down his throat. Now three times a day, Second Nowak stood above him, pouring lukewarm broth into a funnel attached to the free end of the hose.

OUTSIDE, THE STORM grew worse.

A north wind, howling out of Russia, colder than any Lucius had known. Huge drifts built up against the north transept, and the walls creaked with their weight. Branches snapped from the beech tree, skittering across the roof.

The transport of the wounded ceased. There were no new cases, no evacuation convoys to take the wounded to the rear. All efforts turned towards warmth. Firewood details put on three layers of greatcoats and forged their way into the cold. Wet logs steamed against the stoves. Ad-hoc fireplaces blazed in the corners, yet by morning, the slush in the night pots had frozen solid. The soldiers began to sleep together, three beneath their blankets, the outside men rotating to the middle during the night. At mealtimes, the cooks hurried the food across the courtyard, shattering the ice that formed over the soup pots during the short transit through the cold. Lucius took his notes in pencil, because the ink froze in its well.

They moved the kitchen to the church. The smell of boiled onions filled the air, and the soldiers gathered around the bubbling vats of soup.

At times, patrols emerged out of the snow, just seeking warmth. They came on skis, or hand-built snowshoes, their bodies swaddled in blankets, faces wrapped in scarves, even their eyes covered with thin layers of gauze. They told incomprehensible tales of the winter. Trains buried inside snowdrifts. Crows frozen out of the sky like black scythes of ice. There were no wounded, they said. The cold took anyone who couldn't move.

Without new patients, Lucius turned to the drawings they found stuffed in the lining of the silent soldier's coat, hoping they might provide some clue.

Piece by piece, he peeled them apart. There were dozens, their ink faded with the cycles of freeze and thaw, each page bearing ghostly impressions of the next. The man's skill was formidable; he must have been an artist once. Briefly Lucius wondered if he had been hired to document the war. There were lonely pastures, village scenes, sketches of city streets. Camp life with its kaleidoscope of infantry and cavalry. Lancers with their plumed shakos, and infantry in puttees and spiked pickelhaubes, leather rucksacks on their backs. Priests offering the Eucharist to ranks of genuflected men. There were trains and stations, crowds of cheering families, field kitchens, a lone horseman galloping down the road.

Looking through them, it was possible to build a story of deployment, thought Lucius: from town to city, city to camp, camp to plains and on into the forests, to primeval scenes of fallen logs and bracken and filtered sunlight, wild boar and roe deer, sketches of little songbirds, a hare, a winter fox.

And then among these, he began to turn up others, not so easily explained. Eyes hidden in the bracken and the beech leaves. Skies tiled with airships. A lonely wheel perched high upon a pillar in an empty field.

A crowd of naked children with carnival heads of wolves and boar. Serpentine dragons, curling in the corners of the pages. Faces in the torn anatomy of fallen soldiers, and shadowed creatures lurking in the darkness of a crumpled coat.

Sometimes Margarete joined him.

'Does it tell you anything?' she asked.

He didn't know. Save that whatever had happened no longer seemed as simple as the effects of a bomb blast. It went deeper, further back, it seemed.

'Dreams?' she asked, picking up the sketch of a tree, upon which bodies hung like fruit.

A recollection of his journey from Nagybocskó: the open field, the hussar, the carnations blooming from the horses' heads. And in the darkness of the forest, the frozen, turning body. 'Perhaps,' he said.

She set the image down and slowly ran her fingers over the hanging bodies. 'Do you think he will get better?'

Again, he didn't know. If this was madness, he had even less of a chance of curing it. He had been to three lectures on insanity, seen a single patient, a man diagnosed with *dementia praecox*, who believed himself controlled by electric wires emanating from the Emperor. But how were such men treated? Bromides, morphine, cold baths, *gardening* . . . and did any of this even work? Then he thought of other madnesses, of the myths he'd pored over as a child, the sudden assaults of screaming Furies, their victims scuttling back in horror from the beating of their tormentors' wings.

They both looked down again at the page, to where a line of

little dragons curled through a group of portrait sketches, eye-less, with waving manes and cryptic markings on their bellies. The creatures now were strangely familiar, as if Lucius had seen them once before. In some tale of knights and monsters, though he couldn't remember where.

AFTER A WEEK, the soldier began to moan.

It started at night. Eyes wide, back and forth he shook, the nasogastric tube dragging across the blankets rank with piss and broth. The sound was low, less a scream of pain and more a frantic prayer. It rose and fell, a wind of his very own.

Across the church, the other men began to protest. *Quiet! Stop crying, or I'll come and make you stop.* Even the disoriented soldiers in Heads grew agitated, cursing him with stuttering lisps.

'Shhhh,' said Margarete, crouching by the soldier once again, caressing his hair, hushing him until he calmed.

They left. An hour later he began again.

This time they found him sitting up, his hands clenched in his hair. Spittle formed around his mouth; his limbs were tense as pipes. On his wrist, his pulse raced, faster than Lucius could count. Eyes pinched, lids white. The hum horrid, from some-where deep within his throat.

Zmudowski looked out over the ward. 'You have to give him something, or another patient will kill him before the night is done.'

Lucius rummaged through the medicine chest, found some hypodermic tablets of morphine sulphate, dissolved one, and drew it into a syringe. He approached, thumb in the plunger ring, ready to inject.

The humming was constant, louder now. Lucius looked to

Margarete, and she turned to the orderlies. 'Hold him tight,' she said.

But the soldier didn't even seem to register the needle. Half an hour later, they tried another dose of morphine. Then potassium bromide. Atropine. Chloral hydrate. Morphine again.

Finally, after an hour, he began at last to nod off. It was close to two.

AT FIVE, Margarete found Lucius in his quarters.

She was sorry to wake him so soon, she said, but the soldier had begun again.

The snow swirled about them as they hurried together across the courtyard. Inside the church the man lay on his back, his chin contracted to his chest. He looked like someone who'd been bound there, raising his head to watch his torturers. His body was as rigid as the night before, his breath sharp and sudden, the veins of his neck and face so distended that, despite all medical knowledge to the contrary, Lucius feared that they could burst. A nostril was dark with clotted blood, and a stream of blood and mucus had dried against his cheek. 'He was up at four,' said Margarete. 'He tore his nasogastric tube out.' She placed her fingers on his wrist. 'And his pulse, again . . .' Still the man stared past them to his devils in the air.

Again, Lucius rummaged through the cabinet. The soldier seemed even worse now, his eyes wilder than earlier that night. Was the morphine making him delirious? But what were they to do? The army manuals recommended tranquillizing anguished soldiers into sleep. More chloral? Bromides? *Ether?* But this felt like veterinary medicine, and this case was different from the common soldier delirious with pain. But what then? Rub his chest with camphorated oil? Feed him more beef tea? Besides the morphine, the bromides and atropine and chloral, the only drug for nervous agitation was some Veronal they hadn't used for months. He stopped and looked at the vial; half the pills had crumbled into dust. For seizures, but also a sedative, in fashion in Vienna with his mother's set, though not – of course – his mother, who seemed spared of any nerves to calm. He hadn't thought to use it for his soldiers, had no need for it, not with the industrial quantities of bromides provided by the Medical Service. He tapped out a pill, then two, and returned to the soldier's side.

Unable to open the man's mouth, he parted his lips and crushed the tablet against his teeth. Fragments dribbled down his chin. Margarete, at his side, wiped them back up with her thumb and pushed them far inside the soldier's cheek.

The man remained motionless, his face red, his fists clenched so tightly that they would later find his nails had pierced his palms.

From the high windows came a cobalt hint of dawn.

'I think we should make rounds on the other patients, Doctor,' said Margarete. 'Before he starts to scream again. If he is not sleeping in an hour, we'll try something else.'

Their ritual began again in Limbs. They were halfway down the second aisle, when a whistle from the south transept broke across the church.

Hurrying, they found the soldier resting on his side, breathing softly. His eyes closed, but lightly now.

'He spoke,' said Zmudowski.

They crouched at his side. Again it came, a murmur, low and soft.

'I can't understand,' said Lucius.

'*Szomjas vagyok,*' said Margarete. 'It's Hungarian: *I'm thirsty.*'

*

125

THEY BROUGHT HIM a bowl of soup from the kitchen in the transept.

The man let Margarete feed him, opening his mouth to meet each spoonful. He didn't move his arms. He kept his eyes away from her, and from Lucius and Zmudowski, both crouching behind her, more than a little awestruck, as if a soldier eating soup was one of the most amazing sights that they had ever seen.

The effect lasted until shortly after noon.

Then: staring again, body rigid, save the slight rocking back and forth. The same incantatory hum. From his greatcoat pocket, Lucius took the bottle of Veronal and tapped out two more pills. This time he pushed them far back into the soldier's cheek.

Again, after an hour, they found him sitting, staring at his fingers in his lap.

'Soldier?' asked Margarete.

She touched his shoulder. He jumped but she didn't withdraw her hand, and he didn't move away. In Hungarian she asked a question Lucius couldn't understand.

His answer was murmured.

She spoke again in halting Hungarian, her eyes darting quickly to Lucius's, as if unable to contain the miracle of this awakening alone. And again the man answered, his voice slightly louder, occasionally catching on his words.

At last, after what seemed like a very long time, she looked up. 'This is Sergeant József Horváth, Doctor. Hungarian, from Budapest, he says. He thinks it is October, that he's at his garrison in Hungary. That he is just waiting for his mother to come and fetch him. That's all I could get. There is a stammer, as I think you can perceive.'

A stammer. Lucius felt the old twist in his tongue, the metal of the apparatus.

He looked back at her. 'Did you ask him what happened before he came here?'

Margarete leaned forward again and spoke.

They waited a long time, but this time the soldier just stared past them into space.

THEY BEGAN TO schedule the doses twice a day, at the start of morning and evening rounds. They didn't want to wait for the rocking or the moaning or the tension in his body to return. While once Lucius had worried that the man would die before the evacuation convoys reached them, now he feared the opposite: that they would take him back before he could be cured. Through the winter, to the second-level field hospitals with their prowling conscription officers. Or worse, to Vienna, to Budapest. To the specialists, with their electricity and Muck balls.

This weeping, stuttering man, an orb of steel pushed down his throat.

Outside, the snow kept falling. The snow: soldier's curse and soldier's friend. Now, it only was the snow that gave them time.

What is happening seems nothing less than a resurrection, he wrote that first night to Feuermann, rhetoric soaring once again, but needing to share his exhilaration. *I've seen men come out of comas, and others gently thaw to life after being pulled from frozen rivers. But I've never seen such a transformation. Someone so unreachable return with just a little pill. Someone in such despair. Woundless, and yet seeming to bear, like some scapegoat, the misery felt by everyone else.*

But how? Looking down at his thumb, he could still feel the wet pills crumbling as he pushed them deep into Horváth's cheek. He had no explanation for the strange magic he had just discovered. But most advances in medicine involved some serendipity. What was important now was that he watched and studied carefully, and learned.

Like Lazarus, he wrote to Feuermann, then crossed this out, embarrassed by the grandiosity it implied. If Horváth was Lazarus, then who did that make him?

BUT NOW, almost daily, Horváth was changing, awakening, gaining strength.

He began to sit up on his own, to accept the spoons of broth without much prompting, to use the basin for his needs. Soon he was holding his own utensils. He stood. He stood and fell, but then he stood without falling. He took a step. On the first of March, Lucius watched as Margarete walked him, shuffling, up and down the aisle of the church, her arm in his. It's like we're going to be married, Margarete joked, and Lucius laughed, though inside he felt a twinge of jealousy, just a little bit. For Horváth, because of the way that Margarete held his arm, but also for Margarete. It was *my* pills, my Veronal, he wanted to remind her. He felt almost as if there were an unspoken competition for who could be the one to claim this victory. As if they were both falling a little bit in love with their silent visitor or, more, with the cure that they had wrought.

And they weren't alone. The others, who had once cursed Horváth for his screaming, had repented, and in their repentance, now showered him with hope. They filed past to look at his drawings, set him closest to the fire when the men played music, and held out their cigarettes so he could take a puff. When the sun made a miraculous appearance on the fourth, and some of the braver souls took off their shirts to take in the fleeting rays, and others, armless, heads in bandages, played soccer with a bundle of rags, they brought him out with them to serve as a goalpost. He said nothing, only stared up at the great beech tree or watched the playing men. But peaceful now, almost angelic, breath steaming from his chapped, pink lips.

Yes, it was extraordinary, Lucius thought. The joys of diagnosis, the ecstasies of study: none of it could have prepared him for this. He wished not only Feuermann could see it, but also Zimmer, and Grieperkandl, and the rector, even his mother. *See*, he wished to say. Not *your* kind of doctor; *this* is the kind of doctor I will be. And Father, too, would understand the glory of the discovery. Yes, he could feel the presence of the old retired major in his polished boots, standing beside him in the churchyard as they had once stood in the mirrored hallway, the glorious wings of ostrich feathers mounted on their backs.

And I was once content with being just a barber surgeon, a bone-cutter, a setter of broken limbs.

THEY GAVE HIM paper, pencil, and asked him to draw. Slowly, with encouragement, and usually with Veronal, he began to sketch out shapes, fragments of landscapes, faces. He squinted, working with great effort; at times he licked his lips in concentration. By then the apple-like swelling in his face had gone away, leaving the finest craquelure of reddened vessels across his nose and cheeks and slightly puffy eyes. He must have been quite handsome, Lucius realized. There was something almost ethereal in the glow of his skin and the faint tint of plum around his eyes, and Lucius couldn't help but feel another pang of envy as Margarete shaved his beard and combed his wavy hair, and dressed him in a clean pair of salvaged fatigues.

Slowly, Lemnowice began to fill Horváth's pages, like a memory album, and as the village had probably never seen a camera, perhaps the only one. The church. The soccer-playing men, the soldier in the bed beside him. A sketch of Margarete in three-quarters profile, then other sketches of her eyes and mouth and hands. A taller, looming figure in a greatcoat: Pan Doctor, said Margarete, though its features were indistinct. And then: more airships, the portraits of mysterious children, the eyeless dragons crawling everywhere across the page.

'What are these little creatures?' Margarete asked Horváth one day towards the end of his second week of convalescence. But then, all of a sudden Lucius, peering closer, knew.

The long, thin bodies with their manes and eyeless heads. The cryptic markings on their chests. Not manes but gills. Not dragons. Not *on* their chests, but *inside*. Their hearts.

'*Grottenolm*,' said Lucius.

Horváth looked up, and his dark eyes met Lucius's.

'Sorry, Pan Doctor?' said Margarete.

'*Grottenolm*,' said Lucius again. 'As a boy, I used to visit them in the Imperial Collection. They are little salamanders, with translucent skin.' A memory now, of the frightened girl in the Ludwig II suite on that night of his supposed deflowering. But how strange to find them here, he thought, these rarities from the darkest corners of the aquarium, where lonely little boys pressed up against the tanks and harried governesses wiped their nose marks from the glass.

His eyes hadn't left Horváth. Had he been there too, in the museum? And what now did it mean that they had reappeared within his anguished drawings? A nightmare? A hallucination? Or like the recurring faces of men and women he suspected to be Horváth's family, were they something to cling to, an escape? Were they like the shadowed monsters in his sketches, or their antidote?

'You know them, *Grottenolm*,' said Lucius, and with this third utterance, he saw something else register in Horváth's gaze. It was almost imperceptible – a sense of recognition, a flickering of memory – but he had seen it. There had been some kind of connection, not only between the two of them but deeper, to something further back and shared in childhood, suspended in that word.

He turned to Margarete. 'Tell him that we'll get him home,' he said.

THE FOLLOWING AFTERNOON, an evacuation detail arrived in Lemnowice, looking for men sturdy enough to make the journey down to Nadworna through the cold.

Slowly, Lucius and Margarete led the ambulance driver past the patients. They chose a Polish private recovering from pneumonia, a Czech infantry officer from Heads who was ready for rehabilitation, and twelve others from Fractures and Amputations.

'I think he's ready,' said Margarete, when they reached Horváth.

Lucius hesitated, looking down at the soldier, now sleeping peacefully, arm draped across his face. No, he thought. Not before his resurrection was complete. There was little doubt Horváth was strong enough to go. But what would happen then? Nadworna was but a stopping point. From there they would have to take him further, to another hospital, and Lucius worried that the other hospitals wouldn't know how to care for him. There, Horváth could lose everything Lucius's alchemy had wrought.

Margarete listened quietly as he told her this, in more careful, sober words.

'He *wants* to go,' she said at last.

'*Wants* to go? He told you?'

'He asked for *Mama. Haza.* Home.'

Lucius hesitated; he had not expected this kind of opposition. Hadn't Margarete felt the same thrill at his discovery, the first steps of Horváth's rehabilitation, the first inklings of the person who was going to emerge? She had been with him the day before, had seen Horváth's face, the fleeting awakening as Lucius recognized the salamanders in his drawings. Wasn't she also tiring of amputations? Surely, she wished to see what happened next . . .

A whistling came from the walls as the wind picked up outside. 'I'm not sure he understands,' said Lucius. 'It's freezing. And the ambulance is heading *north*, deeper into Galicia. Not to *Mama*. To a hospital in Poland. And if he's better, back to the front.'

'I know. But that's true of any patient, Pan Doctor. He's been here three weeks already. They can give him the Veronal just as well as we can, can't they? We'll send instructions. We can't treat him as if he's different. You know that.'

'But he *is* different, you've seen the progress . . .' said Lucius. He felt now that he was arguing not with her, but with a second presence, invisible, but very near. So he added, 'You've heard what they are doing to such men to get them battle-ready, using electricity, Muck balls . . . It's torture . . .'

'I've heard,' she interrupted. 'But we're a field hospital, not a rehabilitation hospital. Patch and send, no? If a man is healthy enough to make the journey, we evacuate him. If I must remind Pan Doctor Lieutenant, there are Cossacks just across the plains.'

'The front is a hundred kilometres away, Sister.'

'*Pan Doctor*. The front moves fast.'

Outside, the snowdrifts creaked against the roof. They stood facing each other, in the crossing, in the thin light from above. For the first time in memory, he found himself angry with her. He sensed his voice had risen, that he was uneasy that he felt so much at stake.

'I can't,' he said. 'I have an oath. To do no harm.'

'Of course.' Lips pinched, she curtsied, a sign of disagreement he had come to know quite well. She turned to go, then stopped.

'Pan Doctor?'

'Yes?'

'You are keeping him for his sake. Not ours, I hope.'

THE LORRY WAS waiting outside the church.

Snow dusted the hood and canvas shelter. A pair of village children, carrying firewood, had stopped to watch them. Lucius followed the evacuees outside, where they saluted him, one after the other, and climbed into the back. The canvas door was buttoned shut. Were it not for the faint coughing of the Polish private, there would have been no sign of any life inside.

The driver knelt before the engine and turned the crank. The engine wheezed, then failed to catch. Again the driver tried. This time it didn't make any sound at all.

He rose, cursing. 'The hoses have frozen. I'll need hot water.'

He went back into the church, leaving the patients behind. Lucius remained outside, uneasy that the men had just been left out in the cold. And this driver seemed careless, he thought, and he didn't like how small and vulnerable the lorry looked. Inside the canvas shelter, the benches were bare; the men would have nothing but their single blankets, and one another, to stay warm. What if the Polish private's pneumonia worsened again? Was this why he was coughing? And the Czech officer – he still grew confused at times. And now the sun was setting. What if they had to stop at night?

At least Horváth wasn't among them, he thought. Yes, he tried to reassure himself: he was relieved he'd kept Horváth behind.

But the others ... He had half a mind to unfurl the canvas door and get his patients, when the driver returned, lugging a pot of steaming water that heaved and splattered on the earth.

THAT NIGHT, paces away from József Horváth, Lucius poured the remaining Veronal out onto a piece of paper.

Sixteen tablets. Eight days before they began to lose him again; nine, ten if one counted the pills that had turned to dust.

8

AND HE WAS RIGHT. The front was far away. In Latvia and Byelorussia, Italy and Mesopotamia and Verdun. Throughout the winter, fighting had continued in Galicia and the Bukovina, but these were smaller skirmishes, a seemingly endless back and forth for snowy country, downed bridges and open craters, pastures. Little lost, and very little gained.

One day in the middle of March, they thought they heard shelling, and slipped cautiously outside the church. But it was just a village woman, her face red with exertion, replacing a fencepost with the booming flat of her axe.

OCCASIONALLY, evacuation lorries stopped to drop off soldiers injured on the plains. They were mostly from Hungarian regiments, trying to transport the wounded back across the mountains to hospitals in Munkács and Máramarossziget, only to be held up by the snow. There were more cases of war nerves among them, soldiers beset by shakes and twisted postures, who tumbled when they tried to walk. Like Horváth, they had no wounds that he could see, and like Horváth the palsy followed no known pattern. But they were different, more like the cases described by Brosz and Berman. They ate and spoke and wept, and their movements were purposeful; some scurried beneath their blankets with the slightest sound.

Lucius was tempted to try to give them Veronal, which had been resupplied the week before. But Horváth now needed ever larger doses just to keep him from tensing up, and again Lucius feared running out of pills. Now, with Horváth's stay approaching a month, he found himself increasingly pessimistic, even angry, though he didn't know towards whom.

At the end of the month, a conscription detail appeared on horseback.

The commanding officer was a lieutenant called Horst. A tall man, accent from Upper Austria, with pale, almost lashless eyes, a dark-brown moustache trimmed neatly above unusually white teeth, and a scar on his forehead in the distinctive shape of a third, tiny eye. He wore a black cape trimmed with red ribbon over his broad shoulders, and grey trousers tucked into a pair of steel-tipped boots. From Margarete's look of disgust, Lucius sensed this was the same man who had appeared last winter, whom she had cursed so viciously. But Horst gazed right through her. He was accompanied by a pair of Hungarian batmen, granitic specimens, each a good hand taller than Lucius and likely twice his weight.

Inside the church, the batmen sat sullenly at the table and drank from bowls of soup while Horst explained. A year and a half of war had taken a heavy toll on the armies, he said. In Vienna, the draft was expanding. Now they were canvassing the hospitals for men well enough to fight.

'No one here is well enough to fight,' said Lucius, looking past the lieutenant into the dim light of the nave. 'An evacuation convoy just passed through two weeks ago. They took fourteen patients to the rear. The rest are still too ill to leave, let alone return to battle.'

'There are new orders about what constitutes battle-readiness,' said Horst, taking another spoonful of soup. 'Certain doctors do not understand the needs of a fighting army. What constitutes illness in war is not the same as peace.'

A hush had descended over the hospital, and Lucius could sense Margarete watching him. He knew that further protest would only raise Horst's suspicions. 'Whatever Herr Lieutenant thinks,' he said.

Horst downed the last drops of his soup and rose, sabre clattering against his chair. From his pocket, he removed a leather case and extracted a cigarette, which he handed to one of the batmen to light.

They began in Limbs, in the nave, beneath the gilded image of St Michael.

One by one the men lifted their stumps for him. Horst moved quickly, stopping only to inspect a wound. He seemed impatient, Lucius thought, even annoyed to find so many amputees. Halfway down the second aisle, Horst stopped. 'Where are the neurological diseases?'

'Over there,' said Lucius, pointing towards the south transept. 'We haven't many. But they're all quite ill.'

Horst drew on the cigarette and tapped the ash free. 'And I told you I'll decide.'

THE FIRST TWO patients both had head wounds; both were comatose and didn't stir when Horst shook them with his foot. In the third bed was an Austrian private named Berg, a former sapper who'd been buried in his tunnel. His sight had failed him, though Lucius could find no sign of injury to his eyes or brain. At night he woke up screaming, and when they sat him up to eat his meals, he couldn't keep his head from drooping down. He had been there two months, having missed the last evacuation due to a passing bout of dysentery.

But Lucius knew that none of this was likely to protect him from the conscription officer. 'He's blind,' he said.

'Blind?' Horst crouched and tilted the man's head back. 'His eyes look fine.'

'Of course, but on proper ophthalmic exam . . .'

'Stand,' said Horst.

The soldier didn't seem to hear him.

'I thought you said he was blind,' said Horst. 'Not deaf.' He nodded to a batman, who hauled Berg up to his feet.

Berg stood trembling, in half genuflection, as if he didn't know whether to sit or stand. His chin hung to his chest.

'What's wrong with his neck?' asked Horst.

For a moment, Lucius paused, trying to gauge how best to respond. 'Shell-blast kyphosis,' he said at last. He reached out and turned Berg roughly by the shoulder, as if to show that he, too, was no sentimental fool. He ran his thumb over the soldier's spine. 'Probable compression of the vertebrae secondary to the explosion. For a time, we suspected a subdural haematoma. I thought I would have to open his skull.'

This was all, of course, a lie. But the medical language seemed to give Horst pause. As he walked on, Margarete helped Berg back into his bed.

The next patient was one of the new Hungarians, named Virág. According to the story, he been talking to his commanding officer when an errant bullet from a soldier cleaning his gun burst through the CO's eye. Two days later, out of the blue, Virág had dropped to the ground, screaming, clawing at his own face, saying it was burning. For his first few days in Lemnowice, he kept trying to flee into the cold.

Horst told him to stand, turned him, told him to walk.

Virág obeyed.

'Get dressed,' said Horst.

Lucius stepped forward. 'Please. You can't take him, Lieutenant. Even yesterday, he thought we were under attack. He's still sick. He doesn't even know where he is.'

Horst ignored him. 'Dress,' he said.

Again Lucius interrupted. 'Lieutenant. These are *my* patients. I have my duties.'

Now Horst turned to look at him again. He said, '*Your* patients? These men belong to the Emperor.' He paused. For a moment he looked at Lucius as if seeing something he hadn't seen before. 'How old are you anyway? Nineteen? Eighteen?'

Lucius didn't answer that. 'You can't send him back into battle. He's as sick as any of my amputees.'

'Then I will take your amputees, too. I'll take you and your nurse – I'll put you in an ambulance team in a real zone of battle. So you can see real bravery. *Then* you can tell me what constitutes health.'

They had reached Horváth.

'And what is wrong with this man?'

If only I knew. But the lesson from the first two men was clear. He didn't hesitate.

'*Dementia praecox*, Lieutenant. Catatonic type, most likely a primary presentation. Quite classic per the descriptions set forth by Professor Kraepelin of Munich. Highly unstable vital signs with hypertension and tachycardia, which you might know forebodes progression to the fatal form.'

'He's been here a month,' said Horst, studying the manifest.

'Yes, Lieutenant,' said Lucius.

'That's a long time,' said Horst. 'If he is so sick, why wasn't he evacuated?'

'There is always a question of priority. There were other men . . .'

But Horst had turned from him. 'Stand,' he said.

There was silence. Horváth stared up at them. He said nothing.

Again, Horst said, 'Stand.'

Again nothing. Lucius said, 'He speaks Hungarian . . .'

'All soldiers understand basic orders in German,' Horst answered, looking down at the patient on the ground. 'Are you showing disrespect for a senior officer, Private?'

In answer, József Horváth squeezed his eyes shut very, very tight.

Outside, a cloud must have passed before the sun, for the room grew dark.

Horst looked to his batmen and then turned away from Horváth. For a moment, Lucius thought he had decided to leave the soldier alone. Then, with a swiftness that seemed impossible for such a massive person, Horst turned back and brought the heel of his boot down into Horváth's belly.

Horváth doubled over, heaving pale green soup onto the floor. He began to cough.

'I said stand, you piece of shit.'

Again Horst kicked him. Horváth writhed, burying his face in the straw. The lieutenant put his steel-toed boot to Horváth's neck. He pressed. A low groan came from Horváth's mouth.

Beneath his head, beneath the coat Horváth used as a pillow, Lucius could see some of his drawings.

Lucius said, 'Lieutenant, you are going to break his windpipe. I assure you the man means no disrespect. This is classical negativism . . . catatonic symptoms . . . common, Lieutenant, you can find it in every textbook.'

'Insubordination is what it is called. I said stand, soldier.'

'Lieutenant,' said Lucius. 'He is not resisting you. It is a symptom of his condition.'

Horst pushed harder. 'It is a symptom of disrespect,' he said. He drew on his cigarette.

A horrific wheezing rose from Horváth. Lucius looked to Margarete, trying to find some mooring, now afraid that she would try to intervene. 'I said . . .' he began again, turning back to the lieutenant. 'I said he has *dementia praecox*. This is classic catatonic stupor. It is not purposeful. It—'

'And I said I've never heard those words,' said Horst. 'I think you are making this up. If it is a disease, then why haven't I heard of it?'

Now a taunting smile flickered across Horst's lips.

'Because you're ignorant and never went to school.'

The two guards exchanged glances. Margarete took a step forward. 'Herr Lieutenant,' she began in hesitant German.

Horst turned, his face suddenly red with anger. 'A nurse dares speak to me!' He met her eyes and pressed his foot harder into Horváth's neck until she backed away. The soldier gasped and twisted. Horst turned to Lucius. 'Who else are you hiding, Lieutenant?'

'No one.'

Again Horst pushed down harder. Horváth was clawing at the officer's riding boots. The lower part of his body flopped like a fish. 'Who else?' Horst shouted.

'I said, no one,' said Lucius, and against all wishes he felt tears begin to well behind his eyes. 'Take your foot off him.' But then Horváth had writhed off his mat, and the papers were in full view.

Horst motioned towards a guard, who picked them up.

'And what are these?' On the piece of paper, a wreath of little *Grottenolm* circled a sun.

'Drawings,' Lucius said miserably.

'Drawings. He's not well enough to fight, but he's well enough to draw.'

Lucius said, 'It's treatment . . . It . . . distracts him. Otherwise I waste morphine on him. I let him draw because it distracts him. It keeps him from disturbing the other men.'

'He must not be very disturbing if you've kept him for a month,' said Horst. Now he let the papers fall. 'You understand there are punishments for desertion.'

'This man is not a deserter, sir.'

The lieutenant released his boot, and Horváth broke into a spasm of gasping. Horst turned to his guards. '*Anbinden.*'

Lucius looked to Margarete, but she was still as stone. 'Lieutenant,' he said, taking a step closer. 'I take full responsibility for this patient. I . . . I understand the principles of medicine in war. Were there a coward among these men I would happily punish him myself. But this man is sick. He has no visible wound, I know, but he is very sick. He sees . . . spirits. Hears them speaking to him.'

'Then his spirits can tell him how to hold a rifle, how to behave.'

The batman yanked Horváth to his feet. He began to moan, that same cry as when he had first arrived. There was a foul smell, and looking down at Horváth's trousers, Lucius realized to his horror that Horváth had defecated. Horst had also noticed, and his lip curled with disdain.

'Lieutenant,' Lucius begged. 'He's terrified. *Please*. It is twenty below zero. It's too cold.'

Horst turned back to the batmen. 'The doctor, who spends his days in this nice warm church, worries it's too cold!'

Lucius was frantic now. 'I take full responsibility. Send him before a medical review board. If I am wrong, I will take whatever disciplinary measures . . .'

But Horst wasn't listening. He turned and walked towards the courtyard exit. His guards followed, Horváth struggling in their hands, the moans growing louder. Throughout the church, many of the patients were watching. 'Back to your beds,' said Lucius weakly, but bereft of any authority now.

Outside, in the courtyard, the men stopped at the beech tree. They stripped Horváth of his clothing, first his shirt, pulling it over his head without unbuttoning it, then yanking down his soiled trousers. Shit streaked his trembling legs. The soldiers made a sound of disgust and tried to pull the trousers off, but the cuffs got stuck over his ankles, and Horváth tumbled face down into the snow. They roughly yanked each leg off, then threw the trousers into a heap and heaved him up. They tied his hands behind his back and then bound him to the tree. Now the moans became words. '*Kalt!*' he shouted, in heavily accented German. '*Cold. Cold!* Oh! It's so cold!' He struggled against the rope. Lucius looked back at the church. Patients were gathering at the door. Lucius started towards the struggling man, then turned. Then back again. There are forty of us, three of them, he thought. The church is full of weapons. We could overwhelm them.

But no one moved.

'Close the door,' he told Margarete in Polish. 'They don't need to see.'

She started across the yard, but Horst motioned for one of the guards to stop her. 'Let them watch,' he said. 'Let them see what the punishment for desertion is.'

'Close the door, Sister!' Lucius said, his voice beginning to crack.

'If you touch the door, Sister,' said Horst, 'I will need to take another soldier, until the lesson's learned.' She didn't seem to understand the German, but the guard now stood between her and the door. Lucius turned. Five paces away Horváth was struggling. Deep bruises in the shape of a boot could be seen on his belly, a shoe tread on his neck.

As he struggled against the ropes, violet lines appeared on his shoulders. He began to bleed. The blood turned pink as it froze, but he seemed oblivious to it. 'Cold! So cold!' he shouted. He yelled at Lucius now. There was something particularly horrible in how he had chosen German, as if, despite his illness, he was making some final attempt to be understood. '*Kalt! Kalt!* Oh! Oh, oh! My feet!'

'He doesn't sound so crazy now,' said Horst, and one of his guards laughed.

Lucius looked wildly between Horváth and his patients in the doorway. He knew what they were thinking. *You chose to keep him here. This is your fault. Your arrogance, your greed . . .* He lunged forward. The guards restrained him. Again he tried to break loose. He knew they were stronger, but it didn't matter. He wanted to have Horváth see him struggling, to have all his patients see. To prove to them that he had done what he thought best.

To turn back time.

But as the guards fought Lucius, hooking elbows, dragging him down, Horváth wouldn't drop his eyes. He tried to speak but now his lips were trembling too violently to form the words. He made a strange twisting motion as if he were attempting to free his feet from where they had frozen to the ground. The skin began to tear, but he didn't seem to feel it. Spit froze to his lips, his muscles shook, and his penis had shrunken into his pubic hair. His pale skin had gone yellow, then blotched with white and pink, and then the pink began to retreat to pallor once again. The entire scene seemed leached of any colour, the church walls clad in ice, the courtyard bare, even the tree trunk dusted white with snow, as Horváth vanished into it, leaving only a pale pink froth at his feet.

His voice grew quieter, just a hum. Still, he wouldn't drop his eyes.

You did this.

The eyes: Lucius had the horrible thought that the eyes would freeze in place. Again, he begged Horst to cut the ropes. He didn't know how long Horst wished to punish him, but already they were passing the point at which corporal punishment became an execution. A final anaesthesia would be setting in. The pain was gone, the damage by now was probably irreversible. The sounds that came from József Horváth were nothing Lucius had ever heard, thrown up by some monster of physiology, the winter air on vocal cords, a spasm of a palate, he didn't know.

She told you that I asked to leave.

The gaze. *Mama, Haza. Home.*

At last Horváth closed his eyes, very slowly, as if even his eyelids had grown stiff. Across his body, his shivering muscles slowed and knotted up. He was still alive – steam lolled from his mouth. But his head hung down, and his skin gave an unearthly alabaster sheen. He looked impossibly peaceful. Horst told his men to untie him. The rope had frozen to his skin, and as they pulled it off, it tore long red strips. Horváth fell, his feet still in place, frozen to the ground. One of the soldiers struggled to detach them, and when he couldn't, he kicked them free with a sickening crunch.

Horst motioned to Zmudowski that he could bring Horváth inside. To Lucius, loudly, so that all could hear, he said, '*Doktor*, there are thousands of courageous soldiers risking their lives for you and your family. We will not tolerate our medical staff abetting deserters. The next time we come to the hospital, we will execute all malingerers, all of them. You will be court-martialled and your nurse for ever banned.'

Inside, Virág was still waiting silently by the door, blanket draped over his shoulders. Lucius had almost forgotten him. Now, he followed him out to the wagon before the church doors, as if making one final, ineffective attempt to protect this other man. What would they do to him? Lucius wanted to ask, but now he feared that any word he uttered would only worsen Virág's fate.

The driver removed the heavy blankets and the leather pads used to keep horses' eyes from freezing. Then Horst mounted his horse, and the batmen climbed aboard the wagon, and Lucius was left alone.

9

HE REMAINED OUT IN the cold for a very long time.

In the distance, he watched the convoy descend the road, disappearing behind the houses before it reappeared again, a tiny black shape that vanished at last within the drifts.

A southern wind was beginning to stir, whipping the tops of the pine trees. Still he waited. He waited until his hands ached and the tears were frozen in the corners of his eyes, and the burning cold had risen up his feet and into the bones of his legs, and he began to wonder if, by sheer will, he too could wait beneath the beech until it all went numb.

Inside, the warmth of the church drew blood so swiftly to his head that he had to brace himself against the door.

Margarete was crouching by Horváth's pallet. She must have sensed Lucius approach. She turned.

'I don't think you should come closer, Doctor,' she said.

He took another step, but she rose to block him, her voice firmer. 'Pan Doctor, you should rest. You must protect yourself.'

Then he tried to force past her, but she lifted up her arms to stop him. 'Doctor, I don't think that you should see.'

JÓZSEF HORVÁTH remained in Lemnowice for another week.

Margarete moved him to the chancel and hung a sheet around him. Lucius wanted to go to him, to apologize, to explain that he'd been powerless to stop Horst and his men. But Margarete prevented him. Now she was blunt. It was no longer for Lucius's sake, she said. Horváth thought Lucius had done this to him.

'That you wouldn't let him leave. That you kept him. That you brought Horst.'

'That *I* brought Horst?' Lucius protested. But it was the other accusations he couldn't repeat. *That you kept him. That you wouldn't let him leave.* He looked again at her, her face now drawn and tired. But the reasons! he wished to say. The cold evacuation lorry, the Muck balls, the fact that they had come so close to cure. Oh, but who was he arguing with?

'I thought . . .' He tried again. 'I didn't know that this would happen. I thought that it was best . . .'

'I know, Pan Doctor. I know you thought that it was best.'

He waited, trying to decipher the intent behind her words. He expected that she would remind him of what she had said just days before. *You are keeping him for his sake. Not ours, I hope.* That she would tell him what was now so clear to him, that in his hubris, in some fantasy about shared childhood memories of silly little salamanders, he had committed one of the great sins of medicine, choosing to work a miracle over the mundane duty not to harm.

But he heard no blame, only compassion.

He wrung his hands, began again. 'Please,' he said. 'Please, let me see him. I will do anything to . . .'

Again he stopped. To what? Atone? He knew, and Margarete knew, and Horváth, or what remained of Horváth, knew. Barring a miracle, *another* miracle, it was too late.

Alone, Margarete amputated both of Horváth's feet because of frostbite, and then his left leg when a wound infection spread above his knee. As for his mind, after a day Horváth was back to where he'd been before he arrived in the wheelbarrow. He didn't eat. Margarete had to catheterize his bladder, perform enemas when he retained his stool. Behind the curtain, she spent hours with him, murmuring her soft incantations as she'd done before. Indeed, it seemed as if she rarely left him. One night, sick with remorse, Lucius had returned to the church to find that in exhaustion she had fallen asleep by Horváth's pallet. Watching her – sitting on the floor, knees to one side, habit pooling, shoulders slumped, her head resting in her hand – he had wished that he could take her place. It wasn't only his desire for repentance, he realized. He felt as if he were an intruder on a secret, a rite he didn't understand. He wanted to share what she shared, not only with Horváth, but – and this appeared to him now with such clarity – all their patients. Something that he, with his distance, his learning, his diagnoses and orders, could never know. He had not forgotten that in Horváth's drawings, somewhere, were the portraits of Margarete, while the sketch of the doctor was a looming, shadowed figure. As if Horváth had already known.

Alone, outside, at dawn, Lucius dug up the snow around the tree. But no matter how deep he dug, he saw the stain, pink and glistening, like the ice of a fishmonger's stall.

When the next ambulance detail came to Lemnowice, they wrapped Horváth in blankets and carried him out of the church on a stretcher. The detail was heading north, away from Horváth's home in Hungary, but they couldn't wait much longer. His pulse had become irregular; they worried that another infection secondary to his wound had spread. Perhaps, at a larger hospital, they could help him, Margarete said, and Lucius nodded. Now, he had little hope that Horváth would survive the journey through the snow, but he would not disagree with her again.

INDIFFERENT TO all this came April.

Beams of light burst across the nave as one snowdrift after

another slid from the roof. The light, the smell, the melting hills brought back his memories of the Scarcity, the foraging for potherbs in the hills. But by virtue of a supply oversight no one was eager to correct, they found themselves well stocked with food.

Still, he waited, hopeful that he might resume his excursions with Margarete. If only he could walk with her again, return to the ruins of the watchtower, or sit in the forest's slanting light and hear her songs. Perhaps then, and there, they could begin to rebuild what he'd destroyed.

But the new soldiers had begun to come.

LIKE THE SONGBIRDS, like the snowmelt, like the march of wild flowers, they seemed to follow spring.

The first came in the middle of the month, following a brief skirmish in the valley of the Pruth. A nameless, rail-thin, red-haired man found wandering in a tunic but no trousers, eyes empty, grinding his teeth.

From Uzhok Pass: a cook who left his tent at night to urinate and collided with the bayoneted belly of a village girl hanged for alleged spying. Pásztor was his name: Hungarian, a once-dapper moustache now disappearing beneath an unshaven beard. Incontinent of bowel and bladder, fingers constantly fretting his forehead as if there were still something sticking to his brow.

From Stanislau: an infantryman named Korsak, spine arched, pigeon-toed since being thrown by a land mine, neck twisted despite all efforts to keep it straight.

And on. Ungvár: right leg severed by a derailed train car, now unable to move his left. Gesher, from Turka, who had discovered a group of rotting bodies in a granary, tasting flesh each time he ate. Wechsler, Kolmar, blind and deaf, but not.

He thought of what Berman and Brosz had told him about

the Western Front. *An epidemic, something driven up from Flemish soil, now come east.*

Just weeks before, he thought, and they would have fascinated him, these mysteries. But the spectre of Horváth hung over everything. Now he could only think of what Horst would do if he found more of these soldiers without wounds.

HE TRIED VERONAL.

He tried Veronal, chloral hydrate, morphine. He tried potassium bromide to calm them and oral cocaine hydrochloride to wake them up. He tried atropine until they were delirious, adrenaline chloride when they were slow. He massaged twisted arms with whale oil, only to watch the loosened muscles seize back up. He tried pleading, tried walking them, moving the jaws of those who didn't eat. He read to them, whispered, sang. Tried sunshine and cold. Gave them double rations, threatened to withhold their food. Urged them to remember wives and children, sweethearts, parents. Warned them of what would happen if the recruiters came.

But nothing worked. There was no sense to the disease, he thought, no pattern in the damage to their nerves. Now he began to doubt everything. Had he even helped Horváth at all? Had the man's recovery all been Margarete's doing? Or did most wounds, whether of the mind or body, just heal up on their own?

Margarete, too, had changed. She moved slowly now, always watching the door. At mealtimes, they tried in starts to speak, but she broke off with the slightest sound. Twice, falsely alerted, they hurried to the door, certain that Horst had returned. But each time, as they peered out through the arrow slit, there was nothing but the empty street.

*

AND THEN THERE were others, soldiers who could have fought again but now refused.

Their war was over, they told him with finality. They had once been patriots, but all reasons for their patriotism had long been lost.

Why should I shed blood for Austria? the Czech and Polish and Hungarian and Romanian and Ruthenian soldiers asked him. When Austria sends us into battle in front of her own?

With shoes made of cardboard!

And two men for every gun!

'They will hang you for desertion,' Lucius told them.

Ha! Then let them come!

HE STOOD WITH Margarete outside the sacristy. Late April. The days now warm.

She had brought him there so that they could be alone. 'Zeller, the new boy from the dragoons, said that conscription details have been canvassing the hospitals up and down the line,' she said. 'He was in Delatyn, saw them hanging men for desertion. I think it will only be a matter of time.'

She paused. 'Have you thought of what you'll do when they return?'

For the past month, Lucius had thought of nothing else. Now slowly he spoke the words for the first time. 'With the nervous cases? I don't think I have a choice. It's too warm for *Anbinden*, but not for hanging. At least with redeployment the soldiers will stand a chance.'

Nearby, a knot of sparrows were bickering over seeds liberated from the spring melt. She watched them, eyes drifting to a shivering of something passing in the grass.

'Yes,' she said, at last. 'Yes, I understand.'

He searched her face. 'You don't seem convinced.'

She now spoke slowly. 'I think that this time you've done everything you can, to get them well, or home.' Then she paused. Her eyes were dark with sleeplessness, the slight plumpness of her face now gone. The wimple, which she had always worn so crisply pressed, was rumpled and uneven. Yet all about them, in the courtyard, were birds and bright green leaves and flowers, so much life.

When she spoke again, her voice had changed. It was softer now, almost as if offering a valediction. 'Doctor, you know that your duty is to return men to the front. That is your oath. Patch and send. Know that I understand this.'

He turned to face her. 'And what does that mean?'

'Just that. Because I think, for the first time, our oaths are different. That is all.'

MAY.

Hills redolent of peat and mint and wild anise; the clouds cirrus, mosquitoes swarming around the courtyard doors. A mound of fresh soil behind the church. Were anyone to look, drops of candle wax still lay on the earth; the name in the ledger with the rest.

It was afternoon when the whistle rose above the nave. She: south transept, dirty bandage in her hands. He in the chancel. They both stood. Then the words, *Horst, he's back.*

He felt a cold wind, heard a man screaming, saw the eyes.

She ran.

THE REST HAPPENED so quickly that it was only afterwards that Lucius could piece it all together. The rush of her robes as she leapt over the pallets. The soldiers' turning faces. His own swift steps, his hand on her shoulder, her gaze flashing with warning as she tore herself away. Then out from the narthex, door slamming behind her as she burst into the light, leaving but the narrow arrow slit of day.

The lieutenant was in his saddle, finishing a cigarette, when he heard the wailing, caught the grey flash of her robes. A single batman at his side, also smoking. Wagon further down the road. She was upon him before he could react.

'Save us!' she screamed. She seized his leg, kissed him, his horse. 'Save us! Save us! All dead!' In German, her accent slushed and strange.

'What is it?' said Horst. Horse snorting. Two steps, ears erect, flies lifting from its flanks.

But she didn't answer. She wailed, clung to him, as if trying to pull him from his mount. Head now bare, wimple around her neck, her hair cropped short.

Her hair: even in the terror of the moment, behind the door, watching, Lucius noticed. Her hair, auburn, the whiteness of her neck.

Screaming. '*Come, come!* The Beast! The Pest! Oh, it has taken them, oh, God, oh, God in heaven, She has taken all.'

By then Horst had begun to understand. The empty courtyard, the silence, the wailing nurse with her shorn head.

'The Louse! The Louse!'

'Speak sense! I don't understand.'

'Her! Her!'

'Calm yourself! What do you mean? Typhus?'

An inhuman sound rose from her throat. She clawed her face with fingers muddy from the horse's flank. Now Horst stared down at her with unadorned revulsion. A flash of recognition, of other abandoned outposts, other maddened survivors of a plague.

She surged, grabbed him by his riding boots, clawed at his leg. Head teeming with lice, waving her robes rank with pestilence. For a moment it seemed as if she would drag him down, but Horst lifted his crop and struck.

Again she was upon him. 'Don't leave! Save us! Please! She'll kill us all!'

Again the crop. Again she came, now he was ready with his boot. Twice. The crack loud, seeming to echo off the hills.

And that was it. Spray of red, shimmer of horse flank, and he was gone.

She was on her knees when Lucius reached her.

She held her face in both hands, rocked, tried to rise, then fell again, then tried again to stand. Blood ran down her hands and into the sleeves of her habit. She didn't see Lucius coming and fought him off at first.

'Margarete. It's me.'

'Go, hide!'

For a second, Lucius froze, aware now of his incaution. He turned back. The road was empty. Clothes flapped on a washing line. A pair of chickens had resumed their survey of the mud.

'He's gone.' He looked at her. Blood was running freely. He pressed the wimple to the wound. 'Inside, quickly. The bleed looks arterial.'

By then Zmudowski had arrived. *'My God.'*

'Hurry, go and get supplies,' said Lucius.

'Not in the church,' said Margarete. 'Take me to the sacristy. I don't want the pity of the men.'

Zmudowski looked to Lucius.

'Go,' said Lucius, 'Hurry. *Please.*'

HE LED HER, stumbling, through the gate and into the court-yard, and on into her room.

It was his first time inside, and he was struck by a sense of having suddenly entered into a private world, and one quite different from what he had imagined. It seemed almost too empty, too small, too sad even, to think that she passed so many hours there alone. Too *human*, he thought. As if he had stumbled upon her diary only to discover that she thought the same simple, common thoughts as everybody else. Bunches of dried wild flowers decorated the bare walls, her greatcoat hung from a peg, and a single shelf of rough-hewn pine held a blanket and a pile of folded garments. A stool sat at the priest's desk, where several medical handbooks had been neatly stacked. *Wounds and Dressings. Drill Regulations for Sanitary Officers. Field Surgery in the Zone of the Advance.* Her bed sat beneath the single window, and a piece of paper had been pinned to the wall under the sill. As he approached he saw it was one of Horváth's sketches. Movement stopped; the world emptied of air. But it was just a country scene, a little Carpathian village nestled on a mountain slope. Valley of trees and pasture. On a road, a little girl was walking, a bundle of hay upon her back.

If Margarete sensed the tremor that passed through him, she said nothing. By then Zmudowski had arrived, and together they laid her down beneath the window light, placed a towel beneath her head. Lucius leaned over to examine her, slowly peeling off the wimple from where he had pressed it to her face. Slowly, he palpated her head, her neck, then, gently, her face, conscious of the intimacy of it all, how close she was. His first fear, that Horst had fractured her skull, was now replaced by a worry that she'd suffered damage to her eye. In this case, the manuals were firm. *A globe which has been damaged should be trimmed off and the orbital vessels ligated.* He had done this twice before, could do this, but he didn't know if he could do it to her.

He looked. Her lids were now swollen shut. Lacerations circumscribed her eye, black with dirt and blood. 'Tetanus antitoxin,' he said to Zmudowski, who already had the needle prepared. Then, 'Saline.'

Zmudowski handed him the bottle.

'Dressing.'

He cleaned her gently. Beneath her eye, a small artery was oozing swiftly, blood welling with each pass of the rinse.

'Sutures,' he said. Then to Margarete, 'There is a laceration of a branch of the facial artery.' As if she were operating by his side.

'Yes, Doctor. That would explain the quantity of blood.' Her voice calmer than his.

He removed the dressing, placing the little finger of his left hand on the bleeding vessel, while he irrigated the wound again. Then with his right hand, he looped the suture around the vessel and tied it off. Again, he washed the wound. Dirt and dried blood ran over her cheeks and into her ears and hair. Again he irrigated, this time with antiseptic. Gently then, he began to palpate the area for fractures. He saw her wince.

'Cocaine.'

Zmudowski handed him the syringe.

'What do you see?' she asked.

'The bone seems stable, thank God. I am going to check the globe.'

Slowly he parted her lids. He had never seen her eyes so close. A burst vessel on the cornea had flooded the white with a vivid scarlet fan. Against this, the grey iris seemed rimmed in green, gold-flecked. He saw her pupil accommodating to take him in.

'Can you see?' he asked.

She could.

He irrigated her eye again, applied drops of atropine to prevent adhesion of the iris, and let it close. Again, the wound was bleeding, but more slowly now. He placed another dressing and pressed it gently, then held it there. For the first time since the whistle had risen across the nave, he allowed himself a deep, slow breath. Her good eye followed him. He looked again at Horváth's drawing. Then back at Margarete. She looked so much smaller now that she wasn't storming across the ward. Above, in the close crop of auburn, he could see the paleness of her scalp. 'You planned this,' he said.

'What do you mean?'

'Your hair. Shorn.' He felt self-conscious even noticing.

She smiled a little and then winced.

'May he feel Her crawling in his stockings back to Stanislau,' she said.

'Amen,' Zmudowski said.

Lucius removed the dressing to check the bleed. It had stopped.

'Hypertonic dressing,' he said to Zmudowski.

'No,' said Margarete. 'Close the wound.'

He turned back to her, a dripping square of cotton in his hand. 'The wound is dirty. You know procedure. You rest and let the wound close itself. Unless you have invented a way of curing an infection. We can attempt secondary closure once the granulation tissue forms.'

'With respect, Doctor Lieutenant. I'll be bed-bound for days.'

'And if you're walking about, the wound won't heal. We'll manage. It will be good for you to rest.'

'But I don't want to rest. I want you to stitch it up. It won't get infected. I promise.'

'You *promise*!'

'Then I can do it in a mirror if you'd like.'

Lucius looked off, clenching his jaw as if to let her know his disapproval, then turned back and touched the wound again. He considered it . . . Already it looked pinker, cleaner, now that it was clear of all the dirt and blood. He lifted his hands up in surrender. *Okay, you win.*

He turned to Zmudowski. 'Silkworm.'

Margarete slapped the bed. 'Silkworm! God in heaven, Doctor! Can't you spare something a little finer? This is my *face*. I am not going to need to march on it.'

Lucius pinched his lips to hide a smile. 'Okay. Zmudowski, *horsehair* suture. Please.' He looked at Margarete again, trying to capture some of her levity. 'Horsehair. From a Lipizzaner stallion in the service of His Royal Highness. Only the best.'

Zmudowski handed over the thread. 'How about this one, Doctor Lieutenant? From the backside of His Majesty himself.'

Lucius laughed, thrilled at the irreverence, grateful, so grateful now. Margarete glowered. 'I will remind Sergeant Zmudowski that bad jokes are a privilege of rank. If the doctor wishes to try to be funny, we must endure it. We need not join in.'

'Of course not, Dear Sister,' said Zmudowski. He looked to Lucius and, smiling, touched his temple. *Still crazy, if just a little bit.*

Lucius leaned closer. There were three main lacerations, one coursing through her eyebrow, and a longer, deeper cut from the bridge of her nose to the crest of her cheek. As he placed his first stitch, the flesh tented a little, then the needle appeared beyond. He pulled through, and tied and held as Zmudowski cut. Another and then a third. She was very still now, and he realized how close their faces were. He touched her chin to turn her gently, so as to check the symmetry of his work. He placed a fourth.

This time she grimaced.

'Cocaine,' said Lucius.

'No.' She lifted her hand to stop him. 'You just went a little deep.' She paused, then smiled with the good half of her face. 'Someone should talk to you some day about your technique.'

THE FEVER BEGAN some time in the early-morning hours.

He found her in the sacristy, coherent just enough to tell him what had happened. She had awakened sweating, shortly before dawn, wandered into the church and found a thermometer herself. She hadn't told anyone, didn't want to scare them. But back in her room, she'd fallen when she tried to stand.

She wore soldiers' pyjamas, damp with sweat. Her skin glazed, her forehead hot.

He cursed himself for listening to her when she'd asked him to close the wound. A fever could mean that an infection was spreading through the fascia, or worse, was already in the blood. If so, he would be powerless to stop it. Now he worried about more than just her eye.

'I should take the sutures out,' he said.

But she only grimaced and asked him for another blanket, for she had soaked through hers.

FOR THE NEXT week, he scarcely left her side.

He cut the sutures, saw the wound now weeping pus. Her fever rose, then fell, then rose again. She shook, cried out. Her head lolled; they had to take away her pillow, tie her arms, to keep her from rubbing her face against the bed. She rambled, calling out to soldiers long lost to them – Horváth, Rzedzian. Let me go! she told him. She had to care for them. They were so ill!

'Doctor!' she cried, when he was next to her. 'Water! Water!' Then she spat it out. It was so hot there! She'd seen the child. Hurry, it would drown! So hot! So hot!

He sat and touched her hand, her forehead, praying for the fever to relent. Where did it come from, this fire? He'd cared for hundreds of febrile soldiers, but they had seemed so quiet; never had he known that it could be such misery as this. Indeed, disease itself now appeared to him as something different, unrelenting, deliberately cruel. Was this what they all went through? he wondered. All of my patients? But what a question! It felt like the petulant protest of a child, not someone who'd seen so much death. How could he have such a poor understanding of illness? But for all his time in medicine, he realized suddenly, he had worked, somehow, impossibly, under the magical assumption that when he stepped away, the misery abated. When the patient was led out of the amphitheatre, or the crowd of students moved along, or the soldiers were carried off into the darkness of their corner of the church, the misery abated. It must abate. The world couldn't bear it. There must be some relief.

She shook. Cracks opened on her lips; for a reason unclear to him, she began to scratch herself with such intensity that it seemed as if the itching were a torment greater than the thickly weeping wound. Her breath grew short. When he couldn't bear to watch her but couldn't leave her either, he let his eyes shift from her body to her convulsing shadow on the wall. But there his gaze would settle on the little sketch by Horváth, the idyll now so horrible in the way it conjured up the soldier's memory. For it was not too hard to see that Margarete's illness was also of Lucius's doing. If he had allowed Horváth to leave, there would have been no *Anbinden*; if no *Anbinden*, then Margarete would not have risked her life to drive off Horst.

He set up a makeshift bed on her floor. He couldn't sleep. Her breath grew laboured; her pulse was almost too swift to follow. Again he checked it against the ticking of his watch, keeping his fingers for a long time on her wrist. Now his mind teemed with possibilities. Could the spots on her mouth be signs of meningitis? Could tetanus explain the spasms? He had given her the serum; had it been spoiled? Gas gangrene of the face was almost unheard of – and he wouldn't expect it with such pus . . . but then again he'd seen a crackling jaw wound invade a soldier's neck until he choked to death.

He gripped his hair, as if he could extirpate his thoughts. Oh, it was a curse to be a doctor, to know anything! In this at least his patients were lucky, oblivious to the horrors that could happen. Now the possibilities seemed endless. He hesitated over her, wanted to touch her swollen face, palpate it to assess how far the infection extended. But the pain this would cause! And what then would he do? A leg, yes. A leg one could amputate. A face . . . and now he saw the others rise before him, men whose wounds had rotted into their sinuses, their mouths. All dead.

Oh, but she couldn't die! Not her, not like some common soldier . . . He stood and paced and ran his fingers through his hair, collided into a chair and sent it tumbling. Shaking, he bent over to pick it up. The thought was blasphemy. But he would sacrifice the ward, every last one of them. Let them all fall dead but leave her, please.

'Doctor.'

It was Zmudowski. Lucius hadn't heard him enter.

'Of course, it's time for rounds.'

The orderly looked kindly at him. There was nothing urgent, he told him. Two new patients had arrived, but they were stable; for now, the others could manage things alone. 'Pan Doctor has been up all night. You need to rest.'

But he couldn't rest. He paced the church, then went outside. But now, he moved as if through poison. The air was rank and brown, everything he saw seemed cursed. He wanted to go into the little huts and ask the villagers for their icons, beg them to sit vigil with him. In the road, an old woman passed; surely she had watched disease take someone she loved? He wanted to ask her how she had done it, if she had blamed herself.

She pulled a horse cart through the mud. He let her pass, huge clods rising on the wheel, then dropping to the earth. *The mud* ... His sole mercy was the mud, the mire in the passes. That there weren't others to keep him from Margarete. He hurried back.

It was only when it came time for bathing that he left again. Lucius could touch her forehead, auscultate her lungs, he could bear the weight of her breast against his hand as he listened to her heart. But bathe her as she had bathed the soldiers? When he had once touched the rim of his canteen just to feel where she had pressed her lips? No: once in her ravings, her shirt had lifted to reveal her navel, her iliac crest, a little curl of hair above the symphysis, and Lucius had frozen, unable to look away. No, the thoughts of undressing her, the complex mix of fear and yearning, were too much for him to bear.

But she was burning up. Better Zmudowski, uxorious philatelist, responsible paterfamilias. Lucius stood outside the door and watched the sparrows, listening to the slosh of water, the squish of sponge.

Day three: the fever broke. The wound looked better, less purulent, its colour less exuberant. He felt himself buoyed, only to touch her head two hours later and sink. The mercury reached the highest notches on the glass. This was worse, he thought – it meant the infection was within, unseen, a witch's hex.

At night, he dreamed of elixirs, of magical and blessed pills, which when swallowed might clear the bacillus from her blood. She groaned and woke him. She was so hot! He stripped her bed. She was so cold! She shook.

And if she died? he wondered, her body giving up its heat at last? Imagining himself rising, the world now ruined, the spheres shattering as they strayed off course. He now understood why one might die for someone else. It wasn't mercy; it was torture to remain.

But then she didn't die. On the morning of the seventh day, the fever broke again. She lay with one eye sparkling, like someone tumbled by a wave. Scalp wet, cheeks red, goose pimples on her skin.

'What day is it?'

The truth was, he didn't know.

By evening, she was laughing, hungry, eager to get up. Look, the swelling had gone down, her eye was open, just a little. She could see!

Still he didn't leave her. He owed her this vigilance. But something was different. Something vital had returned.

Before bed, she ate and drank and bathed herself. Then sure enough, that night, he heard her stirring once again. The room was dark, the night moonless. From his bed on the floor, he called her name. She didn't answer. He waited, then rose. Looking down at her, he hesitated, not wishing to wake her, but terrified her fever had returned. At last, he gently touched his fingers to her forehead, but it was cool. For a moment he stood and let himself look down at the shadow of her sleeping form. He climbed back into bed.

Later, the sound of movement woke him again. *Margarete?* He sat up on his pallet. More rustling came from the bed, and then her silhouette appeared above him, and before he knew it she had descended to his side. He hesitated; he didn't understand. Now in the darkness, more rustling. Her hand, his hair, his neck, his face, his mouth, then hers.

'Margarete.'

'Lucius.' Not Pan Doctor. *Lucius.* Her breath hot against his lips.

She pressed her mouth again to his. Her cheek smelt sharply, wonderfully, of carbolic.

For a moment, they stayed like that. Outside, he could hear the trill of crickets. Then she pressed herself to him more urgently. At first, he found himself resisting, thinking of her vows, afraid that by acquiescing, he would draw her into something she'd regret. But she seemed a different person altogether now.

She must have sensed his pause. 'I know what I am doing,' she said. She sat up. Her hand was resting on his chest, as if to keep him from fleeing. Then, quietly, she undid the buttons on her pyjamas and let them drop. The blanket was lifted. He felt her shoulders, cool and smooth, her back, her waist. Again, he said her name. She answered. *Lucius, hush.*

10

It was late the following morning when he awoke to find her gone.

Without thinking, he reached out to touch the place beside him where she had fallen asleep. Empty, and nothing but the tousled blanket to suggest that anything had happened. Above him, her pyjamas were folded neatly by her pillow, her bed ship-shape.

A square of light fell on the far wall; the room was already warm. He looked at his watch: nearly ten. He rubbed his face. It had been his first real sleep since she'd been ill.

Missing her already, he found her in the nave, with Zmudowski. By then she had already learned the stories of the handful of patients who'd arrived during her illness, repacked a pair of wounds, and begun to organize the surgery for the amputation of an arm that had grown gangrenous overnight. She was dressed neatly in her habit, indistinguishable from the nurse he'd known, were it not for a slight new gauntness, the scar healing on her cheek.

He had approached them slowly, uncertain how to address her, what to say. She led, of course; he should have known. The doctor had slept well? she hoped. She hadn't wished to wake him. Was he ready to get started? With due respect, she was a bit surprised by how they'd grown lazy in her absence. So many untucked corners. And Sergeant Lukács had stopped doing his exercises? And why wasn't Roth's leg in traction any more? She'd found a chocolate wrapper among the dirty laundry. It was beginning to look like a boarding house, Pan Doctor, with due respect.

'Of course, Dear Sister.' He watched her with some astonishment, feeling a little thrill at the play-acting. 'I will remind you I was attending to another patient.'

In her eyes he sought some flash of acknowledgement. But by then she'd turned.

They began with the amputation. A Hungarian from Munkács, eighteen by his papers, but Lucius suspected this had been an exaggeration so that he could serve. They had removed his hand shortly before Horst's return. The lad had borne it admirably; only this morning it had begun to turn a dusky green. At the operating table, waiting for Zmudowski to apply the ether, he watched Margarete out of the corner of his eye. Still she revealed nothing, and for a moment he found himself considering, briefly, if the night before had been a trick of his imagination. Or if she had come to him still slightly delirious and now couldn't recall . . .

'Doctor?'

He looked up. Zmudowski speaking. 'Your patient has been etherized. Do you want to start?'

Lucius looked to Margarete, who handed him the scalpel. Now, briefly, he thought he saw a flicker of recognition in her eyes. Something insouciant, an awareness of the secret shared. In reflex, face behind his mask, he touched his tongue to the place on his lip where she had lightly bitten him. Then he took a deep breath and turned his gaze down to the work.

But oh, how hard it was to concentrate! By then he'd carried out nearly a hundred amputations, and yet he felt as if he were starting everything anew. Even when he forced himself to keep his eyes from Margarete, he found himself acutely aware of each of her movements, how close her hands came, how long she let them touch.

By late morning, the operation completed, rounds over, he could think of little else.

When the men gathered for their midday meal, he said that he had to complete some old reports, and left for his quarters before they served him food.

Inside, he paced. He was shaken by how easily he'd been unmoored, how his heart had started racing simply when she gazed at him or when her shoulder brushed his arm, how pathetically he had watched her cross the church. He felt like some stupid animal awaiting even the faintest acknowledgement of its master, all while she had seemed so utterly unfazed. Was she trying to tell him something? That what had happened was an error? That the consequences of her breaking her vows were great, too great, and couldn't happen again?

A knock. Before he could reach the door, she'd stepped inside, closing it behind her.

She pressed her mouth to his.

They stayed like that without moving. He was almost too surprised to hold her. Outside, from the courtyard, he could hear the voices of the men laughing as they ate, the tintinnabulation of their spoons.

She broke away. 'They'll suspect something.' She looked up at him. 'My lips, they do not look as if I have been kissing?'

Her skin was flushed.

'A little. Yes.'

Her eyes flashed. She had been there less than a minute. She bowed a little, as she often did when taking leave, and left.

FOR THE NEXT week, they found each other in moments stolen from the day's responsibilities. In the darkness of the narthex, the shadows behind the church, the edge of the garden, amid the jubilating crickets in the arbour of the pears. Never long: a kiss, a brief caress. And then her whisper, Enough now, Lucius, let me go, they'll find us. Lucius, I must . . .

Let them find us! he wanted to say to her, but he had begun to live for those brief moments, and feared she might deny him even them. The first night apart, he had waited in his room, trying to discern the sound of footsteps in the whispering of the wind. She didn't come, and he had gone out into the summer night to watch the sacristy window for any sign that she was sleepless, waiting, like him. Staring at her door, he willed it to open; it would be so easy to cross the courtyard and knock! But he knew already she had decided on their terms.

And so it was she who always came to him, and she who always pulled away. There was no discussion of what was happening. No recognition of the vows she'd broken, of what had changed, and how, and where all of this could lead. Her hours alone, once a matter of curiosity for him, now took on the agonizing quality of a mystery from which he'd been excluded. But he didn't ask. He was terrified of saying something wrong, and that she wouldn't come again.

In the middle of the week, a trio of new patients arrived after a lorry had turned over in a landslide near the pass, and on the second day of their arrival, one of them had begun to seize. For a moment, the flurry of activity broke his spell. To his horror, he discovered a thin fracture in the man's skull that he had missed on his initial assessment. They had to drill the bone, evacuate the blood, and wait and watch until two mornings later, when the man awoke and asked for tea.

He cursed himself. The truth was that he probably wouldn't have done anything different had he found the fracture earlier. But what mattered was that he'd missed it. He was letting his own interests, his own affections, come before those of his patients. It was a warning, he thought. What happened once could not again.

But this was easier said than done. The truth was that, if Margarete was late in visiting, he found himself in a state quite close to frenzy. If only he had a companion to confide in, he thought! But whom? Zmudowski? Feuermann? His father? But he could never betray Margarete to Zmudowski. And Feuermann, now days away, would have congratulated him and laughed it all off so lightly, while his father's chivalry seemed of another age.

Then, just when he doubted he could bear this purgatory any longer, it rained. With the mud, there was a lull in arrivals. Then, when the sun returned two days later, and the wind from the forest brought forth the smell of moss and rotting wood, Margarete, after their rounds, said offhandedly to Zmudowski that she would like to go mushrooming, and as always, the doctor would come along.

And so, once again, they set out into the woods, as they had done the year before. The rain had softened the earth and swollen the streams that fanned across their trail. In the bright light and the glittering refraction of the dew drops, the mats of moss seemed almost phosphorescent. Wood wrens dashed between the tree trunks. The crinkling sound of falling water filled the air.

Again, she led, again she brought a rifle, again her pace was swift. He found himself a little disappointed to see that indeed she wished to gather mushrooms, breaking fresh sulphur shelves from the oak trunks or barrelling off the path to uncover fairy rings of dew-soaked chanterelles. Stopping her on the trail at times, he kissed her, bolder now, and she let him pull her closer, let his hands seek out her form beneath the habit, before pushing him away. Patience, she told him, now having fun with it. We can't come back empty-handed. What would the others think?

From the church, she followed a path up the valley, breaking off towards the river when the trail turned towards the pass. The harvest was bountiful, and to the mushrooms they added clutches of sorrel and sprays of currants and early barberries. She led, keeping them close to the rustling of the water, at times pushing through the high grass when there was no track. He had never been to this part of the river, and unlike the forest, where decades-old paths had been worn through the banks of moss, the route seemed untravelled. Now, alone with her, he felt embarrassed for the fretting he had endured all week, the constant doubts, the fears that she would call off the affair. That evening, they would have to return to their ritual of deception, but now, alone with her at last, it felt like something he could endure.

They had walked for close to an hour, the bags full, their clothes damp and speckled with grass and yellow mustard petals, when at last they passed beneath a willow and she stopped. Outside the shadows of its branches, a bright light swept across a bank of high green grass. Beyond a pair of high boulders, he could hear the babble of the river. He realized that she must have known this spot, known that they could go there undiscovered, and as she set down her gun and bag, and brought out a pair of army blankets, he felt a thrill to think that she had planned it. He hoped then that she would kiss him, but instead she sat on the blanket and began to untie her boots. She said nothing at first, and he watched dumbly as she undid the laces of first one boot and then the other, and then began to roll her stockings down. It had been so dark in her quarters when they'd made love, that the only time he'd seen her skin was during her fits of fever. She had her second stocking halfway down her calf when she stopped.

'What is it? You don't expect me to swim alone?'

Somewhere a frog was croaking. His fingers fumbled with his shirt, a task made unexpectedly difficult by a sudden nervous trembling and his reluctance to tear his eyes from her. She seemed almost unfamiliar to him now, her short hair grown longer since the night she first came to him, her skin pink and pale, one arm pressed modestly across her chest. Unlike his awkward movements, she seemed utterly adroit, somehow preserving a sense of propriety despite her nakedness. It was as if alongside the pious little nurse, the gun-draped forager of mushrooms, he now found himself in the presence of a third person, younger, playful, who laughed as she shimmied from her drawers and disappeared beyond the willow's leaves.

Nearly stumbling out of his trousers, he followed, out into the sun, the dew-wet mustard brushing against his thighs. He followed the path that she had broken in the high grass to where a short bank descended to the boulders. There he saw her disappear between the rocks and heard a splash. He followed. He had to turn slightly sideways to pass through the portal, and coming out onto the short beach, he found her already neck deep in a dark pool of water. He stopped, taken by the vision of the familiar face above the water, the shimmering white form beneath.

The cold water licked his feet. She was staring at him, smiling. He was attempting to be modest, not anticipating that she would catch him so exposed.

'You're scared!' She laughed.

'Not scared. It's cold.'

'It's June!'

'Early June. Very early June,' he said.

'You're stalling.' She took a backstroke away from him, a breast breaking the surface of the water. 'If you don't come in, perhaps we should be heading back.'

Wait! he wanted to shout. The cold was hardly the greatest shock. She began to swim away from him, only a half-dozen strokes, but enough to prove herself a strong swimmer. This too a detail, a secret offered about the life she wouldn't reveal.

He dived. His skin burnt with the cold, but he stayed under, savouring the overpowering sensation, taking swift frog-strokes until he couldn't hold his breath any longer. He came to the surface, spluttering. Around him, sunlight flickered through the branches of an alder, and wisps of cotton spun in an eddy of the pool. She swam to him. He felt her hand touch his forearm. His toes dug into the pebbles of the riverbed; she trod water.

'It's too deep for my feet to touch the bottom,' she said, as he felt her limbs close around his back.

The cold water had made her flesh taut and goose-pimpled, and his hands were so cold they seemed not to be his own.

'Come,' she said, after she had kissed him. 'Your lips are blue already – the bank is warm.'

THEY LAY ON one of the blankets out in the high grass in the lee of the willow tree, sheltered by the swaying ranks of mustard.

Now out of the water, they both found themselves beset by sudden modesty. He didn't know what to say. It occurred to him that he had never seen a woman completely naked who wasn't on an autopsy slab, but decided this unsaid thought was best kept to himself. A breeze came; he shivered, debated asking for a shirt. The ground was stonier than they had expected, and the army blanket itched. Pollen from the pines swept through, and he fell into a fit of sneezing. A scuttling startled them: but it was only a sparrow! Then an invisible sand fly raised pink, vampirish welts upon their necks.

At first this mattered, then it didn't matter very much.

After, they found they had rolled far from the blanket. Laughing, they crawled back. She wrapped the second blanket around her torso and drew out the bread she'd brought along. It crumbled as she broke it open and spread crushed currants with her knife. She took a bite and then a second, before passing it to him. Her hands, despite their swim, still smelt of mushrooms and soil. Neither spoke.

The only questions that he could think of now were questions that seemed too great to ask her. How long she had felt like this. If she'd imagined this would happen. What was next.

He thought of the roads leading away from the hospital, which led to thoughts of distant hospitals, which led to thoughts of Horváth. Against the summer forest, he saw the snow, the evacuation lorry disappearing on the winter road. I do not deserve this kind of happiness, he thought.

Then he shivered. She had touched his back. The winter vanished, the hills burst forth in green. They kissed, then parted. Her lips tasting of currant, her chin dusted with the flour from the bread.

On his shoulder, his skin was bruised where earlier she had bitten him. Was it a specialty of the nurses of Saint Catherine, he almost asked, feeling giddy again. But he had no interest in reminding her of broken vows. Instead, he lay beside her and ran his fingers tentatively up her dirt-flecked calf. He stopped at her knee, now shy again. A cricket trundled across the blanket, below the double arch of her knees. He waited, watching. He broke a blade of grass and ran it along her ankle. She slapped it away. He felt bold, flirtatious. Again, he tickled her.

'The Louse,' he whispered.

'*Lucius!*'

'Oh, no! The Louse!'

She dug her fingers into the earth and threw a clod at him.

A moment later she was picking through his hair. 'I'm sorry! Your poor face! Oh, your eyes!'

She licked a finger and wiped dirt from an eyelid, brushed his lashes gently, kissed him. 'There. You're clean.'

But really, he shouldn't joke like that.

He lay back, looked up where he could see her neck and shoulder silhouetted against the sky.

It seemed impossible, not simply the circumstances, but the change she'd undergone. A month before, he had never seen her ears, would have apologized for having bumped against her in the narrow aisles of the ward. Yet his first impressions of strangeness – the shock of her kiss, the vision of her folded habit beneath the willow, the foreign feeling of her cold, wet limbs – slowly, these had retreated, leaving the sense of something familiar. In the boldness bordering on incaution, in the appetite, even in the ease of her movements, the same physical confidence he had seen on their walks and at the operating table, the same sense that the world was something to be seized and held.

He touched his cheek briefly against her hip and secretly inhaled the scent of the wet blankets and her skin. Again, and deeply, as if it were something he was about to lose.

She shifted, to let his head rest on her thigh. He felt the sunlight on his eyelids and let his gaze run down her legs. Bits of grass stuck to the thin down on her calves. Her toes pale, brushed with sand. Above him, her belly rumbled, a little. He closed his eyes.

It was she who broke the silence, with the words that he'd been dreading. 'They'll be waiting.'

He didn't answer. Looking up, he saw there was a slight rose to her shoulders, as if she had already begun to burn.

'Lucius.'

'Of course.'

THEY BATHED SEPARATELY before dressing and gathering up their belongings, and started back down the trail. A silence fell. Twice, they stopped; both times he kissed her, but now it seemed a little more that she was letting him, that she was impatient to return.

Scattered clouds drifted down the valley, gained and overtook them. His wristwatch showed close to two; they had scarcely been gone four hours, yet it felt as if they were returning from a different world. He recalled the summers in Vienna, the boulevards, the lovers walking hand in hand. But she was always slightly out of reach, and as they walked, he felt a distance open again between them. He fought this feeling, forced his thoughts back to her floating in the water, calling him. But he knew that she was thinking of something she wouldn't share.

At last the trail left the river, and they passed again through the deeper woods. Crushed leaves marked the paths where she had traipsed off for mushrooms. He now regretted that he had let the moment lying in the sun pass in so much silence. Only minutes remained before they reached the road, the possibility of other people. Before he'd lose his chance to speak . . .

In the operas, the novels, he had always been somewhat amused, incredulous even, by the manner in which seemingly sane men and women put so much weight into the words he wished to utter. Three in German, two in Polish, one in Hungarian (though everything in Hungarian seemed to be one word). It had always seemed a bit excessive, he had thought, a bit maudlin and sentimental, a failure of imagination by the poets to put that same phrase upon the lips of dying knights, returning soldiers, weeping maidens, as if worshippers of a faith with but one prayer . . .

Except that now he understood. Three words, or two, or one if he was too self-conscious (for at times self-conscious lovers resort to other tongues). A spell. And like a spell, they'd be transformed . . .

He had wanted to say it the night her fever broke.

And when Horst had come again.

And when he'd watched her care for József Horváth after the *Anbinden*.

And the afternoon when they had gone up to the ruins of the castle, and he had dared to ask her where she'd go after the war.

They gained the road. The first houses of the village appeared just beyond the trees. Steam rising from the thatched roofs and the dark wood of the church. A clattering of squirrels above them. She, too, seemed to slow.

'Margarete.' *I love you.* It would be so easy, just like that.

She stopped. She hadn't even fully turned, when he found himself speaking, so haltingly, so formally, so unsure . . .

'Margarete . . . I . . . I would like to ask you if you would consider marrying me. Not now, of course. Nothing has to change now, I promise. But if you wish, after the war . . .' He twisted his hands. 'Margarete . . . I . . . I . . . you understand that I . . .'

But there he stopped because he saw that she was crying. Impulsively he touched her cheek, and she took his hand and kissed it, first his fingers, then his palm.

'Oh, Lucius,' she said. And then she was running, down the path and around the bend in the road that led to the village and the church.

11

RETURNING TO THE hospital, trousers wet with dew, his cuffs mud-spattered, he went directly to his quarters to change his clothing, holding on to a faint hope that she might be waiting there, that he could see her again before they joined the others. But no, of course she wasn't waiting. She had mushrooms to deliver, a habit to change. And he knew that with the soldiers in the courtyard, she was unlikely to risk a visit to his room.

Alone, he took a moment to collect his thoughts. He was uncertain about what had just transpired. By the way that she had taken his hand and kissed it and said his name, by her tears – which seemed, at least in that moment, to be tears of joy – he had assumed at first that her answer had been in the affirmative. But no sooner had she turned than doubts descended. There had been a sadness in her gaze, and of all the ways she might have responded, he could not expect that she, who rushed headlong into everything, would flee. He didn't know whether it had been a mistake that he hadn't told her he was in love with her. Whether he had already gone too far or not far enough.

In his room, alone, he touched the bruise on his shoulder, on which he could see the faintest marks of her teeth. Now this, too, seemed ambivalent; there are bites of longing and bites of warning. But he couldn't doubt the sun-speckled moment when she had clung to him in the water, or the way she'd said his name.

In new clothes, he headed into the courtyard. The men had begun to gather for supper, and from the kitchen, the smell of cooked potatoes met him as he headed towards the church.

Inside he found Zmudowski.

'You're back.' The orderly was carrying a bundle of linens on his way across the courtyard to the laundry. 'We were beginning to get worried.'

'And Margarete?' asked Lucius, as offhandedly as possible.

Zmudowski stroked his beard. 'I thought she was with you?'

'Yes.' But there he halted, his stomach tightening. Could something have happened in the short stretch between the forest and the village? It seemed unlikely; for all the dangers of the woods, the road at least was safe. 'She *was* with me. Though she walks so briskly, she reached the village first . . .'

This seemed to satisfy the orderly. 'Well, she's probably in the sacristy, or bathing. For a moment I was worried she was on her own.'

By evening rounds, though, Margarete still hadn't appeared. Now Lucius went and knocked on the door of the sacristy, and when there was no answer, let himself inside. She wasn't there, nor was there any sign that she had returned – no sack of food, no habit speckled with mud.

Again, he found Zmudowski.

'Still nothing?'

Lucius shook his head. They were standing in the courtyard, the evening sun slanting across the grass. He wished to tell the orderly about what had happened. That perhaps she wished to be alone, to consider his proposal. That perhaps she simply couldn't face him yet.

'I think that we should try to find her,' Zmudowski said.

Nodding, Lucius let his gaze drift across the hillsides, the high pass, the road that led to the place where he'd last seen her. Then up again, to the hints of trails that led back into the mountains, to other villages, perhaps even to her home. This last thought came suddenly. No, he told himself. She wouldn't have left. She wouldn't have done that, not to him, not to her patients. She wouldn't leave them all alone.

THE SUN WAS just beginning to touch the mountains as they set out, the great underbelly of clouds alight in rose and plum. The kind of sky that presaged something, he thought. Calm or storm. Margarete would know; he wished he had paid more attention to such signs.

Above this, in a clear patch of sky, hung Mars. A flock of crows circled, cawing, as if angry at the presence of something he couldn't see.

There were four of them. Zmudowski would follow the road down the valley to Bystrystya, while Schwarz, a geologist in home life who'd arrived two months before with his hip fractured and his pockets full of Mesozoic ammonites, offered to head upriver. Krajniak, leaving that night's baking to an underling, would search around in the village.

'And Pan Doctor?' asked Zmudowski.

Lucius thought of the ruins up near the watchtower.

Sometimes I used to come here to seek guidance.

'I'll take the trail to the pass,' he said. 'There was a place she liked to go.'

If the others noticed the suggestion of intimacy, they said nothing. They would sound the church bells if she returned, to alert those who were still out looking. In the hospital, Lucius quickly threw together a rucksack, water, bread, a blanket in case she was cold. Papers, as always, in his pockets. A lantern and matches. A pistol from the collection of belongings of the dead.

With Schwarz, he walked in silence to where the valley steepened and forked. There they parted. But once alone, the road rising, he hesitated. His instinct had been that she had gone to the ruins. Now, with night falling, in the silence and solitude, he began to have his doubts.

Just then, a figure appeared on the road ahead of him. For a moment his pulse quickened in anticipation. But there wasn't one figure, there were two, and soon he found himself before a pair of village women in cotton kerchiefs, and then, on a long rope, a cow. He stopped them. *D . . . dobruy vechur.* Ruthenian, mangled, but it worked: *Good evening.* Then, in Polish: had they seen a woman on the road, alone?

They didn't understand. Over the shoulder of one hung an old hunting rifle. The other, her chin propped up by a massive goitre, carried a stick with a sharpened animal jaw fastened to the end. Armed, as always. And now Margarete alone.

He asked again, this time pantomiming a habit, pressing his hands in prayer.

They laughed and shared a glance. *Yes, yes* – this in Polish. *Tak. Tak.*

'Where?'

Again they exchanged glances, turned back to him, and shrugged. Now he pointed up the road. They nodded, smiling, following his gaze.

Yes – again in Polish. One of the women pressed her hands together, laughing toothlessly.

Yes. So perhaps he was right after all.

Dobruy vechur!

He quickened his pace. The trail rose, flattened and rose again. The sun was gone, but thankfully the clouds were high and distant, the peaks alight in alpenglow. A warm wind rustled the trees. He took swift, long strides, trying to think of what to say if he found Margarete. Would she be angry with him? Or just grateful he had come for her? Certainly, she would understand why he was worried: the night, the risks of travelling alone. He hadn't wanted to disrupt her solitude, he'd tell her; he only wished to know that she was safe. On the trail, he hadn't meant to speak so rashly, to ask her questions she couldn't answer. He could be anything for her. A husband, or someone to seek shelter with in the high grass by the water, away from disease and war. Or, if she wished, they could start anew, doctor and nurse.

It took him close to an hour to reach the top. By then it was dark, the moon a sliver. In the distance, he heard the faint, familiar drumming of artillery. But it was far, so far that when the wind picked up, he heard nothing but the trees.

As he reached the ruins, he saw that they were empty. He called her name. An animal scurried on the low wall and vanished into the shadows of the watchtower. Again he called, picking his way through the stones and stunted pines, now with the lantern. But nothing.

At the fallen staircase, he stopped, uncertain where to go. His face felt warm, his hands shook a little; he told himself he must keep calm. He thought back on the villagers, the old woman pressing her hands together in a pantomime of prayer. But had she truly understood what he was asking her? Or was she just mimicking the motions of this stranger with whom she couldn't speak?

Again he felt his worry massing. Had Margarete returned already? But then he would have heard the church bell. Or had she come to the ruins, as he'd expected, but taken another trail from there?

From the watchtower, the path ran either down into the neighbouring valley, or up along the ridge. But neither made any sense for her. The ridge led on to even higher terrain of stone and tarns. It was forbidding country. Soldiers were lost up there, he knew; it was where Horváth was found.

Horváth. The memory surfaced, and he had to fight it off: body, wheelbarrow, the peasant in his sheepskin cloak and hat.

Above him, clouds were moving in from the plains, and light rain began to fall at intervals. He checked the ruins one last time and turned to head back down, when a flicker of grey across the neighbouring valley caught his attention. He stopped and turned down the lantern. He saw nothing; it must have been a trick of his eyes. But then again it was moving, down below, a skirted figure slowly making its way up towards the opposite ridge, a blanket held above her head.

He shouted her name, but now the wind was too strong for her to hear him. So he began to pick his way across the ruins, joining first a narrow descending path, and then a broader trail, which rose up the valley before crossing to the facing slope. He hurried; she was only minutes away, but he would lose her if she passed beyond the ridge.

He called again. The figure halted and then began to climb more quickly through the grass. Again he called. She seemed to hear him, for she turned and looked, then hurried on. Now he found himself confused. He could understand why she might have wanted solitude. But to flee at this hour of night was madness. Perhaps it *was* delirium, he thought, perhaps the fever had returned.

He was running then. The lantern was useless, heavy, swinging, the light reflecting off the mist and making it impossible to see. He left it on the trail, to collect on his return. He stumbled onwards; by the time he reached the opposite slope, she had vanished from sight. But her passage was marked by a clear track in the crushed, wet grass, and he left the trail and followed her path as it rose and twisted, and at last, at the summit, plunged into a dense stand of trees. There, a heavy mist was pushing up from over the other side of the hill, and for a moment he found himself unsure of where to go, when a flash of her habit again caught his eye. He followed through the trees, and out into a clearing, where he stopped. Nothing. He advanced, more slowly now. Again he called. The fog hung low, impenetrable. The air redolent of pine. He could see scarcely see twenty paces ahead.

A voice, *Stij!*

He turned. She was standing off to the side, in the waist-high grass, rifle raised to her shoulder. A girl of perhaps twelve, dew-drenched, panting, kerchief pushed back far on her head. Around her shoulder was slung a heavy bag. From the high-lands, probably, coming home from scavenging for food.

Stij! she said again. *Stop.*

Then more words.

He slowly raised his hands. '*Ne rushume,*' he tried, in Ruthen-ian. *I don't understand.* His doctor's vocabulary, now so useless. *Where does this hurt? Stay still. Breathe.*

She didn't answer. She will kill me, he thought, a strange man pursuing her through the valley at night. Then again, she began to shout. The words were angry, scolding. He had the sense that other grievances were being voiced. He lifted his hands higher. The rifle twitched; he flinched. Again: she was motioning him to move. But he hesitated, afraid of showing her his back.

Again the muzzle twitched, and she made a show of taking better aim. So he backed away, slowly, until the mist closed over.

For a long time he stood in one place, until he felt that she was gone. Rain had begun to fall, and a stronger wind shook the grass. He was soaked now, and he took the blanket from his bag and put it over his shoulders. It was time to head back. He was at the edge of the clearing, about to head into the trees, when the wind shifted, and very briefly, but very clearly, he heard the sound of bells from far away.

*

HE ENTERED THE forest again and began to circle, looking for the path he'd followed after the girl. Again he heard the bells. His spirits lifted. Signalling to me, he thought: she's back. Now the visions that he had fought to keep away – a new fever, a fall, an attack by wild animals or soldiers – all vanished. There was a much simpler story, he thought, hurrying onwards. She went to think over his proposal; now she had returned. She would laugh when he told her about the chase, the windswept slope. He wondered about her answer, what she would tell him, what she had decided. He allowed himself the thought of her beside him, of lying down together in the mist.

The forest, which he had remembered as a narrow stand, seemed much deeper now, and he walked for some time before it opened onto another clearing. He wished again for the lantern. He could not find a path, so he looped back through the grass to a pile of stones that he didn't remember seeing before. He turned and headed back downhill, again looking for the path to the ridge. But the mist was thick and the way was uncertain. He cursed. They would be worried back at the church.

Maybe she deserves to worry a little, running away like that.

Around him pine trees shivered in the wind. He pushed forward, clawed at by the low branches. Now he was certain he hadn't been this way before. He entered another clearing. But this was different from the first.

He stopped. He was lost. His watch read midnight. He wished now that on their walks he had paid closer attention to the land around them and not depended so much on her. But he had enough of a sense of the geography of the mountains to know that all the valleys ran down to the Galician plain. Better to be safe, to head downhill to the flatlands. There it would be easy to walk or get a ride back to the main road that led up to Lemnowice.

So he set out again, this time following the valley down to where a shallow river rushed, a murmuring that seemed to echo against the belly of the mist. Forging it, he found himself on a long, slow descent. This relieved him – soon he would reach flatter country. After some time, the sky began to lighten. The summer night had passed. Despite his worry, the world around him seemed almost out of a fairy tale; the air, heavy with water, glowed like amber.

He crossed a meadow, through neck-high grass. From time to time, he heard something moving, but it went silent when he stopped. A second trail joined his, and the path widened as he left the meadow and entered a new forest, and then an open road – at last – beneath a high outcrop of rock.

He took a deep breath of relief, and, exhausted, stopped and drank some water from his rucksack. The road flanked a curving hillside, above a dense swathe of forest. By the orientation of the sun, the trail ran north, sloping gently down. Tracks rutted the mud. A convoy must have passed recently; perhaps he wouldn't have to wait until he reached the flats to hitch a ride.

He had scarcely gone ten paces when he heard crashing in the undergrowth behind him. He turned. It was still early and the light was dim and so he didn't understand at first what he was seeing, some kind of tank, festooned with camouflage, crackling, snorting through the brush . . .

A bear.

But the creature didn't stop. It barely seemed to register Lucius as it surged forward, its brown fur heaving, casting off a spray of droplets as it cleared a small ledge and disappeared into the bushes. No sooner had it passed than there came more rustling. Two deer burst from the undergrowth behind the bear, tattered foliage flapping on their antlers. Then ahead on the road, more deer, coats red, breath steaming. A slow humming grew louder. A dark grey rabbit shot onto the trail. A flittering of little birds.

He stood there, puzzled, uncertain of what was happening, when a memory came to him, an old memory, of a childhood story, likely told to him by his father, though he couldn't remember when.

An old knight and a young knight were travelling through a dark wood when a wolf broke across their path, followed swiftly by a hare. The young knight laughed. Ha! What is the world coming to? he asked. Are the hunters now pursued by prey?

The old knight just quietly drew his sword.

But how! said the young knight. Don't you also think it's odd? A wolf like that, running from a little hare! What will come next? A mouse! A toad!

The old knight dropped his visor. It isn't running from the hare, he said.

From the far distance came a rumbling.

The knights turned.

LUCIUS TURNED.

Before him, the outcrop disintegrated. The trees lurched towards him and stones sprang into the air. A bright light made itself known.

12

HE AWOKE TO the sounds of hoofbeats and shouting.

He was lying in the underbrush beneath the road where he'd been walking. The smell of earth and gunpowder filled his nostrils. Above him loomed the outcrop, the sky, a great hole ripped in the canopy. He blinked at the light, wiggled his fingers, hands, then slowly lifted his head. Then, with a jolting realization that whatever had just struck the mountain might strike again, he scrambled to his feet.

He looked back up the road. A column of horses had appeared, the riders with plumed helmets, sabres rattling at their waists. *Hussars*, he thought, Hungarian. For a moment he felt relief: *my own*. They were perhaps a hundred feet away, close enough for him to register the golden brocade on their jackets when a second shell whistled through the treetops and struck the road.

He ducked. A rain of mud came down upon him. He heard whinnying, more crashes. When he rose, he found a great crater had replaced the road where moments before he'd seen the first horses. Behind, the column had piled up as the riders tried to lead their bucking mounts down and out of the crater to the other side. He ran towards them, hoping to wave one down. Then, deep within the woods, from down the slope, he heard the rumbling again, now louder. Someone else was coming. He stopped and looked back down into the trees, and then he saw.

Flashes of sabres, high fur caps and dark grey tunics. Shouts now. He knew instantly who they were, the monsters of every

Polish child's nightmares, of the stories he had heard since he was very young . . .

Near him, a horse was struggling up the shell crater, its lifeless rider dragging behind, foot still in its stirrup. Rushing forward, Lucius seized its reins and hurried upwards to the road, clambering on just as they reached the crest. Around him, the fleeing hussars had begun to fire their pistols into the trees. He thought to grab the dead man's weapon, but it was too late, his horse lunged forward, stumbling as the dead rider got caught between its legs. Lucius grabbed its mane to keep from falling. Then the rider's foot broke free from the stirrup and his horse joined with the others just as the wave of Cossacks coalesced out of the darkness of the forest and, in one great roaring instant, struck.

The hussars plunged forward. Lucius clung tighter to his horse. He had no idea where he was going. On their flank, the Cossacks were gaining, the two armies merging now in roiling rivers of blue and grey. The air was filled with the sound of clashing swords and gunfire. Faster now, another Russian artillery charge striking high upon the hillside, showering them with gravel. Then another pulse, another shell, this from the opposite direction, straight into the Cossack charge. Another rain of rock. They swung right, then left again, around a boulder. Behind him he heard a shout, and turned to see two Cossacks gaining. They were close enough for him to see a pair of dark, determined eyes, when machine-gun fire burst from the road ahead and the lead rider whipped sideways, his horse crashing into the other as they spun off, tumbling into the brush.

A crossroads. Austrian artillery. A glimpse of howitzers, a machine gun lighting up the forest. The retreat broke left, zigzagging through trench works and into a clearing. For a moment, he felt a sense of relief, of safety. But the hussars had begun to mass, their horses neighing and fighting their reins. More shouts, and they were off again, to meet the Cossack charge.

His horse followed on instinct. He grabbed at the reins, tried to pull her up, but she pounded headlong after the others. Around him he could hear the scrape of sabres emerging from scabbards, stirrups clanking, the snapping of whips. The horses wild-eyed, their mouths foaming at their bits. Like something from his father's war.

My God, he thought, how the major would be proud: *my son killed in battle with the hussars, fighting the horde.*

He leapt and hit the ground, tucking his head inside his hands. Horses thundered past him, kicking up clods of dirt. He stumbled up, still trying to ward off the flying hooves. Gunfire churned up the ground around him. He ran, swerving through the horses as behind him the armies struck each other with a sound like nothing he had ever heard before. But he didn't turn, he could only think of fleeing. He crossed the clearing and ran up a slope to where an officer was shouting field commands, reaching him just as a bullet struck the officer's neck and knocked him to the earth.

'Down!' someone, somewhere, shouted. Stunned, staring, Lucius hit the ground. A few paces away, the officer clawed at his throat, gasping as blood spurted between his fingers. Out of instinct, Lucius crawled to him and pressed down on his carotid. Blood welled up and over his hands. Around him: bursts of pine needles. Something hot on his shoulder, like a bee sting. He tried to bury himself into the ground, hands stretched above him, still on the man's neck, when the man twitched, a strip of his scalp lifted like a banner and his eyes sprang open in surprise. Another pulse shook the earth. Dirt rose into Lucius's mouth and he rolled away, coughing, as he scrambled to his feet.

He began to run again. Away, faster, head down, until he reached a grove and threw himself behind a tree.

His chest heaved. Still the image of the man's surprised expression hung before him. He drew his hand over his eyes as if to wipe the vision away and found it red with blood.

Ahead of him a soldier was beckoning. Lucius didn't know if it was to him, but he followed, up and over a giant mound of earth. He reached the top just as it erupted with gunfire beneath his feet, and tumbled down the other side. Around him gunners manned machine guns behind an earthwork, firing through gaps of light. Still he didn't stop. It seemed impossible that just a few hundred metres now separated him from the officer with his bleeding neck.

Now, as he continued his retreat, a vast field camp unfolded before him. Soldiers carrying ammunition ran up to the machine-gun nest, while others carrying buckets and entrenching tools fanned out through the forest. A cavalry platoon rode past, flags flapping on their lances. He stared. Where had all this come from? The front was supposed to be far off, still on the plains. Advancing soldiers were staring at him with horror; he realized how gruesome he must have looked covered in blood. A medic approached, but he waved the man away. Around him: munitions trucks, stacks of shells being unloaded. Ad-hoc stables. First-aid tent. A field kitchen. Safety at last.

It was only then that he stopped to catch his breath, chest heaving, hands on his knees.

So that was war, he thought. For two years, in Lemnowice, he had thought he had come to know it, but it was only through its wounds, its scars, its vestiges. Never truly war itself.

Then suddenly he straightened up. Lemnowice. He had to get back to Margarete, before the fighting got there first.

At a communications centre set up inside a farmhouse,

dozens of wires hung down from the ceiling to a rank of radios. In the back, a man in tall boots paced. He wore a cape and a fur shako decorated with a high plume and a silver death's-head. A captain. For a second he took Lucius in, his expression less one of shock than irritation that someone so bespattered had the nerve to enter his tent.

Lucius saluted. 'Medical Lieutenant Krzelewski, sir. Of the Austrian Fourteenth, based at a field hospital in Lemnowice.'

The captain took in his medical uniform, the blood and mud. 'Where?' The skull staring down unnervingly from his forehead.

'Lemnowice, Captain.'

'Never heard of it.'

'Field hospital, Captain. South of Nadworna.'

'God in heaven, Lieutenant.' The man whistled. 'How did you get *here*?'

For a moment, Lucius thought of his march through the mountains, then of Margarete and the river, then Horváth, his winter surgeries, the church, the hussar leading him through the snow. Then Nagybocskó. Debrecen. Budapest. Vienna. *How far back do you wish to go?*

'I am sorry, sir. Where is here?'

'Here! A stinking Ruthenian dunghill not fit for a shitting leper, which somehow Vienna sees fit to defend.'

This wasn't the answer Lucius was looking for. But the captain didn't give him time to ask him more. Instead he turned to a batman, who had appeared protectively at his side. 'Show the doctor back to Field Headquarters. I suspect men like him could be of use.'

THEY SET OFF down the road. The mist was retreating across the plains, revealing a landscape of farms and shallow valleys,

patches of green and yellow and dun. Little black quadrangles
lay like blankets in the distance, revealing themselves on closer
inspection to be advacing Russian companies. It seemed impossible that they could be there, in sight, and he here, walking.
Like the little regiments in his father's paintings, bristling postage stamps that rode across the plains while peasants tilled their
fields. But here, the peasantry didn't seem so indifferent. The
roads were filled with people, some in packs, some travelling
alone, all retreating from the rising sun. They carried bundles
of belongings, children, chickens. A woman nursed a baby as she
walked, blue flies dancing about its mouth.

To the east Lucius could see trails of smoke rising through
the sky. Early harvest lay stacked by the roadsides, smelling
sweetly of cut grass. A soldier was sitting, struggling with puttees that had come undone.

He looked back over his shoulder. There, the mountains lay
beneath their dark green forest. They seemed so quiet. Somewhere, he thought, there, was Lemnowice, Margarete. Less than
half a day had passed since he'd heard the church bells in the
night.

They stepped out of the way for an infantry regiment
coming up the road, their coats faded to different shades of blue.
Further along he could see a scab of town, a train depot. Around
them rose strange towers whose purpose he didn't understand,
thin, tapering pyramids with boxy heads, like ancient effigies of
armless men.

'Oil derricks,' said the aide, following his gaze. 'The town is
Sloboda Rungurska, on the line to Kolomea.'

They had been encamped there for two weeks, the man told
him. He was in the 24th Austrian Infantry Division, under von
Korda. Or what was left of it. The army was in tatters, the men
exhausted. Since the Russian offensive at the beginning of the

month, they had been forced to retreat across the Pruth. It was worse in the north. Lutsk had fallen the week before. And to the south, Czernowitz was under siege, with reports coming in that it had fallen, too. Now they were concentrating defences in the foothills, afraid that they would lose the oilfields, or worse, that the Russians would take back the mountain passes they had last held during the first months of the war.

He stopped. He knew well that if he let the aide take him to Field Headquarters, they could reassign him on the spot.

'Corporal, I must return to my hospital. How?'

'Your hospital, Doctor Lieutenant? But the captain said—'

'I heard the captain's instructions. But I need to get back to my hospital. They have no doctor. How can I get there?'

'The captain—'

Now Lucius looked at him directly. In the batman's eyes, he could almost see the reflection of the captain with his skull and crossbones.

'Corporal – if you take me to Field Headquarters, I will tell them that you tried to bribe me for a medical exemption.'

The man's face turned red. 'But – but I've said nothing!'

'You said you were exhausted. That you would do anything to go home.'

The aide bit his lip. For a moment, he considered this.

'Your captain won't even know,' said Lucius, trying to sound confident. 'I think that I'm the least of his concerns.'

'You said it was near Nadworna?' the corporal said at last. 'Then I would go to Kolomea and then take the train to Nadworna from there.'

'Oh, but that will take too long. How are the roads?'

'What do you mean? To walk directly there? You would have to be mad. You've seen our line. By tomorrow, those roads will be swarming with Russian cavalry.'

Lucius looked uneasily across the valley to the encamped armies, then down at the little town below. Now another long line of soldiers was heading up the road. He closed his eyes and tried to conjure up the map. North-east to Kolomea, west to Nadworna, south along the valley to Lemnowice, this on foot. So: to travel one leg of a rectangle, he would have to travel three.

In the distance, artillery crackled.

'Thank you, Corporal,' he said, but already the man's attention had shifted back to the distant battlefields, the pulsing mortars and the rising plumes of smoke.

HE FOUND THE train depot in chaos. Everywhere, people were running. Soldiers unloaded boxes of shells from the trains and onto motor cars and horse carts. The platform was piled high with bags of foodstuff, boxes of ammunition, barrels of gunpowder left perilously near the track. Soldiers streamed off a train. There were flies everywhere, circling the food, the piles of horse dung. He pushed his way to the stationmaster, presenting himself as formally as he could. He saw the man take in his bloodied face and sleeve.

'It's not my blood,' said Lucius, as if this somehow made things clearer. Then he rushed through his story, how he needed to return to Kolomea, now.

The man, swatting at the flies, accidently caught one. Surprised, he looked about for somewhere to wipe the blue smear on his palm. At last he settled on his boot. He looked up.

'You were saying?'

Lucius again repeated his story. His post, his hospital. Kolomea. The next train.

The man nodded towards an engine idling in the station. 'That's it.'

'Where can I get a ticket?'

'A ticket? Are you kidding?' He jabbed his elbow at the air. 'Like this.' He laughed. 'First class.'

Crowds of evacuees, mostly peasants, were already jostling to get on board. Lucius grabbed the edge of the doorway, then a ladder, climbing onto the roof as the train began to move. There were people covering every inch of the carriages. The train groaned under the weight, and for a moment, with bodies everywhere, it seemed ready to topple. But then they were moving, slowly, out of the depot and through the little town. On the roof beside him, the refugees clung to one another to keep from falling off. A pair of little boys gazed wide-eyed at his bloody face. He had a sense that this moment was being registered, that in their memories of the war, this vision would stand out.

They clutched their bags protectively. He realized he must have lost his rucksack somewhere, though he couldn't remember if he had set it down or if it had been blown off his shoulder by the shell-strike. In a panic, he patted down his pockets, relieved to find his wallet and his identification papers. An old warning from Margarete now stirred up in his mind: *and keep your papers on you – the Austrians have a bad habit of thinking everyone without them is a spy*.

They passed more farms, more open country. The sun was hot; around him people took shelter beneath articles of clothing. He raised a hand to shield his eyes. From his position, he could see far across the plain, to a broad river, beyond which the Russian armies marched. If he stared hard enough, he could even see specks of horsemen galloping across the plain. There were enough infantrymen alone to fill at least three or four divisions. And yet so distant, he could fit them in his palm.

He looked back to see the mountains, now retreating behind the rising smoke. It was almost impossible to believe that at the same time yesterday morning, he had just set out with Margarete on their walk to the river. And now? When would she learn of what had happened? News was slow to make it up the valley, but if the winds were right, they might have heard the shelling . . . How he wished he had a way to let her know he was alive, returning! Again, in his mind, he conjured up the map. If he was lucky, if the trains were running out of Kolomea, perhaps he could get to Nadworna by that evening; from there it was thirty kilometres up the valley. And with the troop movement, perhaps he could hitch a ride. But he would walk if needed, even through the night.

They reached Kolomea shortly after noon. By then his face was burnt, his legs asleep.

There in the station, he asked for the next train to Nadworna.

The agent was a perspiring little man with a flat, broken nose and two missing bottom teeth. There were no trains to Nadworna, he said. All rolling stock had been diverted to supply the army at Sloboda Rungurska. If he needed to get to Nadworna, he would have to first go up to Stanislau, then take a second train south.

'Stanislau?' Lucius felt his heart sink. Stanislau was another seventy kilometres to the north. He felt like someone fighting a retreating tide, carried further and further away each time he tried to take a step. 'There is nothing direct?' he said. 'I'm a doctor – my hospital is there.'

'You could be the Kaiser,' said the man, 'and I still couldn't get you a train.'

HE BILLETED IN a flea-infested boarding house next to the station, its stairways bustling with arrivals and departures. Alone in his room, he stood before a cracked and darkened mirror that overhung the wash basin. At first, he almost didn't recognize himself; his face was bruised and dirty, and flecks of dried blood crusted his ear and hair. There was a hole in the shoulder of his shirt where the bullet grazed him. *Yes, shot by Cossacks, Father,* he thought, mustering whatever humour he could manage. Just above it, he could see the mark of Margarete's teeth where she had bitten him. He touched it. My two scars, he thought.

He closed his eyes. Even his skin contained the memory of her. He could imagine her touch as she listened to his story. *Shot by Cossacks.* She, like his father, would be proud.

A fissured bar of soap sat on the wash table, and he washed his face and hair and scrubbed the shirt until the blood had faded to something vague and nondescript.

THE NEXT DAY's train to Stanislau was in the afternoon, but it was cancelled so they could move more soldiers south. He was told to return the following day. Again, he spent the night in the boarding house, sleepless now, consumed by worries. When he arrived at the station a second time, he was so desperate that he had decided that he would *walk* straight to Nadworna along the railroad, and from *there* to Lemnowice. He could just follow the rails, he told himself; Austria would do anything to keep the rails, though by that same token, the Russians would do anything to take them. But he couldn't wait any longer. In a dry-goods shop he purchased another rucksack, and from a nearly empty bakery, the last pair of crumbling biscuits, at quite an extraordinary price.

To his surprise, however, the next day at the station, the train to Stanislau was scheduled to depart as planned.

He made the trip standing in a car that had been stripped of all its seats. And in Stanislau, he learned the line south to Nadworna was still open, the next train scheduled to depart the following morning. Now he began to grow hopeful again. In a day, he told himself, he would be with Margarete – a day was all he had to wait. He stayed that night in another boarding house near the train station, sleepless, thoughts of her coalescing into a physical longing so acute that he at last abandoned himself to it, closing his eyes and letting the memory of the morning wash over him, her goose-pimpled skin, the coolness of her wet breasts against his chest. In the early hours, his room too small for his pacing, he rose early and walked back and forth across the station until the stationmaster arrived. But he wasn't the only one waiting, and when at last he'd managed to push his way to the front of the crowd, the man asked to see his orders, of which nothing had been said the day before.

Lucius told him this.

'If you don't have orders, I can't let you on.' The man picked his nose with a greasy finger. 'Space is reserved for deploying soldiers.'

'I *am* deploying,' Lucius said.

'Then show me your orders.'

'But I don't have specific orders. I told them yesterday, they said nothing. I'm a doctor. I have to get back to my hospital.'

'And I told you that you need orders. You're a doctor? Medical Office. Kazimierzowska Street, across town. The train is delayed anyway – if you hurry, you'll catch it when it leaves this afternoon.' And he turned back to the crowd.

Outside the station, Lucius looked futilely for a fiacre. Of course: all horses were on the front. So he walked through the old town, breaking at times into a trot, asking for directions along the way. Stanislau was the first city of any size that he had been in since deployment, and alongside his growing crescendo of panic, he found himself disoriented by its mass, the solidity of the apartments, the great paved square.

He, child of the Imperial City: what had the mountains done?

Kazimierzowska was a long street that led out of town. He had walked nearly twenty minutes before he began to doubt his directions. He stopped a Jewish grocer in a kaftan who was pushing his cart. The man nodded with recognition when Lucius asked for the district medical office. But it wasn't on Kazimierzowska Street, it was on Gołuchowskiego Street. He sent his son to lead him, a little boy with long *payess* who discharged his duty with great solemnity, saluting Lucius when they reached the door.

The building was at the edge of a barracks stretching for several blocks. He was sent to three different offices until he finally found himself before the right man, a surgeon major named Karłowicz with a long forehead and eyeglasses scarcely larger than his eyes. He listened thoughtfully as Lucius told him how he had been separated from his hospital, how he needed to get back. To Lucius's relief, the man agreed this was 'important'. If he could just have a minute . . . Then he rose and left Lucius alone.

On the wall was a map, with the locations of field hospitals and a schematic for evacuation that must have been planned by someone extraordinarily optimistic about the constraints of geography: the road from Lemnowice to the Hungarian interior ran straight over the massif, as if there weren't any mountains there at all. He thought how the soldiers, with their dark humour, would have laughed at this. But the map also clearly showed the advancing Russian salient, and none of it seemed so funny now.

Outside, it had begun to rain.

The door creaked behind him. Karłowicz. Again, they sat.

'Lebowice has been evacuated,' he said.

'Lemnowice,' said Lucius.

'Yes, of course, the same. We received the updates yesterday. With the fall of Kolomea, they have evacuated all hospitals in the sector. They've been completely overrun.'

Lucius felt his thoughts spin out, unable to absorb the news. He looked back at the map as if in supplication. *The fall of Kolomea?* It couldn't be – he'd been there two days before.

'Evacuated,' he repeated, his voice breaking, but trying to sound calm. Visions now: the evacuees, the distant fires, the shouts and flashing sabres of the Cossack advance. 'You're certain? But you would know if the hospital had been captured before they got the personnel out, right?'

'I can't speak to every little field station,' said Karłowicz. 'The district was evacuated. That's all they tell me.'

'But do you know *where* they were taken?'

'The patients?' Karłowicz looked through his papers. He shook his head. Perhaps south, he said, truly trying to sound helpful. Back over the passes. Or north, to Stryj or Lemberg. Or west, to Munkács. 'Not east, I'd think.' It wasn't clear whether he meant this in jest.

'And what about the personnel? The nurses.'

The man looked up, a quizzical expression on his face. 'Do I know where the *nurses* are?' He laughed. 'The High Command can't find the Fourth Army.'

'*Please,*' said Lucius, not acknowledging the joke, just desperate now.

Karłowicz threw up his hands. 'Look, if anyone knows about individual medical personnel, it would be the office of the regional commander of your Army Group. In your case, Kolomea.'

'But I thought Kolomea fell,' said Lucius.

Karłowicz paused, seeing the error. 'We've been through this. I've told you what I know . . .' But now Lucius must have looked so miserable that Karłowicz stopped. 'Listen,' he said. 'Do you know at least which regiment she was assigned to?'

Lucius paused. Until then he had spoken in generalities. *Personnel. The nurses.* But Karłowicz must have understood.

He saw no use to hide now. 'She is a volunteer, with a religious order.'

'A religious order? Oh!' Karłowicz smiled briefly at the smell of scandal. He removed his glasses and rubbed his palm over his face before replacing them. 'Then no one knows, my friend. Check with the Pope.'

He pushed a document forward.

Lucius didn't touch it. 'What's that?' he said.

'Your redeployment.'

Lucius shook his head. 'I'm sorry . . . I can't. Not yet. I must get back there.' His voice had risen. 'I must find them. I said I would return.'

Now Karłowicz replaced his glasses. 'She must be quite pretty, Lieutenant. But I said the hospital is gone. *Kaputt.* You've been redeployed. Your transport to Przemyśl leaves this evening. There you will be assigned to an evacuation train. Be grateful – we could have sent you to the front.'

13

He became, then, two men.

In Przemyśl, given his months of service, he was promoted to *Oberarzt*, Chief Physician, of a ten-car ambulance train. He was given a new uniform and sabre, a rise in salary, and the same copy of the drill book he had been given in Graz two years before. Under his command were two assistant physicians, three orderlies and ten lay nurses.

According to the papers with which he had been ceremoniously provided, the train was a state-of-the-art evacuation hospital converted to care for soldiers with advanced injuries. He had seen enough of the war to be sceptical, but even scepticism didn't prepare him for the moment, on the day of his departure, when the district medical officer led him across the rail yards. There were no windows; half the doors were missing. Were it not for the giant red crosses painted on the siding, he would have thought she was destined for scrap. In the hollowed-out carriages, the 'wards' consisted of rows of double-bunked litters hanging on springs from the ceiling. The supplies, in dented metal cabinets, were as scant as in Lemnowice; rat's droppings littered the floors of the latrine. His bunk, behind the engine, consisted of a horsehair mattress that had begun to spill its stuffing. There was a ceramic basin, no mirror, and an abandoned shaving razor that the district medical officer pocketed with embarrassment. The wardrobe opened only with a kick.

In the beginning, they were based out of Kraków, leaving weekly for distant cities, where they picked up patients who had been collected from casualty clearing stations along the Galician front. Slowly, screeching, the train moved through southern Poland, past abandoned fields and sprawling army camps. The light sockets were all empty, and when night came, the train was lit by paraffin lamps, until a jolt sent one crashing into a stack of bed sheets. From then on they rode in darkness, the ceiling flickering with the light of distant fires. There was no oil for the wheels, which screeched so loudly they could hardly hear each other talk. His assistants were a Moravian village dentist and an over-eager medical student from Vienna who had just finished his fifth semester and had so little understanding of practical medicine that Lucius couldn't let him out of his sight.

Like me once, he thought, and were he not so terrified of what the young man would do, he might have stopped to marvel at how far he himself had come.

At times, hurrying through the swaying wagons, Lucius caught a glimpse of the mountains to the south. But while moving, there was gratefully little time to lose himself to memories. There was no order; he attended to whoever screamed the loudest or grabbed him as he passed. Many patients had been only minimally stabilized in the field. Bones had not been set, tourniquets left on for days. Back at Lemnowice, Margarete had taught him to be conservative with his amputations – now he removed many fractured joints just to spare the soldiers the agony of the constant jostling. Sometimes it didn't even seem like medicine. Butchery, again. Carver of flesh, sawyer of bone.

After the amputations, he ordered the nurses to take the limbs to a separate carriage, where – he told the soldiers – they would be incinerated in accordance with a solemn protocol. But there was no protocol, no separate carriage for limbs. There wasn't even a carriage for the dead. If they were near a station, they handed the bodies over, but if not, they buried them by the track.

THIS WAS THE first man. The second had realized something only moments after he had been given his assignment: trains meant travel, and travel meant new stations, new churches, new garrisons, new hospitals, where he could look for Margarete.

He had begun at their very first stop, in a garrison hospital outside Przemyśl. Walking through the crowded wards, he had found his way to the head nurse to tell her the story of the evacuation and ask whether she had met anyone of Margarete's description. A tall woman, with freckled cheeks and wisps of red hair emerging beneath a starched cornette, she looked at him inquisitively, unaccustomed to such a query. Yes, people came and went, she said. But she knew no one with that story, though he was welcome to ask the other nurses. He did. None of them had met her either, nor had the nurses at the No. 113 Garrison Hospital in Tarnów, nor the Sisters of Mercy at the Army Hospital for Officers in Rzeszów, nor the Red Cross Hospital in Jarosław . . .

Still, he wouldn't be deterred. In late July, as the Russian offensive under General Brusilov surged through the mountains, he was in Brünn, far behind the lines, searching the vast wards of hospital pavilions set up in the cornfields. By then he had come to look not only for Margarete, but also for Zmudowski, Krajniak, even Schwarz with his pockets full of ammonites, or any other of the thirty, forty patients he could remember from his last days at the church. It was madness, he knew; there were hundreds of thousands – millions, some said – of Imperial and Royal troops deployed across the Eastern Front, and he was looking for a common name like Schwarz. But still it didn't deter him; with Lemnowice behind the lines, he had no choice. He felt at times as if he belonged among the crowds of kerchiefed women who haunted the stations with portraits of their sons and names painted on placards, endlessly imploring anyone who met their eyes if they had seen their Franz, their David. Like the three old peasants in the Nagybocskó station. Oh, how quickly he'd dismissed their vigil then! But now he understood; he lived for each new stop.

The gravel crunched beneath his feet as he made his way up driveways to baroque châteaux where ballrooms had been converted into rehabilitation wards. He visited converted schoolhouses and sawmills in frontier towns with geese wandering across the yards. Autumn rain thrumming on the tin rooftops, he paced through typhus wards in Kovel, peered over the high, coffin-like walls of cholera beds, and stopped the nurses as they recorded fever curves in the malaria pavilions. While once he hadn't cared for rank, now he wielded it to press lazy clerks to search their books. In September, as the Russian Ninth took Stanislau, he was back in Kraków, on cargo ships converted into floating hospitals on the Vistula. He found Zmudowski's old address through the post office, only to learn from neighbours that his wife and daughter had gone to live with family far away.

In November, he was at a commandeered cathedral hospital in Zamość, when news came that the Emperor had died. It was a grey winter morning, and Lucius stood in the crowd of patients as they listened to the announcement. It was almost inconceivable; Franz Josef had ruled for seven decades, and not a single person present had been born outside his reign. There was a sense, almost palpable, that this was the end, not only of his reign but also of the monarchy, and, perhaps, the war. But then lunch came, and the nursing sisters swept the patients back into formation. Far off, in Vienna, another man would be ascending to the throne.

Lucius registered almost none of this. By the time the Imperial and Royal body reached its catafalque inside the Capuchin Crypt, delivered by decorated horses in silent rubber shoes, he was searching again.

Still no one knew Margarete. In the registers of nursing sisters, he found Renaldas and Anastasias, Elizabeths and Lieselottes, Paolas, Zenias, Hildegardes, Iannas, Anets and Evas, Kunigundes, Katas, Livias, Magdalenas, Rekas and Matilds. In Tarnów, he found a Margarete, but she turned out to be a lay sister in her early seventies, who reddened when the 'gentleman' was presented by the chief nurse. Another Margarete, in Kraków, impossibly plump in that time of hunger, tapped her large fingers together excitedly and asked if he had a wife. There once had been a Margarete in Jarosław, but she had died of septicaemia long before the fall of Kolomea, while Sister Margarete at the Lemberg garrison hospital had just returned to a dying mother in Berlin.

THEN, ONE DAY, in Rzeszów, in December, at a converted leprosarium, a Sister of Mercy smiled at him in recognition. She had bright blue eyes and a happy little upturned nose. Didn't he remember her? He'd asked her the same questions at the hospital in Stryj, where she had been working back in August on the infection wards.

He apologized, blushing. But she had since thought of him, she said; she wished that she could help. Perhaps if he knew *which* Catherine this Sister Margarete was devoted to? There were, after all, several, all worthy of devotion. Perhaps the Italian Catherines of Bologna or Siena? Or St Catherine of Sweden? Or the most magnificent St Catherine of Alexandria, the Great Martyr of the Wheel?

He didn't know. But wait . . . 'The one who ate the scabs of the afflicted,' he said. The words returning to him from that night he first arrived in Lemnowice.

The Rzeszów sister brightened. 'That would be St Catherine of Siena,' she said piously. 'May we all be so devoted.' But she knew of no such convent in Poland. She wasn't from Friuli or Tyrol? Are you sure, Herr Doktor, she was telling you the truth?

'Perhaps Friuli or Tyrol,' he said.

She looked at him for a moment, with an expression that might have been curiosity or might have been compassion. 'Ask at the diocese in Kraków,' she told him. 'Perhaps *they* can help.'

Ten days later, a cherubic factotum of the archbishop ran his finger down the column of a volume bound in calf.

'Here,' he said. 'A convent of St Catherine. In Trieste.'

It was impossible. Lucius had been there as a child, recalled the sun-washed seafront on the Adriatic, the puckered smell of drying fish. A world completely distinct from Margarete.

But he wrote. A simple note at first, in German. *To whom it may concern, I am looking for one of your Sisters. If you know where she is, would you please forward the enclosed?* The second letter was sealed. He wrote first of how he had been separated, of the attack on Sloboda Rungurska, how he had tried so hard to return. He wrote that he thought often of her, crossed this out, wrote, *all the time of you. The truth is, Margarete, I cannot stop.*

He posted the letter that night from Kraków, leaving the regimental office as his address.

But by then he had begun to question.

It was more than just the doubt on the face of the little nurse in Rzeszów. Wandering in the wards, watching the other sisters, their silence, their brisk, efficient deference, he began to consider one final possibility: that she had never taken vows at all.

Of all the possibilities, it stunned him now to think he had never really considered this. On the surface, of course, there was the evidence of their lovemaking. But this in itself hardly proved she wasn't a nun. Vows were broken; indeed, he had inherited a culture keenly aware of all the erotic potentialities of the convent, whether the garden couplings in Boccaccio, or the baser perversities of de Sade. If anything, there was something in the very denial of the flesh that acknowledged the power of flesh's pleasures. He had not needed to read Freud to know this; they took breaths from the same air.

No, it was something else that held him. And something other than the fact that she carried a rifle, or cursed, or drank before her surgeries. Or that she kept *Drill Regulations* on her desk and *Field Surgery in the Zone of the Advance*, but not the Bible. No, it was something subtler, unspoken, something dramatic about her manner when she spoke of God and his angels. Almost as if she were playing at devotion. As she had played at typhus before Horst.

He was in Jarosław when this thought came to him. He was sitting in the office of a mother superior of the Sisters of Mercy, a handsome woman in her early forties with the kind eyes of someone accustomed to being present at the bedside of people who were very scared. He didn't know what it was about the woman's sober, steady manner that made him think, *This wasn't her*, but once thought, he couldn't get it out of his head.

But why? Why would a young woman pretend she was someone who she wasn't, only so that she could spend the next two years surrounded by the horrors of dying soldiers, often sleepless, only hours from the front?

Like me, he thought. He was walking down the steps of the Jarosław hospital. Briefly, he stopped. *Pretending to be someone I was not*.

Outside the hospital, unexpected sunlight coruscating on the snow-wet rooftops, he followed a road that led down to the San

River. Huge ice floes jostled noisily against the bridge columns. Moments from their conversations now drifted back to him. *My vows. My holy service.* The *earthly life I left behind.* But what then was she hiding? He wished that he might have doubted this before, in Lemnowice. To know whom he had truly fallen in love with. He felt as if he'd missed so much, not just to get to know her then, but to know how he might find her now.

Back in Kraków, a letter was waiting, postmarked from Trieste. It was from a nun, a Sister Ilaria. She had never known a Margarete, she wrote to him in German. There were no Polish sisters in her order; nor was it their custom to assume a different name. She would have wished him luck had she not had a Polish shopkeeper translate the contents of his second letter for her. *I cannot dare imagine what has transpired between you and the unfortunate Margarete, Signore. But it is my duty to remind you that all corporeal delights are strictly forbidden by the vows of any Order. Please, Signore. What is at stake is no less than her salvation. Hot are the fires of hell. I urge you to accept the loss and leave our Sister alone.*

THAT NIGHT, FOR the first time since he had joined the trains, he allowed himself to get drunk at the officers' club, just beyond the garrison gates. The room was crowded. On the piano in the corner, a lieutenant of the lancers played military marches, which his comrades urged into a rapid tempo with a banging of their cups. He sat alone in a booth, beneath an old painting of a young Franz Josef that had yet to be replaced by one of Karl I. Twice he unfolded Sister Ilaria's letter, twice he read it, growing angrier each time. It was not just me, he wanted to write back to her. *She* came to me first. *She* kissed me. *She* led me to the river to make love. And now she was not only missing, but had absconded with a part of him he hadn't even known existed before they met.

He ordered another slivovitz. The spirits ran over the top of the brimming glass, burning a scrape that ran across his knuckles. The heat, the smell, the tingling on his fingers now reminded him of the *horilka* which they drank to warm their bellies before surgery. He leaned back and ran his hands through his hair, moist with sweat from the warmth of the room; he couldn't even get drunk without being driven back to her. In his left hand he crumpled the letter on its flimsy ration paper, flagged down the waiter with his right. Another slivovitz, burning his lips as it spilled into his beard.

At last he rose, unsteadily. Now his desire for Margarete was so pressing it was almost clinical. He was infested. The room was small, too small for him, the laughter and the regimental marches seemed to pitch forward in a frantic pace. As he turned, his sabre clattered across the table, sweeping a pair of glasses to the floor. With the songs and laughter no one noticed. The waiter scurried over, apologizing, as if his placement of the glasses had led to such a mess.

Hot are the fires of hell. He had to get outside. Unbuttoning the collar on his tunic, he stumbled, apologizing, pushing through the other officers, none of whom gave any heed. At the entrance, he steadied himself against the wall as the doorman fumbled interminably through the rank of greatcoats. Then he was outside, the air was cold; he paused, breathing deeply, as his breath made spirals through the yellow columns of light. More singing, coming now from a raucous crowd on a wooden pavement outside another establishment up the street. Women's laughter rose from shuttered windows. Now he knew why he had got drunk that night, what he was searching for. Ahead, the crowd churned as the door opened, and a pair of privates stumbled out to the hurrahs and congratulations of the others. They pulled up short, saluting as they saw Lucius approach, a crimson light over the door casting their flushed, warm faces in a devilish glow. But he was an officer, and the red light specified an establishment for enlisted men. He dismissed them with a nod, and they melted back into the crowd. The world deserved its war, he thought. In Lemnowice, he couldn't get the anti-tetanus serum he needed, but there were rules on how to divvy up the whores.

He stumbled on, looking now for the green lantern that would signify an establishment for officers. The cold began to seep through his open collar, and he fumbled with the buttons as he walked on. The streets were dark, clotted with soldiers. Somewhere were the dynastic crypts of the Royal Capital City, but the Kraków that unfolded before him now had the air of a frontier town. The smell of burning coal was everywhere, and a dark bird, a shadow, banked above the scattered nimbuses of light.

At last, before a flickering emerald lamp, he stopped and watched a pair of officers enter a doorway, behind which the sound of dancing music could be heard. A doorman beckoned to him; he hurried off. His heart was pounding in his ears. What had seemed necessary minutes before now seemed impossible. He could not stand the thought of sitting in a parlour getting drunk with fellow officers and singing regimental songs until each of them paired off.

A light snow was falling when he reached the Central Market Square.

Ahead he could see them gathered beneath each of the street lamps. Snow had been falling all evening, and a smooth field of white covered the square. Now approaching, he hesitated, then put his head down, keeping his gaze away as they called out. He saw no one else. Just the women, like sentries, retreating in the distance beneath the spotlights of the lamps.

'It's cold.'

She was tall, almost as tall as him. She wore a black cloak down to the tops of her boots. A strong perfume preceded her as she stepped out of the shadows of the Cloth Hall. She wore a woollen cap, pulled low and decorated with a woollen rose; her cheeks were lightly rouged.

'Yes, cold.' He had stopped. He looked down at his feet, then back along the street, as if there were something of great interest there. 'You have . . . a place to go?'

She named the street.

He nodded, his throat dry, suddenly sober, utterly.

They walked side by side. After a block, she took his arm. For a moment, embarrassed by the intimacy, he resisted. But it seemed less part of seduction than a formality; it would be stranger for them to walk apart. He wondered if he should speak. He felt as if he were already failing, an absurd thought given the nature of the transaction. But the thought was there; it was his duty to entertain. Like a child again. Stone prompts in my pocket. *The portrait of Sobieski means I'm to speak of holidays; the bust of Chopin that I'm to inquire about my guests.*

But his lips were numb, his tongue tied, and she asked for nothing. Indeed, her whole manner projected a professional's indifference, the kind of assuring competence one might feel before a doctor or a priest. He felt, briefly, a kind of relief. They passed another woman, who exchanged familiar glances with his partner but didn't speak. Her gaze, as she took in Lucius, had a strange, almost orchestrated quality, and for a moment, he felt as if there were others watching – his parents, or Margarete. He was relieved when they reached the door. There a price was mentioned, 'for the normal'. If he wanted something else, it would be more.

They entered, a pocket of winter air accompanying him like a second traveller.

Inside, a doorman in threadbare livery greeted them and took her coat. Another portrait of the Emperor hung on the wall behind, and a flowery scene of nymphs pinching each other's nipples was just above his desk. Feuermann would have had a laugh, thought Lucius, as the man briefly disappeared behind what looked to be a hidden panel. Ah, you cultured Poles! A bit of Neoclassicism with your pornography? But the thought was subsumed in a new worry that he had found himself in exactly the kind of establishment he had wanted to avoid. An unmarked doorway! Hidden panels! The doorman in his uniform gave off the sense of a time capsule, the faded decadence of a different age. As if he were about to find himself among a group of masked aristocrats fondling one another in a prelude to an orgy. Or worse, that he would have to dance.

Oh, he was nervous! He shifted, looking furtively at the woman, who was studying the contents of her purse. She wore a plain white blouse, a long, pleated skirt. If not for the rouge, she would have looked like a schoolteacher or governess. Very briefly, he had the wild thought that she was not actually a prostitute. That they had met to read or paint.

The man returned with a key. She thanked him, then stepped through a doorway to a narrow, unlit caracole of stairs.

On the second floor they stopped, turned left, the boards creaking beneath their feet. The hallway was long and branching, rose up a set of stairs, turned and dropped a flight, then zigzagged before rising and falling again. He realized that the hotel must have been built outwards, piercing the neighbouring buildings, twisting like a corkscrew. He told himself to pay attention, in case, like Hansel of the folktale, he might need to find his way out. From around them came sounds of footsteps, voices, but they must have come from another hallway that turned helically about their own and never met.

At last they reached their destination. For a moment the key seemed stuck, and he wondered if they would have to go all the way back. But then the mechanism engaged, and the door opened to reveal a room with peeling wallpaper and a mattress on the floor. The woman sniffed; the room smelt sharply of paraffin. He suspected that whoever had last used it had overturned the lamp. When she lit the bedside candle, he half-expected, half-hoped everything would explode.

She closed the door. From the other side of the walls came a grunted mewling, but she didn't pay it any heed. Without another word she removed her blouse, then, after a moment's assessment of his initiative, took off her skirt, and then her button boots, until she stood there only in garters and brassiere. He was still in his winter coat.

'Do you need help?' she said, after a while.

He shook his head.

'Take your time,' she said.

But the sight of her body brought his thoughts suddenly to the consequences of the act. Memories: his father inspecting the Croatian girl's certificate of virginity with his monocle; a madwoman in the General Hospital, staggering from syphilis in her spine. The warnings of von Holzheim, eminent Professor of Dermatology, finger waving maniacally in the air, that nothing, *nothing*, not antiseptic douches, not leaky prophylactics made of rabbit intestine, nothing – *Nothing, my students, nothing!* – save blessed *coitus abstentia* would forestall this plague.

It eats the brain, devours it, my boys – and you, lady-student – until the patient knows nothing but pain and madness. The most excruciating of pains . . .

Speaking of our patients, of course.

Lucius recalled the woman clinging to him as she had crossed the market square. Had there been a slight shuffle to her gait?

But it already had been decided. Where could he flee to? More dreams of Margarete that left him trembling with longing? More fruitless searching? More humiliating scoldings from far-off nuns who dared to think they understood? No, if Longing were to be extinguished, it must be done so completely. 'Walk for me,' he said, and confused, thinking he was asking her to put on a little show, she sauntered towards him. 'No, walk normally,' he said, but now saw no evidence of tabetic gait, no sign of blue streaks of mercury injections in her buttocks. He placed his palm on her breast and felt no murmur of aortic insufficiency. He lowered his hand to feel for a chancre on her sex. Misunderstanding, she began to murmur, feigning pleasure, then licked her hand and lowered it to his.

In the room next door, the moans were getting louder. There was a candle-lamp; his last thought was that he should bring it between her legs to complete the examination. But the demon inside him was impatient. *Now*, it said. Eradicate her, or she will be with you for ever. He withdrew his hand. The woman lay back on the mattress, exposed. Her breasts fell loosely back from her brassiere, and her abdomen bore the broad scar of a Caesarean. For a moment, the humanness of this – though less the fact that she had once been someone's mother than that she'd been someone's patient – almost scared him off. But he was a persistent person, not used to giving up.

Afterwards, he lay with her. He had fallen to her side. She had long black hair, and he breathed in deeply, drawing its perfume over the clipped, carbolic memory of Margarete. He recalled the hundred depot stations, the thousand soldiers gathering one last kiss by which to remember their wives. He felt that this was somehow what he was pursuing, but in inversion – not to remember, but to forget.

'Come from the mountains?' she asked. For a moment, he

feared that she would tell him she had a husband or a son there, that he would have to consider the possibility that they were one of his. But she said nothing else.

He had.

'I knew,' she said.

He waited a long time for her to tell him why she asked.

'Hour's up, soldier,' she said.

Soldier. But she was talking to him, of course. He could stay longer, she added, but it would cost.

It was close to one when he descended to the night.

Wind swirled the snow around the street lamps as he walked away. It looked like Lemnowice, he thought, in winter, when the snow spun in eddies outside the light of Margarete's room, when hurrying from the church, he would stop and breathe the air and pines, and look back at the shadow of that House of God in all its greatness, when sometimes, sometimes, if he listened closely, he could hear her sing. He remembered this, and for the first time in years, he began to cry.

HE SUBMITTED his petition for leave the following morning.

He was granted two months. So distant did Vienna seem that he could scarcely believe that it was only one long day's ride away.

It had been two and a half years since he left. As he stepped from the train, he was herded by a line of military police towards a pavilion at the end of the station. He protested, impatient.

'You come from the east,' the policeman said. 'Everyone from the field must be deloused.'

Deloused, the word now mystical in all its connections. *As we began.*

In a cold room, separated from the rest of the station by a dirty hanging canvas, he stripped with the other soldiers. They left their clothes in a steam chamber and then walked on, naked. He looked down at himself, his hands nicked and calloused, his long toes pale as a cadaver's, his chest narrow and wiry, its coarse hair seeming, in its whiteness, like that of an old man.

In a new line that had formed in front of him was a small man in a wheelchair, an amputee with Horváth's distant gaze, and for a moment, Lucius felt his heart lurch. But it wasn't him, of course it wasn't him; he was gone, and Lemnowice was gone, and Margarete, and it was time to scavenge what was left. Around him, the soldiers were missing hands and feet and they all were gaunt and filthy, but now, trembling in the cold as they filed forward, they forced themselves to laugh about the meals they'd eat and the girls they'd visit, and what the warmth of beds would be like after so many months on straw. Ahead of him, the amputee had risen from his wheelchair, and Lucius followed as he took great whipping leaps to where they sat on a bare bench beside a disinfectant tanker, where a sanitation officer turned on the spray. There, Lucius kept his eyes open for as long as he could, watching the pink bodies disappear into the fine mist. He could taste the cresol, even through pinched lips.

It was then, in the haze of disinfectant, that his memory of his first night swept up and over him, and through the mist he could see it almost as if he were there again: the disembowelled soldier, the wandering man with his head wound, Margarete running between them, shouting, as he uselessly stood by. He could hear her voice scolding him, see the change in her expression as he saw the understanding settle into her, this rarest understanding of who he was.

'Close your eyes,' said the sanitation officer, and he did.

14

THE VIENNA THAT Lucius returned to that February of 1917 was dark and hungry and tired of war. Gone were the cheering children. Gone the vendors with their barrels of carp and gherkins, the pretty girls in their white dresses from the War Society; gone the bunting and the patriotic orchestras, the glittering piles of the tin drives; gone the blankets laid out with gingerbread in the shape of the Tsar or Russian Bear. It looked, he thought, as though plague had struck. The planted streets, which in his memory had flitted with constant starlings, were now shorn of all their trees.

Outside the North Station, he paused on the pavement and was immediately descended upon by a crowd of grey-eyed children hawking string and buttons. He hurried on. A man in a low hat and high collar approached him, opening his palm to show a murky syringe.

'Looking for a foot infection, soldier? Cow boil, self-healing in two weeks. Guaranteed exemption, no permanent effects.' Repulsed, Lucius turned away to see a legless man with rag-bound hands rowing towards him in a cart. Again he stared, unprepared to see such suffering in the city. Like something out of Bosch, a sinner's hell. He had no sooner handed the man a fist of kronen than another cart-man paddled up.

Memories came then, unbidden, of his soldiers, the grinding plaint of the amputation saw on bone. He saw the wound sites, flaps cut back and tendons gleaming. The hands set free, the heavy legs unmoored. Toes and fingers black with frostbite, Horváth screaming in the snow.

Horváth. So was this the fate to which he'd sentenced him? To be a cart-man, paddling across the ice with rag-bound hands . . .

A scream. A truck passed, tyres confiscated for their rubber, rims screeching on the icy cobbles.

That's all, he told himself. No screaming. Just tyres, just a truck.

Across the square, a cold wind came tearing over the empty planters.

He walked. His home was south, but now after so many months, he hesitated. The memory of Horváth had unnerved him; he couldn't face his parents yet. So at Tegetthoff's column, he turned and walked into the vast park of the Prater. A train was passing over the viaduct as he crossed beneath the arcades. Beyond, as if by some miracle, a few trees had been spared the fate of firewood, the Ferris wheel still towered, and bright colours glittered on the carousel, immobile now. *Karuzela*, he thought. Father once had told him the word meant 'little war'. Only now did this meaning register: the decorated horses, the martial music urging them on.

He had entered the park alongside a group of schoolchildren and their teacher, who officiously bleated a toy bugle when his charges fell out of line. The surprising amusement of the scene – the old man in his loden cape, the little boys struggling to contain their excitement, the stern, maternal scolding of the older girls – served for a moment to distract Lucius from his growing horror at what had happened to the city. He'd seen many children among the crowds of refugees and in the muddy streets outside the hospitals; he'd almost forgotten they could move so lightly, laugh like this.

And so he followed as the teacher trumpeted an out-of-tune cavalry charge and the children burst off, running past the snow-covered fairground amusements, and down a branching avenue into a separate section of the park.

In contrast to the promenade, this hidden section had not been spared the axe. How typically Viennese, Lucius thought, to maintain appearances. Indeed, it seemed to be in a state of incomplete construction. There were broken-down vehicles and shovels abandoned in the ground. Piles of dirt snaked above rough ditches, interspersed with what seemed to be ad-hoc wooden shelters, all dusted now with snow. But then something strange seemed to be happening. A young couple passed the children, the man jumping into one of the ditches before he offered his hand to his sweetheart, who followed. They appeared to be acting out a play, poking up their heads, then giggling and ducking back inside. They laughed, and Lucius watched them kiss before they ran off behind the children, bent over as if under fire. Further along, a little boy was playing on one of the shelters. He was shouting something, but strangely no sound came from his mouth, and it took a moment for Lucius to realize that ever since the bugle call, he couldn't hear a thing. Oddly, for one who had just gone deaf, he wasn't scared by it, just puzzled, and then far more puzzled by the masquerade that seemed to be unfolding. Two boys began to fight, in pantomime, sharing playful punches, while other children, in two neat ranks of three, crawled along their bellies to the trench edge and lifted their hands as if to shoot. A girl spun, the back of her hand on her forehead, as she fell into her classmates' waiting arms. They lowered her down, mouthing words at one another, as two boys trotted over on invisible horses, carefully dismounted, and crouched heroically by her side. Another girl approached them, knelt, and put her ear to the chest of the fallen, lifted her hand to feel her pulse, gazed heavenwards, and let it limply drop.

Before Lucius knew what was happening, there seemed all of a sudden to be an empty space in his mind. He was aware of where he was, of the circumstances of his arrival, his own name – yes, he needed to reassure himself of this – but as he looked out over the playground, he felt he was looking over a blank spot on a map. It was as if simple facts of everyday life – sound, the meaning of the children's pantomime, the laws governing their shadows – all of this seemed suddenly to elude him. Even a sign above the earthworks, which somehow he had looked straight through upon arrival, seemed to be made of words without meaning.

THE 'FRONT' IN VIENNA:

VISIT THE LIFE-SIZE MODEL OF THE TRENCHES!

BRAVERY, HONOUR, SACRIFICE!

They are stone, he thought, looking at the man, the children. Just ice and stone, and nothing beneath, and for a very brief moment, he had the certainty that the world before him was nothing but a void of shapes and silver light.

The bugle blew.

'Enough!'

Sound poured in to him: the rattling of the viaduct, the wail of a steam whistle, the peals of laughter and wind. Footsteps as the children swarmed from the ersatz trenches and climbed down from the ersatz ramparts and the dead girl stood and dusted snow from her dark grey coat.

NOW SHAKEN, HE could only think of getting home as fast as possible. If only so he wouldn't have to see another legless soldier, another child playing dead.

Ice floes creaked beneath him in the canal as he entered the Inner City, weaving through the alleyways off the Fleischmarkt, where he and Feuermann once bought halva from the Greek merchants, the narrow streets all empty now. At the end of the lane, a woman stepped from the shadows, opening a heavy soldier's coat to reveal a threadbare slip. He ducked his head and hurried to the broad street and the crowds. In the dusk, lone figures scurried past the shuttered shopfronts. He saw a queue of people snaking along the street before it turned down an alleyway, and then in the shadow of St Stephen's, another line, this one wrapping nearly halfway around the square.

Everyone was very still. For a moment, he thought that he was having a new attack. He did not know what they were doing, but feared that asking would mark him as an outsider, so he kept walking. Nor did he look up at the cathedral, which now seemed, like the city, threatening simply in its immensity, its steeple large enough to fit the entire church of Lemnowice inside.

It was dark when he reached 14 Cranachgasse. When he rang at the door, a maid appeared, an unfamiliar woman in a high, starched collar, brown curls topped by a small white cap. She looked at him inquisitively.

'I am Lucius,' he said.

'The son.'

The word a single breath, spoken in awe. For a moment she hesitated. She had not been trained for such a moment; he was, in a way, both master and guest.

'If you wish to tell my parents I am here, I'll wait,' he said.

'No, no, Pan Lucius. No. Please. Come.'

The base of the stairs was still flanked by the pair of winged hussars. The carpet the same, but its colour somehow a deeper violet than he recalled.

He found his parents taking coffee with an elderly couple, the man dressed, like his father, in military regalia. They all rose, taking in the pale apparition still reeking of disinfectant. For the first time in his life, he believed he saw his mother unprepared.

'Dear Mother, dear Father, I am sorry to interrupt. Good evening to you, Colonel, Madame.' He kissed them on the hands. They stared, his mother still with her hand partially out-stretched. His father wordless. No Puszek – so, the last one had yet to be replaced.

'If it pleases you, I shall go to my room?'

But he was gone before they could respond. Out of the dining room, past the old familiar statues, past Klimt's portrait of his mother, little Lucius for ever interred beneath the glittering shower of gold. A memory now, of Zmudowski, hidden beneath the rug, holding his little girl. But this was the reverse.

Then up another staircase to his door.

'The bed is prepared, Pan Lucius,' said the maid, still at his side. 'They have kept it that way since you left.'

He thanked her. Her name?

'Jadwiga, Pan Lucius.'

'Thank you, Jadwiga. And Bozenka, is she still here?'

'Oh! They didn't tell you? Bozenka's with child, sir. She's been dismissed.' There was a slight sauciness with which she said it, a brief flicker in her eyes. *Naughty Bozenka, that's what you get.*

With a curtsy, she left him alone.

It took a moment to recalibrate his memory to the geometry of his room, the height of the ceiling, the position of his desk and bed. It had become much smaller in his mind, the light more muted. Now, like the hallway carpet, the colours of his room seemed almost gaudy. The eggshell-blue sky in a pair of painted warscapes gifted by his father. The peach of the bed-spread. The scarlet rug.

On the wall hung his old portrait, his ears lopsided, his neck drowning in his collar. In a mirror beside it, he touched his scraggly beard, stared at the sunburnt cheeks beneath the tired eyes. His shock of hair, for ever pale, had whitened further. In comparison to the adolescent in the portrait, this other person in the mirror seemed like some winter apparition, a memento mori painted to remind one of the proximity of death. When had this happened? He recalled the evening at the boarding house in Kolomea after his separation, washing the dried blood from his hair and face. Cheeks burnt and dirty, but still with life.

He went to his desk. Old atlases of anatomy, lessons scrawled out by hand. *Muscles of the shoulder. Subclavius. Levator scapulae. Serratus anterior. Rhomboid major and rhomboid minor, arising from thoracic vertebrae 1 to 5.*

A ceramic phrenology skull: a gift from Feuermann for his twenty-first birthday.

More lessons. *Bones of the skull. Structure and function of the heart.*

As once he'd taught her, in exchange for learning how to tie a knot.

The paper slightly yellowed, beginning to curl.

Teeth marks in the coloured pencil on his desk. *Mine.*

And did he understand, she asked, how the feeling of a hand remained after the hand itself was gone?

He did not bathe. His bed was so soft that he felt for a moment he would suffocate inside it, and after some time he rose and put his boots back on, curling up on top of the sheets, against the wall. When sleep came, it wasn't sleep as he had ever known it, but something shuddering, as if he were back sleeping on the trains. Awaking, he found József Horváth sitting on the edge of the bed, naked, pine needles sticking to his skin. His head was shaved, his cheeks pink, his thin, snapping tongue the hue of liver. He licked his mouth frenetically, as if trying to lap up every last drop of something sweet. Lucius stared. *Look*, said Horváth, and taking a finger between his teeth as one might the finger of a glove, pulled off his hand.

Lucius must have screamed. Sitting up in bed, catching his breath, he saw a figure in the doorway. Another dream? But it was his mother, still in her evening dress. He had the feeling of being very small again, of waking in a world populated only by adults. For a moment he had the thought that she would come and comfort him, but this had been the duty of his governess when he was young.

Instead, she was very still, resting her fingers on the wainscoting, watching, as if trying to decide what she should do.

'Thank you, Mother. I'm okay.' He closed his eyes and tried to catch his breath. 'I'll be okay. I just need some rest.'

WHEN HORVÁTH RETURNED the next night, and then the next night after that, Lucius began to walk.

He put on long underwear, two sweaters, his greatcoat and his scarf, pulled his regimental cap low over his head, and hurried down the stairs into the street.

He had no destination. What seemed most important was to move, to exhaust himself in the hope that he might also exhaust the dreams. The processes of his mind seemed a mystery to him; he did not understand why this was happening to him now. In the army circulars, they wrote that battle dreams often relented away from combat. *Sometimes all that is needed to restore the soldier to peaceful sleep are a few days behind the lines.* But he *was* away from combat. Was it that these ghosts had found him once he was no longer moving? Had the dreams been there all along, just hidden? Had his search for Margarete somehow kept them at bay?

From his home, he turned out into the dark street and up towards the Inner City. Past the sepulchral palaces of the Landstrasse, the barracks off the Karlsplatz, the prostitutes stirring along the treeless stretches of the Ring. Past the shuttered Opera House and the snow-covered statue of Goethe in the Imperial and Royal Garden, where Feuermann had kissed a girl during the heady days of enlistment. Past the Natural History Museum with the famous Uzhok meteorite that had foretold his father's wounding. *Uzhok*, he thought, the once-empty word now filled with so much meaning: so close to Lemnowice, of all the places for a meteor to land.

He walked. On other nights, he wandered up the Universitätstrasse and out to the hospital, where he entered the courtyard to watch the orderlies hurrying between the buildings, the pleated headdresses of the nurses moving in the yellow light of the windows. They, too, weren't sleeping, he thought. My city of nightwalkers and nurses.

BY THEN HE knew that returning home was a mistake. There was nothing for him in Vienna. For the past months he had been sick with thoughts of Margarete, but on the trains at least he hadn't been alone. Now he had no one. If he saw his parents, it was only in passing. He could sense their worry, and there were times he found them together, silent, and suspected he had been discussed. If necessary, he greeted them, kissed hands, enquired after their day. But these were formalities only, bulwarks against other questions, and to their credit they seemed to understand where the line was drawn. His mother didn't invite anyone to meet her conquering hero. She made no mention of his arrival to his brothers, comfortably positioned behind desks in Graz and Kraków, nor to his sisters, off with their own families. The servants kept their distance, save Jadwiga, always with a cup of chicory, a piece of cake.

It occurred to him that of all of them, he might seek comfort from his father, who followed the war with a great map unfurled over the sunroom table, each army's position laid out in ranks of painted wooden pieces. He, too, must have had a homecoming after being shot by that Italian musket at Custoza, thought Lucius. He, too, came from a world now lost. But there was a difference, immediately apparent and impossible to overcome. Major Krzelewski had returned with a bullet lodged like an encrusted jewel in his greater trochanter, a decoration to be flaunted among his medals, while the younger medical lieutenant had nothing but the memory of how he'd failed in his duty to protect someone from harm.

MORE DREAMS. Horváth screaming. Horváth holding up his amputated feet. Horváth chewing, open-mouthed, a mass of salamanders on his tongue. Horváth placing a pistol barrel between his teeth and laughing, as Lucius struggled towards him on heavy legs of lead.

SHOULD I GO and look for him? he wondered.

But how? He didn't know the name of Horváth's regiment, only that he was an infantryman from Budapest. The name was common; there would be hundreds in the army. But even if he knew the address, he couldn't bear the thought of what he'd find. An image came to him: the trembling soldier in a garret in his city, with marbled, ulcerated amputation sites, bundled on a sunken bed. Mute still? Or had they cured him with their electricity, their Muck balls? Did he still suffer from his dreams? Or now from nightmares of Lucius, just like Lucius dreamed of him? As if some kind of monstrous twinning had bound them across the winter night.

Travelling now, on the invisible currents that coursed between the two imperial cities, Lucius found himself inside the room reeking of dirty bandages and bedpans, saw a mother, kerchiefed, shivering, rise to greet their visitor. *A friend, József, someone here to visit from the war.* And Horváth's eyes widening, mouth twisting, as his doctor, cap in hand, approached his bed.

HE TRIED WRITING to Feuermann in Gorizia.

Their correspondence had ceased after Horst's visit. Feuermann had been the last to write, with three letters after Lucius had stopped responding, each time sounding more and more concerned. *I hope you aren't ill,* he'd written in his final communication, *or that nothing I have written in the past might have caused offence.* But after Horváth, Lucius couldn't bear corresponding about his cases any more. And in his angrier moments, angry at everyone, he blamed Feuermann, for encouraging him to enlist.

Now back in Vienna, adrift and frightened, Lucius regretted this silence, felt it cowardly, and wished to make amends. *My field hospital had to be abandoned,* he wrote that morning. *I lost my nurse, my patients. You will say we all lost patients. That we all lost many, many patients. But I lost someone I should have saved.*

I killed someone I should have saved.

He tore the letter, wrote it again.

It was not my intent to let our correspondence falter. There are reasons for my silence, which I can tell you when we meet again.

He posted the letter. Then, a week later, before any response, he wrote another. Then two days later another, and then daily, apologizing each time for his silence. Again explaining the evacuation, the trains.

Still he did not get a response, and for the first time in their friendship, he began to write of something other than medicine: of the darkness of the city, the loneliness, the dreams that had pursued him home.

Now, with each day that passes, I feel more and more like some of my soldiers, who seemed for ever stuck in their eternal winters. I had thought that returning from the front would ease these troubles. That's what they told us: that battle dreams relent when the risk of battle goes away. But this is not the case. Unless there is a battle that I don't yet understand.

HE FOUND FEUERMANN'S childhood home in Leopoldstadt, across the Danube Canal.

Despite their years of friendship, it was his first time there. An old man came to the door, a tiny, soft-spoken man with the heavy beard of an eastern Jew, though his head was uncovered and he wore a common suit of dove-grey fabric. The single room looked less like the tailor's shop Lucius had imagined, and more like a rag-man's hovel, and at first he could not believe that it was his friend's father. But when the man spoke, he closed his eyes as Feuermann had closed *his* eyes when he spoke, and like Feuermann, he emphasized his words by moving his long, beautiful fingers through the air.

The old man offered Lucius a chair. It was missing its back, sacrificed – Lucius suspected – for heat. As it was the only chair, Lucius demurred, but the old man insisted. He made tea over a hearth. Then, taking a seat on a pile of sacks, Moses Feuermann said he had last heard from his son in August, after his transfer to a field station of an alpine regiment in the Dolomite campaigns.

'But he said he was in Gorizia, at a regimental hospital,' Lucius protested.

'Yes. But he wrote that he was tired of being just an assistant.

He said they treated him like a student, gave him the mentally unsound, never let him operate. He was envious of you, I think. Of all the responsibilities you had.' There were tears in his eyes when he opened them, and Lucius thought how impossible it would have been for his parents to have this kind of knowledge of their son.

Perhaps I could tell Feuermann's father of Horváth, Lucius wondered.

But this was only a fleeting thought. Beyond the empty tables, he could see an unlit parrafin lamp, and beyond that, a bed, or a series of planks lain with blankets, and a pair of pillows, and beyond them a stack of books, the old editions of the anatomy and physiology textbooks he'd bought for his friend. *Loaned* – Feuermann wouldn't accept the charity, though Lucius never had any intention of getting them back. Above them were stacked the notebooks he remembered Feuermann filling at his side. He felt a sudden desire to see them, but this didn't seem the kind of thing one did to the belongings of someone who was alive. So he turned his eyes away.

'He was a tireless writer,' said his father. 'He wrote to me almost every day.'

August, thought Lucius. Before an unrelenting series of battles along the Isonzo had resumed.

'The lines of communication are poor in the mountains,' he said.

'Yes,' said his father. 'That is what they say.'

Lucius might have promised to visit the War Office or use his mother's contacts to try to find his friend. But Feuermann's father did not ask for this, and when Lucius at last bid him goodbye and stepped out into the crowded, narrow street, he knew what he would learn. It was then that he knew he would return to medicine, if only because he could not survive this news alone.

He petitioned that afternoon for redeployment.

In the Medical Division Office for Field Operations in the East, the clerk noted down his name and address. It would take some time, he said, his voice high and nasal. They had to communicate with his regiment in Kraków; he would receive his summons in the next few weeks.

'But I don't need to return to Kraków,' said Lucius. 'I'll go to any theatre. Whatever is available the soonest. If you need a medic . . .'

The clerk leaned back in his chair and peered at Lucius over his reading glasses. 'A medic? Are you suicidal? Why so urgent? Aren't the Viennese girls good enough?'

It was a Monday. On Friday, he returned home from his walks to find a letter waiting. But this wasn't from the War Office. Instead, on faded university stationery, he found a note in the shaky hand of Zimmer, his old professor. *Your mother says you're home and set for re-enlistment. I now direct a rehabilitation hospital for neurological injuries in the old Lamberg Palace, where I think your services are needed. If you will reconsider . . .*

Mother. So he *had* received his redeployment letter. And once again, like some *deus ex machina*, she had intervened. He recalled how back during the heady days of mobilization, after she had done the same, he had defiantly discarded Zimmer's letter. But this time was different. *Your services are needed.* He was desperate to return to medicine, any medicine. And perhaps he could tell Zimmer about Horváth, and his dreams.

He found his professor in the palace that evening, in a vast ballroom converted to a ward.

In nearly three years, Zimmer had scarcely changed. He had

the same puff-of-smoke sideburns, the same pebbly smile. Perhaps a little shorter, a little more piratical. His eyes now marbled with a slight sheen of cataract, and on his pate was a waxy scarab of a scab.

He was making his rounds with two nurses and an orderly when Lucius found him. He held a fly-swatter with an ivory handle, which he tucked into his belt as a soldier might a sabre. He held out his hand and Lucius took it. His fingers were smooth and twisted with an arthritis Lucius didn't remember being so severe. They shook. 'My student,' said Zimmer, and held Lucius's hand long after they had stopped shaking before he let it go.

LIKE THE CHURCH in Lemnowice and the schoolhouses and châteaux Lucius had visited across Galicia, the Lamberg Palace Army Rehabilitation Hospital for Neurological Injuries was one of countless civilian buildings converted by the Austro-Hungarian Medical Service into wards for the wounded. It had been set up under the personal patronage of an archduchess, Anna, a cousin of Franz Josef. It was a family palace, dating from the reign of Josef II, with a high slate roof, gilded pilasters, and frescoed ceilings with *trompe l'œil* crenellations and a *trompe l'œil* sky. To this, the archduchess had generously donated personal touches from her family's collection. The theme was martial – there were statues of St Michael, tapestries of the Turkish siege of Vienna, and a great canvas showing the corpse-strewn marshes of Marathon. A painting of Cadmus, sowing the earth with dragon's teeth, overhung the chair for minor surgeries. Aloud, Lucius wondered if these were wise decorative choices for a room of injured soldiers, but Zimmer said that the archduke, a great believer in the curative power of manliness, had been adamant. After all, hadn't the dragon's teeth turned into even fiercer warriors, who eventually had founded Thebes?

Moreover, said Zimmer, to Anna's credit, she even volunteered. Of course, mostly she read war poetry, and when she tended to the men, it was above the waist only and not on the face, and she didn't like any wound with blood or pus.

'What kind of wound is that?' asked Lucius.

'So mostly she reads war poetry,' said Zimmer. But still she volunteered.

It was a testament to the remarkable constancy of medicine that such a setting might be anything like the little church with a crater in its floor. But within hours of arriving, he found himself back in the familiar rhythms. There were differences, yes. The wounds here were old, the injuries more stable, more recalcitrant to cure. Fewer dressings, more scars, more contractures. Little blackboards at the foot of each painted metal bed upon which were written names and diagnoses. A bewildering array of metal and leather strengthening devices. A phonograph, of course: this was Austria, land of Haydn, Schubert, Mozart. But so much else the same. Morphine for pain. Phenobarbital for seizures. Camphorated oil for everything. Chloral for sleep.

The first night he stayed long after Zimmer had gone home. There were close to a hundred and twenty patients, and unlike many of the simple fractures and amputations he'd cared for in Lemnowice, all were cases of great complexity. So when the lights went out, he took a stack of the thick charts and began to read. The summaries were mostly typed up by the transferring hospitals, with annotations in Zimmer's unsteady hand. Head wounds, all of them, and as he read, he felt briefly, with a pang, that Margarete were there with him, introducing them as she had introduced the soldiers that first night in Lemnowice. This, Pan Lieutenant Doctor, is Gregor Braz of Prague, blind after being shot behind the ear; this is Marcus Kobold, a sapper from Carinthia, tremor following near-burial underground. This is Helmut Müller, infantry, an art teacher, burnt at the Marne, self-inflicted gunshot wound after being told he'd lost his eyes. Samuel Klein, Pan Doctor, a cobbler's son from Leopold-stadt, blunt crushing trauma just above the ear. This is Zoltán Lukács, a hussar thrown from his horse, an epileptic. This is Egon Rothman, loss of memory since close-range penetration of a magnesium flare. This is Matthias Schmidt, with penetrating trauma through the left temple. This is Werner Eck, with drop attacks, and this is Natan Béla, paralysis of his left arm and leg after being wrongly hanged for spying and cut down before he died. This is Heinrich Rostov, lance wound, right temple, inability to swallow. This is Friedrich Til, Doctor. This is Hans Benesch. This is Bohomil Molnár. Maciej Krawiec, Daniel Löw . . .

'Doctor.'

He opened his eyes. A nurse, holding a steaming cup of chicory.

'You fell asleep. There is a cot in the old library.'

An older woman, perhaps his mother's age. A stiff cornette shaped like a ship's keel soared above a face coarse with smallpox scars. She looked at him with worried eyes.

'Thank you. I'm sorry . . .'

'There is no need to apologize, Doctor,' she said softly. 'The men here will be grateful to have someone so dedicated. But there are one hundred and eighteen patients. You will confuse them unless you take your time.'

It was close to four a.m. He followed her to the library, a small wood-panelled room, its ceiling frescoed with the constellations. But the books were gone, and in their place were dozens of half-formed faces, some bare, some painted. Foreheads, noses, cheeks.

'I hope you don't mind them,' said the nurse, following his gaze. 'They are prosthetics, made of copper and gutta-percha. To cover the deformities. The room serves as a workshop in the day.'

For a moment, his eyes scanned the shelf. He had the strange feeling that he was meeting the patients they belonged to, Klein and Lukács, Molnár, Eck.

'No, no, I don't mind. It is good that they have these.'

'It *is* good, Doctor. Many of them have wives who can't bear to look at them. And the little ones scream when they see their fathers. We are very lucky to have the masks. When the men leave us, people won't avoid them in the streets.'

He waited for her to say more, but she had finished. For a moment, he wished she hadn't spoken; he was prepared for the patients, not their families. At Lemnowice, it had been possible to care only for his patients, without imagining the worried people waiting for them at home. Now this omission seemed almost inconceivable. What had he thought? That they came from worlds devoid of other people? It seemed almost a failure of compassion; the doctor he had been now seemed so young.

He thanked her, and she left him with a neatly folded blanket, army-issue, the rough texture and sour smell familiar. Like his blanket from Lemnowice, on which he'd lain with Margarete that morning by the river. He buried himself beneath it, still in his shoes. He worried that he wouldn't sleep, that thoughts of Horváth would come again, but before he knew it, the same nurse had returned to tell him it was six, that Zimmer was ready. It was only then, walking swiftly with her down the marble corridor beneath the ceiling painted with cherubs and clouds of bursting lilac, that he realized he hadn't dreamed.

15

IN THE MONTHS that followed, he found shelter in medicine's routine.

Days began at six, with rounds; at ten they took the patients out to the palace grounds for rehabilitation exercises. At noon they ate. Two o'clock brought leisure time for cards or music. There was a marching band for one-armed soldiers, table tennis for the one-legged, and a theatre group for those regaining the ability to speak. At four they bathed. At six they ate again. Those able enough helped clean the wards at seven. Lights were out at eight.

He scarcely left the hospital, choosing to sleep on the cot in the library, at times eating with the patients. They were quiet affairs compared to the Lemnowice meals fuelled by song and schnapps, but nonetheless companionable. Other times, he just took surreptitious bites from a hunk of *kielbasa* he kept in a pocket of his coat.

He worked mostly alone. Only a week had passed when Zimmer, manifestly more interested in exploring the archduchess's cabinet of curiosities in the third-floor study of the palace, turned clinical responsibilities over to him.

This, Lucius had come to understand, was probably for the best. With the physician shortage, the Imperial and Royal Army had not only graduated students early and enlisted dentists and veterinarians for medical duty, but had also brought men like Zimmer out of retirement, pathologists and comparative anatomists who had long ago given up their white coats for post-mortem aprons. Despite the well-stocked medicine cabinet, Zimmer seemed to think most problems could be cured with atropine, insisted on patent medications that no one had ever heard of, and still prescribed milk diets for pneumonia, though every respectable textbook since 1900 said that oatmeal was the best. He liked the mantra, 'Death is part of life'. And there was the matter of his vision, the oily monocle he had a habit of misplacing, the flies he chased with his ivory fly-swatter, flies that Lucius soon realized only Zimmer could see.

At first, alone again, Lucius had the vertiginous feeling that he was back in Lemnowice, far out of his depth. Most of the nurses had been there since the founding of the rehabilitation hospital and carried out their duties with a brisk, if stern, efficiency. Like Margarete, they didn't hesitate to correct him, though quietly, with fewer interruptions, exhortations and general bossing-about. But as the days went on, he began to settle in. He created regimens of sleep and exercise and diet, ordered applications of turpentine and eucalyptus oil in cases of bronchitis, and painted infected tonsils with perchloride of iron. For constipation, he prescribed castor oil, and bismuth for diarrhoea. He gave strychnine for heart failure, beef tea for skin infections, and morphine for pain and melancholy. For listlessness and nostalgia, he relied on cigarettes, unless the patient had an irritable heart, in which case he gave bromides, almond milk or brandy, depending on what the nurses could rustle up.

For the more complicated patients, Lucius sought out his old professor, finding him in his gilded consultation room, smoking tobacco in a pipe scavenged from the *wunderkammer*, with a bezoar bowl and scrimshawed stem that Zimmer claimed had been hollowed from the coccyx of the favourite servant of Franz II.

'With due respect, Herr Professor, really, I wouldn't put that in your mouth.'

He blew rings as Lucius told him about the patients with mysterious patterns of pain or palsy. At times he drifted into reveries, and at times Lucius worried if he'd had a stroke. But then, when the answer was needed, the old man's face lit up, and his fingers traced the paths of cranial nerves or the twisting decussation of the pyramids, as he extracted an explanation of great beauty and precision from the air. It was like being back in the lecture halls again, thought Lucius, watching those old men so gifted in diagnosis, so ignorant of cure.

Other times, his professor asked him about his cases at the front.

Then, Zimmer leaned back in his chair, chewed his pipe stem sensuously, and crossed his hands over his belly like a man who has just enjoyed a filling meal and is preparing for dessert. Certainly, Lucius must have seen some extraordinary pathology!

'Yes . . . some extraordinary pathology, Herr Professor.'

'They say there were such magnificent, beautiful cases of war nerves. *Our* head and spine wounds seem so common in comparison, so dull . . .'

Lucius looked down into his hands. 'Such *cases*, Herr Professor, yes . . .'

And he told him of the infantryman with his pigeon toes and twisted neck, the Czech sergeant who tasted rotting bodies in his broth, and the cook who had collided with the bayoneted belly of the hanging girl.

He could not bring himself to speak of Horváth. Zimmer, he knew, would focus on the anguished rocking, the seemingly miraculous response to Veronal. But Lucius wasn't asking for a scientific explanation, and he had no wish to discuss miracles. His belief in miracles was what had led to Horváth's *Anbinden*.

What he wanted to know was whether Zimmer had ever committed such an error, if he had lost a patient, how he'd atoned.

Briefly, he thought: I could tell Zimmer of the case of a young doctor suffering from guilt and dreams and winter visions. How once the doctor had been in love and this had seemed to save him from his crimes, but then he'd lost the woman that he loved. How still he felt her presence with him always, watching, bidding patience with the sickest soldiers, marvelling at the healing of a wound. How he missed her. How now he spent his free hours wandering, wondering how life could begin again.

Instead, he told him of his patient who had lost his right leg to a derailed train car, and then was unable to move his left.

'Extraordinary,' said his professor. 'No wound at all. At least not one that you could see.'

IN APRIL, Lucius was examining a patient with pneumonia named Simmler, when a new patient was carried in by stretcher, a man who looked so much like Horváth that Lucius felt a darkness lower itself across the world and thought he might be sick.

'Doctor?'

Simmler was looking at Lucius's hand, the bell of the stethoscope now shaking. Hastily, he pressed it to Simmler's torso and gripped his shoulder. 'Breathe,' he said. 'There. Deep breaths, just breathe.'

The new man was an Austrian, his skull broken by a shell. Like Horváth, he remained curled up in his bed, though Veronal did nothing to loosen him. Sometimes, they could get him to straighten out his legs, to take some steps, but mostly he just stared back in confusion. There was little urgent about the case; the soldier had been that way for months. But throughout the day, Lucius constantly returned to him, checked and double-checked his medications, and took the man's vital signs himself. Sitting at his bedside, he helped him eat, spooning his soup as Margarete had done for Horváth, and walked him, as Margarete had walked Horváth, along the palace halls. At last, the nurses stopped him. His dedication was commendable, they told him, shortly before the soldier was discharged home, unchanged. But feeding, walking, speech therapy: this was *their* responsibility. He need not involve himself so intimately in the care of any single patient. It was his job just to tell them what to do.

As THE DAYS lengthened, he found himself increasingly at 14 Cranachgasse.

It did not seem deliberate at first. He went there at times to look at his old textbooks, to eat, or check for post that never came. But slowly, he felt himself dismantling the ramparts he'd erected.

He began to join his parents for their meals. Despite the food shortages, they ate well; the food came from the black market, purchased by Jadwiga from girls who lingered in the Naschmarkt with perambulators filled with beetroots or plaits of garlic. Sometimes there was not enough, and sometimes the rye was spoiled or the milk rancid, but compared to the rest of the city they were very lucky. He had been hungry enough at times to feel guilty that he was eating while in the streets people attacked and overturned the food wagons, and when he could, he brought chocolates and pralines to share with his patients, smuggled all the way from Warsaw. Then, in June, the police turned up to question him about rumours that the Lamberg Palace was getting dessert while the rest of the city was starving. He lied; the gift of a grateful patient, he told them, but they persisted until he realized they wanted some themselves.

At the table, the nightmares of his first few days were never spoken of, nor did his mother ever mention her interference with his commission. Instead, increasingly busy with new steelworks in southern Poland, she listened with curiosity when he described the derricks at Sloboda Rungurska. It was helpful, she said, to have a 'first-hand' observation, and she quizzed him on what he remembered of the bridges and the rails.

But of all the changes, Lucius sensed the greatest was with his father. Seeking Lucius out alone, Retired Major Zbigniew Krzelewski still spoke of cavalry skirmishes vastly different from the war Lucius had experienced. And still, when Lucius found the courage to ask the hardest questions – Did he dream of the fighting at Custoza? Had he seen things he couldn't forget? – the retired major mostly answered with enthusiastic tales of heroic comrades who crawled bleeding over the bodies so they could fire one last musket bullet into the Italian charge. Indeed, for months his father had persisted in a seeming unawareness that Lucius had served as a doctor, not a soldier. But as this sank in, something else seemed to be happening, as if talking to his father about uniforms and heraldry could return him, briefly, to the place he'd left behind.

Was it true that German dragoons wore the same pickelhaube as the infantry? his father asked him. And the Guards Cuirassiers no longer wore a breastplate? Ah, but Lucius was in the east, and the Cuirassiers were mostly in the west. And how did he think the Hungarian cavalry compared to the Austrians and Germans?

The lancers Lucius described from an early firefight near Lemnowice were of particular interest to him. *His* lancers. But how appalling that they weren't wearing their *czapkas*!

'It makes them easy targets for the sharp-shooters, Father.'

His hands went up. 'You think we didn't have sharp-shooters!' And no plastron, either?

'It was twenty below, Father. They wore greatcoats like everybody else.'

'You think we didn't have the cold?'

But nothing excited him as much as the seven or eight minutes Lucius spent fleeing Cossacks. An uphill charge! Through the woods! And were they carrying sabres or muskets? Both! God in heaven. Did he see their saddles? Did their jackets have the ornamental cartridge loops? He had heard the Russians had abandoned them in the name of saving thread.

'I couldn't see. I was being chased.'

'On a hussar's horse.'

'Yes. The rider was killed. I took his horse.'

His father's eyes sparkled as he stroked his moustache. 'That is extraordinary. You just leapt on. Like that.'

Still his father was appalled to think of brave hussars on the run. If they still wore wings, surely the Cossacks would have given it second thought.

'Have I told you the advantages of wings?' he asked.

'You have.'

'Can you imagine how terrifying it would be to see a winged horseman charging you with his lance?'

'It would be really, really terrifying, Father.'

It was then that Lucius sensed that, in his father's gaze, he was seeing something close to love. And Major Krzelewski did something he had never done in Lucius's memory: he reached out and gently touched Lucius's cheek.

'A hussar's horse! That means he died, and you survived. My son! A doctor, and even Cossacks couldn't chase you down.'

BUT NOTHING pleased his father more than huddling over the war map in the sunroom with his friends. Indeed, he had never been so industrious since the beginnings of his unemployment in 1867. But the map, Lucius realized, was more than just the quaint pastime for a group of old nostalgic soldiers who liked to dress up in waxed riding boots and tasselled parade helmets. Many of the old nostalgic soldiers still had positions in the army, and all of them had old nostalgic friends with positions in the army, and during the long hours playing *tarock* and drinking, they spoke of little else. The maps printed in the newspapers were often wildly inaccurate, and of course subject to censorship, while his father sometimes updated his several times a day.

As the months passed, Lucius watched the little green, blue, red, yellow and black cubes murder each other for tiny swathes of cardboard. And while he let his father explain the western trench systems, or the Alpine battles in Italy, his eyes kept returning to one spot, to the left of the *T* of the word *KARPATEN*, and below the *w* in *Nadworna*. There, a tiny hatch mark like a thousand others marked a change in elevation. *There*. As if something magical linked this tiny scratch of ink to the mountains far away.

Thinking, *When the fighting retreats, when the rails open, I'll go back to find her. There, in the one place I have yet to look.*

Through the first six months of 1917, the Russian Seventh Army – a blue piece the size of his finger – sat on Kolomea, its shadow falling ominously over the hatch mark that was Lemnowice. In June, to his dismay, the piece began to advance even further: another offensive, again led by Brusilov. But then word came that Russian soldiers, sick of fighting, were beginning to desert.

By July, the Russian cube had inched back east. By August, it no longer even cast late-evening shadows, as the Carpathians once again fell under German black and Austrian green.

*

BUT THERE WAS no way for him to get to Lemnowice. Quietly, not wishing to ruffle Zimmer, he had enquired about a transfer east. At first the clerk in the Medical Office had seemed receptive to the proposal. It should be easy to find a volunteer replacement who wished to serve back in the comfort of Vienna.

Fearing the interference of his mother, Lucius gave the address of a café. Then, for a month, he waited, only to hear his transfer was 'no longer considered a priority'; with the war quieting in Galicia, and the slow shift of soldiers from frontline hospitals, even Vienna was seeing shortages of physicians. This already confirmed what he had suspected with growing dread. Through the summer, he had seen their census grow; by September, new men were coming daily, forcing them to open wards on the second and third floors.

Then, in November, Bolsheviks seized the Winter Palace in St Petersburg, and peace negotiations began between Russia and the Central Powers, culminating in the Brest–Litovsk treaty in March. Neither event should have had much of an impact on the timeless practice of medicine, had there not been by then, according to the rumours (for the official papers gave much lower numbers), nearly two million Imperial and Royal prisoners of war in Russian camps ready to come home.

The flow of soldiers, already heavy by the New Year, became a flood. They came by the trainload, piling into freezing cattle cars and clinging to the roofs. Platforms in the North Station were soon transformed into ad-hoc wards because there weren't enough hospitals to take them in. By then, the palace, its rooftop glinting with snow, had all but ceased to be a neurological service. It was like working in the field again. In addition to fractures and amputations, the men brought malaria and Volhynian fever, frostbite from the Russian winters, and cholera caught in the camps. Zimmer had come down with pneumonia, and together, Lucius and the nurses dragged away the clanking rehabilitation equipment to make more space for beds. They laid out cots, then blankets on the floor. When the first cases of typhus appeared, they received a mobile delousing and disinfection station, with a tent and rusty boiler, set up beneath the plane trees on the palace lawn.

Surely, thought Lucius at times, there couldn't be this many soldiers, but he had seen them in their splendoured millions as they'd marched out towards the front. It was as if the war was contracting under some mysterious force of gravity. As the winter drew on, it was almost possible to read events in distant places by the mud on the men's shoes and trousers: the dark, rancid earth of Belgium, the white clay of the Dolomites, the pine needles embedded in the wool socks of the men from the Carpathians. Overwhelmed, he petitioned the War Office for another doctor, begged the archduchess, and asked his mother to use her influence. But even his mother was no match for typhus. Eventually, the archduchess secured a consultant for relief on every second Sunday, an Austrian from Innsbruck who listened to the tales of Zimmer with scarcely disguised horror. Lucius was given a portable bacteriological laboratory to quantify wound organisms, but no eosin to stain them; an X-ray machine to aid the extraction of foreign bodies, but never enough film. The rubber on the nasogastric tubes was old and cracked, and flies drugged themselves on mixtures of glucose and morphine that leaked down onto the patients' beds. Every week brought another shortage of the phenobarbital he used for seizures. In March, in the middle of another fuel shortage, and unable to wait for spring, they chopped down the plane trees to heat the stoves.

*

IN APRIL, exhausted, he received a note from his mother, inviting him to dine.

It arrived at the hospital by messenger, a little man in livery and a Tyrolean hat, a spray of blackbird feathers in its corded band. This was the first time she had written to him there. There was no explanation. 'She said nothing of an emergency?' asked Lucius. In his hands, he held a large syringe to draw off the blood that had slowly gathered around one of his patient's lungs.

The man shook his head. 'She said you might ask. No, no emergency. She only misses your company, the lady said.'

This was highly unlikely; and his mother knew he would think so, too. But it left no room to turn the invitation down.

IT HAD BEEN two weeks since he had stepped outside the hospital. In the streets, the last snow had melted, and little bursts of willowherb and pimpernel had appeared between the cobbles. On the Beltway, a small parade of children from the War Orphan Society was marching behind a stern drum major. The air was cool, cut with the smell of horse dung that plopped unceremoniously in a line of listless fiacres waiting for their fares.

His mother was alone when he found her, at the long dining-room table that the family had brought with them to Vienna. She wore a dress of pleated pale-blue silk. A webbed necklace of pearls spanned her bare neck; her bracelets were of silver filigree. Nothing she would dare wear out, among the crowds in all their threadbare, lest she be set upon as unpatriotic. Posture martial; hair pinned tightly to her head.

A corner of the table had been set, intimately, for two, near where – his mother liked to boast – a lovesick Jagiellonian prince once carved the initials of his beloved, though everyone in the family knew it had been Lucius's oldest brother Władysław.

He kissed her hand.

'And Father?'

'Hunting, with Kasinowski.'

Duke of Bielsko-Biała and Katowice.

'The blind one?'

'Not *completely*, Lucius.'

'Mother isn't worried he may shoot Father accidentally?'

She smiled with her perfect teeth. There was no way faster to gain her affections than ridiculing other aristocratic families. 'As long as we don't have to mount his head,' she said. 'After the zebus, we've scarcely any space.' She nodded towards the line of trophies in the neighbouring sunroom.

'*Ibexes*, Mother. Ibexes.'

'Of course.' She touched her temple. 'My son the scientist.'

Then she withdrew her hand. 'You must be famished, with the slop they feed you at the hospital. Shall we eat?'

They sat. A satin cushion rested at the small of his back, a detail which did not escape his notice, for she prized the chairs ornamented with rococo roses, which kept her guests from getting too comfortable to dislodge. *This will not be brief*, he thought. The table was set with white damask and white and yellow tulips. China and crystal had been arranged so that he sat at her right hand, while she sat at the table's head. Behind him the vast fireplace. Large enough, she liked to say, to cook Franz Josef, *figure of speech*. A joke, of course, but he was aware that she had replaced the commemorative ceramics from the Emperor's jubilee that once sat proudly on their mantel. His view gave out on to the window; hers to the expanse of the table, the portraits of her bloodline in their furs and armour, the pillars of yellow marble that marked the entrance to the sunroom.

Jadwiga appeared in a high black collar and decorative lace apron, pushing a service tray loaded with dinner: cabbage rolls in tomato sauce and sour cream, a plate of blood sausage, potatoes spiced with marjoram and onion, pork sirloin in mushroom gravy. A row of dumplings, stuffed with duck.

'My,' said Lucius, looking up at her. 'You must have canvassed half the city.' He knew the risks of the black market. The papers loved to report the arrests of smugglers. Even 14 Cranachgasse hadn't known beef in months.

Jadwiga curtsied proudly and vanished behind a swinging door. Usually she waited; his mother must have asked to be alone.

'Eat, Lucius,' his mother said.

As he ate, she spoke of politics, the civil war in Russia, the slowly accumulating treaties, the squabbles among the Austrian command. She praised President Wilson, his Fourteen Points, and the promise of an independent Poland. A *true* independent Poland, she said, '*her territories inhabited by indisputably Polish populations, which should be assured a free and secure access . . .*'

'. . . *to the sea.*' Lucius had joined her. 'I know.'

It was only a matter of time, she said. The sea! Poland hadn't dipped her toes since 1795.

But by then he knew this was all a prelude to something else.

She broke off and briefly touched the pearls around her neck. Her gaze drifted across his face, the fireplace, a decorative porcelain clock of Hannibal and his elephants that graced a far credenza, the hanging portrait of Sobieski with his panther cloak and laurels. There she stopped, as if she were conferring. Then her eyes turned back to Lucius. He had the sense of a bird of prey, circling, feathers shivering, before a strike.

'I think that you should take a wife.'

His knife paused, mid-dumpling. *A wife*. He managed to swallow what he was chewing. 'Mother, yes. Go on.'

The House of Habsburg, she told him, was at death's door, as certainly he knew. The future no longer lay in Title, but in Capital. His brothers' countess wives, his sisters' margrave husbands: all bearers of titles to a world that wouldn't survive the year. She had seen the future; it sat prettily on the plush sofas of the drawing rooms of men with controlling stock in steelworks, oilfields and mines.

He forced himself to take another bite. 'You can't be serious, Mother.'

'My son knows me as someone who likes to joke?'

She had not touched her plate. He saw that she was waiting. Cautiously, he advanced. 'I still have to spend most nights at the hospital. With the POW return, things have only got worse. It is hardly what one would expect of a devoted husband—'

'I'm sorry,' she interrupted. 'Did someone use the word *devoted*? My son is one of the few men in Vienna who isn't a cripple or a shirker. I'd think your wife would be quite happy with whatever she is getting.'

He stared at her, trying to assess the degree of her conviction. She was smiling at him, though it seemed more a baring of her teeth. Now he understood why this needed to await his father's absence; his father still held to notions like romantic love.

'This is quite sudden,' he said. 'Of course, I will need time to think about it.'

'No, Lucius. Actually, there is no time to think about it. Men are already returning home. Marriage is a market like any other. And a very liquid market, I should add. You can imagine the effect that armistice will have on supply.'

He leaned back and crossed his arms. Above him, candles

flickered on a massive antler chandelier. He looked past them, to the window, the square of evening sky.

'Mother isn't anything if not blunt.'

'My interest is yours,' she said, now utterly still. 'You are how old?'

'Please, Mother. You don't need me to say it. I believe you were present at my birth.'

'I *do* need you to say it.'

'Mother—'

'How old?'

A sigh as he relented. 'Twenty-six.'

'Tell me about the girl you left in Galicia.'

'Sorry?'

Now, for the first time, she picked up a fork and knife, transferred a single pierogi from the warmed platter to her plate, and cut into it, its corner yielding with a tiny burst of steam.

'I am waiting, Lucius. Tell me. It is either that, or I must take you for an invert, though you have none of the *panache*. There was a girl.'

In the window beyond her, a flock of starlings rose slowly from the shingles of the neighbouring rooftop, lifted like a conjuror's cape. It soared upwards, curling upon itself before it burst into a larger, fluttering orb. He said slowly, 'I worked in a field hospital. I've told you many times.'

'Yes, yes, of course you have.'

'There was no girl.'

'No, of course not. Not a single nurse. Quite a hospital, without a nurse.'

'There was a nursing *sister*. From the order of St Catherine.'

Briefly then, he saw her, laughing, skin cool with water, warm with sunlight, as she rose above him on the riverbank.

'Pretty?'

'Mother. I can't believe we are discussing this.'

'Polish or Austrian? Do I dare ask about her family? Lucius, your ears have turned bright red.'

'There was no one, I said—'

'No? Then to whom were you writing those letters you tore up so diligently? Why were you constantly checking the post?'

A pause; no answer. He could claim that it was Feuermann, or another comrade. But he knew, and knew she knew when she had won.

'Lucius . . .' She leaned forward and placed her hand on his. 'May I offer some motherly advice? You've been home for almost two years. If she had wanted, she would have written to you. Unless she couldn't read.'

The door behind them opened, as Jadwiga's head emerged to survey the table. His mother waved her away. Outside, the starlings had returned, a vortex, a lens, a greater bird. Not two years, he wanted to say – just fourteen months. But this didn't count the time that he had sought her from the trains.

Softer now, his mother said, 'You act as if I'm against you. But this . . .' She pushed down on his hand. 'This is *me*. This is my flesh. You can't hide in the hospital for ever. We are talking about your life.'

She withdrew, sat back, her posture still impeccable. From a silver case, she extracted a long cigarette.

He said, 'And I thought we were talking about Capital.'

'I didn't say marry a laundry girl. I'll select the menu. You choose the dish.'

BACK ON THE wards, he waited for the messenger to return with another summons. But Agnieszka Krzelewska, he later realized, was cleverer than this. She had said what for the passing months he'd been unable to admit. How long was he to sit in mourning?

He'd canvassed half the hospitals in eastern Galicia for Margarete. Short of heading off to Lemnowice himself, which, without permission, essentially meant desertion, he'd reached an end.

And there were other thoughts, at first ignored, now unavoidable. Margarete could, after all, have sought him out. If she couldn't travel, she knew his name, knew how to write. This would have been easy. A nurse might be lost among the great movements of people, but not a medical lieutenant. If mail could find him at a mountain field hospital, it could find him in Vienna. He'd written to Feuermann with just his name and regiment; by field post, she wouldn't even need a stamp.

For another week, he waited for his mother's messenger, but nothing. This wasn't, he knew, an oversight. His mother did not commit oversights. The seed had been planted; she was just giving it time to grow.

And it was spring. Around the city, on the boulevards, in the public gardens, he saw soldiers reunited with their sweethearts. Hemlines had risen, just a little. Whether it was the cloth rations, or the weather, or a kind of recklessness unleashed by so much deprivation, he didn't know. But ankles were everywhere, and necks. Because all jewellery had ostensibly been donated to the war effort, the girls began to decorate themselves with little wild flowers, plucked from untended gardens and tucked into a collar button or a hat. Now, when his patients' families came to visit them in the hospital, he found himself looking at the young wives doting on their injured husbands and felt a twinge of longing. It seemed like madness to feel envy for a soldier paralysed below his neck, or a man forced to wear a tin-face prosthetic so as not to scare his children. But the wives always made themselves so pretty when they went to see their husbands, and the accents of the Czechs and Slovenians were really lovely, and sometimes when they thanked him, they even offered him their hands. Just for a moment, and only for him to grasp their fingers lightly while accepting their gratitude, and not to raise them to his lips, as if meeting among friends.

Other times, he spied the rustling of bed sheets in a corner. A blush, skirts shifting, a button opened on a blouse. It didn't matter, he tried to tell himself; he should be happy that the soldiers could find even some fleeting pleasure. But by then it was undeniable, the longing, right here in his chest.

WITH SPRING, the crowding, his mother's offer, the arrival of the soldiers' pretty wives, he began again to walk. Past the palaces of the Landstrasse, the barracks off the Karlsplatz, the prostitutes stirring along the treeless stretches of the Ring. Past the shuttered Opera House, the statue of Goethe in the Imperial and Royal Garden, daisies bursting about his feet. To the canal, to St Stephen's, to the North Station to watch the trains come in.

One afternoon, in late April, relieved for several hours by the visiting consultant, he found himself in the Maria-Josefa Park, near the Arsenal and South Station. It had rained much of the week, and with the respite, the park was filled with families and strolling couples and small crowds of furloughed soldiers who flirted with the governesses and trinket-selling girls. He had brought with him a pair of volumes from the *Army Medical Journal*, and settled on a bench in the middle of the park, not far from an empty fountain, where Neptune, whitewashed with pigeon droppings, rose upon a school of dolphins bursting from marble waves. It was humid; the sky was low, the colour of burnished steel. He tried to read, but his mind was constantly returning to Margarete and his mother's offer, when the sound of laughter rose from a crowd gathered in the broad walk just beyond the laburnums, near the entrance to the park.

He ignored it at first. The streets were full of buskers: violinists and accordionists, practitioners of sleight-of-hand. They were often veterans, and he usually approached them with caution, worried about the memories they stirred. But the people in the distance seemed to be enjoying the performance far more than he was enjoying his article on starvation psychosis, so he rose and joined the crowd, which had gathered around an organ grinder and his bear.

The organ sat on what looked like a converted pram, with large, black stagecoach wheels, a lacquered chassis and a push-handle of iron filigree. The organist had left the blanket over the top of the organ, and the box itself was decorated with glossy green tendrils and little painted strawberries, and a name, illegible at this distance, in gilded baroque script.

The bear was in fact a man of small stature, dressed entirely in a real bear's skin, save that the paws had been removed to make space for the man's hands and feet. There was something quite primitive and horrid about it. Much of the skull had been removed, and the bear's skin had contracted unevenly: the nose was twisted, and one ear sat higher than the other, reminding Lucius uneasily of the twisted grimaces of his patients with facial wounds. In place of the eyes were white shells with painted crimson irises.

The dancer looked out of the mouth, which had been propped open, the bear's lips pinned up to make a snarl. The organ played a tarantella. The bear tumbled, cartwheeled and had just danced off with a busty girl in frilled pink calico, when the light sprinkle turned to rain.

There was a groan; at first the organist just adjusted the blanket on the organ, and the bear kept dancing. Here and there umbrellas burst open, couples pressed together, and women pulled their shawls forward on their heads. Lucius tucked the

Journal inside his coat. Then the sky grew darker, as if something great had passed in front of the sun – a Zeppelin or a giant bird. A heavier rain began to fall. The tarantella halted, the organ grinder hurriedly tucked the blanket around the organ, the bear decapitated itself, and the empty head made rounds for tips.

Lucius, who prided himself on a sense of the weather not particularly borne out by experience, hadn't brought an umbrella. There was a gazebo at the end of the walk, and he was hurrying towards it in a giddy crowd of factory women, when his eyes caught on a figure walking past a rank of drooping lilacs, in the direction of the South Station.

He froze.

White blouse. Skirt of rough blue flannel. Dark blue shawl, and gold remembrance ribbon around her wrist.

No habit any more, he thought; but this was the least of the mysteries that needed to be explained.

The crowd broke around him.

'Margarete!'

But she was too far away, the shouts and laughter of the crowd too loud. He began to walk faster, skipped, and broke into a run, colliding into a young couple scurrying off beneath a newspaper glistening with rain. Another collision, this time with a man carrying his dog. The crowd seemed to converge: a policeman in black oilcloth, a trio of young men in bowlers, a woman heaving a kicking child. He pushed through them, now not bothering to apologize, as little eddies of outrage exploded in his wake.

She had entered a wide river of humanity hurrying from the park and towards the shelter of the train station. He followed, the *Army Medical Journal* now sheltering his eyes, desperate to keep her in his sight. Crossing the street, he was nearly disembowelled by the decorative metal bumper of a fiacre, whose caped driver cursed and snapped his whip inches from Lucius's face. Another horse, another fiacre, creaking wheels spitting up water, another shout. Then a wagon, a motor car – it seemed at once as if all the conveyances of the Imperial City had contrived to block his path. He ducked at last beneath a whinny and the flicking of a mane. The station now before him, an opulence of grey and white, columns rising to the ranks of marble knights and griffons, Victory high and hazy in the falling rain. About its base, the crowds. His eyes scanned the headscarves, the ranks of multicoloured skirts and blouses. Umbrellas collapsing as their owners gained the arcades. He'd lost her. Now a second time.

Journal still raised, he made his way slowly forward, his body still and quiet, but inside frantic, alert to everything, his eyes trying to take them in. And everywhere the people! How many people in this cursed city! How many shades of blouse, how many prints of calico! How many flannel skirts, how many ribbons, shawls, and how many faces floating beneath them, pink faces and grey faces and dun faces, faces lined with age, jowled faces, faces long in tooth and short in neck, long in neck and low in brow, dolichocephalic and leptorrhine, harried faces, imperious, voluptuous, insouciant faces, heat-flushed, and pale and glistening from rain . . .

And: nowhere. He broke from the masses and trotted partway down the length of the arcades, staring into them, searching for the shawl, the ribbon. The rain fell harder. Someone pushed him from behind. A bell – a tram had disgorged its passengers, making quickly for the dry.

He followed them inside, through the main lobby, with its tall gas lamps flickering in their amber globes. Fluted pillars rose to the high ceiling; crowds streamed up and down the grand staircase that led up to the tracks. He was being carried towards the platforms and had to fight his way out of the current, turning, eyes trying to take in all the people moving past. The questions now unavoidable: why here and how, and why the remembrance ribbon, worn for someone dead or missing, unless she wore it for him?

A powdery odour drifted from the baskets of a pair of dried-flower peddlers, who had taken defiant seats in their ample petticoats on the corner of the staircase steps.

Back through the crowds, and now out again to watch the shivering arrival of another tramcar, silvery in the rain.

And then again he saw her: blouse, gold ribbon, passing out of the arcades and hurrying along the path that flanked the train tracks, towards the underpass. Skirts swaying as she hurried, a familiar shift. High grass, dark wooded trails. Like that day she fled him, crying. He ran.

Past the ranks of pavement planters, empty except for tree stumps. Weaving between the painted bollards, the travellers descending from another tram. The tunnel dark, a feathered shifting in its beams, the air heavy with the smell of wool and human breath. Back in the light he saw her on the far side of a traffic circle, still out of earshot, heading into an alley off the boulevard. His face was hot; he felt the weight of the months, the years upon him, saw all that would be returned. She was tangible now, a block away from him, and already he could feel what it would be like to hold her, to comfort and be comforted, to kiss her lips now wet with water, as once along the river's bank.

He called, but his voice was lost beneath the whistle of a train. He hit a puddle, turned an ankle, stumbled, then was back upon his feet. He called for her again. But she was speaking to a man who leaned against an open doorway, and then she disappeared inside. Around him, Lucius had only a second to take in the flanking street crowded with crates and horse carts, the torn awnings of the shops and terraced balconies strung with dripping clothes. And then the man pushed off from the doorway and stepped out to meet his path.

White shirt, patched elbows, maroon vest jacket frayed about the collar and the arms. Long, well-tended moustache, smooth dome of head. One eye frozen, the outlines of the iris melting in a milky blur. Accent unfamiliar. 'What do you want?'

But Lucius was already looking past him to the figure inside.

In the safety of the doorway, she stood on the third step of a stairway, beneath a sconce that cast her shadow against the opposite wall. She had dropped her shawl, and now her hair hung wet about her neck in tangles. Faint steam came off her blouse; her chest was heaving.

It was easy to see how he'd made the mistake, with the high cheeks, that angle of gaze, that mouth.

The rain had relented; around him, the small street had begun to stir. From a window came the smell of cooking oil. A voice in an unfamiliar language was calling down. He looked back to the young woman, who had advanced to stand between the pair of twisting caryatids that flanked the doorway. She reached up to brush her hair back, the ribbon sliding down her wrist.

A memory now, of the night he'd left Margarete, chasing the grey figure through the mist, the young peasant with her rifle in the glen. The shouts, the way she gripped the stock and aimed. A warning, he thought. Which he hadn't heeded, now chasing ghosts again.

His hair was plastered to his face, and his coat was soaked; he could feel the rain running off his nape and down between his shoulder blades.

'I'm sorry,' he murmured, embarrassed now at how hopeful

he had been. Again he looked at the girl, and as a man of science, he understood how it had happened – the rain, the ghost, the chemistries of memory, the magic way that crystals appeared out of solution, before dissolving once more into its haze.

He gave a little bow, as if in deference, as he had been taught once as a child to greet new acquaintances. It was absurd, given the circumstances. But it was the custom of his station, and he remained his mother's son.

16

THIS TIME IT WAS Lucius who sought out his mother. Grimly, now determined to complete what she'd begun.

He found her in their sunroom, reading from a trade journal of the Mining Association, which she folded neatly before setting down. She seemed genuinely pleased to see him. And how delightful that he had made his decision, she said, almost offhandedly, as if they had both known it was but a matter of time before he came around.

Within a day, she had set the dates and hours of the appointments. There would be a visit to the tailor first, of course, then to the barber, to take care of – she tapped her head to mirror his cowlick – *this*. Then they would start with four, so that he might compare his options; were he still unsatisfied, she would consider adjustments to accommodate his taste.

'Smile,' she told him. 'You're going to a matchmaking, not an exorcism.'

And he smiled thinly, inwardly marvelling at her choice of words.

AS EXPECTED, she joined him, and together they made their rounds.

Four meetings, on four Saturday afternoons, in four parlours brimming with gleaming marble statues, overstuffed sofas and gaudy, tasteless family portraits that elicited such a haughty twitch of his mother's nostrils that he thought she might call off each meeting before it even began. They were daughters of industry all. Katherina Slovoda, Maria Rostoklovsky, Wilhelmine Schmidt, Krisztina Szűcs. Solitary daughters of a Czech smelt-works owner, a Polish rail-carriage manufacturer, a German-Austrian weapons concern, and the largest producer of Hungarian lignite. And pretty, all of them. Of course, said Madame Krzelewska: they all had pretty mothers who had married wealth.

They were also, as his mother had predicted, terrified of spinsterhood, and knew they faced a competitive field. But neither she nor Lucius had anticipated the degree of desperation. Katherina, perched between her mother and her father, was so nervous that her nose began to bleed, and Lucius was soon attending to her in a reclining chair, pinching her nostrils with a handkerchief. Maria, in a hat decorated with the feathered carnage of a dove, squeezed her lapdog so hard that it tried to bite her and fled beneath the Biedermeier chair. Krisztina asked their parents to leave them, exchanging a knowing glance with her mother as she left the room. When the door was closed, she leaned forward and told Lucius that he wouldn't have to wait until their wedding night. For a moment, he didn't understand. Her eyebrows rose up and down in insinuation. A nervous tic? But *bilateral*? Of the occipitofrontalis muscle? No . . . but . . . oh, he understood!

Even poor Wilhelmine, whose reading habits would have killed the archbishop with piety, wore a dress so low that his mother could not restrain herself from muttering to Lucius in Polish that someone needed to notify the girl of the invention of the brassiere. Patriotic medals flanked her décolletage. For ten minutes, as Frau Schmidt sang the praises of her daughter, Wilhelmine thrust out her chest, and Lucius forced himself to stare at the spray of rubies in her tiara. Misreading his inattention, the poor girl shuffled even further out on the sofa until

Lucius's mother, her lips pursed in an expression of supreme annoyance, motioned her back. 'That's quite enough. Your mother has apprised us of your assets, dear.'

'Sorry?'

'Your bosom, child. It is – how do you say in German – *threatening* us? You'll fall out of the chair.'

There was a moment of stunned silence. His mother, of course, spoke beautiful German, perfect German, and this was not lost on their hosts. 'Well . . . I . . . but . . . I . . .' began poor Wilhelmine, her patriotic medals trembling, before her mother shouted, *'Apfelstrudel!'* as she plucked one from a silver tray of pastries and took an explosive, powdery bite.

He left each failure with a feeling of vindication, a vague sense of loyalty to Margarete's memory, and just a little disappointment. Which is what he expected with the announcement of his fifth audience, with one Natasza Borszowska, the youngest daughter of General Borszowski of the Polish Legion, rumoured among the circles preparing for Polish independence to be in line for the Polish Southern Command.

They met on the third of May, at a party held by his parents in honour of the Polish constitution of 1791. Lucius was with his father when Natasza entered on the arm of *hers*, an old man in a plumed helmet and so many decorations that he seemed from a distance to be wearing chain mail. She smiled gratefully to the doorman as he took her stole, and for a moment Lucius felt certain that conversation in the room had stopped. Part of him wished this wasn't her. She was too beautiful; the vague terror he felt at most social occasions seemed to concentrate itself cruelly in his throat. He thought to leave. But his father had also noticed, turning in almost clockwork coordination with Lucius. And his mother, across the room, had registered both the general's arrival and her husband and son's response.

She wasted no time. Gliding swiftly across the parquet floor, she brought them together. Lucius: Natasza Borszowska. Natasza: my son. But old Zbigniew, still charming in his *fin-de-siècle* kind of way, had already taken her hand.

'*Enchanté.*'

Gently, Madame Krzelewska prised her husband off. Perhaps the two youngsters would like to get to know each other? She believed the sunroom was unoccupied. Jadwiga could bring them something to drink.

SHE WORE A silk dress, sky blue and loose and sleeveless, and long silk gloves. A string of pearls dangled low beneath her breasts, knotted at her sternum. He would later learn her hair was long, but that day it rose in a complicated manifold of pleats that bared her neck.

They sat at the corner of a low table decorated with a forest scene of inlaid wood. A nymph fled, pursued by Cupid's arrows. He was speechless, terrified by that resurgent hint of stammer, trying to decide whether it was ruder to stare or look away. He stared. She inhaled deeply from a cigarette of cloves, taking in the room with its hanging ferns and black-and-white-chequered floor, the piano in the corner, the table with its war map.

Then she turned to him and smiled. 'Hello.'

'Hello!'

It came out a little loud. For a moment, he thought the interview might end there. But she was a quick student of his limitations. She had been hearing about him ever since she had returned from holiday, she said. Her father said that he had been a war hero, survived a Cossack assault in the Carpathians. That he now ran the archduchess's charity. She was fascinated by medicine, by neurology. Had he read *Interpretation of Dreams*?

He hadn't, yet.

'That's too bad. I'll give you my copy, if you don't mind the annotations. Perhaps you could tell me what you think.'

If she saw his ears reddening, she didn't let on. His mother had told her father that as a student he had made great advances in the studies of X-rays. Did he still do this research? Once, right before the war, she had been radiographed for fun; she still had the image – one could see the outline of her rings, her necklace, *everything*. She felt that as Poles, they had a patriotic commitment to radiation. As a child she had even met Madame Curie, in Paris, and for years she was certain that if she had a daughter, she would name her Marie. Had Lucius ever met her in the course of his studies? Oh, but how silly of her to think that just because they both studied radiography . . .

But he had!

Her eyes flashed as he told her the story. A *mermaid*? He couldn't take her to the Medical School to see it, could he?

'No, but . . . *wait*,' he said.

He took the stairs three steps at a time.

The film was still there, on the highest shelf, in a paper sheaf, tucked among the books. He nearly tumbled as he ran back down.

'How extraordinary!'

She held the image to the light.

'Truly, who would have made such a thing? *That* is the interesting part of the story. And who was it that they were trying to fool?'

He realized all of a sudden that he had never stopped to wonder.

An ashtray sat at the far end of the long table between them. She could have asked for it. Instead, she held her blouse modestly against her chest as she leaned far forward to tap the ashes off her cigarette, and then, reaching up to brush away a fallen curl, she let it very briefly go.

THE COURTSHIP WOULD be, as Natasza put it, *very eighteenth-century*, consisting primarily of negotiations between Lucius's mother and General Borszowski. They were married in early August 1918, shortly before her twenty-first birthday. The ceremony was modest; both parties felt that a display of ostentation would be tasteless given the political situation. At first Natasza had asked to honeymoon at a family estate near Salzburg, but for Lucius, this meant leaving his patients with Zimmer, who, after his pneumonia, had returned more befuddled than before. So they spent their wedding night at the Hotel Impérial, after a boisterous dinner at which both fathers got drunk and sang songs from the lancers and his mother finally motioned for the newly-weds to go.

Up in their room, Lucius and Natasza fell into silence. She had brought her own glass flask of almond schnapps, and poured them each a tumbler. This helped a little. Throughout the day, he had the image of Margarete appearing in the little church, or at their dinner, or running into him with his new wife as they ascended the stairs. It was almost impossible to imagine: Margarete with her heavy soldier's boots and greatcoat, Mannlicher over her shoulder, her fingers still muddy from rummaging for roots.

It was Natasza who led him to bed, who first disrobed. She was tanned from sunbathing in the mountains, all angles, smooth-legged, like someone sculpted out of bronze. He stared, while above them the fan spun quietly. The feeling came to him that he didn't deserve this kind of fortune, that he was still the child with the stutter, exiled with Feuermann from the student associations, an accidental son.

'You do not need to be gentle,' she said, after some time.

She was the only person apart from Margarete whom he had ever kissed. At first, he was taken aback by the firmness of her tongue, and his lips resisted in reflex, before he let it in. There was an unfamiliar taste to her mouth, almost metallic beneath the sweetness of the schnapps.

After a few minutes, she rose and took a *gummi* from her handbag. He didn't mind, of course? She didn't want a baby now. She had such plans for skiing that winter; there was so much to do now that the war was coming to an end. He shook his head, scandalized a little by the sheath he had seen only in soldiers' belongings. But no, he didn't mind. Of course he didn't mind.

What happened next suggested she was vastly more experienced than him.

Afterwards, he lay beside her, looking at the gold of her skin as if he had come across some kind of treasure. Faintly, he could see the evidence of a sleeveless tennis outfit and a swimsuit, and he allowed his fingers to trace the tan lines, feeling almost bold. It was enough even to retain him, for a moment, there with her, without his thoughts flying back across the mountains.

She was sleeping, and he rose to turn off the lights. At the bedside, he paused, now struck by the novelty of returning to warm sheets where someone else was waiting. It seemed impossible, this absurd luxury of hours – *hours* – unmenaced by discovery or interruption. Beyond the fleeting moments when Margarete had rested beside him after lovemaking, he had never truly slept beside another person. But now, moonlight drifting over Natasza's sleeping body, the novelty of it gave way to something else. For weeks he had anticipated his wedding night, but so distracted by the exquisite promises of consummation, he hadn't really considered the sleeping part that must come next.

But sleeping remained an uncertain proposition. The relentless dreams of Horváth had remitted somewhat after his return to medicine, but there were nights, many nights, he lurched awake.

He looked down at her, her warmly glowing shoulder.

Tomorrow, he thought, tomorrow he would tell her about his dreams. Not now – this moment couldn't be ruined. And so he gingerly slipped back into bed and waited, vigilant, watching the window turn to dawn.

It was late in the morning when she woke and kissed him. How had he slept?

'Sweet as a soldier on night watch,' he joked. And closing his eyes, he kissed her back.

They moved into an apartment belonging to her father not far away, on Hohlweggasse. For the first week, he waited for an opportunity to tell Natasza about his nightmares, but there never seemed to be a moment to bring them up. Instead, at night, after their lovemaking, he waited until she fell asleep and then went to the living room, returning to their bed before she woke. To pre-empt the awkwardness of any discovery, he told her he slipped away to deal with the endless paperwork he brought home from the hospital. It couldn't last, he knew, but during the war, he'd become an expert at stealing scraps of sleep during the spare hours of the day. And he was used to exhaustion. No, he thought: she was his wife, but still a stranger. He couldn't burden her so quickly. To speak of dreams meant speaking of Horváth and the beech tree, of what he'd done and what he'd failed to do. With time, they would grow closer, as he had with Margarete.

She spent the days reading and calling on acquaintances and playing tennis at a sports club. In the evenings they went out. The first week, his mother, anticipating that he wouldn't know what restaurants to go to, had arranged for reservations. A gift, she said, but he knew it was more of a command. She sent French champagne, patriotically re-labelled as sparkling Rheingau, and in the booth at Grand-Hôtel, bubbles rising to the backs of his eyes, he felt bold enough to ask Natasza more about her interests, her childhood, her family. To his surprise, she answered at length. The next night, drunk again, emboldened, he asked her more, about her friends, her schooling, her plan to apply to art school in Paris after the war. Then on the third night Natasza said he sounded like a doctor taking a medical history, and suddenly he felt it all come crashing down.

By the second week, their meals had grown silent. 'What do you like to talk about?' Natasza had exploded in frustration, and he stammered, 'M-medicine,' before he could keep the word from coming out. Her lip curled, and he thought that she would laugh. *Once*, he wished to add, defensively, once there was someone else who might have listened. But he feared mentioning Margarete's name in the presence of this other woman, as if her memory were something fragile and might be harmed.

When they got home, Natasza had a letter from a friend. What luck! she said: she had been invited to the Salzkammergut with Princess Dzieduszycka. And Lucius, irritated, at last finding a way to deploy his mother's encyclopedic registry of the Polish nobility, told her that there hadn't been a single princess in 'Princess' Dzieduszycka's family since the death of Sobieski (1696). Then, feeling both relief and an impending, ineluctable loneliness, he bid her go.

He slept easily the next week on the wards. When he stopped at their apartment on the day she was to return, he found a telegram from her saying that the lakes were lovely, he should come. He couldn't, of course, and he knew she knew this. When he thought of her bronze body moving through the lake water, he felt a stab of pain. She returned the next Monday with a small book of photographs of her friends, all tanned, the women in striped swimsuits, the men with smooth hair and cigarettes. The photos were a montage of such perfect human beauty that they seemed almost staged. Her neck was covered by drops of water, the suit was thin, revealing the outline of her breasts. Now, looking at it, he felt himself in the presence of a superior creature who had the power to bestow either a final blessing or disapproval. He had spent the day trying to stop the seizures of an eighteen-year-old soldier who'd been asphyxiated by phosgene blowback. At the end of the week she asked to go again.

Once more he returned to the hospital to sleep at night. He had hoped Natasza might be a solution to his loneliness, but now what was happening was even worse. He did not want to think of her, then spent the night imagining where she slept. Five days later, she called the Lamberg Palace to say she had returned early, and with some hope, he hurried home. There he found her with her sister, a long-armed lookalike, and her sister's husband, a German industrialist's son named Franz. For four nights Lucius allowed himself to go with them to restaurants, if only to lay claim to Natasza when they got home. He wished that they gossiped or slandered, so as to at least grant him some sense of moral superiority. But Franz was a veteran of the Marne, who'd spent a year in a field hospital with a festering infection after a hip fracture and then founded a home for orphans on his return. He had a pearly, perfectly placed scar across his cheekbone, was as quick and clever as Natasza, and irritatingly aware of his appeal. Yet still he was solicitous of Lucius, which somehow made matters even worse. What kind of patients did he care for? Did they need new rehabilitation equipment? His friend, Dr Sauer, had written in his textbook

that horseback riding was the quickest way back to health after
bed rest – what did Lucius think?

Lucius didn't know. He hadn't read Dr Sauer's textbook,
hadn't even heard of Dr Sauer, actually. The three others waited
for him to say something else. So he added that he thought
doctors who made broad generalizations without considering
the specifics of each patient often did more harm than good.
Natasza studied her food. Her sister smiled thinly. Franz said,
'Spoken like a true expert,' and lit a cigarette. Lucius sensed
they all had turned against him. Across the dining room, he
could see his own reflection, his pink ears, his shock of white
hair. How ugly and foreign he seemed among them! Angry
then, at them, at himself, at his mother for thinking he could
belong, he turned back to Franz.

'But I will consider using horses for our patients, thank you.'

And then he wondered aloud whether Germany would like
to donate them for the rehabilitation of the Territorial soldiers
they sent in first to battle, without helmets, two men to a single
rusty gun.

That night, Natasza asked Lucius why he had been rude
when Franz was simply trying to include him, after he'd passed
hours saying nothing at all. How annoying! Lucius was a genius,
she said, with the faintest tone of mockery. A doctor, an expert
on the human soul! Madame Krzelewska had showed her father
Lucius's assessment from back in 1913. *An unusual aptitude for
things that lie beneath the skin.* If he could make conversation with
a bunch of stutterers pretending to have shell shock, he could
clearly speak to Franz.

With these words Lucius felt own his stutter returning, and
something must have crossed his face, for she smiled with a
smile that only the very beautiful can manage, wicked and con-
ciliatory at once. He should just not sit so quietly, she said, lest

someone mistake him for one of his mutes. Then she asked offhandedly if she might spend the weekend with her sister in Trieste.

This time, Lucius said he wanted to go as well. She laughed it off. He insisted. She said it would be dull for him. He didn't play tennis, didn't dance. He insisted again. She said she didn't want to go to restaurants with him, that she had seen him staring at a waitress once, not because she was beautiful, but because she had a limp. If the waitress had at least been beautiful, that she could understand! But a cripple? She said her sister had mistaken Lucius's coat for Franz's, found *kielbasa* in his pocket, and thought it was part of a patient. She said she didn't care what he did at the hospital, but that at least he must change coats. She said her sister said Lucius's smell reminded her of the sanatorium where she had once gone to take a nervous cure, and now she, Natasza, couldn't get this out of her head.

He asked if there would be another man in Trieste.

'Yes,' she said. She didn't even hesitate. She added, 'And in the Salzkammergut, and in Berlin. Why do you think my father was so insistent I get married? At least *they* stay in bed with me. *They* sleep, *they* eat, like humans.

'What kind of monster are you, anyway?' she asked.

She had used a word in Polish that meant less a creature of evil than a sorry, accidental creation, a word one uses for a defective child, or a goat born with two heads.

If only you knew, he thought, but now he couldn't speak. Even the very grammar of his language seemed to mock him, for it occurred to him that she was the only person in his life with whom he used the informal, and this was coming quickly to an end.

She lit a cigarette and held it to her lips, as she often did after their lovemaking. 'Don't look so distraught,' she said. 'You married to placate your mother, too.'

But he hadn't, he wished to tell her. *This time it was my decision.* But he couldn't give her the pleasure of this victory. I've lost much more than you, he thought, as she took another draw from her cigarette, and left.

Compared to demobilization, his return home this time was easy.

'My wife has not been loyal,' he told his mother, and of all the explanations, it shamed him the least. There was no need to mention the sullen dinners, the impossibility of sleep. To his surprise, he found his mother kind, even apologetic. Briefly, it occurred to him that the scandal of the separation might somehow be more useful to her than the partnership of marriage; now she possessed some very compromising gossip about the daughter of the Polish Southern Command. But he stopped this thought before it went much further. No, Mother was ruthless, but such machinations were cruel beyond conception, and he knew she maintained allegiances to her blood. Still, she must have known that something like this would happen. She knew her son.

THIS WAS LATE September. His belongings were delivered to his parents' address; he hadn't even entirely unpacked. But he had little time to think about Natasza. During the final, failing days of his marriage, the full force of a simmering outbreak of influenza had arrived at the Lamberg Palace Army Rehabilitation Hospital for Neurological Injuries. By November, he'd lost twenty-seven patients and three nurses, and himself spent nearly two weeks in the third-floor quarantine, delirious with fever, listening to the gasps rising from the neighbouring beds.

When at last his fever broke, he rose and walked down to

the main ward. It was late in the afternoon, and strangely silent. A dim light filtered in through the high windows; with the fuel shortages, they had turned off the chandeliers. At the far end of the ballroom, in the shadows, he could see his nurses, and as he approached them, he found that they were gathered around a breathless, ruddy orderly holding a broadsheet, still in his snow-dusted winter coat.

THAT NIGHT HE returned home to Cranachgasse.

'You've heard?' his father said as Lucius met him in the sun-room.

Armistice, the abdication of the Royal Family, the Empire's end.

And they walked slowly to the map table, where the old retired major drew out the sabre he had worn at the Battle of Custoza and, with a flourish, swept all the armies to the floor.

17

He returned to the hospital late that evening, through empty streets.

The night was strangely warm, and he let his coat hang open. The electricity was out, and in the windows, shadows moved in the yellow glow of lamps and candles. Silence everywhere, but inside, he knew, the same word was on everyone's lips.

Armistice. Like him, they'd all been waiting, each one for something different: the return of a son, a long-promised wedding, the chance to see a baby who was now a little girl. The end of food queues – though with winter coming, this wasn't certain. The loss of titles, lands. For his mother and his father: a new Poland, or – as they might correct him – the rebirth of an old one. But for Lucius, in the months he had been waiting, the word had come to mean the single place that might yet yield the secret of what had become of Margarete.

Lemnowice. For two long years in Vienna, he had felt as if every obstacle had been placed in front of his return: the Russian Army, the flood of POW returns, and now, and this at his own bidding, Natasza. But Natasza was gone, vanished from his life as if she'd never been there, and Brusilov was back in Russia. Now, finally, after the trains, the listless wandering, the days spent dreaming of Margarete, his chance had come.

Yet in many ways the world that met him the Tuesday morning after Armistice was even more complex than that of Monday. There was the practical issue of the trains, still packed with homecoming soldiers. The sudden appearance of borders within what used to be the Empire. The need for travel papers from the newly declared 'German Austria', which for effective purposes of governance was little but a name. There was also the matter of politics. His father's clearing of the table had been a dramatic gesture. More accurately, they should all have sat down with little brushes, repainted the Austro-Hungarian forces in eight different colours, and turned them to fight each other. Already, the week before, Serbia had attacked Hungary, Czechoslovakia had attacked Hungary, and revolutionaries had stormed the Reichstag in Berlin. There were murmurs that the border between Poland and Czechoslovakia was mutually unacceptable; Russia, of course, was still in civil war. And, most worrisome for Lucius, in Galicia, skirmishes had broken out between Poland and Ukraine.

It was, his father told him, as though someone had stomped on a fire, scattering the burning embers before they put them out.

But all these obstacles seemed surmountable, all save one. Since his pneumonia, Zimmer's mind had continued to decline, and for Lucius to leave his patients alone with his old professor as their only doctor was no less than abandonment. Almost immediately after Armistice, he began to petition for a temporary replacement. He would not need long, he wrote in various letters to various ministries. The flu had receded, it had been nearly two years since he had taken any leave. Two, three weeks was all he wanted. That would be enough, he thought, to get to Lemnowice, to find anyone, anything that might lead to Margarete. Now, short of searching all of Galicia again, short of knocking on the door of every hut in every village, only Lemnowice remained.

But he received no reply. And soon, with the Medical Service

of the Austro-Hungarian Army no longer even in official exist-
ence, and Archduchess Anna, fearing some Jacobin revolt,
decamped to Switzerland, he didn't know whom to ask.

AND THEN, at last, in May, a letter came.

He received it at the hospital. At first he thought it might be
a reply to one of his petitions. But this was from an unfamiliar department. The hospital was moving, the letter said, the
patients transferring to a government sanatorium in Baden. It
had come to their attention that he was not a medical graduate,
that the wartime degrees were null and void, and that if he
wished to practise medicine, he would have to re-enroll at the
medical school that autumn. The tone was severe; it was a trav-
esty of the imperial government that he had been given such
responsibility. The archduchess would be selling the palace.
They would close the wards later that month.

He found Zimmer in his office.

'Herr Professor Doktor has heard the news?'

His old professor nodded as he chewed a toothpick, and for
a moment Lucius feared it was more plunder from the archduchess's *wunderkammer*, some scrimshawed urchin spine or
gilded rodent penis bone, or the exquisite little sceptre of a doll's
house king. But it was just a toothpick, and for the first time in
recent memory, there were no jarred monstrosities on his desk.
Zimmer's fingers clasped each other as if searching for something that had been taken from him. He reminded Lucius of one
of his great-uncles, a baron, who had spent his last years tending
the geese in the ponds behind his castle, clapping as simply as a
child when they snapped the bread out of his hand. But Zimmer
seemed to understand what was at stake.

'Where will you go?' he asked.

Behind Zimmer hung a faded tapestry showing a unicorn

sipping from a rushing forest stream. Snowy peaks rose high above it, the sky filled with soaring birds. Strange, thought Lucius, that he had never noticed it before.

He saw her walking, figure swaying in her habit, her fists full of roots and pot-herb, saw her lowering herself to him that sun-dappled morning, beneath the willow on the bank.

'To find a friend,' he said. *At last.*

THE ARMY AMBULANCES arrived the following week.

They were the same lorries he had grown familiar with at war, and pairs of porters appeared carrying the same stretchers. One by one the patients left, bowing or saluting, or kissing Lucius's hand. *This is Zothar Lukács, Doctor, a hussar thrown from his horse, an epileptic . . . Matyas Kraczki, Samuel Klein . . .* Now, saying goodbye, there was part of him that doubted his departure, and he had to remind himself that it was not his choice. His expression must have betrayed his emotion, for one of the nurses appeared at his side. 'There, there, Herr Doktor,' she whispered. 'They'll be taken care of. The hospital of Baden is lovely, state-of-the-art.' He nodded. He did not say what he was thinking then, that it was the fate he wished he could have given his patients at Lemnowice, a discharge to a sanatorium at Baden, not to more horrors of the war.

The ambulances departed, gravel crunching beneath their wheels; then more returned. When the men were gone, movers came and carried out the beds and the cots, cleared out the supply closet, and disassembled the nursing station in the centre of the ballroom.

Zimmer left in a fiacre for his old office at the university. Lucius would visit him, he hoped, and Lucius nodded. They shook hands. Over the past month, the cataracts seemed to have grown even thicker, like inlaid pearls. Then the nurses followed, bowing neatly in sequence to Lucius as they filed out. Soon there were only a few small scattered pieces of furniture, but still Lucius waited. The room was empty then, the light from the high windows illuminating the frescoes of the ersatz sky. Once, in the days before it was the hospital, there would have been grand balls and dinners, but it seemed as if it had been abandoned centuries ago. Scratches and stains covered the parquet floor. Cobwebs on the chandeliers. The painting of Cadmus and the dragon back in its place high upon the wall.

A door at the end of the great hall opened. For a moment he expected a new arrival, a patient who hadn't heard the news. But beside the race of warriors emerging from the dragon's teeth, he was alone.

Outside, a cold wind had begun to blow.

THE QUESTION THEN was how to return.

His best hope was to go by train to Dolina, by then the closest stop in Polish-controlled territory to Lemnowice. At the North station, crowded with travellers, he enquired about tickets. Yes, the old Emperor Ferdinand Northern Railway to Kraków was fully open, the ticket seller told him; from there one could go as far west as Lemberg, now known by its Polish name Lwów. But with the Ukrainian insurgency, the railway south of Lwów was under Polish military control. Civilians were forbidden.

'Thank you,' said Lucius, leaving the ticket window as another traveller pushed into his place. From Lwów, he might hire a motor car, but from what he'd heard, the roads were in such disrepair as to be almost impassable. And, just that month, his mother, not one to be intimidated, had cancelled a trip to Drohobycz after vigilantes had held two of her agents until she paid their ransom.

Thinking of his mother, he wondered if he might approach her, asking for her influence in securing passage from friends in the Polish Army. But he knew she wouldn't permit such madness. Think what kind of kidnapping target you would make, she'd tell him. And for your pretty little nurse, who likely isn't there at all.

A rowdy flock of pigeons was scuttling in the station rafters above. Around him the crowds continued to press towards the ticket windows. For a moment, he felt his hopes again collapse, before his thoughts circled once more back to his mother, to the army, and he knew what he could do.

HE FOUND NATASZA at her apartment on Hohlweggasse.

It was a hot day. She came to the door in a kimono, a cigarette between her fingers, her hair done up in a chignon.

'Lucius. What a surprise.' By the old laws of the state, she was still his wife, but she waited for an explanation for his visit, as if she could dismiss him without inviting him to come inside.

But this time he was not so easily disposed of. He looked past her. 'May I?'

'Of course. Do enter. It's been some time.'

They sat together in the living room, where he used to pass the hours of the night. If she remembered, she gave no indication. Now, she was coldly civil, asking crisply after his family, his work. He told her about the hospital closing, how he planned to return to medical school that autumn.

'You! Back at school!'

He didn't mind, he said. What he had learned was war medicine; it was time for something else.

In turn, she told him how she had lived the past six months in Italy. Now that the new Austrian government was supposedly planning to reform the imperial marriage laws, she was secretly engaged again, to an Italian, a sculptor. Yes, truly an Italian sculptor; it was so predictable. The wedding would happen as soon as paperwork for the divorce was put in place.

Our divorce, he thought. He said, 'I suppose I should offer you congratulations.'

She stubbed out her cigarette. 'Well. I am guessing you're not here just to pay a social visit.'

Across the room stood a mirror, paints, a canvas. Briefly he wondered as to their purpose. But he, too, was finished with small talk. 'I need a favour.'

'Oh?'

'From your father.'

She listened coldly as he explained the situation with the rails. All he needed was a letter, he said. He could get to Lwów alone; but from there he needed permission to travel south on the Polish Army trains.

She lit another cigarette and shook her head. She was sorry. Her father was in Warsaw now, meeting Marshal Piłsudski. There were wars with Russia and Ukraine, hadn't he heard? And if Russia wasn't enough to deal with, the general wasn't happy about her new fiancé, always having wished she might marry another Pole. The last thing she wanted was to remind him of Lucius.

As she spoke, Lucius could feel his temper rising. 'It would take nothing but a telegram,' he protested. 'All he would have to do is dictate a letter to an aide.'

'And I told you, he can't be bothered. Maybe in a couple of months, when I see him in Kraków.'

'Just a letter. A single sentence. Eight words, maybe ten. He dictates hundreds a day.'

'And I said not now. Why do you need to go there anyway?'

Lucius leaned back, fighting the urge to raise his voice. After everything, he thought, at least you owe me this.

She had grown silent, her way of saying she was finished. But he didn't move.

'Is there anything else?' she asked at last.

Lucius looked down at his hands, then back at her. 'My mother says the general's reputation is impeccable. Especially in a time of so much graft.'

Natasza eyed him cautiously. 'And what does that mean?'

'Just that I was always surprised to hear your story about his buying champagne from the enemy, or how you and your sister were escorted by soldiers of the Third Brigade to Zakopane to go skiing during the war. Soldiers diverted from the front.'

She froze. The tiniest movement, almost imperceptible. But he saw, and she knew that he had seen.

She drew on her cigarette. 'Blackmailing us won't work, Lucius.'

'Oh, I have no interest in blackmailing you,' he said. 'Not me.' He paused, realizing that for a brief moment, he was actually savouring the revenge. 'But then, it's the kind of story that my mother *loves*.'

Across the room, he noticed the image on the canvas for the first time, a self-portrait, a nude. He waited briefly for the pang, but there was none.

IT TOOK A WEEK for the letter to arrive.

A single sentence, guaranteeing *Lucius Krzelewski, friend of Poland, passage from Lwów to Dolina, and return.*

The *return* was a nice touch, he thought. Generous of her. He hadn't asked for that.

He went directly to the train station, buying a ticket departing the following morning for Lwów, through Oderberg, now called Bohumín, in the nation of Czechoslovakia, just eight months old.

That night he slipped into his father's study. Both of his parents were out at a reception somewhere in the city, and Jadwiga had been given the week off to visit her family. A menagerie of lances, arquebuses and bayonets covered one of the walls above a case of handguns. There, among the antique duck's-foot pistols, three-barrel volley guns and Italian hand cannons, was the old service revolver his father had tried to teach him to use when war broke out.

The case creaked as he opened it.

On the shelves built into the walnut panelling, he found an imperial atlas, thumbing through the pages until he found a map of the Carpathians. 1904. But the mountains hadn't changed. He tore it out. From his father's hunting kit he took a compass. He'd been lost once. This time he couldn't take the chance.

Deep in his wardrobe, he found the rucksack and old canteen he'd been reissued with on the trains. He ran his fingers over the buckles; despite the months that had passed since he had worn it, he could still recall its weight, the way that snow collected in the seams, the creak when it was loaded. He slipped it over his shoulder. He had almost forgotten this other part of him, unbound from the house on Cranachgasse. This other person, who had spent two years with only what he could carry on his back.

From the kitchen: a round of heavy rye, a jar of pralines, and a piece of cheese. From his desk drawer: a stash of kronen, and then, uncertain if he could use Austrian currency in Czechoslovakia or Poland, his boyhood collection of silver coins.

Back in his room, he pored over the map, tracing the knuckles of the hills. Lemnowice was unmarked, but he found Bystrystya and, following the valley up, the bend in the river where the village perched. From there the thin blue line wound through the green swathe of forest. A willow, somewhere there. Two boulders by a riverbank.

With one of his old medical school pencils, he marked the village with a little x.

His parents returned late that night while he pretended to be sleeping. He slipped out early, before they woke. On the table in the dining room, where his mother had proposed he find a wife, he left a simple note. He was going to Galicia to see an acquaintance from his army days. *Don't worry about the ransom*, he thought of adding, but the letter alone felt spectacularly defiant. She would know exactly what it meant.

On the Ringstrasse he hired a fiacre to take him to the North Station, where, within the crenellated arches, his train was waiting.

THE SUN WAS beginning to rise as they left the city.

He sat by the window, facing forward. In the compartment: a family of six, four wide-eyed children piled onto two seats; a soldier; a young man, dandied for the voyage, theatrically solicitous of his young, pregnant wife. Outside, a low light fell across the stockyards, where rail workers loaded up a car with rusted pipes. Further along they passed a row of decommissioned trains, paint peeling now and windows empty, grass tufts growing from the narrow sills like old men's eyebrows.

They slowed as they crossed the Danube on a rattling iron bridge.

They picked up speed. Across from him, the children ate sunflower seeds, neatly spitting out the wads of shells into a tin can they passed back and forth. The light was bright now, warming the window in an amber glow; he had to squint to watch the country pass. Boys played along the railway, miming aim at the passing carriages, then gesticulating dramatically as if they had just been shot. Passing Deutsch-Wagram, he recalled a visit long ago with his father and two older brothers, to see where Napoleon had gone into battle. A memory now, his brothers searching the fields for bones and bullets. Father scanning the horizon with binoculars, while a sunburnt Lucius held out the Orders of Battle like a little aide-de-camp.

Can you imagine? said his father. *The bodies, the horses. This would have been bodies as far as the eye can see.* But no, Lucius couldn't imagine then.

At the March River, the railway turned north, leaving the floodplain, and the land began to rise.

It was noon when they reached the border. At Břeclav, once Lundenburg, the train was boarded by Czechoslovakian police, wearing old Habsburg uniforms, the imperial insignias torn from their epaulettes. They had an air of make-believe, as if they were imperial officers *playing* officers of the free nation of Czechoslovakia. They stopped briefly in the compartment and collected passports, though neither the passengers nor the policemen seemed to know what for. Lucius thought briefly of his father's revolver in his rucksack on the rack above him, the stories of militiamen, the shifting loyalties, now wondering what the police would think.

They didn't check.

Beyond the city, the fields gave way to forests. The Morava appeared, dark blue and beaded with little hamlets. Barges moved in the distance. Across from him, the young man and his pregnant wife began to eat a pungent sandwich of egg and onion. The domesticity of the scene seemed almost impossible against the knowledge that within hours they would be entering territory once racked by war; but with the warmth, he soon found himself beginning to doze off.

It was evening when they crossed the Oder, and night when they entered Bohumín.

IN BOHUMÍN, he was told the train to Lwów would be leaving in the early morning.

He left to look for lodgings. It was hot, and the air was heavy with smoke from factories flanking the track. An oily film seemed to coat the buildings, the peddlers with their carts of pears and leeks, a pair of skinny horses who fought their bridles at the entrance to a dry-goods shop. There were beggars everywhere; only seven months of independence, and already it had the air of a frontier town, the sense that things had been pushed there only to get stuck, like the detritus gathering at the corner of a wall.

A light rain began to fall, and the streets exhaled a fetid breath. At the station, he had been given the name of a hotel in an imposing imperial building off the main street, with a thick red carpet leading up the stairs to the reception. A heavy woman sat at the desk, dressed in a kind of black nightgown that seemed to have been cut from mourning cloth. Her arms were bare and dewlapped, her face plethoric, her breath laboured and wheezy as she passed him a key from the pigeon holes behind her desk.

He slept fitfully. The walls were covered by peeling, blood-red paper, and the light came from a candle, stuck directly to the bedside table in its wax. The sheets were pilled and dirty, and twice he turned on the light, certain that he would find them full of lice. But there was nothing. Just my imagination, he thought, trying to find some lightness in his panic. *Once you feel Her, Pan Doctor, you can't escape.*

Around midnight, he was aroused from half-slumber by hammering and shouts of authority, and he braced himself for someone to burst through his door. Later he heard weeping. It rose, gasping, so loud and urgent that he ran into the hall, thinking someone was dying or giving birth. Then it went silent. By then it was four. He did not return to sleep.

Back at the station, he made his way to the platform for trains heading east. Even in the two hundred paces that separated the eastern and south-western lines, the difference was palpable. More and more people speaking Polish, more scraps of Galician costume: vests, embroidered blouses, the occasional woman in a highlander cap. It was not hard to imagine Margarete there, among them. He was getting closer. If not to her, to the place where he would begin to search.

At the platform, he learned that the train to Lwów had been delayed because of problems with the gauge changes on the Breslau line. From a station vendor, he bought a dry piece of cake and a cup of roasted chicory advertised as coffee.

The train came.

The compartment sat six and was full when he entered. On the far wall, a pair of old women sat side by side in identical dresses of a coarse brown muslin, buttoned to the chin. There were two old men in stiff green vests, whom he took to be their husbands, one reading a Czech newspaper, the other Polish, each creased neatly along a column. The other two seats were taken by a woman in a light-blue blouse and a sleeping child in a gown.

Lucius stepped back out of the door to check his ticket against the number of the compartment, but by then the young woman had gathered up the child in her arms. 'I'm sorry,' she said in Polish. She shifted over to the window, freeing the middle seat.

Lucius nodded to her in thanks, set his rucksack on the rack above them, and took his seat. Outside there was a long whistle and then the train began to move.

Through the pipe yards again, the brick factories and smokestacks giving way to smaller workshops. It wasn't yet nine, and already the day was warm. He removed his coat and folded it on his lap. Outside, the city began to drop away. Fields again. In the distance he could see low hills, and perhaps the hint of mountains through the haze.

'I noticed your ticket. You are going to Lemberg . . . I mean, Lwów?'

He turned. Her hair was honey-coloured, loose down her back. Eyes dark brown, skin pale, a little burnt. The child sleeping in her lap.

'Have you been there before?' she asked.

He hesitated, uncertain of her intentions. It was a bit brazen, he thought, for a woman travelling alone to solicit conversation. But he was grateful for someone to speak to.

'Only during the war,' he said.

'You were a soldier?'

'Not quite. A doctor.'

'Oh. You weren't in the Fourth Army, were you?'

He paused, struck by the specificity of the question. 'No,' he said, more hesitantly now. 'The Third. Later the Seventh.'

Her face lit up. 'But after the Brusilov Offensive, many of the companies from the Fourth Army were integrated into the Seventh. Perhaps you *met* men of the Fourth?'

If her voice didn't seem suddenly plaintive, he would have smiled at the incongruity of this young woman sounding like his father talking army organization. 'You seem to know more than me,' he said. 'I left the front after Brusilov. I was in the medical corps, on the trains, then at a hospital in Vienna.'

'I see.' But it didn't really seem as if she'd heard him. Carefully, so as not to wake the child, she leaned forward to a canvas sack at her feet and extracted a package bound with yellowing twine. With one hand she untied and unfolded the wrapping paper, which clearly had been folded and unfolded many times. She withdrew a photo, mounted on cardboard.

She handed it to him. On her hand he saw a wedding band, the nails on her fingers bitten to the quick.

'Did you ever see him? His name is Tomasz Bartowski – he was in the Ninth Corps, Tenth Infantry Division.'

In the photo, she was sitting with a young man in an outdoor café. A decorative cloth was spread over the table, and there was a single, extravagant piece of cake with two forks buried in its flank. His hand rested on hers, and both of them were smiling; he wore a boater, jauntily angled, and her striped white blouse rose all the way to her chin. Behind them stood a waiter with a tray of cigarettes and chocolates, his torso bisected by the frame.

'I'm so sorry,' said Lucius, now understanding why she knew so much. 'I don't recognize him.'

'Can you look more closely? If you were a doctor, you must have taken care of many men.'

Many, many men, thought Lucius.

But still the face was unfamiliar.

'I've been looking since the war,' she said, as she took the photo back. 'I even went to Vienna, to the War Office. He isn't on their casualty lists. So I have hope. They said he may have been taken prisoner of war, that even though most of the prisoners have returned, the Bolsheviks have kept some of them for labour. Then in Kraków, I met a man from his company who said he was pretty certain Tomasz had been injured at Lutsk, but lightly. That he was probably at the regimental hospital in Jarosław. He wasn't there. But a nurse recognized him, said she was certain she had seen him among the wounded at the Przemyśl hospital. Except he wasn't there either. Now I've heard the hospitals are being emptied, to make space for the wounded from the Ukrainian war. So I'm going back to Jarosław, to start again.'

'Maybe you just don't recognize him,' she added, when she saw he didn't have an answer. 'It's an old photo, from long ago.' Then she handed him another photograph. 'I have this one, too.'

The second was from their wedding, the young woman dressed in a traditional wedding dress from the Galician lowlands. For a moment Lucius let his eyes linger. There was something striking about the image: her face a little flushed, her eyes darker, wilder. Her hair was plaited, the braids folded upon on her head and bound in a tumble of white damask and flowers. The skin of her neck glistened, and the weight of a breast pushed at the cotton pleats of her blouse. She had been dancing, he realized. Right up until the moment the wedding photographer had taken their portrait, and here she was, a little out of breath.

He felt as though he had been looking too long, but she didn't seem to mind. If anything, she seemed proud of her laughing self. 'I was fatter then,' she said. She touched the photo affectionately. 'The baby, and the worry, made me lean.'

He shuffled the photographs. Out of the corner of his eye, he was aware now of her neck, bare that warm morning, and the fine sprinkling of freckles that ended just above her collar.

The third photo was a studio portrait, probably taken at the time of Tomasz's enlistment. In it, he wore a crisp uniform and deeply serious expression, while at his side his young wife smiled as if she had just been teasing when the bulb went off.

'And this is the card he sent me.' She turned it over and showed Lucius the postmark. Tarnów. He couldn't help reading, *Dearest Adelajda! We are all well. I am still with Hanek; he too is well. I think of you always and carry your photograph next to my heart. Tomorrow we go to*—but a blue censor's pen had cruelly removed the following two lines. She peered at it, as if, after so many tries, the words might suddenly appear. Then she placed it in the stack and folded the paper back up. The child stirred in her lap.

'There, there,' she whispered. 'Shhh, sleep. We will find Papa. Sleep.'

She turned back to Lucius. 'He's had a fever for almost five days now. I had thought it would have gone away. But you're a doctor, maybe you know what's wrong.'

He hesitated. I *was*. Not any more, according to the new Republic. But this mattered less than the fact that lectures and clinics in paediatrics belonged to the seventh semester, which he had planned to start that first autumn of the war.

He thought of the village children back in Lemnowice, trying to teach them to listen to their hearts.

'My patients were all soldiers,' he said.

She didn't seem to register his answer. 'I've been giving him this.' She took out a bottle of patent medicine, its miraculous effects prominently advertised on a bright red label. 'The pharmacist said three drops whenever he's crying. But all it does is make him sleep.' She touched his forehead with the back of her hand, then touched her own, then again touched his. 'He's still so hot.'

For the first time since the start of their journey, Lucius looked closely at the child. He must have been around two years old. He was barefoot, and the gown, probably his nightwear, was of cotton, stained about the neck and hem. He slept with his arms thrown up above his head, like a pantomime of a person falling. Cheeks pink, fingernails almost translucent, ears like porcelain.

Lucius felt the attention of the other passengers as he

examined the boy, but the child was so flushed it was hard to discern a rash. Were there any other symptoms? he asked Adelajda. Cough? *Oh, yes.* Diarrhoea? *Yes, a little.* Bumps in his mouth? *Not that I have seen.* But he's not eating? *He just takes a little milk.* He tried to open the boy's mouth, but the boy resisted. He pressed an ear against his ribcage. *A murmur?* But with the rumbling of the train, he couldn't hear. Glands swollen, but not to the degree he might expect in quinsy; though he was thinking of adults.

'Has he had his smallpox vaccination?'

She shook her head; there had been shortages, the doses had been reserved for soldiers. But she'd seen smallpox; he didn't have the blisters.

Not yet, thought Lucius grimly. The cough made it less likely, but just the thought made Lucius's ear and cheek feel warmer, where they had touched the child's chest. But I've also been vaccinated; he had to remind himself of this.

Fevers of childhood. Roseola, scarlet fever, measles, rubella, influenza . . .

Feuermann, with his internship at the rural clinic, would have known.

He looked at the tincture, which appeared to be a preparation of laudanum, without any mention of a dose. She said she gave it to him whenever he was crying? She was lucky she hadn't killed him. So he *could* help, at least a little. He gave it back. 'I would stay away from this.'

They were passing fields again. Beyond, he thought he could see mountains. They entered Tarnów. Now the signs of war were everywhere. Broken artillery filled the junkyards outside the station, and the grass traced discarded skeletons of trucks. Adelajda had returned the packet to her bag, and after a time he realized that she was crying softly. One of the old women watched her, emotionless, but the other passengers made an effort not to stare. He had the impulse to comfort her, but he didn't know what to say. That she should stop looking for her husband? Go home, at least until the little boy was well?

'I am also going to look for someone I lost during the war.'

The words came unplanned.

There was silence. She sniffed, then turned, eyes beseeching. 'Your wife?'

Almost. Perhaps one day . . .

'No, not my wife.'

'You loved her, though.'

She said this with such naturalness, that he answered, 'Yes. I did.'

She brightened almost immediately. 'Then you're like me,' she said. 'You know, a customs officer once told me that half the continent was looking for the other half. Now you, too. See?'

He nodded. There was something in her hopefulness that touched him like a balm. He could almost see her as she had been the moments before her wedding photo, a swirl of colour and laughter, her eyes flashing, her flower-embroidered tresses swaying as she danced.

She said, 'And you think she is in Lwów?'

'Not Lwów. I don't know where she is. I last saw her at a field hospital, in the mountains. So I was going to return there first.'

'Oh, and when did you last see her?'

'June.' He paused. 'In '16.'

'*16?*' He sensed a sudden slackening of her optimism. '*16. And you haven't given up.'

He did not know whether she had meant this in admiration or in pity, and was about to add that he hadn't been searching this whole time, when the train lurched and, shuddering, began to slow. The luggage rocked above them; the little boy nearly tumbled from his mother's lap. He began to cry.

They came to a stop. Outside, a lone road led off through fallow fields, blotched with scattered clumps of wild mustard. The passengers looked at one another. One of the men took out his watch.

'I didn't know we were stopping,' Lucius said.

'We're not. Not until Rzeszów.' Adelajda leaned against the window to try to see. 'Sometimes they have trouble with the rail. We have to wait. Sometimes for quite some time.'

Outside, a group of horsemen rode past, and Lucius sensed Adelajda tensing. Then the men rode back. There was shouting in Polish further up the line, something about boarding, but Lucius couldn't make out everything they said. Behind them there was a clatter as the door to the carriage opened and a voice called out. Then footsteps, banging on compartment doors.

In Polish: 'Everyone in your seats!'

Adelajda's son, who had finally quietened in her arms, began to cry again. As she stroked his hair, she leaned towards Lucius, and said, very softly, 'Militias, loyal to Poland. The same thing happened last month. They are looking for enemy sympathizers. Because of the wars with Ukraine and Russia.' Then in a much lower voice, 'Last time they detained all young men travelling alone. Say that I'm your wife.'

He thought of the detailed map to the province of Galicia, his father's revolver, tucked neatly in the bag above his head. His old army papers, from before Natasza. 'But my passport says that I'm unmarried.'

Now Adelajda didn't drop her gaze from him. 'No. We were married in Vienna in 1916, but the new Austrian Republic asked us to resubmit our marriage licence before travelling. But they bungled it; Poles love stories about how the Austrians bungle things. This is our son. His name is Paweł Krzelewski: that is your family name, right? I saw it on your ticket. And my maiden name was Bartowska, like it says on mine. We are going to Jarosław to visit my aunt, Vanda Cenek. She is a war widow; her husband died fighting for Polish independence in the Pripet, a great patriot. We plan to spend a month with her at a small farm belonging to my cousin. It is too hot in the city for our child who, we must remind them, is very sick.'

'My ticket says my destination is Lwów.'

'Your ticket says your destination is Lwów because the ticket office in the Nordbahnhof bungled it. You will disembark at Jarosław with me, to visit my aunt.'

'But . . .' Lucius began, as the carriage door slid open.

'Papers,' said a young man in an unmarked uniform.

Adelajda put her free hand on Lucius's arm.

Lucius removed his passport and ticket, and passed them over with those of the older couples. 'Yours,' the young man said to Adelajda.

'They're in my bag,' she said. She leaned over and leafed through it with her free hand, struggling with little Paweł, who had begun to cry again.

'Hurry,' the guard said. At last she handed them over. The soldier studied the papers of the older couples before handing them back. His cheeks were pink, covered with peach fuzz, his eyes bright blue. He looked perhaps sixteen. A rifle was slung around his chest, and a pistol sat in a holster on his belt.

He looked at Lucius.

'You two are travelling together?'

Adelajda didn't give him time to answer. 'My husband met me in Bohumín. I was in Rybnik with my family. We're going to Jarosław, to see my aunt.'

'You ticket says Lwów.' He was staring at Lucius. 'And your papers say you're single. But this is your wife.'

Again Adelajda was faster. 'We filed papers in January.'

'Really?' The young man smiled as if he'd unearthed a dirty secret. 'The baby must be what, two years old? Three?'

Her face hardened. 'That's none of your business.'

'I'd say it is – your story doesn't hang together.'

'And I'd say that not everyone had the leisure to file papers during the war.' She paused 'Or perhaps you wouldn't know? My husband didn't even meet his son until demobilization. You look like a baby. Were you playing with your dolls while your brothers served?'

Lucius looked at her. He had thought at first that her taking offence was calculated. But now he worried that something else was boiling over, that she was no longer in control.

He interrupted. 'My wife means no disrespect,' he said. 'I . . . I . . . it has been hard for all of us, you see . . .'

But the young man had retained their papers. 'Come with me,' he said.

Lucius's heart pounded; he began to rise.

'Not you. This one.' The young man pointed at her with his chin.

Adelajda shook her head. 'On whose authority?'

The young man took a step towards them. Now Lucius thought of General Borszowski's letter in his bag. *Friend of Poland.* Surely this would mean something, as would the signature of the general. But the letter made no mention of a wife.

'I can explain.'

But the young man ignored him entirely. 'I'm waiting, *Pani* . . .'

She looked off in defiance. 'I will not put up with this. I was born a Pole. I lost a brother for Poland, nearly gave my husband. My baby has drunk my love of Poland in his milk . . .'

'Good. You can explain that to my captain.' He paused. 'Let's go.'

'I'll come,' said Lucius, louder.

'Not you,' said the young man, angrier now. 'You can stay with the baby while this patriot comes with me.'

Adelajda looked at him. He knew, just as she knew, that not to pass him Paweł would risk betraying them entirely. She leaned over and whispered something Lucius couldn't hear. Then, 'Stay with Papa. I'll be back.'

But the moment she moved, Paweł began to grab wildly at her, her arm, her hair, her blouse. She had to pry him off. He grabbed a finger, then again her hair. A wail rose from him. 'Please,' she said to Lucius, who reached over to help. But the boy, despite his illness, was fierce in his resistance, and it took a few more tries to pry him out of Adelajda's arms. 'Shhh . . .' Lucius whispered, but the wailing only grew louder. He struggled to contain the child, at last enfolding him in his arms. It occurred to him that he had never truly held – not just touched, but truly held – a child in his life. It seemed impossible. There must have been a younger cousin, a nephew, some time in the past, but the force of the little limbs was something he had never anticipated. And the fever was nothing like he had felt in his patients, a dry, searing heat that radiated through the light gown. Still Paweł twisted for his mother. 'Shhh . . .' Lucius whispered again. He could feel every eye in the compartment upon him. What would a father do?

Roseola, scarlet fever, measles, rubella, influenza . . .

'Shhh . . .' he said, lips touching the hot skin of Paweł's head.

'Let's go,' the soldier said.

Again, Adelajda looked to Lucius, her eyes betraying desperation. He had a sense suddenly of a new realm of loss that he had never really known existed. He looked up. 'In my bag . . . I have a letter . . .'

But the soldier put his hand on his holster. 'Do you want your son to see me make him an orphan, *Pani*?'

She rose.

'Now!'

She made it to the door. Life had left her; her skin was almost green, and for a moment Lucius thought she would collapse. She turned again. 'Paweł,' she said. 'This is Papa. Stay with him. He'll care for you until I'm back. He'll care for you . . .'

Her voice broke. The boy was screaming, his face scarlet, twisting with such a force that Lucius could scarcely hold him. He could see his little teeth, the trembling vibrato of his tongue.

But Adelajda couldn't go any further. She turned and lunged for him. The soldier grabbed her by the shoulder and hurled her against the far wall of the corridor.

A shot.

Then voices, footsteps pounding through the train. More soldiers, pushing past them. Lucius saw Adelajda's hands go up, covering her head. More shouts. *Hurry!* The soldier grabbed Adelajda and threw her back into the compartment, tickets and passports scattering on the floor. Paweł broke free and tumbled into her arms. Lucius looked back to the door, but the men were all gone, storming out into the fields, where a figure now was running. Another shot. He saw the figure go down in the grass, then come back up again, now at a slant, then fall again. Then three men were on him.

They lifted him, carried him back struggling towards the front of the train and out of view. Then from the rear came more shouts, then two more men were marched forward, hands on their heads. A horseman rode past, his open greatcoat waving in the wind.

Then silence.

In the distance, a hawk circled above the fields.

At Lucius's side, Adelajda held Paweł tightly to her, pressed her face against his cheek, his forehead, his hands. She let her hair fall around him, willowing them together in its shelter. Around the little boy's wrist was a rosary bracelet, and at times she stopped and kissed it, murmuring, 'Mother Maria, Mama, Mama, Mama . . .'

Across the compartment, the old twin sisters watched them impassively. They would have heard much of the earlier conversation, Lucius knew. They could have betrayed them. He wanted to thank them for their silence, but to do so seemed to implicate them, to put them all at risk.

Another of the horsemen rode past. 'Lower your blinds,' he shouted. 'All passengers! Blinds down! What are you staring at? Countrymen, lower your blinds, there is nothing here to see!' Lucius rose and pulled the cord. His shirt was soaked with Paweł's tears, and a strand of mucus spanned his arm.

Engines louder now.

Adelajda's murmurs growing softer. 'Mama Mama Mama Mama.'

They lurched forward, on.

THE SUN WAS beginning to set when they reached Jarosław station.

For the rest of the journey they'd been mostly silent. She had retreated into the child, holding him and cooing, chastened, Lucius suspected, by the risk she'd taken, by how perilously close she had come to such extraordinary loss. He sensed, and sensed she sensed, that perhaps they had committed some transgression. For all the gravity of their previous conversation, there had also been something unspoken, not quite a flirtation, but a hint of possibility.

Say that I'm your wife.

This is your son; his name is Paweł Krzelewski.

There was more than one way to understand these words.

My husband met me in Bohumín.

But now they both had retreated from whatever dream they'd tested. He to his world; she to hers. In Rzeszów, where the train was swarmed by children selling fistfuls of currant sprays, he had purchased some for Paweł, but beyond a whispered *Thank you*, Adelajda said nothing else.

He looked out the window at the approaching station. The beginning of the journey – with the young couple and their egg-and-onion sandwich, the old men with their stiff jackets and crisply folded newspapers – this moment, almost from an older, pre-war age, had lured him into a kind of complacent fantasy about what lay ahead. But the encounter with the militia had cast the true recklessness of what he was doing into much sharper relief. Again, he had to remind himself that all reports said that the fighting was concentrated around the rails and cities. That in the mountains he'd be safer. Or so he hoped.

The train had stopped, and Adelajda began to gather up her belongings. Lucius watched her, waiting for words to be exchanged. But she acted now as if she didn't know him, and it was only at the door that she looked back. The little boy was sleeping on her shoulder. With a flicker her fingers she waved goodbye. She left.

A moment later she returned. As she sat, her arm brushed against Lucius.

For a moment, he thought she had decided to travel on.

Then, very softly, she whispered the name of a street in Rybnik. 'Perhaps,' she said, 'if you don't find the person you are looking for, you can come and find me.'

She didn't wait for an answer. Again she rose. Across the compartment the old women watched him. He heard Adelajda disappear down the corridor. He turned back to the window as the train began to move. She was there, amid the crowd mingling on the platform, and he wanted her to cast a backward glance, but she seemed resolute now in her decision not to turn.

IT WAS CLOSE to midnight when he reached Lwów. Now, everything moved swiftly, without a hitch. He presented himself the next morning to the garrison, where soldiers took target practice on the same slate-grey dummies he remembered from the years before. By midday, letter in hand, he was on the train to Dolina, in a cattle car with a drunk, deploying Polish rifle battalion heading off to their new war. They reached the station late in the evening. There, a small hotel was advertising vacancies, but he no longer wished to delay his journey, setting out on foot along the overgrown rails.

18

HE PASSED THE night in an abandoned station, on a decommissioned railway south of Dolina. It was of standard imperial construction, and not yet stripped of its Habsburg double eagle. Were it not on the other side of the mountains, it might have been the same building in which he found the hussar waiting with their horses years before. The same board for posting timetables, the same bench that once had sustained the troika of waiting mothers. Roof now caving. Walls already beginning their crumbling return to earth. Otherwise empty, save for a tall trapezoid of goldenrod in the light cast by the empty door.

He slept inside on his jacket, on earth wet with summer rain. It was a tentative sleep; in a dream that seemed to cross into his waking moments, he found himself back on the train, running through the corridors, searching compartment after compartment for Margarete. At last, the dream was broken by a pittering reconnaissance about his rucksack, whiskers on his cheek. Nose to his nose: he lurched awake.

Outside, the mountains were beginning to declare themselves against the early summer dawn.

From his bag, he extracted the page torn from the imperial atlas and spread it over the bench. Back in Vienna, he had focused his attention on a highway that skirted the foothills before joining the road that climbed through Bystrystya to Lemnowice. But after the attack on the train, he wanted to get away from the flatlands as soon as possible. Light dashes through the mountains suggested roads passable by horse. Assuming they were still there fifteen years after the atlas was published, they'd serve well for someone on foot. It was lonelier, but he now worried much more about men than wolves.

From the station, the road south was broad, the mud thick and heavy. In the fields, high grass crowded out the maize and sunflowers. My God, thought Lucius as he stared into the green expanse, he had almost forgotten the land's fecundity. Great heaps of flax and St John's wort rose on the roadside berms, and the road itself, a paisley of mud and tyre tracks, was overgrown with brome. Ahead, the mountains rose before him in their grandeur, looming, massive, like the rumpled repose of a stage curtain with its rich, brocaded pleats.

So here he was, in the little hatch marks on his father's map, the word *KARPATEN* splayed before him across the land. But a finger's-breadth to travel yet.

He walked swiftly, his eyes alert for the possibility of other travellers, but he saw no one else. After an hour, at a crossroads, he came across the remains of a field camp, deep in mud, as if half-buried by a deluge. There were dented tins, a bent fork and an old decaying tarp. A band of sparrows argued in the shadow of a rusting field oven, where a burst of hound's tongue had begun to seed. Beyond this: some scraps of uniform, flapping in a morning breeze. A skull and scattered teeth, a rind of scalp, a pair of ribcages, white as stone.

Like Cadmus, he thought, recalling the painting hanging above the chair for minor surgeries, the earth sewn with the dragon's fangs, from which would grow a fiercer race of men.

It was not yet nine, and already the grass was seething with heat and life. He rolled up his coat, tied it below his rucksack, and pulled up his sleeves, still dirty with their snail's track of snot. Butterflies had settled on his shirt collar, and he shook them off; then, feeling generous, let them remain there. After another hour, he saw his first people, two farmers in a distant field. They stopped their work and watched him, without greeting. Then two young boys, leading a pair of reluctant, mud-caked sheep.

He walked until dusk, stopping only to eat, staying clear of settlements, wary of how they might treat an unfamiliar visitor at night. At last, alone, exhausted, he turned off the road and, near a narrow stream, laid his coat down within the shelter of a willow.

A frog was croaking. As he rested, memories, stirred by the day, descended. The crushed-grass smell, the hint of pine sap drifting from the distance. The way the sparrows swayed balletically on the umbels of the wild carrot, snipping at the insects they encountered in their orbits. The way the mud caked on his boots. Yes: wrapped in the rustling of the willow he could almost hear Margarete's laughter. She seemed so close now that he had to remind himself that he couldn't expect to find her yet. That he couldn't lose himself to hopes and expectations. If he was lucky, very lucky, there would be a villager who knew what had happened, or perhaps a clue left in the church. Like a seam running through the great mass of possibilities. And from there he would push on.

There were other possibilities, of course, he realized. He could find the village ransacked, destroyed like so many others. The church in ruins. Corpses left behind to decompose across the Cadmean earth.

He stared up at the night sky and fought very hard to keep this from his mind.

He began again before dawn.

The land grew hilly, and he checked the map and compass, following a narrow, rocky road. His stomach growled. His feet, in his old army boots, began to ache, and when he stopped to readjust his socks, he found blisters on both his heels. Inside his shirt, a spray of insect bites had appeared after his night sleeping in the grass. His face was burnt; his head throbbed. He'd forgotten a hat. He, with his Icelander's complexion, had brought a half-century-old revolver and forgotten a hat.

He passed a man leading a donkey and a wagon, piled with belongings and a pair of children. Its wheels were spokeless, cut from solid blocks of wood, like something out of a children's encyclopedia entry on the ancient history of transport. He recalled the family he had encountered with the hussar, the pilfered rabbits. As if they had been wandering ever since. But now there was no mother, and the children's summer clothing was ragged, sustained by fraying knots of string.

He had been taking small bites from a loaf of bread purchased two days before in Bohumín. Seeing them, he felt ashamed in front of their hunger, so he offered it. They looked to their father, who nodded, and then they scrambled down from the wagon to seize it, retreating to the safety of their bags.

'Where are you going?' their father asked, in something halfway between Polish and Slovakian, after trying out two other tongues.

'Lemnowice.'

'Ah.'

'You know it?'

'Yes.'

'Far?'

'Not as far as where you've come from.'

The children gnawed at the bread, watching him.

'And you're alone?' the father asked.

'Yes.'

A long pause.

'You have your reasons,' the father said.

THE ROAD WOUND on, through meadows and scattered copses of trees. He finished his water and the last of his food. The land was steeper now; the earth shimmered with run-off. Rain clouds came, opened and left.

Soon he began to regret his fit of charity. He was hungry, and the water in the rivers was too muddy to drink. Instead, he grabbed clumps of high grass and sucked the rain, as Margarete had taught him. Calamus on the banks – he ate the shoots. *See, I still remember.* Beyond it, the earth was chalky, greedy for his boots.

In the early afternoon, he passed a pair of villages, both destroyed. The first must have been of some size in 1904, for it was there in the imperial atlas, unnamed but recorded with a little square. In the second, the walls of a synagogue were charred and broken. An old man in a black hat and robe was pushing a plough through a garden behind one of the ruined houses, and a young boy led a frail old woman down a path. Who had done this? Lucius wanted to ask them, but the child panicked when he saw Lucius, disappearing with the woman into the ruins.

Later, he passed another hamlet, this one completely burnt to the ground. This time there was no one, and by the size of the trees growing up from the remains of the houses, he guessed that it had been that way since the first days of the war.

After that he stayed away from the villages.

Sometimes, far off in the trees, he sensed the presence of other people, and once, in a far-off valley, he saw a figure on horseback, with a plumed helmet and lance, uniform glittering. For a moment Lucius blinked, wondering if it was an illusion, but the man remained, seemingly lost and wandering in time.

Dusk fell. Clouds of midges lifted from the high grass. A flock of blackbirds appeared above the valley, dived and rose again in teeming ranks, unfolded, colonnaded, burst.

Now the woods grew denser, pines and spruces appearing among the oaks.

Her woods. Around him, everywhere: *her* bracken, thistle, goosefoot. On a ridge, he found a foxhole and a machine gun, its barrel bent and rusted, draped with a muddy scarf. A line of grave mounds, now covered with a thin growth of pine trees. A half-torn pickelhaube, a leather glove.

The ground was thick with old, spent shells, like acorns after a masting.

Darkness had fallen, and he spent the night inside the fox-hole, in a corner worn smooth in the shape of a sleeping man. It was empty, save for a discarded canteen, half-full of water. How long had it rested there? he wondered, and though he was thirsty, he didn't drink.

It was raining when he awoke. Droplets drummed down on the oak leaves. He walked faster now, hungry, not trusting him-self with the mushrooms and too impatient to stop and strip the cambium from the bark. For everything told him he was getting closer, memory a landscape with a topology of its own. Some-thing faintly different in the smell of the forest, in the softness of the earth. The rushing streams now lined with horsetails. Stones of familiar shape. He began to walk more swiftly. Yes, he recognized it: here was the ridge where Margarete had once stopped to remove a pebble from her boot. Here was the rocky overhang where once they'd taken shelter. Faster, off the trail, twigs snapping as he hurried towards a light. And then before him, where the land began to drop and the forest opened, he stopped. There, he saw it. The church, the houses, the valley, the thin stream of mist rising through the same trees through which it had risen on the night he'd left.

He stood for a moment, almost in disbelief. Heart pounding from the exertion, taking in the vision before him, preparing for what he was about to learn.

In the wind from the valley, the leaves rustled, hiding the sound of the footsteps behind him as three men stepped out from the woods.

They were very gentle, considering. A dusty sack came down over his head, and the fabric was pushed into his mouth and bound there with a stone. He had no time to speak. Then his rucksack was stripped, his hands tied. Standard Imperial and Royal procedure for moving a POW, he later thought, though the stone in his mouth seemed a local innovation. Images, then, of hooded prisoners, marched off into the snow, prodded with the barrel of a gun.

He waited. There it was: cold against the bare base of his neck.

THEY LED HIM down the hillside and into the valley, one man on each arm, the third behind him, reminding him of his presence with intermittent nudges of the muzzle. The path was muddy, and he stumbled constantly. From time to time he could hear the men speaking in Ruthenian, but what he could understand helped him little: *morning, captain, bag*. He assumed they were remnants of Ukrainian units, having taken to the mountains after being pushed out of the plains by Polish forces. By then they would have found the gun, the sundry coins, the map, and, if they could understand Polish, they would have read the letter from the general. *Lucius Krzelewski, friend of Poland*. His story, that he was a doctor returning to the village, now seemed completely improbable. They would be fools to believe him. If they even let him speak.

His stomach knotted, and for a moment, he was afraid that he might soil his trousers. Like so many of his patients – this sordid fact never mentioned in the manuals. But the heat passed through him, sparing him. He felt his face flush, and in the dusty chamber of the sack, he sneezed.

The trail began to level out. They left the woods. In the light that filtered through the fabric, he could vaguely make out the shapes of low-slung houses. He could feel the sun's warmth now, smell the musty odour of a farmyard, hens. Some children's voices, the sound of more footsteps on the road. This comforted him a little. They wouldn't shoot him in front of children, would they? They turned from the road and climbed a short path and stopped. A door creaked. They entered a darker room. Smell of stable dust and linseed and manure. He was shoved down onto a stool. The rope was untied from around his head, the stone removed. They left the sack. His lip had been wedged between the stone and his teeth, and now he licked it, salty with blood.

An old memory, the metal apparatus in his mouth, his bleeding tongue.

They bound his feet.

Now the men addressed him directly, but again he didn't understand. The gun barrel moved from neck to head. He had to speak, he knew. Roughly, he tried what he could remember of Ruthenian. I am a doctor. Worked here, wartime.

'*Polyak?*' said the soldier.

Pole. It depends who you ask, he thought. By name, but not by passport. He took a gamble. '*Avstriyets.*'

Austrian. There was silence. Whispers. Then the door opened and someone left.

Now he could vaguely make out features of the hut. A guard sat by the door, beneath a rank of farm tools. It occurred to him that they might be useful in an escape, but he knew this was an insane fantasy. The truth was that he probably couldn't have fought off a single guard, even without a sack around his head. Now his thirst and hunger began to grow acute. *Voda*, he said to the soldier. *Water*. But no answer returned to him from across the room.

Alone, his head bound, sitting uncomfortably on the stool, he found his mind surprisingly empty, slowing, as if somehow preparing to meet death halfway. He was scared, very scared, but very tired, too, and he found the thoughts of what would happen to him now almost too difficult to bear. He wondered if this was what others felt. If so close, death seemed almost welcome, not something to be feared. Perhaps it would be easier, he thought, if his journey ended now. There would be something fitting to this: back at the church, where his new life had begun. Was this what he'd been drawn towards, a kind of ending, a release?

Then panic surged in him, he felt his eyes fill with tears, and his stomach seized again. Now, more than fantasies of fleeing, he felt a wish to fall and curl upon himself until someone came to carry him away, light and elemental, like a shell or husk.

It was afternoon when at last he heard the sound of horses outside, and then someone dismounting. The door opened again. More steps.

'So you're the Austrian?' This, surprisingly, spoken in German.

'Yes.'

'What are you doing here?'

He hesitated, trying to gauge his answer, but the vastness of the war and its allegiances were too great to outmanoeuvre.

So he decided on the truth. 'I once lived here, during the war. There was a field hospital. I was the doctor. I've come back to look for a friend.'

Silence. Through the sack, he saw the newcomer turn to the guard and say something. Probably asking for papers, for he heard a rustling. He braced himself.

'Krzelewski.'

Pronounced correctly, though with a faint Ruthenian hum. He answered. 'Y . . . yes?'

Then, suddenly: the light.

A one-handed man stood there before him, his good hand holding the sack, while he sniffled and wiped a runny nose with the stump of his other wrist. A colourfully embroidered high-lander's jacket covered an old grey Austrian uniform. On his head, despite the heat, a sheepskin cap, with upturned ear flaps. A thick moustache overhung his mouth.

'Doctor!'

Lucius stared, uncertain how to respond.

'It is I, Krajniak! Krajniak! By God's beard, don't you remember?'

Ah, yes: the missing hand, the sniffles. *The French dine out on foie gras. The Brits beef in a pot.* Saluting with his stump that final evening when they went looking for Margarete. The cook.

But now the face was sunburnt, hardened, and the moustache long.

'Of course!'

Krajniak turned to the guard and motioned him to untie the rope that bound Lucius's hands and feet. Then he approached, cupping Lucius's cheeks in palm and stump. 'Pan Doctor! Oh, my friend, you're lucky. They were debating whether to hang or shoot you first.'

*

KRAJNIAK TOOK HIM outside to a table that was set up at the back of the house, where a bottle of *horilka* and two cups of hollowed wood quickly appeared. A village woman emerged from inside, in a smock and patterned kerchief. With one arm, she pinned a long grey piglet to her breast, while the other held a curved, thin knife. A little girl of six or seven followed, carrying a baby, nearly bald with a mottled skin infection of the scalp.

'My wife,' said Krajniak, placing his hand on the small of the woman's back. 'From the village, perhaps you remember. The little one is ours.'

He spoke to the woman in Ruthenian, and her face opened in recognition. Vaguely, Lucius recalled her: heavy epicanthic folds, a pale mole in a crease of her nose. She laughed. Then, still holding the pig, she drew back the shirtsleeve of her free arm with her teeth, and presented Lucius with her wrist.

For a second, he wondered if this was some sort of highland custom he had never learned. Was he supposed to kiss her wrist, perhaps the knife? She waited, shook it at him, and spoke again. Then Krajniak said, 'You lanced a boil on her arm, remember? Gone! It never came back.'

Lucius was fairly certain that he was not the one who lanced the boil, but he saw no reason to dampen his reception. He touched it with his finger.

'How it's healed!'

The woman spoke again, and Krajniak answered. He turned to Lucius. 'Tomorrow, you will go, but tonight you are our guest. You're hungry, I imagine?'

The pig twisted, as if it understood.

'Only if you're cooking,' Lucius answered, as lightly as he could. He watched Krajniak as he poured out the *horilka*. Now I'll ask him, thought Lucius. Now I'll learn. But the fact that the cook had yet to mention Margarete's name made him pause.

Hastily, Lucius took a gulp, as if to fortify himself for what was coming next. The smell familiar, reminding him of the moments in the surgery when they sterilized their hands. But he had forgotten how hot it was. He coughed.

Krajniak laughed and pinched the nose of the piebald baby, who broke into a grin. 'Ah, the city made the doctor soft.' His single hand dived into his breast pocket, removed a metal cigarette case, and held it out to Lucius, who, still hacking, shook his head. Krajniak flipped it open, extracted a cigarette between his fourth and fifth fingers, closed the case and palmed it, lifted the cigarette to his lips, then exchanged the case for a matchbox in his pocket, bracing it with his little finger as he struck a flame. A deft, practised motion, suggesting an unexpected physical confidence. He puffed. A cat leapt onto his lap, and he stroked it with his stump.

For a moment, Lucius wondered if Krajniak would explain the men, the weapons, the coloured jacket he wore over his old uniform. By then the absence of livery or any sign of field organization suggested the men were not part of either the Polish or Ukrainian armies. Then who? Krajniak, if he remembered, was from a nearby village. The men had the air of a local defence force; with the fall of Austria, even highlanders had begun to proclaim their own republics, Lucius knew. He thought of his father's words that evening by the war map in the sunroom, of the burning embers splintering into ever smaller flames.

But Krajniak said nothing, and his gaze seemed to catch on the steeple of the church just up the road.

'You said you came looking for a friend,' he said, turning his dark eyes on Lucius. 'I assume you mean our sister nurse.'

SHE HAD RETURNED late the night the men went looking.

She did not explain her absence. She was distracted, said

Krajniak. Something clearly had upset her, but she wouldn't tell them what.

They rang the church bells. Zmudowski straggled back, then Schwarz – you remember, Pan Doctor, with the fossils? All save Lucius. When a few hours passed, Margarete and a group of others set out to look for him. But by then the fog was so thick, they could scarcely find the path. Still they searched. Our good sister wouldn't quit.

It was only later the next morning that they heard the first sounds of artillery. Again they sent a search party. But still they couldn't find him, Pan Doctor knew that part. And with the fighting over the hills, they didn't dare go far. She was frantic then, said Krajniak. She paced the church, the road, went back up the river to look again.

By afternoon, a messenger had appeared from down the valley. Russian cavalry was advancing across the foothills, he told them. Their orders were to evacuate the patients into Poland, on intelligence of a Russian pincer movement to the south.

Krajniak took another swig. 'But still she didn't want to leave.'

How she was stubborn! But by the time the evacuation crews arrived, there were reports that Cossack cavalry were already in Kolomea. Chaos descended on the church. One by one they transferred the men into the lorries. Margarete waited until the very last ambulance was loaded with the sickest patients, then climbed on board. By the time they reached the mouth of the valley, they could see smoke on the plains, and the roads were filled with marching troops. In Nadworna, the soldiers were separated based on their injuries, the frailest men sent on to Sambor; Zmudowski stayed, she went along. It was the last time that Krajniak saw either of them. No sooner had he reached

Nadworna than he'd been sent back towards the front. Not as a cook this time, but as a soldier.

'With this.'

He held up his stump.

But Lucius had scarcely heard anything after the word *Sambor*. Now the railway map, burnt into his mind during his time on the ambulances, appeared before him. *Sambor*. He'd been there shortly after his new commission. *Our paths had crossed*. He felt his mind yield, buckle in accommodation as this fact was taken in. Summer, August. Yes, he could recall the sweltering wards.

'Do you know which hospital?'

'Which hospital? I told you, we were separated.'

'But perhaps you heard from someone else . . .'

Now a look of sympathy crossed Krajniak's face. 'No, Doctor. I didn't hear from anyone. I told you – a week later, I was carrying a gun.'

Lucius nodded slowly, still reluctant to accept that this was all. But *alive*, he told himself. And last in Sambor. This was what he had hoped for: a glowing pebble left on the forest floor.

Sambor, safely in what was now Polish territory, just west of the Lwów–Dolina line.

The sun was beginning to go down behind the hills, and above them, the sky had turned a coral red. In the yard, a hen summited a dung heap, a glistening yellow grub twisting in its beak. Nearby, a cat watched it hungrily. In a neighbour's yard, one of Krajniak's comrades was cutting wood. Now food came: beetroot soup, rye bread and onion dumplings. They grew silent as they ate from old tin army plates, spoons clanging as they had at mealtime during the war.

Then Krajniak spoke. 'Pan Doctor? Do you remember

Zmudowski's story, about the stamps?' He took a bite. 'You know, it wasn't true.'

'No?' Slowly, Lucius set down his cup. Wondering what this had to do with Margarete. Why Krajniak was telling him this now.

'Not the way he told you, at least,' Krajniak continued. 'That Russian soldier? He couldn't have cared less for stamps. He wanted something to send his girlfriend. So one day, when Margarete was out, Zmudowski sneaked into her room, hoping to find something, a pair of stockings, a chemise, anything he could trade. As you could guess, there wasn't much other than the habits of the other sisters who had died. But beneath her pillow, he found a handkerchief, a silk one, with the names Małgorzata and Michał, joined at the "M". The kind a young man might buy for his betrothed. So he took it. That's what Zmudowski gave the soldier for his stamps.'

Małgorzata, thought Lucius, turning the word over in his mind. Polish for Margarete. So it wasn't really a new name.

A pair of different children had materialized, chasing a hoop from an old food barrel across the rutted yard. The summer sun had long set. They moved in shadows.

'And what did she do when she found out?' asked Lucius.

'That's the strange part,' said Krajniak. 'She wasn't one to keep quiet, but she never said a thing. If it was from a brother or a father, or even a friend, I think she would have asked us if we'd seen it. Or denied the soldiers their morphine until someone gave it back. It made me think that there was a story she was hiding: of a husband maybe, or perhaps she was engaged. But she never mentioned anyone, never received a single letter. She never said anything about home, but I knew, just by the way she spoke, that she was from the mountains. If this man of hers was still alive, she would have gone to see him. But nothing. For two and a half years.'

'And what do you think that means?' asked Lucius. Thinking: *Małgorzata*. The earthly life I left behind.

'What do *I* think?' The cook paused and watched the children. 'There are many ways for young men to die in the mountains, even before the war. I think she lost him. Maybe before she entered the convent. Or maybe there was no convent – maybe she just came straight to us.'

Lucius looked up towards the steeple, now a shadow against the sky. He nodded slowly. A memory of her came to him, standing at the door to share the news of Rzedzian's passing. *One should not grow attached to other people, Doctor.*

Her forest songs of weddings and midsummer festivals.

Her tears, her flight, when he asked for her hand in marriage.

'I understand,' said Lucius slowly, his memory of her shimmering, like a body in the water, threatening to break apart. 'I've also wondered who she really was.'

Krajniak blew his nose again. 'If I may, Doctor? You were rather in love with her, weren't you?'

The children sprawled over each other; the hoop bounced loose.

'A little,' Lucius said.

BY THEN IT WAS past midnight, but Margarete's mention had released memories of their time in Lemnowice and neither of them wished to stop. Now the stories tumbled out of them. Lucius spoke of the food they gathered during the spring scarcity, the hasty winter sunbathing, the games of soccer in the snow. Krajniak reminded him of Margarete's breeding programmes – 'Cats everywhere now, Doctor! Don't eat the goulash!' – and the way everything seemed covered in powdered lime. Lucius recalled the drunken summer singing, the card games played out beneath the stars. Krajniak waxed poetic about the accidental pickles, the wine pilfered from the summer estates. Together they recalled Rzedzian and the way his tears would gather on his moustache, and Nowak with his fear of handwashing, and Zmudowski's photo of his daughter, and all the others they could summon up from memory: the chastened Sergeant Czernowitzski, the clarinettist with his instrument of tin and wire, the Viennese tailor, the cobbler with the dented head.

By then, Lucius's wristwatch read four, and a hint of dawn was in the sky. He felt the fatigue of his journey, but still he didn't wish to stop. He was starving for this, he realized. It was more than simply recollection; it was as if Krajniak contained a part of him that he had once thought lost. Now he was hungry to reconstruct that person, greedy even, given the knowledge that he would probably never see this man again. Do you remember when I first arrived? he asked. And that first night? The soldiers, with the missing jaw, the belly turning inside out?

Krajniak remembered.

And those first surgeries?

Yes, Pan Doctor. Truth was there were some of us who didn't think you knew what you were doing.

And the doctors Brosz and Berman?

He remembered.

The first shell-shock cases?

Yes.

'Do you remember József Horváth?'

The words came out almost without his knowing.

There was a long pause. Even the name sounded impossible; it had been two years since he had uttered it aloud.

And Lucius said, though it wasn't necessary, 'The Hungarian that peasant brought in by wheelbarrow that first winter, who'd been found up by the pass.'

Whether Krajniak's eyes were watery from the *horilka* or the memories, Lucius didn't know. He was sitting sideways with one arm on the table as he gazed off to the lightening sky. Now he nodded slowly. 'I remember. Of course I remember, Pan Doctor. I can't forget.'

There was a long silence. Then slowly, without premeditation, Lucius began to speak. He told Krajniak about the nightmares that had begun upon his return home, the blame he placed on himself for not letting Horváth leave, thinking that he could cure the man himself. He spoke of the many times he thought that he'd seen Horváth among his patients and on the Viennese streets, the impossibility of finding any peace with memory, or any absolution or release. He feared, he told Krajniak, that he would be stuck for ever in that winter. That even if he found Margarete, he would not be able to escape the fact that Horváth had been sacrificed for any joy he might attain.

Strangely, for thoughts that had possessed him for years, it took no more than a few minutes for the story to come out.

He was silent. He waited for Krajniak to answer.

But Krajniak did not say anything at first. Lucius felt suddenly ashamed that he had burdened him, had let their stories stray from memories of cats and pickle barrels. Or did Krajniak blame him for Horváth? Was that why he'd said nothing until Lucius brought it up? In the half-light, a pair of bats flitted in and out of the shadows. Krajniak poured another cup of *horilka*.

Lucius was about to speak again when Krajniak lifted up his stump.

'I can still feel it, Pan Doctor.'

It took a moment for Lucius to realize that Krajniak was

referring to his hand. 'Yes . . .' said Lucius, wondering now whether this was a way of changing the subject, or whether Krajniak's thoughts had drifted off. Perhaps they both were lost in their own worlds. 'Some of my patients say the same . . .'

Krajniak's voice was strained now. 'Sometimes it feels as if it's burning, and other times I feel as if it's touching something, my fingers moving over something on their own. The fur of an animal, a coin, a piece of meat. For a long time, I couldn't stand it. I'd close my eyes and squeeze at the place where I felt my hand to be. I'd punch and stab it, and once I tried to remove it with a knife. Not the stump, Pan Doctor: the hand, my missing hand.'

He stopped and finished off his cup. Lucius waited, for Krajniak to say something more, to offer some kind of redemptive wisdom, to share how he'd gone on.

The bats returned, now visible in all their flitting detail in the morning twilight.

But Krajniak just poured the last of the *horilka*. Now when he spoke, his voice was steadier. Lucius would have to leave soon. He could escort him down to the mouth of the valley, though unfortunately no further. But the territory north of them was well secured by Polish forces. *You'll* be safe there. And on the plains, with the letter, Lucius would find frequent Polish convoys that could take him to the Sambor rail.

So that was all.

'I would offer for you to stay, Doctor, but there are many reasons we should go our separate ways.'

'Of course.'

Krajniak stood. He'd get the horses. It would take an hour to get everything together. Lucius must be tired. If he would like to get a little bit of sleep . . .

But Lucius's thoughts were elsewhere. A light breeze had

arisen, and in the distance he thought that he heard branches rustling. In his mind, he saw the beech tree, the courtyard crowded with patients, the winter soldier vanishing into the white expanse. Krajniak was right; there were some wounds that couldn't be amputated. But he had respects to pay.

HE WALKED the last hundred paces alone.

The sun had just begun to peek above the hills. Around him, from the yards, came snorts and clucking. Faces of old women turned to watch him pass. Smells of cooking oil and onions rose from the huts, and smoke seeped through the thatch. He recalled the days that he had gone with Margarete to visit the soldiers distributed among the rooms musty with feathers and tallow, the children bearing silent witness. He wondered how they remembered him: friend or invader. He heard a clattering, and a pair of jays alighted on a fallen fencepost. Then the road opened before him and he was there.

It had changed little from the outside. The wooden facade still dark and faded; the base of the walls now a little overgrown. A pair of black storks were nesting in the belfry, and tufts of wallflower had begun to creep up around the door frame. But everything else was otherwise unchanged. In the arrow slit, a haunted darkness hovered, as it had hovered four years before.

The doctor? she replied, still staying back, deep in the shadows of the world that awaited him. *Didn't you just say you're him?*

THIS TIME it was unlocked.

It was, in many ways, how it had remained in his memory, only smaller now, and this time light spilled in from a southern breach, not from the north. And empty. Gone were the soldiers, of course. But also the blankets, the pallets, the operating table built from pews.

All used as firewood, he assumed. Fitting, even. He begrudged no one; hopefully it had kept somebody warm.

The air was cold, also empty of that old familiar smell: the lime, the iodoform and carbolic, the straw beds, the spoiled wounds.

He walked slowly up the centre of the nave, following the path he had grown used to taking through the patients, and turning at a right angle when he reached the crossing, he entered the old ward for the dying. The floor was bare; he could have walked there directly at a slant, but the daily circuit was entrenched in him, and it felt wrong to step where men once lay.

This is Brauer, Pan Doctor Lieutenant, frostbite; this is Czerny of the 14th Fusiliers. Moscowitz, Gruscinski, Kirschmeyer. Redlich, professor of Vienna, shot by Cossacks near his tail . . .

He could see the outline of the crater in the floor. The roof they had repaired still held, though in the south wall a new shell had burst a hole.

Nature had followed, ferns and grass sprouting from the shattered wood. The floor was littered with dung and leaves, and a pair of stunted saplings stretched up towards the light. Streaks of bird's droppings painted a scene of the Crucifixion, and following it upwards he saw movement in the rafters, a face, an owl, looking down. As he took a step closer, the bird, perturbed, awoke and, with its great wings out, fell towards him, banking skywards in a silent puff of down.

He walked on. Water had crept in behind the Annunciation in the chancel. The paint was blistered, cracked, bursting around Gabriel, as if Mary had fallen in ecstasy not at the visitation of the angel, but the rift in her gilded world.

He stopped at the cabinets that once had held the medicine. Empty, now, save for a handful of ampoules of atropine and chloral hydrate amid the rat's droppings. No Veronal. He found a package of old bandages, gnawed open. Cats aside, the rats had probably wasted little time once Margarete was gone.

He paused before the door to the sacristy as if he might yet find her inside. But it was empty, completely empty, stripped just like the rest of the church. On the floor, he could see the indentations where once her bed had stood. Now it, too, had been taken. Even Horváth's country sketch was missing. In the chaos of the evacuation had she thought to bring it with her? That was one great difference between them. That for Margarete, József Horváth was a patient she might remember with affection, even love, as one could love a person one had cared for, even if they couldn't be saved.

For a moment, he stopped and looked out of the window, the square of sky he had beseeched so many times when she was ill. Through branches he could see the outline of his old quarters, which now seemed so close to hers. How often had she sat there, looking towards his door? Then he touched the sill and froze.

There someone had placed two small, white, almost perfectly round stones.

It could have been anyone, he thought, his world contracting to these points. Any soldier, any village child.

They were cool in his hand and left bare circles in the dust.

Then he had one place left to go. The door to the courtyard from her room creaked as he pulled it open, through a scrim of gritty soil that had been washed beneath the moulding. Outside, the yard was thick with uncut grass. The air hummed with mayflies and little moths, gnats and butterflies. The beech tree was in leaf, its towering branches garlanded with catkins. His oracle, his monument of memory, the bark grey and smooth and utterly unscarred. No soldier. No disfigured revenant. No screams, no tinted snow. Nothing at its base but high green grass, now swaying in the wind. Just the old, indifferent monument to what was lost.

He thought of the city's war memorials, and the way the mourning knelt before them, laying wreaths and candles and praying for a son's return. But what he was seeking was forgiveness and atonement, and he couldn't think of any worthy offering to give.

Another shiver passed through the beech's branches. High above, a squirrel chattered.

Yes. I know. It's time.

THEY RODE OUT on a pair of Carpathian ponies, small, mouse-coloured creatures who ambled amiably through the mud. The forest was damp and warm. Billows of midges hummed in the light shafts that descended through the canopy. Krajniak ahead, rifle across his saddle, watching, silent now. By then it was clear he would not tell Lucius who his men were, or what they were fighting for. But Lucius didn't press him. The little band seemed so vulnerable against the armies of the plains. Perhaps they all were safer if he didn't know.

Once, in a clearing, Krajniak whistled, low, and an answer came from somewhere in the woods. But they saw no one else, and the forest was so still that at times Lucius nodded off to sleep.

It was evening when the land opened and Lucius dismounted. Krajniak followed. Standing at the edge of the forest, Lucius searched for the right words to thank the cook. But what to say? That somehow in their drunken chatter about pickles and games of winter soccer and a soldier who carried fossils in his pockets, Lucius felt as if something had been returned to him? That Krajniak was the only one of all of them to whom he had truly bid farewell?

'Goodbye!' said Krajniak. He kissed him once, twice, on the cheeks, and a third time on the head.

'Goodbye!'

And taking the reins of Lucius's pony, the cook wiped his nose and disappeared back into the woods.

It was midnight when Lucius reached the empty highway to Dolina.

He slept off the road, a deep sleep in the shelter of an overturned wagon. In the morning, a Polish convoy passed him heading west. When he presented Borszowski's letter, they hoisted him on board, without even bothering with the elaborate story he had prepared.

Two days later, he was in Sambor.

He spent the night at the Hotel Kopernikus, near the centre of town.

It had been over a week since he had bathed, and his shoes and clothes betrayed the journey. He found a shave just down the street from the hotel, from a squinting man with raw, pink hands and a suspicious absence of customers, who berated him with a conspiracy theory about the shortage of badger hair as he drew a dull blade across his throat. Freed, he found a clothes shop across the square. The racks were mostly empty; the longest trousers still fell short. Pale khaki, like some tropical explorer. But they would have to do.

He found the district hospital in the same building as the old army regimental hospital, which itself had occupied the site of an even older cholera hospital, behind centuries-old ramparts that gave the impression it was under siege. He had been there once before, during his service on the ambulance trains. But inside the walls, the grounds were nothing like the place of constant movement he had remembered from the war. A tall statue of a man with an unfamiliar name stood along the entrance path, presumably the cholera-fighter of old. Some goats wandered over the grass. A family was picnicking.

He stopped. Beyond them, a nurse sat by a young man in a wheelchair and gently fed him from a bowl. In his throat Lucius felt that same familiar quiver that he felt each time the amputees back in Vienna reminded him of Horváth. It wasn't *him*, of course, or her, but there was something to the nurse's gentle manner that reminded him of Margarete with their soldier, so long ago. This man was missing both hands, both feet. Frost-bite, most likely, Lucius thought, finding shelter in clinical considerations. Though by his stillness, by his vacant stare, Lucius suspected frostbite wasn't all.

Near the entrance to the building, a group of old men played *tarock*, and didn't seem to notice when he passed.

He walked up a short flight of stairs and went inside. During the war, he recalled that even the foyer had been filled with patients, but it was empty now. There was an unmanned desk and chair, and a small sign that indicated visiting hours. On the far wall was a low display case, flanked on either side by the annual staff photos that hung on every wall of every hospital he had been to in his life. Over the doors that led into the wards were the words *Oddział 1*, and *Oddział 2*. Ward 1 and 2.

Through the small windows in the doors, he saw movement. But now he hesitated, as he had hesitated back with Krajniak. It was less the chance of finding that the trail was cold again, and more the other possibilities he might learn. All he knew was that in 1916 she had been alive in Sambor. Before the full brunt of the Russian assault, before the typhus outbreaks in the crowded hospitals, before the flu.

He walked over to the display case, as if somehow what it held could help prepare for what came next. Inside were photographs related to the history of the hospital, an old brick used in the first foundation, a medieval-looking tooth extractor, and a pair of stuffed birds without a label, one of which had fallen on its side. He looked above, at the pictures on the wall. The first showed a pair of sombre doctors, standing on the same steps he had just climbed, flanked on either side by nurses. And on the frame, the year, 1904 . . .

Quickly, he began to scan the dates, 1905, 1906 . . . He followed them to the other side of the door. They stopped in 1913, resumed in 1916. By now the people had changed: gaunter, the intricate wimples replaced by the simpler habits of the Red Cross.

1917. And there he stopped.

She was standing in the first row, second from the right. Even in the poor light of the foyer, even with the dark long hair that hung down beneath her simple nursing cap, she was unmistakable. The same wonder-filled eyes, lips parted, ready for laughter, her gaze off and to the sky. She wore the costume of a lay nurse. No more habit. But he was no longer surprised.

He looked to the neighbouring photo. 1918. Gone. There were many explanations, Lucius thought, but only one he couldn't shake from his mind. The full force of influenza had begun to build that autumn. 1918.

In the photo, there was snow upon the ground; but was this January or December?

He stopped himself. There were so many other explanations! But he recalled the fury with which the flu had swept through the ward, the soldiers and nurses who had succumbed.

He took down the photo and removed the print, part of him now wishing that it wasn't her at all. On the back, he hoped to find a name as if to prove it, but there was nothing other than the address of the studio, stamped in decorative lettering.

'Is that someone you know?' From behind him. Polish.

Lucius turned to see a small man in a white coat. Balding, tiny circular eyeglasses neatly repaired with wire. A thin moustache over his lip. He motioned to the photo in Lucius's hands.

'Yes,' said Lucius. He realized he owed an explanation. 'So sorry not to have introduced myself. I entered, and I saw this and . . .'

He took a breath, stepped forward, and held out his hand. 'Doctor Lucius Krzelewski of Vienna.' *Doctor*. No need to mention he was a medical student again, and technically, given classes had yet to start, not even that. His only hope rested on professional courtesy. 'I served at a hospital in the Carpathians during the war. I've come to look for my nurse. I was told that she was here.'

For a moment, the doctor considered this apparition, the too-short trousers, the bruised lip, the sunburnt skin flushed now by barber's blade. The bare photo in his hand, its empty frame behind him on the cabinet.

He came and looked.

'Here.' Lucius pointed. 'This is her.' The doctor leaned forward, wrinkling up his nose to keep his glasses from sliding off. A healthy bramble of grey hair filled his ear. He straightened. 'I don't recognize her. But I've been here only for a year.' He paused, then pointed to another nurse in the photograph. 'But *this* nurse is here. Perhaps she knows.'

The doctor led him through Ward 2. It was a men's ward, crowded, but clean and tidy. Patients' names and diagnoses were written on little chalkboards at the foot of every bed. There were many families, sitting with the patients, playing cards or reading newspapers, or holding squirming children as they talked. The nurse was at the far end of the hall, carrying a stack of bedpans. When she saw them approach, she stopped.

The honourable Polish doctor from Vienna was presented, the story told.

The nurse studied the picture for a moment before beginning to nod. 'Yes. Yes. Małgorzata, yes. Last name Małysz, I think. She came with the evacuees in '16, right? She was good. A little bossy, acted like she knew more than the doctors. But good, especially with the shell-shock cases. If I remember correctly, there was a group that went that winter to a rehabilitation hospital in Tarnów.'

'That winter?'

'March, I think. I remember only because it was around the time the army began to use the gas, when we began to see all the men with phosgene blowback and needed to make space.'

''17, you mean?'

'Yes, Doctor.' On her face there was a question of why it mattered. But it mattered. Tarnów, 1917. Flu and typhus still lay between them, but he knew that he'd drawn closer. To where, and when, and who.

Małgorzata Małysz. A stranger's name.

Downstairs, the doctor handed the photograph to Lucius. 'Take it. I think you need this more than I.'

AGAIN HE WAS moving, back on the train. Chyrów, Jarosław, Rzeszów: These towns now part of him, the familiar stations from his ambulance days. Again the crowds, the children with their sprays of currants. He felt as if he were on some pilgrim's route, only this time not stopping. This time only one place mattered: Tarnów.

But would he find her there? In Jarosław, waiting for what seemed like hours for some unexplained problem on the line, he took the photo from his rucksack and looked at it again as if to reassure himself that it was her. No phantom, no fleeing peasant, no South Station apparition. How astounding that it had preserved that gaze familiar from the moments she had looked up at him across the surgery, a gaze that now suggested astonishment at the great game that she'd been playing. In the seat next to him, his neighbour, an older woman in a winter coat despite the summer, made no attempt to hide her curiosity about the image that commanded such absorption. Should I ask *her?* he wondered. Like Adelajda, interrogating everyone she met? For who was to say that his search would end in Tarnów? That it would not be just another stop, another hospital? *Yes, Doctor, we remember her. She went to Kraków. No, she went to Jarosław. No, to Sambor. No, to Stryj. She was from the mountains, Doctor, wasn't she? She was going home, she said.*

Perhaps if you go there, they will know.

And on. And he would continue, a ghost searching for its flesh.

'Let me see,' said the clerk in the Tarnów District Hospital, running an efficient finger down a staff register. 'Yes, here's her name, just as you said. Rehabilitation pavilion, up the street.'

'I'm sorry?'

'She's here. Unless it is someone else by that name. But if you want to catch her, then I'd suggest you hurry. She's on the day shift. They are about to come off work.'

A NARROW STREET led between the complex of hospitals, signs pointing to Maternity, Paediatrics, Surgery, Tuberculosis. It took him a moment to find the path, flanked by box hedge, that led to the Rehabilitation ward. Dusk was beginning to fall. Now, from the building, far up the path, the nurses began to file out. He stopped as they broke around him, hurrying in pairs and threes, some still in nursing caps, others having loosened their hair. They laughed or chatted, passing without paying any heed.

He stood there, eyes jumping from one nurse after another. Uncertain of what he would do when he found her, what he would say, how to begin.

'Lucius.'

She'd seen him first. Not Pan Doctor. *Lucius*. Like the night she had descended to him in the dark.

They stood in the path, between the hedges, facing each other a few feet apart. Behind her, others were still coming, parting around the two of them like water around stones. On either side of the path, brick buildings rose to their slate roofs, to the early-evening sky of midsummer, now salmon, mauve.

Over his shoulder, were he to look: a scoop of moon. The air gilded with the pollen from a line of pines beyond the buildings. A fringed white curtain fluttering in an open window. A pair of sparrows, garrulous, as if urging their terrestrial counterparts to speak.

'Lucius.'

She was asking for an explanation. But once again she was more prepared than he. He needed just to stand there a moment and take her in. He hadn't anticipated that she had changed, that life, of course, had carried her along as well. It was her, Margarete, yes . . . And yet! Her face was fuller now, the worried circles gone from beneath her eyes. She still wore a nurse's uniform, now white, different from the familiar grey from Lemnowice. And she had thrown a light-blue blouse over it, buttoned over her chest. In the place of her old sturdy winter boots, she now wore laced white patent shoes, with heels.

And her hair! Long and smooth, and russet-coloured, now clearly styled, though he couldn't name the fashion. It was combed back over her ears, where it tumbled in smooth waves to her shoulders. She must have combed it just before she left the hospital. For someone else: this should have been his clue.

Across her cheekbone, he saw the scar from Horst's boot, bone-coloured against a blush. She clasped a handbag – no Mannlicher! – and squinted slightly, as if she too were trying to take him in. Should he embrace her? There? Before the others? Memories rising now of soldiers descending from the trains with arms outstretched to meet their wives.

The footsteps sounded on the gravel as the nurses continued to stream past. He waited for her to take his arm, or ask him to follow, to somewhere quiet, where they could sit or be alone. He hadn't imagined it like this, amid so many other people, before the open windows of the ward.

'Lucius. How?'

Her lips parted, as if in wonder. She touched the scar. Still he wanted just to stand there in her strange, new presence, not to speak. But she was waiting, and so he stumbled through his story: the Brusilov offensive, the ambulances, the hospital in Vienna, his trip to Lemnowice. Then: Krajniak, the hospital in Sambor, the photo, the other nurse, the train. Details that now seemed so unimportant. But that was how.

'*Lemnowice* . . .' She said the word with some astonishment. As if it had been a long time since she had thought of it. While he had thought of nothing else.

'Yes.'

'And you came for me?' Now in her voice he heard a different timbre, less slushed, less song.

'For you, yes.'

'Oh, Lucius. Oh, Lucius.' For a moment, she just stood there and shook her head. Again she touched the scar, a habit apparently acquired since they last parted. He had the impression of some confusion, then of someone mourning something delicate that had just been broken. 'Oh, Lucius. I don't know what to say.'

Now most of the day shift had moved off. They were almost alone. He recalled their sudden, surreptitious kisses, outside the church, in the darkness of the forest. He stepped closer, ready to take her in his arms.

She closed her eyes. 'Please. Please, don't.'

A line then, from the nun Ilaria's letter he'd read so many times. *I urge you to accept the loss and leave our Sister alone.*

But her hair, her shoes . . .

'I didn't think . . . You've kept your vows?'

'No. No . . . Oh, Lucius.' She worried her hands. 'There is so much to tell you. So much, but where can we start? There were never any vows.' She took a breath. So there, another question had been answered. 'No vows,' she said again. 'But . . . Oh, but I'll just say it! I have a daughter, Lucius, a little girl.'

The sparrows had fled. Suddenly, he felt very cold.

'A daughter.' He let the word sink in.

That moment by the river lay before them. Her legs cold from the water; the trundling cricket. Neither able to speak of what he wished to ask.

'And she . . . is . . .' But he couldn't say it. *Mine?*

'She's six months old.'

This also answered it. He looked now at her hands, God's little hands he'd come to know so well. A simple ring, no stone. 'You're . . . married?'

'A year ago. But yes, *we* . . . oh, Lucius!' she exclaimed, her voice now plaintive. 'You'll understand! You were lost . . . and then . . .' She paused, closing her eyes. It seemed as if she were trying to prepare him, to do this kindly. 'He is someone that you know. He . . . Oh, the world is very strange and wonderful . . .'

But now, for once, she was at a loss for words; now she had begun to tremble, too.

'Lucius, I tried to find you. I dreamed you were alive. For months, I dreamed I saw you. I knew! I sent a letter, *two* letters to you, care of the army. I thought of going to Vienna, but the hospital, it needed me. And then . . . then I found him.'

She stopped. 'I should be so happy!' She forced this, her words breaking. 'My friend is alive. You are alive. I thought I would never see you again. I am a mother, and my child's healthy, beautiful . . .'

But he was having trouble hearing everything she'd said. He repeated, 'Someone I know.'

She looked off, now unable to meet his gaze. She took a breath. 'I found him, by chance, in Sambor,' she said. 'In the hospital. Among the other amputees.'

Still she couldn't say his name.

'He was so ill,' she said. 'For three months, he couldn't even move. His amputations had healed, but he was like he was that winter day the peasant brought him to us. I knew my duty wasn't over then. I knew. I asked to be his nurse. It wasn't hard; the others didn't want to work with him, moaning like that. I was with him for almost six months in Sambor before he was transferred. I went with him. First to Przemyśl, then Jarosław. I couldn't leave him, after all that'd happened, I couldn't let him go. By then, he'd begun to recover. By the time we were transferred here, to Tarnów, he had begun to talk again, and for the first time he could tell me about his life before the war. I helped him write to his family in Hungary. They came to see him. His mother and his brother – he lost his father when he was very little – and a sister from his mother's second marriage, a beloved little girl he often drew. But when they left, he chose to stay here, with me. By then he was so much stronger. Still there are nights when he wakes screaming. Days of sadness, or when the trees or clouds call out to him in ways that I can't see. But that will take time, you know. Many soldiers take such time to heal. We have a fine wheelchair for him, and in the day, while I work, he looks after Agata, the baby. He loves the baby. He's become an illustrator of children's books, for a publisher in Warsaw, and . . .'

But there she stopped. It had been said.

She was a little out of breath from the story, as when they first had met those years ago. Now, she looked up at Lucius, eyes full of concern about how this news would land. But something extraordinary was happening. It seemed to him as if the world were changing, as if some great force was gathering about him, in the cobbles and buildings, in the rails, the trains, the clouds and light, the distant mountains in the sky.

A shadow moved; a great winter bird unclenched him from its talons and exploded into flight. And then a drifting, a sparkling, silvered drifting down.

And he was there.

'I should like to meet your daughter,' he said.

Margarete looked up at him, with the gaze of patience and understanding he had come to know so well. 'I would like that more than anything else in the world,' she said. 'But I can't. For József. He's come so far. I can't. If he were to see you . . . You remember . . . You understand.'

Then suddenly, she began to cry.

'Margarete.' Lucius took a step towards her. Not Małgorzata. Her old name, her *nom de guerre*.

She looked at him. Tears were running down her face. 'Look what you've done,' she said. Then she began to laugh. 'Oh, how silly all this is. Look at you, you're crying, too! Oh, Lucius, he loves our little girl. He laughs, can you imagine? After all that's happened to him. Oh, what I would give for you to hear him laugh . . .'

What I would give, thought Lucius. He watched her wipe the tears from her eyes with the back of her hand. Then she sniffed and rubbed her nose with her palm, a familiar motion, from the coldest days.

In his pocket, he felt the little stones. *I will keep these*, he thought. Then, very slowly, he leaned slightly towards her, as if what he was about to say should be a secret, though there was no one else around.

It was still there, he thought, that faint smell of carbolic. I did not forget.

'Thank you,' he said.

In the distance, a train whistled. She looked up one last time at him. Then, for a brief moment, he sensed that she would ask him something else, about his life, or more of what had happened since they had parted, or where he'd go from here. For there was so much left to say. But something she saw must have given her his answer. She lowered her gaze. Then quickly, as if she was worried she might change her mind, she hurried off, hesitant at first, then more determined, the stride of someone expected somewhere, someone going home.

He watched her as she walked down the street and turned the corner. In the sky, the clouds continued their march. A cold wind passed. At his side, the curtain snapped and billowed. The sparrows returned now, chattering. He took a step. The world received him.

ACKNOWLEDGEMENTS

For their support during the long writing of this book, I would like to acknowledge the generosity of Beatrice Monti von Rezzori of the Santa Maddalena Foundation, the Camargo Foundation, the MacDowell Foundation, and the National Endowment for the Arts.

I have benefited from the advice and kindness of Robert Mailer Anderson, Reagan Arthur, Nadeem Aslam, John Barry, Chris Bennett, Justin Birnbaum, Katy Black, Zuzanna Brzezinska, Daniela Cammack, Adam Chanzit, Melissa Chinchillo, Sallie de Golia, Robin Desser, Grainne Fox, David Grewal, Chris Hayward, Rona Hu, Anna Jarota, Jovana Knežević, Karen Landry, Shannon Langone, Tanya Luhrmann, Gitte Marx, Jed Purdy, Laura Roberts, Tim Roytman, Katherine Sanborn, Anna Spielvogel, Hans Steiner, Éva Soós Szőke and Thomas Weiser. Ellis McKenzie and Peter Houghteling believed in this book when it was in its earliest pages, and I deeply feel their absence upon its completion.

Over the past twenty years, I have been fortunate to have Tinker Green, Kevin McGrath and Josh Mooney as not only friends but also the most thoughtful of readers.

For the wisest counsel, I am deeply grateful to my agents, Christy Fletcher and Donald Lamm, and to my editors, Lee Boudreaux and Asya Muchnick at Little, Brown and Company and Maria Rejt at Mantle and Picador in the UK.

Finally, thank you to Debbie, Emma, Fiora, Susan, Charlotte, Sylvia, Pearl, Ed, Aaron, Cotton, Bob and Elizabeth; to my sister, Ariana, and niece, Selah; and to my parents, Robert and Naomi, for welcoming this book into your lives. Thank you, Raphael and Peter, for reminding me always of the power of stories, and for lifting me in winged ways I hope you one day understand. And above all, thank you, Sara, to whom I owe each one of these words.